THE GINGERBREAD MAN

"[A] gripping story of small-town secrets. The suspense will keep you guessing. The characters will steal your heart."　　—*New York Times* bestselling author Lisa Gardner

DESTINY

"An altogether stunning book, *Destiny* lives up to the expectations created by *Eternity* and *Infinity* and then some."　　—*Old Book Barn Gazette*

"Maggie Shayne's books just keep getting better and better!"　　—*Romantic Times*

INFINITY

"[A] dark, enthralling brew of love, danger, and perilous fate."　　—Jayne Ann Krentz

"A superb fantasy romance . . . The story line, especially the historical segment, is stupendous. . . . Nicodimus is a wonderful hero and the supporting cast adds dimension while propelling the tale forward to its exciting climax . . . Ms. Shayne augments her growing reputation for some of the best fantasies on the market today."　　—*Painted Rock Reviews*

"A heartfelt and believable love story . . . Maggie Shayne's gift is that she creates believable characters who react very humanly to unbelievable situations. . . . If you like lush romances set in well-conceived fantasy environments, don't miss *Infinity*."　　—*All About Romance*

continued on next page. . .

ETERNITY

"A rich, sensual, and bewitching adventure of good vs. evil, with love as the prize."   —*Publishers Weekly*

"A hauntingly beautiful story of love that endures through time itself."   —Kay Hooper

"Maggie Shayne's gift for melding the mystical and the magical into her novels has made her one of the preeminent voices in paranormal romance today. *Eternity* is an awesome start to a series that promises to be richly textured and powerfully rewarding."   —*Romantic Times*

"Ms. Shayne's talent knows no bounds when it comes to romantic fantasy; her latest is a hauntingly exquisite tale . . . lush . . . heart-stopping suspense, spellbinding romance, and enchanting characters. *Eternity* is to be treasured like the precious gem it is."   —*Rendezvous*

"[*Eternity*] is one of the best books of the decade, as the magnificent Ms. Shayne demonstrates why she is ranked among the top writers of any genre."   —*Affaire de Coeur*

THE
GINGERBREAD
MAN

MAGGIE SHAYNE

JOVE BOOKS, NEW YORK

THE GINGERBREAD MAN

A Jove Book / published by arrangement with
the author

PRINTING HISTORY
Jove edition / October 2001

All rights reserved.
Copyright © 2001 by Margaret Benson.
This book, or parts thereof, may not be reproduced in any form
without permission.
For information address: The Berkley Publishing Group,
a division of Penguin Putnam Inc.,
375 Hudson Street, New York, New York 10014.

Visit our website at
www.penguinputnam.com

ISBN: 0-515-13167-9

A JOVE BOOK®
Jove Books are published by The Berkley Publishing Group,
a division of Penguin Putnam Inc.,
375 Hudson Street, New York, New York 10014.
JOVE and the "J" design
are trademarks belonging to Penguin Putnam Inc.

PRINTED IN THE UNITED STATES OF AMERICA

10 9 8 7 6 5 4 3 2 1

Author's Note

In New York State, the death penalty was reinstated in September of 1995. For the purposes of this novel, I have pushed that date back in my fictional world to 1993.

This novel deals with issues of child abuse. If you would like more information on how you can help protect our children, visit the Center for Missing and Exploited Children at www.missingkids.com.

ONE

⸎

"ARE my children still alive?"

Sara Prague asked the question in a quiet, steady voice that he heard very clearly despite the noise around her. Cops coming and going, keyboards clicking, phones ringing. She looked haggard. Hard. She hadn't always, Vince figured. The worry lines bracketing her eyes, her mouth, the dry skin, the chapped lips, the sense that she really didn't give a damn what she looked like—those things had been strangers to her that first day. The day her kids hadn't come home from school. Now those lines, that hardness, had made themselves at home. It looked as if they planned to stay awhile. This shouldn't have happened to Sara Prague, a PTA mom whose world revolved around her kids. It shouldn't have happened to her husband, Mike, full-time plumber and part-time Little League coach. It shouldn't happen to anyone. Ever.

Vince walked around his desk and eased Sara Prague into a cracked vinyl chair, ignoring the chaos around them. He poured her some stale coffee from the pot on the nearby stand, just as he had every day for the past three weeks. She came in here like clockwork—something the Center for Missing and Exploited Children had probably told her to do. He thought she would keep doing it, too. For years, if necessary.

It wouldn't be necessary, though.

She took the foam cup and sipped automatically. It was all part of their daily ritual. "You haven't answered my question, Detective. Are Bobby and Kara still alive?"

"Mrs. Prague, we're doing everything we possibly can." He walked back around his gray metal desk, pulled out his chair, sat down. It gave him a chance to school his face. It gave him a chance not to look at hers. She was just . . . bleak. Looking into the woman's eyes was like looking into a black hole. Nothing left. "Every lead is being meticulously followed. We're pursuing every avenue of—"

"I don't want the party line you give to the press, Detective O'Mally. I want the truth."

Things crossed his mind. Things every cop knew—like the fact that, in most cases, kids abducted by strangers are either found in the first twenty-four hours or not found at all. Not alive, at any rate. He shook the thought away. It was irrelevant. This was *his* case. The outcome would be different this time. He wouldn't fail.

He forced himself to look her in the eye and managed not to shiver at the dead gray chill of her gaze. "I do think they're alive," he told her. "And I'll keep thinking it until and unless I have a reason to think otherwise." He painted his face with a hopeful expression, reached across the desk, and squeezed her cool, limp hand. "Try to hold on to hope, Mrs. Prague."

"I have to, Detective. I don't have anything else left." Pulling her hand away, she set her coffee cup on his desk, adding a new ring to a file folder already covered with them. She reached inside her purse.

Vince bit back a groan. God, here came more pictures. He couldn't take much more of this daily torture. Then again, he didn't imagine it even began to compare to hers.

"I brought this for you." She pulled it out—a silver

frame that folded in half, like a book. With her free hand she pushed aside some papers—the ring-marked file folder, the wrapper from his mac-breakfast—making a single bare spot on his desk. Then she set the frame there so that it faced him. One side held a photo of five-year-old Kara. Dimples. Freckles. Carrot-colored pigtails and sky-blue eyes. She held a scrawny tiger kitten in her lap. The other side of the frame held a photo of seven-year-old Bobby, posing in his Little League uniform, bat at the ready.

Keeping a professional distance had never been what Vince O'Mally did best. Hell, it was the one thing he wished he *could* do by the book. But he wasn't a by-the-book kind of a cop. His methods were more instinct than science. His gut had gotten him further than any procedural manual or training course ever would. He trusted it. But sometimes it got him too close.

And this was one of those times.

This woman—coming in here every day, with her photos and her red, puffy, lifeless eyes—was dragging him into her anguish. He barely slept nights anymore. Every spare second, on duty or off, he was working this case. It gripped him in a way nothing ever had.

Sara Prague was a needy woman. Not a weak woman, but needy. He didn't do well with needy women. He tended to want to save them. Always a mistake.

"Mrs. Prague . . . ," he began.

"I notice the other photos I've brought aren't on your desk anymore. What do you do with them after I leave?"

He got up and paced away from her, pushing a hand through his hair. "I keep them. Just . . . in a drawer. It's too distracting to have them on the desk like that." Turning, he faced her again. "I understand what you're trying to do, but I need to focus on the case. On chasing down leads and analyzing evidence. Not on how . . ." His gaze strayed to the photo against his will, and his throat closed up. "Not on how goddamn bad I'd like to come to a game next spring, and see Bobby hit a homer."

Sara Prague nodded, her huge haunted eyes never leaving his. "I suppose it seems cruel of me to keep bringing photos. Please understand, I need to know you won't forget that these are my children, Detective O'Mally." Her hand moved to the largest pile of paperwork on his desk, settling atop it. "They aren't in these files. They aren't a case number or a statistic or an investigation. They're Bobby and Kara Prague." She moved her hand to the photo, forcing his gaze to it again. To Kara's baby teeth. To Bobby's unevenly trimmed bangs. "They're *my children.*"

He tried to look away from her, from the need, the plea in her eyes. But he couldn't. She didn't speak, but he heard her anyway. Her eyes said it all. *Tell me it's going to be all right. Tell me you're going to find my babies safe and sound, and put them back in my arms where they belong.*

He knew better. He knew damn well better.

Tears welled in her eyes. Something deep inside him quaked. He said, "It's going to be all right, Mrs. Prague. I'll find your kids. I promise you."

He saw a hint of light come into her eyes, dull, dim, flickering, but fighting its way through the fog of despair. He'd given her hope. It would help her get through the day. Maybe even a couple more beyond that. But at what cost?

Vince O'Mally didn't make promises he couldn't keep. How the hell was he going to keep this one? The photograph tugged his gaze back to it, like a supercharged magnet pulling shards of metal.

She reached across the desk, squeezed his hand. "Thank you for that." Then she got up and left him standing there staring at the photo. He heard the door swing closed when she left, and he still couldn't look away. Even when his vision blurred, he kept staring at those little faces staring back at him.

Then a big hairy hand swung into his line of vision, and swiped the frame off his desk in one brisk motion.

"That woman isn't gonna let up until she drives you right over the edge, is she? Dammit, Vince, you're letting her get to you. I can see it."

Vince sank into his chair, cleared his throat and tried to shake off the grimness that squatted on his shoulders like a lead demon. "Hell, no, I'm not letting her get to me," he told his partner. "I know better." It was a lie and he knew it.

"I used to think so." Jerry tossed the frame onto his own desk, leaving it folded closed. "But look at you, pal. You haven't been right since they handed us this case, and you're getting steadily worse."

"That's bullshit."

"Is it?" Jerry shoved a stack of file folders aside, and perched on the edge of Vince's desk. He wore a white shirt that could've been whiter, and a striped tie that he'd tugged loose. His belly hung two inches over his shiny black belt, and he had less hair on his head every day. "So, what else are you working on, Vince?"

Vince shook his head, ignoring his partner.

"You're not working on anything else, are you? Nothing but this."

"Get off my back, Jerry."

"I heard you just now."

That brought Vince's gaze up. Jerry looked worried—a little scared, even. "Why the hell would you make a promise like that? You know better."

"It helped. The woman is barely standing these days."

"Yeah? And what do you suppose it's gonna do to you if you can't keep it?"

Vince's fist clenched. "We'll never know, because that's not gonna happen."

"Vince—"

"I'm gonna find those kids, Jare."

Jerry sighed, studying his friend's face for a long moment. But when he spoke again, his tone was closer to normal than it had been before. "Still following up on registered sex offenders?"

"Only the pedophiles. And, hell, I've only made it through the first five hundred or so. You know how many convicted perverts we got living like normal people in this city?"

"No, but I'm sure you're gonna tell me."

Vince just looked at him. "I meant what I said. I'm gonna find them."

"Because you're Detective Vincent frigging O'Mally. Decorated supercop who always gets his man. You know, my friend, this case might be easier on you if you'd ever once failed at anything in your entire life."

"You don't know what the hell you're talking about."

"I know this. You're not infallible, Vince. And if this one goes bad, it's not gonna be because you fucked up."

"It's *not* going to go bad," Vince said, meeting his partner's eyes. "And I *don't* fuck up."

The telephone on his desk shrilled. Jerry grabbed it up before Vince could, probably just to piss him off a little and distract him from the case.

"Detective Donovan," Jerry intoned automatically. Then he listened, and his gaze shot to Vince's, and his face went pale. "Shit. Okay, yeah. We're on it."

Jerry put the phone down. "Maybe you'll want to sit this one out, buddy."

Vince got to his feet, grabbed his coat, and tried to fight the dread building in his belly.

———

"THERE'S NOT GOING TO BE ANYTHING IN here." Vince stood just outside the door of a dilapidated house on Syracuse's east side and said words he didn't really believe. Jerry was on the other side of the door. Their guns were raised, their backs to the outer wall. The light wasn't good. Overcast skies tinted everything in sepia. A stiff autumn wind rode herd on dried-out leaves, so they crackled over the sidewalk like rattling bones. "We checked this place out already."

"The caller said there was a bad smell," Jerry said, keeping his voice low. "I don't smell anything, do you Vince?"

Vince didn't really sniff the air. He couldn't make himself do it. He said, "No, I don't smell a damned thing. Probably the same neighbor who reported seeing that beat-up van near here the day the kids were taken. Probably just likes calling the cops. Makes her feel important."

"We checked it out that day," Jerry said. "We didn't miss anything."

Vince looked at his partner. "We didn't miss anything."

Jerry nodded, and Vince turned and pushed the front door open, backed away, then entered cautiously. The place was falling down. Not a piece of glass remained in a single window, but plenty littered the splintered floors underneath thick layers of dust and plaster.

There was a closed door on the far side of the room, its once-white paint peeling off it in great strips. Boards lay here and there, and the floor creaked under their feet. Vince took another careful step. A floorboard broke and his foot went right through. He swore under his breath and yanked his foot free. Then he looked in the hole his foot had made, frowning. A child's storybook lay under the floor, its cardboard cover warped and bent, colors faded. It looked as if it had been lying there for years. Still, Vince carefully picked it up with two gloved fingers to take a closer look. A thick coat of dust covered the title. *The Gingerbread Man.* Odd place for a children's book. There were gaps in the floor all over the place. It must have fallen through one of them, who knew how long ago? Opening the cover carefully he saw a library card pocket. The words "Dilmun Public Library, Dilmun, NY" were stamped there, along with a series of dates. He yanked an evidence bag from his coat pocket—he always carried a handful of them—and dropped the book into it, telling himself it was probably unnecessary, because this place had nothing to do with Bobby and Kara Prague. Nothing. He wasn't going to find a damn thing here.

His instincts were disagreeing vehemently with his mind on that, but he refused to hear them. Still, he jotted a note about the book on his notepad.

Stuffing the bagged book and the notepad into his coat pocket, he looked at the closed door, took a single step toward it. Then the pungent scent hit him and his entire soul recoiled.

"Ah, shit," Jerry said, turning his nose into his collar. "Vince, the smell . . . it's coming from in there." Jerry nodded toward that same closed door at the far end of the place.

Damn, he didn't want to do this. Everything in Vince was screaming at him not to go over there. Not to open that door. Just to turn around and leave. He stepped forward even as his partner reached for the broken door with a trembling hand.

Vince put his own hand on Jerry's shoulder, stopping him. "Why don't you check the other rooms, partner?"

Jerry frowned at him.

"It's my case, Jerry."

"It's *our* case."

Vince lowered his hand. "You've got kids."

"And I've got a partner. We'll go together."

Finally, Vince nodded. Swallowing hard, Jerry pushed the door open. The odor sprung from the pitch darkness and hit them both like a physical blow. Jerry turned his back on it, a knee-jerk reaction. A second later Vince heard his partner's staggering footsteps as he headed back through the house and out the front door, then he heard him retching someplace beyond it. Hell, it looked like Vince would be doing this alone after all.

Stiffening his spine, Vince pulled the lapel of his coat up over his nose and mouth, pulled out his flashlight, and flicked it on.

The beam pierced the darkness, the floating dust specs, the invisible veil between blessed blindness and hell. The pale light spilled onto the bodies of Kara and Bobby Prague, and Vince turned away, but not before the image had burned itself into his brain. He lurched out of the room, and a second later he was outside, on his knees beside his partner. He wasn't puking. Just kneeling there, ice cold, his entire body rigid, eyes wide and unable to erase what they had seen. Unable to silence the voice in his mind telling him he had failed. He'd promised to find those kids—but not like this. *Goddamn,* not like this. He kept seeing Sara Prague's eyes, the hope he had put in them.

"Vince? Vince, what the hell was it . . . ?" Jerry wiped his mouth with a handkerchief, getting to his feet to lean over him. "Was it the Prague kids? Was it them?" When he didn't answer, Jerry swore and turned to go back inside.

Vince got up, grabbed his partner, jerked him around. "Don't go in there."

"The hell I won't." Jerry pulled free.

Vince punched him. Just like that, he clocked his partner in the jaw, knocked him flat on his back. Jerry lay there, blinking up at him in shocked silence.

"No man with kids has any business seeing what's in that room," he muttered. Then he stepped over Jerry to reach into the car for the radio mike, and, keying it, requested a coroner and a forensics team.

<hr>

THREE DAYS LATER, VINCE AND JERRY SAT in Chief Rogers' office. Jerry and the chief seemed to be taking turns shooting worried looks Vince's way, but he did his best to ignore them.

The chief didn't waste a lot of time before coming to the point. "You two are off the Prague case."

Vince surged to his feet. "What do mean? Jesus, chief, we don't even have the autopsy report yet!"

The chief held up both hands and kept talking. "The FBI has it. They've taken over. There have been other cases with what they say are striking similarities in Pennsylvania, Massachusetts, and Jersey. They've got a task force in place to deal with it, and they don't want any locals stepping on their toes."

"That's bullshit," Vince snapped. "I've been working this case for almost a month, dammit. I have to get this guy."

"You're off the case, O'Mally."

"I have to get this guy."

The chief glanced sideways at Jerry, then focused on Vince again. "Sit down."

"I—"

"Sit. Down."

Vince sat, but stiffly. He braced himself on the edge of the chair, his hands balled into fists on his knees.

"When's the last time you shaved, O'Mally? Huh?" The chief eyed him, looking more concerned than stern. "How long since you've eaten a full meal, or had a few hours' sleep? Have you walked by a mirror lately?"

Vince averted his eyes. "I've been busy."

"You're running on empty. You can't possibly be thinking clearly. Now, I know that crime scene got to you. It got to all of us. The forensics team that went in there is undergoing group counseling, and they admit they're having trouble. And these guys have seen damn near everything."

"I'm fine," Vince insisted.

"No. I don't think so. Do you think he's fine, Jerry?"

Jerry shook his head. "No sir, I don't think he's fine at all."

"Jerry, for crying out—"

"I'm sorry partner, but you've been messed up since you came out of that room. I don't know what the hell to do about it. You insisted on talking to Sara Prague yourself—breaking the news, when I begged you to let someone else do it. When you came out of her house that day you looked . . . dead, Vince. You looked dead. You're drowning in this case, man, and I don't know how to pull you out."

Vince tipped his head back, rolled his eyes at the ceiling.

"I'm gonna give you a choice, O'Mally," the chief said slowly. "Take a thirty-day leave, get out of here, get away from this thing, and see if you can shake it off."

"No way. I'm seeing this thing through to the end, Feds or no Feds. What's behind door number two, Chief?"

"An hour a day with Dr. Feltzer."

"The shrink from hell?" The chief nodded. "For how long?" Vince asked.

"Until she says you're passably sane."

"Hell, she didn't think I was passably sane the day they hired me."

"Your decision. Either way, you're off this case. I want everything you have on my desk in ten minutes. That goes for you, too, Jerry."

"So you can turn it all over to the Feds?" Vince asked, disgusted by the thought.

"Those are my orders. After that, I want you to go home. Take the rest of the day off, and let me know what you decide—the leave or the shrink."

"But—"

"I'm done talking," the chief said. "You can go now."

"But, Chief, I—"

"Go. Now." He lifted an arm, pointed at the door.

Vince stormed out of the chief's office and headed for his desk. Jerry was right on his heels, but he ignored his partner as he pulled file folder after file folder off the sloping stacks on his desk and dropped them into the little wastebasket beside it. Papers flew like confetti. He could feel everyone in the place looking at him as if he'd lost it. He ignored them all, opened drawers, rummaging through them, gathering up every scribbled note and every paperclip that had any connection to the Prague case. Slamming one drawer closed he yanked open another, and then another, until at last, he opened the drawer with the pile of framed photos inside.

He stopped, frozen, and stared down at the freckled

faces. His shoulders quaked, but he caught himself, held himself in a hard, merciless grip.

"Those . . . probably ought to be sent back to the mother," Jerry said, his voice hoarse.

"Yeah."

"I'll take care of it for you."

Vince nodded, then reached in and picked up the most recent photo. He handed it to Jerry. "All but this one, okay?"

"Vince?"

"I want the Feds to have this one. Tell 'em to look at it every day. Tell 'em this is what that bastard killed, not that pile of paperwork. This."

Jerry nodded and took the framed photo. "So . . . you gonna take the time off, or the treatment?"

"I don't know yet." He picked up the wastebasket, handed that to Jerry as well. "Give this to the chief for me." Reaching for the computer on his desk, he peeled off a half dozen yellow sticky notes, wadded them up and tossed them into the trash can as well. Lastly, Vince hit a button, and a disk popped out of the A-drive. He took it, and tucked it into his shirt pocket.

"What's that, Vince?"

"What's what?"

Jerry scowled. "What did you do? Did you keep a copy of your files on this case?"

"Shit, pal, when did you ever see me organized enough to think of something like that?"

"Vince. You gotta let this one go."

Vince met his partner's eyes for one long moment, then looked away. "I'm going home. I'll see you later."

Jerry sighed as Vince left the office.

Halfway back to his apartment, three miles from the police station, Vince glanced down and noticed his coat lying on the passenger seat. It had been warm for this late in the fall. He hadn't worn the coat since . . .

The kids. The house. The book. His senses prickled.

He'd turned the book in, and then forgot he had. But there had been something . . .

Slamming on his brakes, he jerked the wheel and brought the Jeep Wrangler to a jerky stop on the shoulder. He grabbed his coat, searched the pockets and found his dog-eared notepad. Flipping it open, he read what he had written there: *The Gingerbread Man.* Dilmun Public Library, Dilmun, NY.

TWO

꧁꧂

IT took fifteen minutes to walk from the neat little house on Lakeview to the Dilmun Police Department on East Main. Holly knew this because she walked it every weekday—unless there was a blizzard or something. It was one of her favorite parts of the day, her walk to work. Mostly because of the little girl who walked beside her.

She looked down at Bethany, seven going on fifteen, as the little girl waved to her mother standing by her front door. Her mother blew her a kiss, and Bethany blew one back, her blonde curls gleaming in the morning sun.

God, she reminded Holly so much of Ivy.

Holly glanced east toward the crooked finger shape of Cayuga Lake, partly to hide the rush of emotion from her favorite next-door neighbor. "Look at the way the sun gleams on the water," she said. "It's the most peaceful thing in the world, isn't it?"

"Especially now that all the summer people are gone," Bethany said.

Tourist season was over. There was no breeze as they walked along together, but the tangy scent of dead leaves and a crisp autumn bite flavored the air. It was good here. Nothing bad ever happened in Dilmun.

She let her gaze travel farther along the lake's shore, past a half-dozen empty rental cabins that lined the southern shore, to the hulking shape of Reginald D'Voe's Gothic mansion on the far side. "Look, Beth. The leaves have fallen enough so you can see Reggie's house from here."

"Creepy!" Bethany remarked, with a smile that said she loved it.

The house hunched above the town on a small hill, separated from it by a thick stand of woods, and the narrowest part of the lake. That mansion had always reminded Holly of an aging vulture.

"Have you ever been inside?" Bethany asked.

"No. Have you?"

"No, but they say old Reggie is going to have a Halloween party this year. Every kid in town is invited. I might go."

Holly glanced down at the girl with her brows raised. "A party? Really? I thought Reggie was a recluse." Bethany wrinkled her nose and tilted her head to one side. "You know, a hermit?"

"Oh." Bethany shrugged. "I don't know. Mom says he used to have a Halloween party every year, way back in the old days."

Holly nodded. Reginald D'Voe, the town's favorite claim to fame, had moved away for several years, but just the year before last he'd come back, taking up residence once again. As little as anyone saw of him, Holly figured most of the locals never even knew he'd been gone.

"Have you ever seen any of his movies?" Bethany asked.

"Hasn't everyone?"

Bethany giggled. "He comes to school sometimes. He is a great story reader."

"Is he?"

"The best!" Bethany exclaimed with an enthusiastic nod.

"So you haven't decided if you're going to his party?"

"I don't know. Everyone who goes has to wear a costume, and I don't have a costume for Halloween yet." She shrugged. "Still, Mom says it will be the biggest party of the whole year."

They came to the intersection where Bethany had to turn off to go to the school. Last year, Holly had walked the girl every step of the way. Now, Bethany insisted on traveling that last block alone. And in deference to her pride, Holly had to let her, though it almost killed her to release the girl's hand every time.

Bethany waved. "Bye, Holly!"

"Bye, hon. Have a good day. Be careful."

Grinning, Bethany skipped off, blonde hair flying behind her. She joined several other kids heading for the school at the far end of the block. Holly didn't start walking. Instead she stood near the corner and watched them all the way to the school building. And she kept watching, until they got safely through the front doors.

Only then did she continue on her way to work.

She had to walk through the tourist section of town to get to the police station at the other end, but she didn't mind. She loved walking the tourist strip this time of year, when it was all but deserted, other than a few shopkeepers just unlocking their front doors, or sweeping colorful fallen leaves off their section of sidewalk. The trees were nearly bare now. Skeletal.

The strip ended suddenly at the intersection of Main and Fairfax. Here was the barber shop, the small grocery store–slash–gas station, the library, Mr. Lee's Ice Cream Emporium, which was closed now that the tourist season had ended. It closed at the same time every year.

She liked that about this town. Its predictability. Its regularity. She thrived on calm, order, and a good solid routine. Serene waters were the kind she needed in her life,

she mused, glancing toward the ever-present lake. She
didn't do well in stormy seas.

She was so intent on looking at the lake that had become a fixture in her life that she didn't see the man
standing outside the police station until she heard his impatient thumping on the door, and his deep voice, saying,
"What the hell is the *matter* with this town, anyway?"

Great. A stumbling block in the path of her daily routine. She *hated* when that happened. Scowling, she picked
up the pace, walking right up behind the man. He was
bending over, hands cupped on either side of his eyes as
he peered through the glass, trying to see between the
lettering of the words DILMUN POLICE DEPARTMENT.

"Actually, there's *nothing* the matter with this town,"
she said, coming to a stop behind him. "Not to those of
us who live here, anyway."

He straightened, not turning around. "And to those who
don't?" he asked, meeting her gaze reflected in the window. She couldn't make out much of his face. The glass
was tinted. Her impressions were three. Big. Dark. And
moody.

"Those who don't," she quipped, "are free to leave if
they don't like it here."

He finally turned and faced her. Holly shivered as a
cloud passed over the sun, and its shadow slid over her.
The man frowned and nodded once. "I didn't mean to
insult your town. I was just surprised to find a sheriff's
office closed."

She crossed her arms over her chest, the way her
mother did sometimes, and she just looked at him. His
face was craggy—far from handsome. His jaw was too
hard, and his chin too clefted. His nose was too big, and
his eyes too far apart. He looked tired and worn down . . .
but that was more a mental impression than a physical
one.

"Maybe I should start over again," he said.

She shrugged. "The tourist area is back that way," she
told him, pointing.

"I'm not a tourist."

"Well, you're not a resident." Frowning, she glanced at her watch. "And you're really lousing up my schedule. Do you mind?" She reached into her pocket for her keys, and motioned for him to move aside.

He moved, then stood there while she unlocked it. "Don't tell me you're the police chief," he said.

She shot him an irritated glance. "Why couldn't I be?"

He held up a hand, ticked off his list on his fingers. "Too young, too pretty, too mouthy, too unfriendly, too—"

"Do you have some kind of business with Chief Mallory?"

"Then you're not him?"

She opened the door and walked inside. "No," she said. "I'm not him. He'll be in at eight. If you want to see him, come back then." She released the door, letting it fall closed on the irritating man, and turned to get herself back on track. Damn, the clock read 7:50. She always got in by 7:45. Okay, okay, just focus, she told herself. She stood there for a moment and drew a deep breath. Then she moved through the small police department with brisk efficiency, quickly resuming her established routine. She snapped on the reception area lights, opened the blinds . . . then paused again to look out at the lake in the distance. Something had changed. Tiny whitecaps crisscrossed the surface now, as if the glassy stillness of a short while ago had been shattered. "Must be a storm coming," she muttered, glancing worriedly at traces of dark clouds just beginning to gather in the sky.

Turning, she unlocked the next door and went through it to the larger part of the station. Her alcove to the right had a sliding plastic bifold shutter over the window between it and the reception area. To the left were files, weapons locked in a big case, and Bill's and Ray's desks. Straight ahead was the chief's office, and beside that a small restroom and the stair door. The cells were farther along the hall, with a clear line of sight all the way back to the reception area when the door was opened. Holly continued turning on lights, opening blinds. She unlocked the chief's office door and fired up his computer for him. Back in her own area, she turned on the lights, the radio, then the computer, in that order. A quick check of her desk told her everything was exactly as she'd left it. She straightened her pencil cup, moved a paperweight an inch to the left. Then she opened the sliding plastic barrier between her desk and the reception area.

That man was standing on the other side, looking right at her.

She almost jumped out of her skin, jerking backward. One hand pressed to her chest in reaction.

"I decided I'd rather wait for the chief in here. It's getting kind of nippy outside."

She closed her eyes slowly, waited for her heart to resume its normal beat, consciously controlled her breathing, then opened her eyes. Focusing on the man again, she said, "Do you have a crime to report or something Mr. . . . ?"

"It's detective, ma'am. Detective Vince O'Mally, S.P.D."

She lifted her brows. He said "S.P.D." as if it was supposed to mean something. He said it the way TV cops said "N.Y.P.D." or "L.A.P.D." He was that full of himself. "S.P.D.?" she asked. "Would that be . . . Scranton? Saratoga? Sherburne?"

"Syracuse."

She nodded, averting her eyes. For some reason it didn't surprise her he came from there . . . or that he'd brought foul winds with him. She didn't like him. She wanted him to leave. "Have a seat, Detective. The chief will be here in . . ."—she looked at her watch—"five minutes. And thanks to you, his coffee won't be ready."

"Thanks to me? What did I do?"

She just frowned at him and hurried back to the restroom, snatching the water pitcher from her shelf on the way. She flicked on the restroom lights and then filled the pitcher with tap water. Finished, she carried it back to the reception area. The coffee pot stood on a cart against the west wall, between two small leather sofas. She poured the water into it and rummaged underneath for the coffee and filters, while the man observed her every action. She could feel his eyes burning holes into her back, and she was so rattled by his presence that her hand shook as she measured the French roast into the basket, scattering bits of coffee all over the cart's surface. "Damn." She slammed the basket into place, hit the ON button, and immediately looked at her watch. *"Damn."*

"Are you okay, Red?"

She pivoted to face him. He wasn't sitting as she'd told him to. In fact, he was standing only a foot or two behind her. "My name is not Red. It's Holly. Holly Newman."

"And you make the coffee."

"Among other things."

"And you take your job very seriously."

Her glare heated. She felt it heat. It should have wilted him by now. He should have smoke curling from the ends of his dark hair. "Excuse me?"

He smiled, but it never reached his eyes. There was something dark about the man, and his eyes seemed hidden among shadows. They were blue, but not vivid. Dull, though she felt that was not their natural state.

"It's not like the coffee being five minutes late is going to bring about the ruin of Dilmun, is it?"

He didn't look sarcastic or teasing. He just looked . . . tired. She felt her lips narrow. "Just what is it you're doing here, Detective? I know it's not anything official, so—"

He held up a stop-sign hand. "Wait a minute. How do you know that?"

She shrugged. "We don't have any real crime in Dilmun. Much less anything important enough to bring you all the way down here from Syracuse. Nothing bad ever happens here. And besides, I know everything that goes on in this office. The chief hasn't had any official communications from . . . um . . . *S.P.D.*" She smirked when she said it. "So what are you doing here?"

"You're sharp, Red. You oughtta be a cop."

"You're changing the subject."

He held up both hands. "You going to arrest me?"

She rolled her eyes and turned to head back into her office. He stopped her at the doorway by speaking. "Actually, you're right. I'm not here on business. At least, not officially. The truth is, I'm on vacation."

Narrowing her eyes on him, she battled a shiver. "And what is your unofficial business?"

"I can't tell you that."

"And if I should call S.P.D. and ask them?"

"You'd probably get me fired."

He wasn't kidding. His manner was completely matter-of-fact. Something weighed on the man. Something big.

The bell jangled as the front door opened, and Chief Mallory walked in, making the room seem immediately smaller. He stopped where he was, his brows drawing together, his gaze moving from Holly standing nose to chest with the big, full-of-himself detective, to the coffee cart, with puddles of water, a dusting of grounds, and a pot that was only half filled. His frown grew deeper.

"Holly?" he asked, one hand inching toward the gun at his side.

"Whoa, wait a minute, now . . ." O'Mally backed away from her, holding both his hands up to about shoulder height and looking from Chief Mallory to her and back again. "I'm a cop, okay? For a town with no crime in it, the residents are sure as hell nervous."

"It's okay, Chief," Holly said. "This is Detective O'Mally, down from Syracuse. He's been waiting to see you, and irritating me." She shook her head in disgust. "Sorry about the coffee."

"Honey, I can wait five minutes for my coffee." The chief relaxed, and walked forward, extending a hand. "Sorry about the reaction, Detective. I'm not used to seeing Holly flustered."

"I was not flustered," Holly called as she headed into her office. "Just distracted!" She returned with a roll of paper towels, and proceeded to clean up the coffee cart.

The two men shook hands and the chief said, "We can talk in my office. Holly, will you bring us back some coffee when it's ready?"

She nodded, smiling easily at the chief, then gritted her teeth and held the smile in place with effort as she asked, "How do you like it, O'Mally?"

He pierced her eyes with his. He just said, "Black." And for some reason the word sent a chill right up her spine.

There was something dark living inside that man. It had peeked out at her just now. Holly recognized it at once, because she had seen it many times before.

In the mirror.

THREE

<small>◆◆◆</small>

DILMUN was one strange little town, nestled at the southern tip of the Finger Lake named Cayuga. Part of it was quaint to the point of "tacky tourist trap" status, and seemed designed to fool you into thinking you were on the New England coast. Cross a street and you found yourself in a typical small town that could have been Mayberry. Walk the other way and you might think you'd been dropped into the middle of a scene from *The Last of the Mohicans,* with the wild-looking forests and that dark-water lake. Vince had rented a cabin along its shore for a remarkably reasonable price. He'd found lodgings easily, with no more than a couple of phone calls. He figured this late in the fall, with the water too cold for swimming, and with the leaves past their peak and rapidly vacating their gnarly branches, he wasn't facing much competition for the space.

The redhead was almost as contradictory as the town. Cute as hell, though certainly no raging beauty. She was small, slight, with a pageboy cut and bright green eyes. She had secrets, that redhead. She'd been shaken when he'd said where he was from. A blind man could have seen it. Maybe she knew something about his case.

Or maybe he was just so damned eager to find some answers out here that he was seeing things that weren't there. He'd gone back to his apartment in Syracuse only long enough to pack what he needed and make a few hasty arrangements. He'd placed a quick call to the chief, and another to Jerry saying he had decided to take that time off—that he was going to the country for some R and R. He couldn't very well say where he had really gone, much less why. Hell, he was out here on a whim. A hunch. A children's book at a crime scene, which could have been left there by anyone. School kids hanging out where they shouldn't. Vagrants. The former residents of the condemned house. A freaking pack rat could have dragged it in, for all he knew.

He was reaching. He had no plan, no outline, no standard operating procedure. All he had was his gut. And his gut was still so knotted up over what he'd seen inside that dilapidated house that he wasn't even sure he could trust it anymore. He was staggering under the weight of his own broken promise and the knowledge that he'd missed the book the first time he'd been inside that old house. It did little good to rationalize that it had been out of sight. He knew the weight of his conscience wouldn't ease. Not until he found the monster who had killed those kids, and made him pay.

And he wondered if the weight would ease, even then.

The Dilmun police chief leaned back in a chair that must have had to strain to hold him. He was a big man. Not fat. Just big. "So what brings you to Dilmun, Detective O'Mally?"

"Research on a case. Technically I'm off duty, but you know how that goes. You wear a badge, you're always on."

"You got that right." The chief nodded toward a chair, and Vince sat down knowing he had a foot in the door. Reminding the man of the vocation they held in common ought to go a long way.

"Actually, the chances of there being any connection between the suspect I'm looking for and this town are slim to none."

"Probably," Mallory said, smiling. Believing.

"Still, I thought as long as I was here, enjoying some down time, I may as well check it out."

"Makes perfect sense to me."

Mallory seemed totally relaxed and not the least bit suspicious. He leaned back even farther, crossing his arms behind his head, and thumping his boots onto the desktop. "So who is it you're looking for?"

"Don't know. What I *do* know, is that he was in possession of a book from the Dilmun Public Library. A long overdue book, by the looks of things."

Chief Mallory raised a brow. "Is that what he's wanted for, son? Delinquent library fines?"

"Nah, but it's almost as trivial." He would keep it light. At the first mention of child murders, he figured he'd be screwed. The entire town would clam up in panic, and every rat in it would scurry to his hole. The sheriff would probably run Vince out on a rail. So he wouldn't mention it. He had his cover story ready. He'd had time to think about it on the drive down here. "This guy stole a car, went joyriding, and wrecked it. If the heap hadn't belonged to a judge's son, I wouldn't even be bothering with this." He lied as smoothly as a politician, he thought. And yet something flickered in the chief's eyes. Was that a hint of suspicion behind the friendly smile? Had there been the slightest narrowing of those worry-free eyes? No. Not now, at least. If there had been such a flash, it was gone fast. "I tried to talk to Ms. Baker, over at the library, last night, but she wasn't too inclined to help me out. And it's not as if I have a warrant or anything, so I didn't push. Like I said, I just figured as long as I was in town . . ." He left the words hanging in the air.

The chief's feet came down with a thump and he sat up in his chair. "Local folks around Dilmun are a little bit wary of strangers. Oh, they don't mind the tourists much—but they don't mix with 'em, either."

"I see."

"Tell you what. You give me the title of that overdue library book, and I'll get the information for you—that is, if the library even has a record of the book being missing." He reached for a pen, held it poised and sent Vince a questioning look.

"It was a children's book. *The Gingerbread Man.*"

The chief blinked. "You're joking."

"Nope." Vince shrugged. "I told it you it was a longshot."

He looked at Vince for a long moment, then his face split in a huge grin. His hands slapped the desk. Gusts of laughter burst from him, and Vince wasn't sure, but he thought the man's eyes began to water. "That must be one badass car thief," he gasped, between bouts of hilarity, "with readin' material like that!"

Vince smiled, too, shaking his head as if he found it all just as funny. "Well, we found the book in the vehicle, and it didn't belong to the owner. So we figured . . ." Vince lifted his hands expressively.

The chief got his laughter under control, wiped at his eyes, drew a steadying breath.

"I don't plan to worry too much one way or the other," Vince told him. "I'm gonna laze around the cabin and look out at the lake, and anything more strenuous than that will have to wait till my vacation time is used up."

Grinning broadly, the chief nodded. "I hear that. So you rented one of Marty Cantrell's cabins, did you?"

"Sure did. It's gorgeous out there."

"Fishing's not bad, either."

"No?"

The door opened and the redhead walked in with the pot of coffee. She reached up to the shelf behind the door to take down two real coffee mugs—no foam cups for the chief of police around here—and, setting them on the desk, began to pour. "Must be something pretty funny going on in here," she said as she filled the mugs. Her gaze slid over Vince's face, seemed to catch on his eyes before she managed to jerk it free.

"Detective O'Mally is looking for someone with an overdue library book," the chief said, laughter still in his voice.

She lifted her brows. "Really?" She sent him a glance that was almost teasing. He found he liked it on her far better than the irritated expression that was all he'd managed to induce in her earlier. "They must think very highly of you at S.P.D. to send you out here on such a delicate case."

He gave her a smirk. She only smirked back.

"You haven't heard the best part yet," the chief went on. "This must be one hardened criminal he's after. The missing book—it's *The Gingerbread Man.*"

Vince saw something change in her face. Like the light in her eyes just blinked out, or some kind of shade came crashing down to block it out. Her cheeks paled.

" 'Run, run, run, as fast as you can. You can't catch me, I'm the gingerbread man,' " Chief Mallory chanted.

The redhead dropped the coffee pot. It shattered, and hot black liquid splashed onto the legs of her jeans. She stood there, staring down at the mess as if she didn't quite know what it was.

Vince and the chief were on their feet instantly, the chief coming around the desk to grip the woman's shoulders. "Damn, Holly, you could've scalded yourself!" He pushed her backward a couple of steps, out of the mess. "You okay? Hmm?"

Pounding feet brought two other men to the open door. The officers must have arrived since Vince had been in the chief's office. One was tall and blond, the other stockier, dark. Both wore uniforms and shields.

"What happened?"

"You all right, Holly?"

She looked up at them and nodded, but she still seemed rather dazed. "I . . . don't know. I guess my hand slipped."

The frowns those two men sent to one another and then

to the chief said they flat out didn't believe that.

The redhead gave a shrug that pretended to be casual, and pushed past them to head to the restroom beyond the door. When she came back, she was using a mop's handle to push a rolling pail along, and she looked as if nothing unusual had happened.

"Okay, clear out, boys. Let me get this mess cleaned up."

The two officers backed out of the way, and Holly mopped up the spilled coffee and pushed all the broken pieces of the pot into a pile. "Too bad about my timing," she said. "I didn't even get a cup yet."

"I'm sorry," Vince said, watching her more closely than before. Because now he'd stopped doubting his twisted-up gut. She had just confirmed his hunch. She knew something.

"Don't be silly. You were nowhere near me." She pulled a whisk broom and a dustpan from the basket attached behind the mop pail, and briskly swept up the traces of the accident, dumping them neatly into the chief's wastebasket.

"I got the feeling it was something I said," Vince said, watching her face.

She brushed off her hands, "You weren't the one speaking."

It was not, he realized, any kind of an answer.

"Maybe it's just that I haven't had my coffee," she added with another carefully casual shrug, and she backed out of the room, pulling the mop, pail, broom, and dustpan with her into the hall, and then reached back to close the door.

Vince stared at the door for a long time after she closed it. "She's a jumpy little thing, isn't she?" he asked.

"No, as a matter of fact, Holly is the steadiest, calmest person who's ever worked for me," Chief Mallory admitted, and there was real concern in his tone.

Vince turned slowly toward the chief. "Was it me, do you think?"

The chief's worry lines didn't ease much with his smile. "Nah. She must just be having an off day. It happens to all of us once in a while . . . I suppose."

He frowned at the door in a way that told Vince it *didn't*—at least not to Holly Newman. It told him something else, too. Holly was a fragile sort of woman. Or at least that was how the men in this office perceived her. Weak and fragile.

"I'll . . . uh . . . I'll check in with her mother, all the same. Just to make sure nothing's going on."

It was an odd thing to hear a police chief say. A personal thing. It crossed Vince's mind that there were more differences between Dilmun and Syracuse than the 60 miles on routes 81 and 13.

A *lot* more.

<hr />

CHIEF MALLORY WAITED UNTIL HE'D watched the stranger go. Then he picked up the phone and dialed Maddie Baker over at the library. She answered crisply, but her tone softened when he said, "Maddie, hon? I need a favor."

He could almost see her smiling at him, perfect false teeth looking a size too big for her mouth. Maddie could seem as mean as tar to outsiders. Only the locals knew what a sweetheart she was. "What can I do for you, Chief?"

"There was a fella over there askin' about an overdue library book last night, as I understand it."

"Why, yes. Yes, there was. I *told* him any records we might have dating back that far would be in the basement, but he just wouldn't give up. I didn't like him. He was pushy, that fellow."

"Back how far, Maddie?" Chief Mallory asked.

"Oh, near to twenty years. Said the date due stamped on the book was nineteen eighty-three, for heaven's sake."

Mallory nodded. "I'll tell you what, Maddie. How

about you let me come on over and take a look through those files in the basement, hmm? See if I can figure out what this pushy young fellow is looking for."

"Well, if you think it's important, Chief."

"I do. And Maddie?"

"Yes?"

"Let's just keep this between you and me for right now. All right?"

THE WIND OFF THE LAKE HAD KICKED UP during the morning, and it didn't seem too eager to let up. When Holly walked the fifty-three steps from the police station to the Paradise Café, she had to tug her denim jacket's collar up, and bow her head. Leaves flew like flocks of brittle birds, and the air was heavy with unshed rain. Holly walked into the café at one minute past twelve, closed the door against the wind, and reached up absently to finger comb her hair. A leaf drifted loose and floated to the floor, landing squarely in the middle of one of the neat square tiles. For a moment her gaze remained on the floor, its perfect checkerboard pattern, straight, predictable lines, square corners.

Glancing up, she saw her mother sitting at their usual booth, and waved to her as she started across the red-and-white tiled floor. She felt out of sorts and distracted. Even after Vince O'Mally had left the station this morning, her routine had never really fallen into place again. She'd answered the phones, filled out forms, paid bills, done some filing—all the usual things, but she'd done them with the feeling that something was off. She was running behind. Her pattern, broken. And she kept wishing she could undo the day and start it over again, the way she could have done with a row of knitting. Just take the end of the yarn and pull it all out, all the way back to the spot where the pattern had become altered—then start over again from there.

If she could do that, though, she'd pull that thread all the way back to October 10, 1983. Start *that* day over.

She forced herself not to think about that. Things were off today. And there was a niggling in the back of her mind, but she was ignoring that, as well. She was very good at ignoring things. It only took concentration. She'd had lots of practice.

"Honey?"

She looked up, realizing she had walked all the way across the diner to the table where her mother waited, and shaking herself, she managed a smile as she slid into the booth. "Hi, Mom. How did your morning go?"

"Holly . . . honey, are you all right?"

Startled, she searched her mother's face. "Of course I am. Why would you think otherwise?"

"Well . . ." She reached across the table, covered Holly's hands with her own. "You were counting just now."

Holly rolled her eyes. "Oh, I was not."

"You were. You were counting as you crossed the room. Your steps, I think. Very quietly. Sweetheart, did something happen this morning?"

Holly tensed and gazed around the diner, wondering if anyone else had noticed her odd behavior. Counting. Dammit, she had stopped counting *years* ago.

Oh, hell. *He* was here, sitting on a red vinyl-topped stool at the counter, and watching her. He lifted a hand in greeting. She pursed her lips, nodded hello, and looked away.

"Should I make an appointment with Dr. Graycloud?" her mother asked.

Holly bit her lip, swallowed her anxiety, and turned back to her mother with a forced smile. "I was thinking about floor tiles for the dining room," she said. "Like these—different colors, of course—but the texture and the quality of these are just what I had in mind."

"Floor tiles." The words were heavy with doubt.

"Uh-huh. I was thinking about square footage just before I walked in here. I just didn't realize when I started figuring how many tiles we'd need, and what it would cost, that I was counting out loud." She made her smile broader. "I guess I was more into my planning than I thought I was."

Her mother still looked doubtful, but Holly knew she would believe her. Her mother would want to believe her too badly to give in to suspicions. But if this nonsense kept up . . .

Her mother looked past her, distracted by something. And Holly turned to follow her gaze.

Vince O'Mally was bearing down on them, carrying a coffee carafe he must have charmed away from Tracy, the teenage waitress. Not saying a word, he reached for the coffee mug in front of Holly, flipped it upright, and filled it. "Coffee's on me, Red," he told her.

"That isn't necessary," Holly said.

"Sure it is. You told me yourself you never got a cup this morning." He glanced across the table. "You haven't introduced me to your friend." As he spoke he lifted the pot and arched a questioning brow. Doris nodded and Vince filled her cup as well.

Doris smiled at him. "I'm Doris. Holly's mother."

Holly didn't like the man. Something about him set her teeth on edge. Still, she said, "Mom, this is Detective O'Mally—"

"Vince," he said.

"Right. Vince. He's with the Syracuse Police Department. Their special library crimes unit or something." He shot her an amused look as he took her mother's hand in greeting.

"It's a pleasure, Ms. Newman."

"Call me Doris," she said. Then she turned to Holly. "And how is it you two know each other?"

"I had some business with the chief this morning," Vince said before Holly could answer. "There was a mishap with the coffee, the pot got smashed to bits, and I think it was partly my fault. I doubt Holly ever got her morning caffeine."

"Really?" Doris looked from Vince to Holly and back again. "And, um . . . are you here at the café all alone?" When O'Mally nodded, Holly knew what was coming but couldn't speak quickly enough to prevent it. "Well, why don't you pull up a chair and join us?"

Vince glanced at Holly, but where she expected to see a smirk of triumph in his eyes, she saw only a question. Reluctantly, she nodded. Only then did he say, "Thanks, I think I will." He pulled up a chair from a nearby vacant table, and sat down at theirs.

"What brings you to Dilmun, Detective?"

"Oh, just vacation time. I have a couple of weeks to fill. Thought someplace quiet would do me good."

"I'd say you came to the right place. We used to live in Syracuse, you know. Liked it so much down here we never wanted to go back."

"Really?" Vince glanced at Holly. "You didn't mention that."

She only shrugged. But she sent her mother a pleading look. They didn't talk about that time, that place. They just didn't. Her mother was breaking a sacred, if unspoken, vow by even mentioning it.

"How long have you been living here?" Vince asked.

"Gosh, must be going on five years now."

"And where in Syracuse did you live?"

Holly set her cup down on the table. Hard. Her mother, who had been about to answer him, closed her mouth and they both looked at Holly, brows raised. "Will you two excuse me for a minute?" She got to her feet. "I just . . . uh . . . I'll be back." Holly hurried into the restroom, closed the door behind her, stood there, and realized she'd counted again. She'd counted the steps to the restroom, and she had no idea if it had been aloud or not.

She braced her hands on the sink, and stared into the mirror. "Okay, so what's going on with you, huh?" she asked her reflection.

"You okay, Holly?" a small voice asked.

Holly turned to see Bethany Stevens standing there looking up at her with eyes big enough to swim in.

Holly swallowed hard, and plastered a smile on her face. "Hey, you. What are you doing out of school?"

"Half day today. Good thing, too. It's tough this year."

"Yeah, I'll bet. I heard you got Mrs. Predmore."

Bethany nodded. "She's not mean or anything. Just gives lots of homework."

"Second grade is like that."

Bethany came up to the sink, turned on the tap, and washed her hands. "Me and Mom decided to have lunch out. Dad had to go out of town this week, so it's just us." The little girl stood on tiptoes to look into the mirror, fussed a bit with her long blonde hair.

"So, have you decided yet?" Holly asked. "About the Halloween party?"

Beth shrugged. "What do you think, Holly? Do *you* think I'm too old to dress up for Halloween?"

Holly smiled, and wished for the times something so small was the major dilemma of the day. "Bethany, *I* still dress up for Halloween," she said.

"I sure would like to see the inside of Reggie's place."

Holly lifted her brows. "Me, too."

"Mom says he used to have one of these parties every single year, before he moved away. She says they were the best parties anywhere, when she was a kid."

"My aunt Jen told me the same thing. That spooky old house of his has to be the best place around for a Halloween party."

"Yeah." Bethany nodded hard. "Maybe I will go. If you really think I'm not too old."

"You're definitely not too old."

Bethany smiled up at her. "Will you help me figure out a costume?"

"We will put together the best costume Dilmun has ever seen." She clasped Bethany's hand, led her to the door, and they walked out together.

Halfway to the table, Bethany looked up with her bright blue eyes and said, "Having you next door is like having my very own older sister. I always wanted one, you know."

Holly's smile froze in place as Bethany turned and ran to join her mom at their corner booth.

FOUR

<small>⚯⚯⚯</small>

HIM. *It's him! What the hell is he doing here? I know his face. He's the cop who found the bodies. His face was splashed all over the papers. And now he's here. Jesus, sweet Jesus, does he know? Is he onto me?*

Oh, God, he's talking to her *of all people!*

Okay, wait. I need to get a grip, here. He may not know anything at all about me. About her, maybe, but that's okay. That's okay, that won't tell him a fucking thing. It would explain his coming out here. Talking to her. But that's all. Maybe that's all.

Son of a bitch found my place. Found my sugarpie and her goddamn brother before I could out them to rest. Of course, the boy wouldn't have gone beside her. He didn't belong. He got in the way.

Holly is a basket case. She's crazy. He'll find that out soon enough. She won't be any help to him at all. She's fucking crazy. Everyone knows it.

But why is he here? Why is he lying about what he's doing here?

To protect the crazy bitch, maybe. Yeah. Yeah, that could be it. He has to know I won't let her talk to him.

He figures if I know what he's really after, I'll have to shut her up, just in case. But she may not know, either. If she did, she'd have run her mouth about it long before now, wouldn't she? Fucking ungrateful little brats usually did if you let them.

Still, that nosy cop might not know a damn thing. Not yet. Not yet.

But what if he does?

Hell, I've got to be sure.

HOLLY DIDN'T GO STRAIGHT HOME FROM work. She started to. She walked along her usual route, back through the strip, where the shops were mostly closed now, all the way down to the leading edge of Lakeview Road. Her home, her safe, comfortable haven, was five houses ahead on the right.

So why did her eyes keep wandering along Shoreline Drive's beach-hugging loop? Why was her body turning to take that stretch of road, even though it meant turning right into the brisk, chilly wind? And why on earth were her feet carrying her amid the rustling leaves, along the gravel road that was all but deserted at this time of the year?

She didn't know. She did know that it was a mistake. Disaster always followed when you took the long way home, she'd learned. You just didn't veer from your routine. You stuck to a plan, and in that way you could be in control.

She wasn't in control right now. And that scared her.

The lake was dotted with dancing whitecaps, and the wind nipped at her nose and cheeks, razing them. The closer she walked, sneakers crunching over gravel, the more intense that wind became. Trees lined the left side of the road, their limbs shedding any remaining leaves rapidly, their colors fading like the color of an old man's eyes. Tall reeds, cattails, and muck stretched for several yards along the roadside. As she passed those waving, whispering rushes, the sky seemed to darken by degrees. It was as if every breath of wind blew a little more of the daylight away. It was completely unlike her not to go straight home. And she hadn't gone through all those years of therapy not to know why that was, but she refused to think about it. She'd come this far. She might as well keep going.

She needed to find out what the weary, craggy Syracuse cop was really doing in her town.

She finally passed by the marshy area to where the ground became firm and dry and green with tall, lush grasses as it sloped gently down toward the lake. The water was dark today. Every whitecap seemed designed to contrast with the midnight hue of the water. The ill wind that had kicked up with the stranger's arrival only grew stronger.

She rounded a curve, and the grasses stopped standing tall and lush and became neatly clipped. Crewcut lawns on duty, and every fifty feet or so a small square log cabin at the ready. Each had a narrow gravel driveway, and a small wooden dock of its own. Each had a porch. She knew the cabins well. She had spent a few weeks of every summer in one of them as a child.

She'd always loved the way they smelled, and she inhaled that same scent now. Aging cedar touched by freshwater and a hint of fishiness.

Holly sighed. "So get on with it, already," she muttered. She veered off the road onto the private drive that lined the row of lakefront cabins. Most of them were obviously vacant. One or two were occupied by fishermen out for a long weekend. Those were the cabins with oversized, four-wheel-drive SUVs parked in their gravel driveways, and small motorboats tied to their docks.

She knew which cabin Vince O'Mally had rented the second it came into view. The very last one at the end of the row. The most private one, out of plain sight of the others because of a curve in the drive. Its curtains were all drawn tight, not a bit of light coming from within. His car was nowhere in sight, either. Nor was there a boat at the dock.

Holly bit her lip and took a quick look up and down the driveway. No one was around. Swallowing hard, she cut across the lawn, and ducked around to the rear of the building. Nothing back there but weeds, a giant propane tank, and a stack of nicely seasoned firewood. Squatting low in the weeds, she waited, listened. Her heart was pounding so hard she couldn't hear much else, and it wasn't from exertion. Hell.

She caught her breath eventually and, gathering her courage, rose. She still didn't see anyone. Standing on her toes, she leaned close to the nearest window, and tried to find a spot where the curtains parted enough to give her a glimpse inside.

Something moved in there. The barest shadow among the shadows.

She jerked backward so fast she lost her balance, and fell, hitting the ground hard, then scrambling to her feet again, her heart pounding as her mind sought answers. What had she seen, exactly? A dark form, a man, or was he the nightmare that kept replaying in her mind? She stood motionless, listening, waiting. The woods were at her back, the lake to her left, and the road to safety, right. Straight ahead was the house, and she didn't know if the shadow man was even now coming around it after her, or if he was, which way he would come, or if he were even real. So she froze there, questioning her mind, her senses, with her breaths rushing in and out of her lungs uncontrollably. She crouched and waited.

Something creaked.

It could have been a tall tree, bending in the wind.

Or it could have been the creak of a screen door opening and softly closing again.

Oh, God, he was coming, he was coming! Her heart hammered her chest mercilessly. She was gulping each breath. He would hear her if she didn't quiet down.

Something moved, off to the left. A twig broke, and she launched herself around the house to the right, running full tilt, pushing her legs as hard as she could manage.

She slammed into something hard. Heavy arms dropped what they'd been carrying, came around her and held her. "Red? What the hell?"

She lifted her head, and saw the damned Syracuse cop frowning down at her as she sucked in breath after gasping breath. This was all his fault. She was going to die. Her heart was going to explode and she was going to die.

"Someone," she gasped. "There." She pointed.

He looked where she pointed, and she jabbed her finger insistently when he looked back at her. So he let go of her shoulders, and ran to the rear of the house. Seconds later, he was back. "There's nothing there, Red. Okay?"

"No." She was still panting, her heart still hammering like a runaway train.

He knelt down, and she saw what he'd been carrying. A paper bag of groceries. He dumped out what remained in the bag, though most had already spilled, and then he squeezed the bag shut around its neck, and held it over her mouth. "Breathe slower," he told her. "Come on, slow down. Easy."

Her lungs expanded the paper bag and deflated it, over and over, and the dizziness eased. Too much oxygen would put you on your back fast, she knew it from experience. It had been a long time, but not long enough that she had forgotten.

He was talking. Saying the things her mom used to say to talk her through the panic attacks. "You're perfectly safe. I'm right here. Nothing can hurt you. You're safe, and everything's all right."

She fought to control her breathing, tried to consciously slow it down. He led her toward a tree, and she put one hand flat against its rough bark. Her breathing finally slowed. Her heartbeat eased. She sat down, leaned against the strong tree trunk. It helped, for some reason.

"There was a man . . . in your cabin."

He nodded, looking around them. "If there was, he's long gone now. Did you get a look at him?"

"Not really." She took another breath, and another.

He was still standing, but no longer examining the area quite as intensely. "You didn't see him?"

"No."

"Then how do you know he was there?"

"I . . ." She averted her eyes. "There was something . . . a shadow. And then the door creaked."

He remained silent, studying her face.

"And a twig snapped," she added for good measure, refusing to back down. "I didn't imagine it."

"Okay. All right. You didn't imagine it." Again he looked around, and she noticed he'd unbuttoned his denim jacket. Better to reach his gun, she thought.

"And I'm not crazy."

He looked at her sharply. "Did I say you were crazy?"

"I'm not."

"Are you all right now?"

"Yes." She reached a hand up, and he took it and pulled her easily to her feet. "You . . . should call Chief Mallory."

He nodded as if considering her words. "Do you have panic attacks often, Holly?"

She looked at the ground. "Not in years."

Taking her by the hand, without even bothering to see whether she objected, he led her to the cabin and up the three steps to the front door. He tried to be casual about it as he searched the place to be sure it was safe. It was a small cabin, so it wasn't a major job. Bedroom, closet, bathroom, kitchen, that was it. But she got the distinct impression he was only doing it to humor her.

She sank onto the plaid camelback sofa, embarrassed to the roots of her hair, wondering what he thought of her. He came back, went to the door, and locked it. Then he brought her a glass of water.

Sitting up a little straighter, she took it and sipped. But

she nearly choked on it when he said, "So you wanna tell me what you were doing snooping around my cabin?"

"I wasn't," she lied.

"No?"

"No. It's a . . . a shortcut. To my uncle Marty and aunt Jen's place. There's a path through the woods. It forks in the middle. Left goes to my uncle and aunt's place. Right goes farther, all around the west bank of the lake."

"Uh-huh." It was obvious he didn't believe her.

"Look, I come out here all the time. My uncle Marty owns these cabins. I used to stay a couple of weeks in one of them every summer when I was a kid."

"Should I assume that means you'll be out here snooping often?"

"No!"

His mouth narrowed. "Do you have a key?"

"Oh, don't be ridiculous." She sighed, sipped more water, set the glass down. "How did you know what to do?" she asked, partly to change the subject, and partly because she was curious.

"About the panic attack, you mean?" He shrugged. "It's not the first time I've seen one."

"Because you're a cop?"

"Yeah. Partly that."

They looked at each other for a moment. Then he took a cell phone from his pocket and dialed the chief's mobile number as Holly recited it to him.

While he spoke to Chief Mallory, Holly looked around the cabin. There were a half dozen foam coffee cups around, most of them with coffee still in them. There were newspapers spread on the table, a T-shirt flung over the back of a chair, and she could see the unmade bed through the open bedroom door.

The man was messy.

She was uneasy. She disliked questioning her own senses. She disliked it more than just about anything she could think of. But for the life of her she couldn't be sure of what she had actually seen, and what her mind had embellished.

"No," he was saying on the phone. "It looks like Holly scared him off before he had time to take anything. Okay, sure. Thanks, Chief." He hung up and turned to face her. "Chief says to wait here. He'll be out in a few minutes to take a look around. Then he'll take you home himself."

She nodded. "I should have known better," she muttered, half to herself. "Bad things always happen when I take the long way home."

—◦◦◦—

THE CHIEF ARRIVED WITH ONE OF HIS OF-ficers right behind him. Bill Ramsey, the lanky blond one, and that was a good thing because it provided someone to sit with the still-shaken redhead while Vince and the chief took a look around. Though Vince really didn't expect to find anything.

And he was right. There wasn't much to find. One decent footprint in the soft ground underneath the rear window that probably belonged to Holly. It was too damned small to be a man's. And there wasn't anything else.

The chief glanced back at the cabin. "You working on anything that might make someone nervous, Detective?"

Vince shook his head slowly. "I told you, I'm here on vacation."

"Right. And this library book connection . . . ?"

"It's probably nothing."

"Right," the chief said. "And you say Holly didn't actually see anything?"

Vince shook his head. "Does she . . . um . . . have a history of this sort of thing?"

"What sort of thing is that?"

Now the man sounded slightly defensive.

"Well, seeing things that aren't there."

"No. She's honest as the day is long. But . . . delicate."

"Delicate in what way?"

The chief sent him a look that told him that was none of his business. "What I want to know is, what was Holly doin' out here in the first place?"

"Don't know. She never really said."

The man was too sharp for Vince's comfort, but he supposed he was going to have to tell him the truth sooner or later. He just hoped it would be later. He wasn't altogether sure he even trusted the man yet.

Finally, the chief realized he wasn't going to get any more information, and took Holly home.

It was a relief to be alone. For a long moment, Vince just stood on the small porch, arms braced on the railing, staring out at the water and trying to get a grip on his blood pressure. If he'd needed a warning, this had been it. He hadn't talked a woman through a panic attack since the runaway teen he'd tried to help last year. He'd known better than to get too involved, but he had let the kid hole up at his place until he could get her into a good halfway house. Why? Because she was needy. Homeless, unstable, and had the crap beat out of her the night she stumbled onto his path. He did not do well with needy women. He'd put his heart and soul into seeing Shelly through her crises, and he thought he'd helped. He really did.

Until she turned up on a restroom floor with her wrists slashed.

And here was another one—maybe not just like Shelly. None of them were just alike. But he'd been around long enough to know damaged goods when he saw them. Red was on shaky ground, and there were deep secrets haunting her eyes.

He had a weakness for needy women. A tendency to get involved, to try to fix things for them. He knew it, recognized it as a character flaw, and recently had managed to walk the other way every time a needy woman had crossed his path. Up until he met Sara Prague.

He wasn't going to make that mistake again. No more playing the hero. No more promises that would haunt his nights when he couldn't keep them.

Cute or otherwise, Holly Newman was strictly off-limits. It was important that he acknowledge this up front. It would save complications later on. He hated complications.

What he needed to do was analyze the woman's behavior from a purely objective point of view. She was obviously nervous about him being in town. She'd come out here to snoop and apparently had interrupted someone else who was also nervous about him being here, and snooping. Or she'd imagined the intruder, which seemed just as likely. There was no evidence anyone had been inside the cabin. The lock hadn't been broken, but it wasn't much of a lock. He supposed Holly could get hold of a key easily enough, since her uncle owned the place. He wondered if she had been inside rummaging through his stuff. Nothing too revealing in here. Not yet anyway.

Her fear had been real, though. Whether she was lying, imagining, or had really seen someone, she had been scared into a panic attack. And it seemed unlikely a shadow and a snapping twig were enough to bring that on all by themselves. No, they'd probably acted as a trigger for something else. Something old. She told him as much when she admitted she hadn't had an attack in years.

He wondered briefly about the source of her fear—the kind of fear that could come back to knock her flat on her ass, years later, at the slightest scare. Then he reminded himself that was beyond his strictly defined area of interest. Back on track.

Just suppose there actually had been someone in the cabin. Who could it have been? Hell, he'd only been in town just over a day. Who could know what he was up to? He headed out to his car, unlocked it, and slid his laptop case out from under the passenger seat. He noticed his groceries still scattered in the dying grass out by the side of the cabin. A can of coffee. Coffee filters. A six-pack of beer and a few other essentials. They would have to wait.

Inside the cabin he dialed his cell phone while he waited for the laptop to boot up. A woman picked up on the fourth ring.

"Katie? It's Vince, I need to talk to Jerry." He could hear his partner making motor sounds in the background, his four-year-old twins mimicking him and squealing with delight.

"Nice to hear from you, too, Vince," Kate muttered.

Chagrined, he said, "Sorry. How are you, hon? How are the kids?"

"Molly wants her ears pierced, and Sydney is arguing her case for her," she replied. "I figure I have a fashion model and a litigator on my hands."

"Just as long as they don't grow up to be cops," he said. "I really need to talk to Jerry."

He heard the phone shift hands, heard Katie call to her husband, and then Jerry's voice came. "Vince? Where the hell are you, anyway?"

"I'm fine, lounging in a nice little rustic cabin on a lake. It's freaking paradise, pal."

"So what's wrong, Vince?"

Vince frowned at the phone. "What makes you think anything's wrong?"

"You called me."

Vince drew a breath. His partner knew him too well. "I need a favor."

"I knew it."

"A discreet favor, Jerry."

"You're working the Prague case, aren't you? Dammit, Vince—"

"I have a name I want you to run for me. Not just for a criminal record—I really don't think you'll find anything there. But check anyway. And newspapers, too, old files. I'll take anything you can come up with, going back . . ."—he paused to flip open a notebook, for the date he'd found stamped on the library book—"go all the way back to eighty-three, just for the hell of it."

Jerry sighed and said nothing.

"You want to put away the creep who murdered those kids or not, partner?"

"You know damn well I do. I'd also like to keep my job long enough to collect my pension, you know what I mean?" Another sigh. "What's the name?"

"Newman," Vince said. "Holly. Mother's name is Doris. They lived in Syracuse until five years ago. That's about all I have."

He heard Jerry scribbling. Then, "Vince, you know most of these types of crimes are committed by men."

"I know. But this woman knows something, I'd lay money on it."

Silence, long and drawn out. Then, finally, Jerry said, "Tell you what. I'll run the info if you'll tell me where the hell you are."

"Place called Dilmun, on Cayuga Lake," he said. "That's between you and me."

"For now, it is," Jerry replied. "What are you doing there, Vince?"

"I told you," Vince said. "I'm on vacation." He hung up the phone, and told himself he wasn't interested in Holly Newman's background for any other reason than how it might tie in with his case. He couldn't care less what kinds of demons haunted her. It was no concern of his.

※

"SO JUST WHAT HAPPENED OUT THERE, Holly?"

Looking sideways at the chief as he drove, Holly shook her head. "I was just walking." She tried to keep her voice from trembling, and giving away her true state. She was shaken, right to the core. She was scared on so many levels she couldn't begin to take stock. And her sense of security, which she'd built so carefully and so strongly here in this town, was shattered. Something was happening. Something was bringing it all back, and it seemed as if she had no control over it whatsover.

That was what shook her most of all. That feeling of things moving beyond her control.

"You don't *go* walking. You go straight home, every day, same route. You know it and I know it."

Holly sighed and faced him. "I'm trying to get over that," she said, and she knew damned good and well it was a lie. She didn't want to get over it. She needed it. "I'm trying new things, breaking old habits. It's good for me."

"I wouldn't say it was all that good for you today."

He was almost pouting. Big, strong Chief Mallory, looking like a scared kid. She forced a smile that was far from genuine. "You sure did get there in a hurry," she said, trying to change the subject. "What did you do, fly?"

"I was on my way home. When O'Mally called I was just around the corner. I called Bill and told him to meet me here." He shook his head slowly. "Your mother is going have kittens over this, Holly."

"Not if you don't make a big deal about it, she won't."

He pursed his lips, turned the car onto Lakeview and slowed to a crawl. "I'm not gonna say a word. It's your call. You're an adult." Finally, he stopped in front of Holly's house. She saw her mother part the curtains and look out at them, and she waved.

The chief said, "Holly, try to keep clear of this O'Mally character, will you?"

Startled, Holly turned to face him again. "Why?" He avoided her eyes, and she caught her breath. "You know what he's really doing here, don't you?"

"No. Not yet. But I don't have a good feeling about him. Just . . . be careful, all right?"

She nodded. "I will." Then she sighed. "Stop worrying about me, will you? I'm fine."

"You sure?"

She nodded. "See you at the bonfire tomorrow night?"

"You bet."

Holly got out of the car and closed the door. The chief watched her all the way into the front door of her house before he drove away. Inside, she smelled chicken roasting in the oven, and smiled at the familiarity of it. It was Friday. They always had chicken on Fridays. She closed her eyes, her relief so intense she was near tears.

CHIEF MALLORY DIDN'T GO HOME. HE went back into town and had Maddie Baker let him into the library's basement. He was the chief of police here; he was also one of a few remaining eligible bachelors. The other two were Dr. Ernie Graycloud, and Reginald D'Voe, the retired actor, but old Reggie didn't socialize much, and Ernie had publicly declared his intent to remain single to his dying day. Maddie Baker was a spinster whose voice always softened when she spoke to the chief. And she was only ten years his elder, so she probably held out hope, despite his relationship with Doris. It didn't take much talking, and only minimal flirting, to convince her to hand over the key, and trust him to lock up for her when he left.

It took him three hours to find what he was looking for, but he finally did. The library had three copies of *The Gingerbread Man* through 1982. In 1983, one copy went missing and had to be replaced. The last person to check that book out of the Dilmun public library . . .

Mallory read the name, closed his eyes, shook his head. Holly Newman. Dammit straight to hell.

FIVE

⚒⚒⚒

CHIEF Jim Mallory sat in a rocking chair on the front porch of his log cabin. A wicker table sat beside him, with a glass of iced tea and a cordless phone on it. He liked his cabin. It sat just a little bit above the town, and gave him the feeling he was watching over Dilmun, even when he wasn't in his office.

He was troubled tonight. And he knew there were other men in this town who would be just as troubled when he let them know what was going on. There was no use stirring all this up. He needed to let them know, though. They needed to figure out how best to deal with it.

Sighing, he picked up his cordless phone, and keyed in Ernie Graycloud's number. Ernie answered on the third ring, just about the time Mallory was beginning to wonder if he was busy with a patient or had been called in to the hospital or something.

"Yeah, what is it?" he asked by way of a greeting. He always sounded slightly grumpy on the phone. It was his way.

"It's Jim. Listen, we need to get together. Something's going on, and I don't like it."

He heard Ernie's sigh. "This got anything to do with that cop who showed up in town?"

"Yeah. He's showing way too much interest in Holly Newman. It's not good, Ernie."

"I was afraid of that. Heard he was sniffing around her. He digging into the past?"

"It looks that way."

Ernie made a sound, halfway between a grunt and a clearing of his throat. "Have you talked to Marty about this?"

"No, but I'm gonna call him next. We should get together, talk face-to-face."

"That would be best," Ernie said. "It won't do to have this stirred up."

"Agreed."

"Good. Let me know when and where, I'll be there."

"I knew I could count on you, Ernie." Mallory hung up the phone, leaned back in his rocker, and looked toward the town spread out in the distance. It was his town. Nothing bad ever happened there. It was up to him to keep it that way. And he damned well intended to do just that.

—⊗⊗⊗—

DORIS NEWMAN STACKED THE LAST plate in the dishwasher, added detergent, and closed the door. "I don't like it. No, not one bit. Does your uncle Marty know about this person you thought you saw creeping around Detective O'Mally's place?"

Holly was elbow deep in soapy water, scrubbing the roasting pan. Helping her mom with cleanup after dinner was part of her daily ritual, and she was trying hard to lose herself in it. "I have no idea. I imagine the chief called him by now. I mean, it's his cabin. He'll have to be notified." She kept on scrubbing. "Besides, like I said, I'm not even sure anyone was there. I mean, I was at first, but . . ." She shrugged, and sighed heavily.

Her mother glanced at her, a touch of worry clouding her eyes. "You mean you think you might have imagined it?"

Holly controlled her expression. "Of course not. I saw *something*. I wouldn't have made Vince—Detective O'Mally—call Jim if I hadn't seen *something*. I'm just not sure what."

Her mother nodded, but Holly didn't know if she was convinced or not. God, she didn't want to worry her mom. Her mother had been through enough in her life. If the scales of justice were to be balanced, her mother would know nothing but sheer bliss for the rest of her days.

"I just don't understand," Doris continued, speaking slowly now. She came to the sink, took a sponge and dipped it in the soapy water, then she took it to the round table and wiped it off. "What in the world were you doing out at the lake anyway, Holly?"

Holly felt herself stiffen, but kept her back to her mother. "I just decided to take the long way home for a change. There won't be any foliage at all soon, and it's always prettiest around the water."

Doris stopped wiping. Holly heard the cessation of movement and felt her mother's eyes drilling into her back. "Please don't lie to me, Holly."

Forcing a smile, lifting her chin, hoping her eyes appeared shadow free, Holly turned to face her mother. "It's not a lie."

"You decided to take the long way home—something you haven't done since—"

"Don't." Holly turned back to the sink too quickly. "Just don't, don't bring it up."

Her mother was silent for a long moment. Then she spoke again. "You decided to look at the foliage, on the most overcast day we've had in weeks, when most of the trees are all but bare."

Holly swallowed hard. "Fine, you don't have to believe me. Why do *you* think I took that route home?" She scrubbed harder on the pot.

Her mother sighed long and slow. Then she spoke, and

her voice seemed a bit lighter than before. "*I* think you went out there to visit Detective O'Mally."

The relief that washed through Holly that her mother was so far from the real reason, was short-lived. Disbelief followed on its heels. "That's the most ridiculous thing you've ever said to me."

"Is it?" her mother came closer, leaned over Holly's shoulder. "Then why are you scrubbing the finish off my best baking pan, Holly?"

Holly stopped scrubbing. She let her mother shoulder her aside, rinse the pan, and set it upside down in the dish drainer. What was she supposed to say? That she suspected the man was here for reasons he wasn't giving? That his very presence seemed to be stirring to life her most deeply buried ghosts? No. No, she wouldn't put her mother through that.

"It's all right, hon," Doris said, pulling the plug, wiping the sink as the water ran down the drain. "To tell you the truth, I'm thrilled to see you showing some interest in a man. I was beginning to think you never would."

She blinked and looked at her mother. "Interest?"

"He's not exactly handsome, is he? It's more a charismatic sort of thing, I think, that makes him seem so attractive."

"*Attractive?*" She thought he looked burned out and tired.

"And he *certainly* returns your interest."

She released a burst of air that was almost a snort.

"He *does,* Holly. It was obvious at the café. You should have heard him asking me all about you while you were in the restroom. Listen, I'm going to call your uncle Marty and make sure he knows about this break-in incident. But after that—"

"What was he asking?"

Her mother was halfway to the telephone on the opposite wall, but she stopped and turned back with an inquiring expression.

"What did he want to know about me?"

"Oh, the usual kinds of things. How long you'd been working for the chief, what you like to do with your free time, whether you were seeing anyone." She smiled knowingly.

Holly had a knot in her stomach. Why was this man asking about her? It wasn't for the reasons her mother had concocted. He was in this town for a purpose, and it had something to do with her. And maybe . . . maybe with Ivy, too. The idea sent her pulse racing. She felt the blood rushing in her temples, thudding there.

"After I get off the phone with Marty, you should give that man a call," Doris went on. "Why don't you invite him to the bonfire tomorrow night?"

Holly searched her mind for a reason. "You know the phones aren't turned on at the cabins."

"He had a cell phone. I saw it at the café."

Holly tried to remain calm. "I don't have his number."

"Marty will have it. He rented the man the cabin, after all." Wiping her hands on a dishtowel, Doris walked with a bounce in her step the rest of the way to the telephone on the wall, and dialed her brother-in-law's number.

MARTIN CANTRELL SEEMED MORE UPSET about the alleged intruder than Vince was, when he showed up at the cabin. Vince hadn't met the man face-to-face yet. The arrangements had all been made by phone, and the key had been waiting under a flowerpot when Vince had arrived.

Marty, as he insisted Vince call him, was a friendly fellow with a ready smile, a paunch of a belly, and a reddish horseshoe of hair surrounding a shiny patch of scalp. He wore plaid flannel and carried a toolbox. You had to like a guy who wore plaid flannel and carried a toolbox. Right now he was crouching near the door, examining the lock the way a surgeon examines a tumor, and shaking his head. "You're right, you know. These locks are jokes. Any twelve-year-old with a Swiss army knife could get in, if he wanted to. It just never occurred to me we might need serious locks out here. I can't even remember when there's been a break-in."

"Right," Vince said, "Nothing bad ever happens in Dilmun."

Marty smiled broadly. "It's practically the town motto." Then he sighed. "Guess we've let ourselves get a little complacent out here."

"Maybe. But we aren't even sure there was anyone in here. There's no sign of an intruder, and Holly didn't actually see him."

Marty nodded, looked troubled for a moment, opened his mouth to say something, then seemed to think better of it.

Vince took note of all of it. "What?" he asked.

Marty brushed off his hands, got to his feet. "Holly . . . no. Nevermind, it's not important. Look, I can get a decent deadbolt on this door for you tomorrow. Hardware store is already closed tonight, or I'd take care of it right now."

"Not a problem," Vince told him. "You want a beer, Marty?"

"Love one. Thanks."

Vince walked to the kitchenette, grabbed a beer out of the fridge for each of them, talking as he did. "I appreciate you're coming over so fast. Chief Mallory must have called you in a hurry." He was in no hurry to get rid of the guy, now that it seemed he knew something about Holly Newman that he was keeping to himself.

"Nah, the chief knew he didn't have to bother. Doris called me just a little while ago."

"Oh." Vince handed Marty his beer while his brain processed the information.

"Doris is my wife Jenny's sister," Martin explained.

Vince nodded. "Holly mentioned that her uncle owned the cabins."

The man looked at him and grinned. "I'm feeding the

small town stereotype, huh? That everyone's related."

Before Vince could answer, his cell phone bleated. "Make yourself at home, Marty, while I get this." Marty sat down as Vince pulled the phone out of his pocket, answering as he always did, with a terse "O'Mally."

There was a hesitation on the other end, and his skin started to prickle. Was it the same guy who'd broken in here earlier—if there had been a guy at all? Then a soft breath whispered from the phone and he could almost feel it on his ear. He was just beginning to wonder if this was going to turn into an obscene phone call when she spoke at last.

"Hi. It's Holly Newman."

He glanced toward Marty, saw the guy grinning even wider than before, and carried the phone into the kitchen. "Did you remember something more about the guy you thought you saw, Red?"

"No. I . . . look, my mother wanted me to invite you to the community bonfire, so I'm inviting you."

He lifted his brows. "You don't sound happy about it."

"I'm not. It's tomorrow night, down by the lake. You'll see the crowd gathering from your porch around sundown."

"And when I do, I should . . . ?"

"Meet us down there," she said.

He thought for a moment. It would be a good chance to poke around some more, he figured. Meet more of the locals. Dig a little deeper into the mind of the strange little redhead. "Fine," he said. "It's a date."

"No," she replied. "It's not."

The click told him she'd hung up the phone. He looked at his phone, scowling, and wondering just why Holly Newman disliked him so much. There was something motivating it, and it was connected to his case, he felt it right to his bones.

"So, you're going to the bonfire with Holly then?" Marty asked as Vince walked back from the kitchen. He was sitting on the sofa just to the left of the front door, one arm stretched across its back, sipping his beer.

Vince frowned. "You psychic, or do you just have a bionic ear?"

Marty grinned. "Doris asked me for your cell phone number. Told me Holly was gonna call and invite you."

Vince said, "Now you're feeding another one of those small-town stereotypes. The one where everyone knows everyone else's business."

Marty's grin faded. "Yeah, I guess so. It's just that, uh . . . well, you know she *is* my niece."

"Yeah. I know. Do you mind that she asked me?"

"No. No, it isn't that. I just . . . look, Holly's . . . fragile."

Vince nodded. "I kind of picked up on that."

"You could tell, huh? I didn't think it showed so much anymore."

"It doesn't," he said quickly. "Not in her, anyway. But everyone else around here acts likes she's made of glass." It wasn't entirely true. He did see it in her, during that episode outside his cabin. But there was something rubbing him the wrong way about the protective attitudes of those around her. He wasn't sure why, but it bugged him.

"Look, you only just met her. If we seem a little protective of her, we have reason," Marty said. Maybe a touch on the defensive side now.

"I picked up on that, too," Vince said. "Would I be out of line to ask what the reason is?"

Marty looked him in the eyes for a moment, then tipped back his beer, draining it, set the can on the coffee table, and got to his feet. "I'll come by in the morning to put that new lock in."

Vince was aware he'd stepped over the line. "I might not be here in the morning. I have some errands to run. But don't let that stop you."

"Didn't plan to," Marty said. "It's my cabin." Then he picked up his tool box and headed out. "Anyway, I'll see you tomorrow night at the bonfire."

Vince nodded. Then he realized he'd just answered the

man's initial question as to whether or not he'd accepted Holly's invitation.

"Not bad, Marty," Vince said. "You'd have made a decent cop."

"I make a better uncle," he replied. "You watch your step with Holly. I don't want to see her hurt." He gave a nod of good-bye, and walked down the steps to the path.

"Don't you worry, Uncle Marty," Vince muttered as he watched the man vanish around the curve. "I like my women tough as nails with a hide like old leather. I don't do fragile."

<hr />

VINCE HAD SOME SERIOUS SHOPPING TO do on Saturday. Marty had arrived early, ready to install the new lock, just as Vince was heading out to run his errands, which gave Vince a chance to ask him about the vacant phone jack in the bedroom wall. He learned that a call to the local telephone company and payment in advance could turn it on, giving him two lines to work with. He folded up his laptop, pocketed his cell phone, and headed out.

He drove all the way back to the city. It took longer than he'd hoped it would, to pick up supplies at home, and find most of what he needed at the retail outlets. He then met Jerry for a quick lunch and an even quicker conversation.

Jerry nodded toward Vince's Jeep beyond their booth window. Boxes stacked in the back showed through the tinted glass. "Been shopping?"

"Yeah. Gave the old plastic a workout this morning."

"So, what's the connection you're onto, buddy?"

Vince shook his head. "Can't tell you that. Not yet, anyway. Did you get what I asked you for?"

"Yeah. And it's damned interesting, Vince." He slid a fat manila envelope across the table, and Vince picked it up. But before he could ask what was inside, a uniformed cop walked through the door.

Vince took the envelope and slid out of the booth. He was supposed to be on vacation. If anyone saw him in town, much less meeting with his partner and exchanging large envelopes, questions would surely come up. And Jerry could get into as much trouble as Vince.

Jerry started to get up, too, but Vince held up a hand. He'd just slip out alone while the cop's back was to him.

Jerry understood, and gave a nod. "Be careful, buddy. And call if you need me."

"I will."

Vince walked out of the diner with the envelope under his arm, got into his Jeep, and headed back to Dilmun. He glanced at his watch and knew he was going to be late.

HOLLY PACED AS MORE AND MORE OF THE locals gathered, and she tried to keep her gaze from drifting toward Vince O'Mally's cabin. She wasn't having much success. His Jeep had been gone most of the day. Maybe he'd decided that whatever he'd come looking for wasn't here. Maybe he'd gone back to Syracuse for good.

"It's early yet, hon." Her mother's hand curled over Holly's shoulder with a reassuring squeeze. "He'll be here."

"Who?" Holly pasted an unconcerned expression on her face. She couldn't very well tell her mother she half hoped the man was gone for good. Or that the other half only wanted to see him tonight, to try to find out what he was really after.

Doris just shook her head and moved away, toward the heap of deadwood that had been piled up for the bonfire. Around the pile, in a concentric circle, people milled. Picnic tables littered the area, and the early arrivals claimed them. Others spread blankets on the ground, or unfolded lawn chairs. Off to the left, on the round pavilion, a local band set up their instruments. Farther from the woodpile, some of the locals were erecting dome tents, planning to make a full night of it.

Already the sun was drooping low beyond the hills out past the lake. It had been a nicer day today than yesterday. Chilly and breezy, but dry. The sky was dusky now, violet and pink as the sun sank lower, and the wind stirred the water with its breath.

And still not one sign of life from O'Mally's cabin.

"You looking for someone?"

His voice came from right behind her, and she jumped. Then she bit her lip and closed her eyes, still not facing him. Damn, he'd caught her staring off toward his place. He would probably reach the same conclusions that her mother had.

"I . . . was just wondering if your burglar had come back." There, that was better. She turned, trying for a smug expression.

He said, "He might have for all I know. I haven't been home all day."

"I know." She frowned, and felt a stirring discomfort because he stood so close.

"Did you see anything suspicious?" he asked.

Holly shrugged. "It's not like I've been watching."

"No?"

She shook her head.

"Then how did you know I hadn't been home yet?"

"Lucky guess." She saw his Jeep now, in the vacant area they used as a parking lot for lakefront gatherings. He'd parked there and come straight here, rather than going back to the cabin first. Almost as if he were in a hurry. He wore jeans and a brown leather jacket, unzipped so that his blue button-down shirt showed underneath. It wasn't tucked in tightly, so it bagged. She wondered if he ate enough. A cop his age should have a paunch. He had a haggard look to him—eyes slightly heavy lidded, and shadowed. He didn't have laugh lines around his eyes. He needed them.

His eyes met hers, and she knew he was aware of her perusal.

"Oh, Detective O'Mally, there you are!" Doris called, hurrying from the table she'd commandeered to where the two of them stood, gazes locked. "Holly was getting impatient, wondering where you were."

That was enough to make Holly break eye contact. She jerked her gaze toward her mother and felt her face heat. "I was not."

Vince could have smirked at her, but he didn't. He shifted his feet, maybe a little uncomfortable. "Sorry I'm late, Ms. Newman."

"Doris, please. And there's no need to apologize."

"Doris," he said. "And there is. I had some errands to run, and it took longer than I expected."

"Have you had any luck tracking down your library book bandit?" She asked the question, Holly thought, as if he were chasing down an armed bank robber, and it was the most interesting case in the history of criminal justice.

"None at all." He worked up a smile for her. Holly thought his smiles always looked as if they took effort to produce. "Fortunately, it doesn't matter, since I'm on vacation."

"So you keep insisting," Holly muttered.

He glanced at her sharply, about to say something rude, she was sure, but then his eyes widened on something beyond her, distracting him. "You're shitting me. Is that who it looks like?"

Holly turned to follow his gaze, and spotted the town's reclusive celebrity settling into his lawn chair, as his niece draped a blanket over his shoulders. He'd barely got himself seated before several children made a beeline for him. He was surrounded in a matter of seconds. "You didn't know Reginald D'Voe lived out here?" Holly asked.

He shot her a glance. "I knew he had a place here, years

ago, but I read that he moved to the west coast."

"You never would have struck me as a fawning fan, Vince," she said, fighting a smile.

His brows creased. "I don't fawn." Still, it was the first time she'd seen him lose that preoccupied scowl of his. "I grew up on horror flicks, though, and I think he starred in most of them. I was planning to drive by his house while I was out here, just to see what it looked like."

"It looks like something out of *Scooby Doo*, just about like you'd expect, I suppose. It's that creepy-looking one on the hill." Holly pointed across the lake, to where the house loomed, its windows dark, its shape like a phantom against the night sky.

"Of course it is," he said, shaking his head as if he should have guessed.

Doris chimed in, "Reggie's something of a recluse, you know."

"Yes, I know, I read that somewhere, too."

"You're right that he moved away. Oh, it must have been fifteen years ago, give or take. But he never sold the place. He and his niece only moved back here the year before last." Then she nudged her daughter. "Hon, take Vince over and introduce him to Reggie."

Holly sighed. "Okay, just don't go asking for an autograph or fussing. He doesn't like it. Frankly, I'm surprised he even showed up for this."

"So am I. The celebrity scandal sheets make him sound borderline agoraphobic."

"They exaggerate," she said, looking at him in surprise. "You really are a fan, aren't you?"

"Not a fanatical one. But, yeah, if I see his name on the cover I'll usually buy the magazine and read the article. And I have several of his films on tape. Not the full collection or anything, but . . ." He shrugged.

She thought he seemed almost embarassed to admit to having followed the old actor's career, and it did seem a little out of character. But somehow, it made him seem a little more human. A little less intimidating. She walked across the sand with O'Mally at her side. A little too close, maybe. She wouldn't have minded, if he had been anyone else. But she seemed to feel his closeness more than she felt anyone else's.

"He's really not the hermit the press makes him out to be," she said, just to get conversation going again. She didn't like silence as a rule. Less so with him nearby. "He's reinstating his annual Halloween party for the kids this year, you know."

As she spoke, little Bethany Stevens climbed up onto Reggie's lap.

Vince stopped walking suddenly, and when Holly looked at him, his expression was hard and cold as he stared at Reggie. "He likes kids, does he?"

Startled, Holly studied him. What was that in his voice, just then? It hadn't sounded like a casual question. "It's not the kind of thing they'd play up in the press," she said at last. "Not in keeping with his dark, menacing image, I suppose. But yes, Reggie loves kids. They say he always has."

SIX

"ACCORDING to local gossip, he's always loved kids," Holly went on. "Aunt Jen says before he moved away back in the eighties, he had a Halloween party every year for the little ones. It was the biggest event of the year in this town. And Reggie always had lots of special effects and spooky surprises. They still talk about those parties around here."

"And who's the woman?" He nodded toward where Reggie sat, with the young woman standing at his back.

"That's his niece, Amanda. She came to live with him when she was little. Mom says her parents were killed in some kind of accident. Poor thing."

Vince seemed deep in thought. She wasn't even sure he was still listening. "So, do you want to meet him, or what?" she finally asked.

"Yeah," he said. "I do."

Odd, how his attitude seemed to have changed all of the sudden. He'd been almost relaxed—or as close to it as she figured he was capable of being—and now he seemed tense and tight again. Even more tense and tight than usual.

Go figure. Normally, she and her mom would be enjoying snacks with Uncle Marty and Aunt Jen by this point in the festivities. But not this year. Nothing was normal this year, nor had been since O'Mally had come into town.

They continued to where Reginald D'Voe sat. They had to pick their way among the small bodies all around him. Most of the kids were sitting. Bethany was saying, "Tell us the one about the werewolf, Reggie. Like you did when you came to story day at school!"

"No, no," another child piped in. "The vampires. Tell us one of the vampire stories."

Reggie held up a hand as he saw Holly and Vince approaching. "Be patient, my friends, be patient. We have grown-ups to contend with first." But he said it with a smile, as he nodded hello to Holly.

Bethany jumped off his lap to run up to Holly and grab her hand. "Holly's here!" she said, grinning ear to ear. Then in a conspiratorial whisper to Reginald, "She's gonna help me make my costume for your party, Reggie! It's gonna be the best one in town."

"I can't wait to see it," Reggie said in a stage whisper.

Amanda D'Voe sent Holly a smile, as well. But she didn't hold her gaze long. She never held anyone's gaze long. Her eyes were usually cast slightly downward. Amanda was slim and pretty, with hair a light shade of brown that was almost blonde, but not quite. Sweet and painfully shy, she was as much a recluse as her uncle.

"It's so good to see you both here," Holly said to the two of them.

"And you, as well," Reginald replied. "Holly Newman, isn't it?"

Holly smiled. "I'm surprised you remember!"

"I try to make it a point to know all my neighbors." The man was thin, his face harsh and lined, but he still had that star quality that had made him so famous, and the distinctive appearance with the sculpted features and angular brows. His hair was silver now, but his eyes were just as clear and blue as ever they had been on the big screen. And he still spoke in that unidentifiable accent that was some cross between British and Romanian. "How is your dear mother?" he asked.

"Oh, she's great. She's here," Holly gestured toward her mom, who was unloading a picnic basket with help from Chief Mallory. She leaned down to Bethany. "My mom brought some of those oatmeal chocolate chunk cookies you like so much."

"Really?" The little girl's eyes widened. Then she spun on her heel and ran toward Doris and the chief.

Reginald laughed softly, a deep, quiet sound she'd heard a thousand times in his films. Usually with a diabolical undertone to it, though. There was none tonight. "Your mother is luring my audience away with those cookies," he said, his tone teasing. "She shouldn't make me angry." And that time he used his most menacing inflection, narrowing his eyes and bending those angular brows in a way that had sent shivers up countless spines in the past. The kids seated on the ground around him laughed with delight.

Amanda shook her head. "Uncle Reggie, you're impossible."

He patted her slender hand on his shoulder. "Fortunately, I'm quite possible. Now, as for you,"—he said, addressing Holly again—"do you intend to introduce us to your companion or did you bring him as some kind of offering?"

"Oh, yes, right," she said with an apologetic glance at Vince. "This is Vincent O'Mally. Vince, Reginald D'Voe, and his niece, Amanda."

Vince extended a hand, and Reginald took it, still smiling. But his smile seemed to freeze when Holly said, "Vince is a detective from the Syracuse Police Department."

"It's an honor to meet you, Mr. D'Voe," Vince was saying, his tone reserved, his eyes watchful. "I'm a longtime fan." Then he turned slightly, offering his hand to

Amanda as well. But before he could touch her, Reginald reached up and grabbed hold of her wrist.

"Amanda, I seem to have left my books in the car. Do you mind?" Reginald asked.

"Of course not," Amanda replied in her soft voice. "It's very nice to meet you, Detective. Good to see you again, too, Holly." She leaned down to kiss her uncle's cheek before rushing off to the parking area.

Vince's eyes followed her, the look in them intense. Holly felt suddenly like so much chopped liver. Oh, great. What was up with that?

" 'Again'?" Reginald asked, addressing Holly. "I wasn't aware you and Amanda were acquainted."

Holly tried to stop watching Vince watch Amanda, and drew her gaze back to Reggie. "We only knew each other in passing, up until a couple of weeks ago. Mom was late for our lunch date, and Amanda was in the café picking up takeout. We ended up having coffee together while she waited for her order."

"I see," Reggie said.

"She came to live with you as a small child, Holly tells me," Vince said, his gaze returning to D'Voe only when Amanda was out of sight.

"That's right." D'Voe pulled his blanket closer and changed the subject. "What are you doing in Dilmun, Detective?"

"I'm here on vacation."

"How nice. I hope you enjoy your stay." Reggie turned his attention to Holly so totally, so firmly, it felt as if Vince had been dismissed. Holly had never seen the retired actor behave so rudely. It was completely unlike him—at least, she thought it was. She didn't know him well, but any time she had run in to him he'd always been polite. Almost exaggeratedly so. "Do tell your mother to come over and say hello, Holly. I haven't spoken with her in months."

"I will," she said.

"And now . . ." He looked at the children all around

him. "That story I promised you, hmm?" The kids cheered and shouted requests. Holly turned to go, realizing it was time. But Vince didn't seem inclined to follow. Amanda was on her way back now, three or four books in her hands, and Vince's attention seemed riveted. Holly finally grabbed his arm and gave a tug, snapping his reverie. He followed her as she left the group.

———

THE DARKNESS WAS COMPLETE, AND someone put a torch to the pile of brush. The fire caught and blazed hot, snapping and sending sparks and flames high into the night sky. The band, which consisted of two guys with acoustic guitars and passably decent voices, and a third guy on drums, began to play. Vince walked around with Holly, let her introduce him to people, tried to sound mildly interested in their small-town small talk, but he kept his eyes on Amanda D'Voe and her famous uncle. Something wasn't right there. The old man had tensed up the minute Holly told him Vince was a cop. Why? What did he have to hide? And why had he sent his timid niece scurrying away?

Vince sat on a blanket with Holly, her mother, and the chief. He ate cold fried chicken and potato salad. He said all the right things, complimented the cooking, talked shop with Chief Mallory, kept it light, and steered conversation away from anything to do the alleged break-in at the cabin, or the real reason he was in town. He thought he was doing great, right up until the chief of police took Doris's hand and led her out to where people were pairing up to dance. That was when Holly turned to him and said, "Do you want to dance?"

Her face was slightly flushed, her eyes sparkling with something. Not excitement. Not happiness. Something else. He didn't think his dancing with her was all that great an idea, but didn't know how to say so without offending her, so he nodded. "Sure, why not?" He got to his feet. Holly didn't. He held out a hand. But Holly remained sitting.

"I thought you wanted to dance," he said, confused.

"Who me? No, Vince, not me. Amanda."

He blinked. "I . . . I'm not following."

"Go ask Amanda to dance," she said. "You've been staring at her all evening. Don't rein yourself in on my account, Vince, I really couldn't care less."

Okay, so maybe he hadn't been handling things as well as he'd thought. And this was a problem. Because, while he didn't want to alienate Holly Newman until he'd learned what the hell she was hiding, he didn't want her getting ideas about him either. She was the furthest thing from the kind of involvement he wanted or needed right now. And that edge in her voice just now had sounded like a hint of jealousy. He was walking a goddamned tightrope here. But, solving this case was the most important thing. More important than anything else, and if she wound up getting her feelings hurt in the process, that was a small price to pay. He had resolved to do what he had to in order to find the truth, and that included using Holly Newman. If it seemed slightly heartless to his more compassionate side, all he had to do was remember the Prague kids. The way they'd ended up. The nightmare he'd walked in on in that abandoned house less than a week ago.

He gripped Holly's hand and pulled her to her feet. "If I wanted to dance with Amanda D'Voe, I'd have asked her. What do you think, I'm shy or something?"

She shrugged, but let him pull her along into the area where couples were dancing. "Hey, it's nothing to me either way."

He claimed a spot for them, and the band immediately ended the upbeat ditty they'd been playing and switched to their rendition of "Lying Eyes." Slow and mellow. He almost groaned because he knew slow dancing with her was an even worse idea, but he couldn't very well say so. So he pulled her closer. Not too close, though. He fit his hands to her waist, and tried not to notice any physical reaction to her arms linking around his neck as they started moving to the music.

Although he *felt* one. And he attributed *that* to it having been a long time between one-night stands.

"So what is it then?" she was asking.

"What is what?"

"The reason you've been watching Amanda all night."

He looked at her sharply. "Just curious, I guess."

"Why?"

"Why do you want to know?" he asked.

"Just curious, I guess."

She was good at sparring, witty and quick. This was not the same Holly Newman who'd been damn close to hysterics over thinking she had glimpsed an intruder at his place. She was complicated. He had to remember that. When he'd met her he had labeled her weak and fragile, then he had decided she was a snoop. More recently he'd been thinking of her as fearful and troubled. Now she was something altogether different yet again.

Finally, she sighed as if in capitulation. "Fine, I'll fill you in. Amanda was orphaned when she was a little girl. Of course I didn't live here then, but gossip has an unlimited life span in this town, so I've heard all the stories. She came out here to live with Reginald after her family died, and they say she wasn't quite right. Probably just the trauma of losing her parents, but the rumor is that she didn't speak at all when she first moved in with Reggie. Doc Graycloud spent a lot of time with her when they still lived here. Then they moved out west somewhere. The press said L.A., but the locals say it was Arizona and the California story was just to keep the paparazzi off their backs. The move was for Amanda's health, they said. And now they're back. End of story."

Vince nodded. On the far side of the fire, Reginald D'Voe was still surrounded by kids, his niece at his side, as he read to them from one of the books. He used his hands expressively, and his face, bathed in the red-orange glow of the firelight, conveyed one emotion after another. Vince couldn't hear him, but found himself almost wanting to pull up a lawn chair and listen in. Amanda seemed rapt. "How old is she?"

"I don't know. Around my age, I guess." Holly tipped her head up slightly so she was looking him in the eye. "You really can go talk to her if you want. I wasn't being flip when I said I didn't care. I only asked you to come here tonight because my mother backed me into a corner. It won't bother me in the least."

He arched a brow, focusing on Holly now. "I think I've just been insulted."

She dropped her gaze. "Don't take it personally, Vince. You're just not my type."

He almost smiled. She was a lousy liar. When he'd first arrived, he'd seen her watching the cabin so hard her eyes must have been watering. She was attracted to him. He felt it like an energy sparking from her skin when she got within a few feet of him. He felt it now. It was setting off his warning systems, telling him to back off. Hell, he was attracted to her, too. There was an almost magnetic pull between them as they slow danced to the old Eagles tune. He had to exert an effort to keep space between their bodies. But he'd expected that. She was needy. He was always drawn to women like her. Usually to his own detriment. It was good she was denying the heat. Nothing could come of it.

"So, tell me how your mother managed to force you into inviting me to this thing, Red."

She sighed. "Mom wanted to know what I was doing out at your place earlier, when I saw . . . whatever the hell I saw."

"And you didn't want to tell her you were snooping?"

She widened her eyes and put on the phoniest innocent expression he'd ever seen—and he'd seen plenty—then she quickly lowered her head. As if she knew he could see through the act. "I wasn't snooping. Exactly. But Mom would have blown it all out of proportion and started worrying about me if I had tried to explain."

"Seems like a lot of people do a lot of worrying about you," he said.

She shook her head. "Not because I enjoy it, believe me. At any rate, my mother assumed I'd been at your place because I had a crush on you. I decided to let her go with that. It's better for her than the alternative. And that led to this."

He nodded slowly. "That almost makes sense."

"What do you mean, almost?"

She tipped her face up to ask the question, and he felt his body react again. He hadn't noticed the ripeness of her lips before. They were full. Plump and juicy looking. He forced his eyes up to hers instead. He was a cop and she knew something connected to the crime he was here to investigate. He felt it right to his toes. He needed to focus on that and nothing else. Anything else was too dangerous. *She* was too dangerous. She had secrets. Those haunted eyes told him so. Maybe he needed to remind himself of that—maybe once she verified it for him, his body would listen to the warnings his mind was sending. And maybe her secrets were all tied in with his case.

"Why does your mom worry so much about you, Red? I mean, what would she have thought about your coming out to my place to spy on me that would have caused her undue concern?"

She only shrugged, but she looked away from his eyes, he noticed. "Mom's a worrier."

"I think there's more to it than that."

"What makes you think so?"

"I've seen enough to know a woman with a past when I see one. I think you have a history, Holly Newman."

She shot him a look that should have knocked him flat. Like a bullet. "So what if I do?"

"I want to know about it."

She shook her head. "Don't go there, Vince."

He held her gaze for a long moment. It was deep and

shuttered. And more. It was afraid. "Why not? What do you have to hide?"

She jerked free of him, stood there with her hands clenched into fists at her sides. "I don't want to talk about it."

He shrugged. "I am a cop, you know. I can find out anyway."

She looked suddenly stricken. As if he'd scraped a nerve with a sharp blade. A throat cleared beside them, but Vince didn't shift his gaze. It was still locked with hers.

"Is, uh, everything okay here? Holly?"

She looked away first. "Fine, Uncle Marty," she said. Her voice was a little coarse.

"You don't look fine." He glanced at Vince. "This guy giving you a hard time, honey?"

Vince waited, watched her face. It was amazing the way she could compose it. Within a second the agitation was gone, and an easy smile replaced it. She looked at her uncle, and sighed. "Oh, it's not him. Heck, him I can handle. But I'm not feeling very well for some reason. I think I'm going to go on home."

"Want me to call Doc Graycloud over here? Have him take a look at you?"

"No. I'll just go say good night to Mom. Enjoy the rest of the party, you two." She didn't look at Vince again before she turned and walked away.

Her uncle did, however. And his expression wasn't kind. "You know, her father died in ninety-four," Marty said. "So it's up to me to look out for her."

Vince met the guy's stare. "Look, I know where this is going—"

"Do you? Then you know that I'm going to tell you I don't think it's a real good idea for you to be seeing my niece. I tried to tell you to be gentle, take it slow, but it doesn't look to me like you listened very well."

Vince shook his head. "You've got it all wrong. She's not my type, Marty."

"No? Then it shouldn't be any hardship to stay away from her. Look, Vince, I like you. But Holly—she's been through a lot. I'm not going to stand by and see her get hurt again. I'm not sure she could take it."

"What, exactly, is it that she's been through that has everyone in this town hovering over her as if she might crack at any moment?" Vince snapped. "If you don't mind my asking, I mean," he added, not bothering to hide the sarcasm.

"I do mind your asking." Marty looked mean for just a moment, leaning closer. Then he caught himself, backed off and pushed a hand through his scant hair while blowing out a sigh. "Sorry. It's a family matter. A private one, and we don't talk about it. Just do what I tell you, okay? Trust me on this, Vince. It's for the best." He patted Vince once on the shoulder, then turned and headed back to where his wife was talking and laughing with some neighbors near the fire.

Okay, fine, Vince thought. He had a big fat envelope in his car right now that might very well have plenty to say on the matter. In fact, judging from Holly's reaction when he'd suggested checking official records to get her story, he was ninety-nine percent sure he would find something. Maybe everything. And suddenly he was dying to get some down time so he could read every word. He started to leave, but got waylaid every ten steps by locals wanting to chat. Friendly bunch, or maybe just curious. They all asked plenty of questions, he thought. Any one of them could have ulterior motives.

Ernie Graycloud held him up the longest. He was obviously Native American—he reminded Vince of the fellow who used to do the pollution commericals in the seventies. Long hair, black with streaks of silver, pulled behind his head and tied with a thong. He wore faded jeans and a denim jacket.

"You're the cop, right?" he asked. He stepped into Vince's path and asked the question. Just like that.

"Did someone pin a sign on my back, or what?"

"No need. Small town. I'm the local M.D., Ernie Gray-cloud." He thrust out a hand.

"Vince O'Mally, in case you didn't know." Vince shook his hand.

"You look like you're leaving," Graycloud said.

"Yeah, I was hoping to turn in early," he lied.

"But you don't want to do that yet. You'll miss the best part of the autumn bonfire if you do. I bring my drums every year, lead the kids, and most of the grown-ups, too, around the bonfire in a tribal dance taught to me by my grandmother."

"Wow, that must be something to see."

"Oh, it is." He leaned closer, as if sharing a deep secret. "Now D'Voe, over there, he thinks his spooky stories are the highlight of the bonfire. But in truth, it's the drumming and the dance."

"Sounds like you have a little friendly rivalry going."

Graycloud nodded, grinning. "You shouldn't miss it."

He was honestly tempted to hang around. But those files were calling to him. Before he had to make up an excuse, though, someone called his name.

He turned at the soft voice. Doris Newman stood behind him. "I need a word with you."

He glanced back at Graycloud, who nodded once, and walked away with a wave. Then he turned back to Doris, noting her tight expression. "What is it?" he asked.

"I'm worried about Holly," she said.

"Oh, I'm sure it's nothing. She said she didn't feel well and wanted to go home." He looked past Doris but didn't see Holly anywhere in the crowd.

"Yes, I know, but I don't like the idea of her walking home alone. Not after that intruder she thought she saw at your cabin yesterday."

Vince felt his brows draw together, and his gaze shifted to the dark, winding road in the distance. "She's walking?"

"She left already. I couldn't talk her out of it—I swear that girl can be so stubborn."

He nodded, tried not to look as exasperated as he felt. "I'll go after her," he said. "Don't worry, I'll see her safely home." He thought about adding, "and don't tell your brother-in-law," but decided against it.

Doris smiled, looking relieved. He might have suspected her of matchmaking, but there was something in her face. Something truly concerned. It was like a very dim reflection of Sara Prague's face, looking at him from across his desk, asking him to find her children. And just like before, he promised he would make it okay. The realization made his stomach twist painfully. Damn, when was he going to learn?

"Thank you, Vince," Doris told him. "You're a good man. I can tell."

HOLLY LEFT THE PARTY EARLIER THAN she'd expected. She had never done that before in the five years she and her mother had lived here. It wasn't a part of the detailed plans she'd made for tonight. She'd had it all worked out. After all, annual events weren't as easily controlled as daily ones. You could get into a habit, a routine, of doing certain things in a certain order every day, until it became second nature. But events that only happened once a year took more time. More effort. She was supposed to have spent a half hour catching up with Uncle Marty and Aunt Jen. She was supposed to have taken a minute to talk with Doc Graycloud. And she had planned to spend some time with Bethany, too, to start planning that Halloween costume, so she could go in search of a pattern on her Sunday shopping trip with Mom.

But, no. No, her well-laid plan was destroyed, her carefully calculated outline of the evening's activities, torn to bits. All because of Vince O'Mally.

What interest could he possibly have in her past?

She walked away from the lake, from the cars in the

lot, from the cabins. She walked until the fire's glow no longer reached her. The road was dark. No streetlights, not here. And no stars tonight, either. It was as if the sky matched her mood. Dark.

That cop was up to something. Something involving her, and her past, and that book. That damned book. That damned, damned, damned book. It had triggered something, when she'd heard the title of the missing book. It had set things into motion in her mind, things she'd locked away and managed to keep contained for a long, long time.

A little girl's voice starting singing in her mind. *Run, run, run, fast as you can*—

"No," Holly whispered. But it came again. *You can't catch me*—

She pressed her hands to her ears, closed her eyes. "No, no, dammit, no!" She wasn't going to think about it, she wasn't. It was in the past, and that was where it belonged. But then she was gone, sinking into an abyss of memory, and suddenly she was small, and carrying a backpack as she walked. The gravel was replaced by a sidewalk, the night sky by daylight. And a little girl with dimples and blue eyes and golden blonde hair in braids skipped along beside her, clutching a copy of her favorite book in her hands . . . and she was singing . . .

"Run, run, run, fast as you can, you can't catch me, I'm the gingerbread man."

Ivy sang the words she'd memorized from her favorite story as they walked home from school together. Holly used to walk home alone, but now that Ivy was in kindergarten, she had to walk with her. She was supposed to hold her little sister's hand all the way, but she rarely did so until they got within sight of the house.

"I can't believe you brought that book home, Ivy. It was supposed to be returned to the library before we came back from the lake!"

"I wanted to keep it."

Holly rolled her eyes. "Yeah, but it was on my library

card. I only just got it this year. If you don't return your books on time, they don't let you take out any more."

Ivy looked up at her sister, her huge eyes wide. "I didn't mean to get you in trouble, Holly."

Holly softened. The kid looked near tears. "Never mind. I guess it'll be okay, so long as we take it back next time we go down to the lake."

"Yeah!" Ivy smiled, her worry gone, and continued walking with her big sister, until Holly turned left instead of going straight at the end of the block.

"Holly?"

"It's okay, sweetie. I just want to take the long way home this time."

"Why?"

Holly looked around. "Because that new boy lives over this way, and I want to go past his house."

Ivy's smile spread wider. "Ooh. You like him, don't you?" She added in a sing song voice, "Holly and Johnny, sittin' in a tree—"

"Don't even." Holly scowled. "And if you tell a soul, I'll never get you another library book ever again. You hear?"

Ivy giggled, and skipped ahead. "I won't tell." Then she chanted, "Holly's got a boyfriend, Holly's got a boyfriend . . ."

They walked down the street they didn't usually take. And then the van came around the corner. . . .

"No, no, no, no, no . . ."

"Holly!" Hands gripped her shoulders, shook her. "Holly!"

A sob welled up and she bit her lip, fighting the nightmare of her past, telling herself to pull out of it, but the words burst free anyway. "Mom told us to come straight home!"

"Holly, open your eyes and look at me. Right now." His tone was firm and level and strong. She opened her eyes. Vince O'Mally was kneeling on the gravel road in front of her, looking at her as if he thought she might be dying. She was sitting down on the side of the road with her hands pressed to her ears. Her face was wet. Really wet. So wet that tears were dripping off her chin onto her blouse.

"What the hell happened to you? Was someone out here? Did he—?"

She held up a hand to stop him. "I'm okay. I'm okay, now." Her hand decided to grip the front of his shirt. She'd been crying so hard her chest kept heaving with spasms, even though she'd forced the tears to stop. His arms came around her, and she didn't resist, although she remained stiff, holding herself together by sheer will. He'd seen her out of control—twice now—but only briefly. It was not pretty. He wouldn't see it again. No one would.

He picked her up, carried her to his Jeep.

She closed her eyes. "What's happening to me?" she murmured. "Why now?"

He opened the door, set her on the seat, then hurried around to get in the other side. "I'd like to tell you it's all right, Holly, but I'm damned if I can do that until you tell me what the hell is the matter. Did someone—?"

"No." She curled her legs beside her, and turned her face into the seat. "No one was out on that road but me. Me and my shadows."

"Look . . ." he said. She felt his eyes on her, sensed his hesitation. Then she felt his hand lower to her hair, very gently. She thought maybe it was shaking just a little. "Look," he said again, more softly this time, "if you tell me about it . . . then, maybe I can help." He said it as if the words were being pried out of him.

"No one can help me, but me." She forced her voice level, refused to let it waver. It was broken by the occasional sob, but that couldn't be helped. "I thought I was past all this. Apparently, I have more work to do. And that's really all you need to know."

Seconds ticked by. She felt him watching her, felt the Jeep moving after a while, took comfort in the darkness.

She wished she could curl into it and never emerge. But she couldn't do that. She had beaten the past into submission once. She would simply have to do it again.

And she would do it on her own.

"I need to know a hell of a lot more than that," he said as he drove her to her house. "And I'm afraid I can't take no for an answer, Red."

SEVEN

H E didn't know what the hell to make of the woman. He'd hurried to his Jeep, grabbed the envelope off the front seat and tucked it underneath, and then driven out in search of her. He had damn near run her over.

She'd been sitting there, right in the road, rocking back and forth and sobbing the word "no" over and over, never taking a breath in between. Her hands were pressing so hard to her ears it looked as if she were trying to crush her head between them, and she was crying so hard her back shuddered.

His first thought was that she'd been attacked. That some son of a bitch had mauled her, or raped her. But, no. That wasn't it.

He carried her into her house, cursing at the fact that the door had been left unlocked as he carried her through. She worked at a police station, for crying out loud. Oh, but wait, he thought. Nothing bad ever happens in Dilmun. Yeah, it certainly looked that way.

He carried her to her bedroom, or what he thought was her bedroom. There were only two in the house, so he figured he had a fifty-fifty shot at being right. They were directly across the hall from each other, both doors open, and he'd glanced quickly left then right. The first bedroom was neat. The other was immaculate. He chose door number two, and took her in there, yanked the covers back and laid her down in the bed.

She curled onto her side, buried her face in the pillows, said nothing.

Vince pulled the covers up over her. "You want some warm milk or tea or . . . anything?"

She said nothing. Just burrowed in more deeply, hiding her face.

Sighing, he said, "Fine, have it your way." He backed away from the bed, but he didn't go far. Just pulled up a chair and sat down.

She didn't turn. But she did speak. She said, "Go."

"You're a mess right now. I'm not going anywhere."

"Please."

He got to his feet, went to the foot of her bed, and yanked the blankets up. Then he bent and pulled off her shoes. "Tell you what, Red. I'll go as far as the next room. I imagine you like a little privacy when you get like this. I know I do. So I'll go out there, and I'll close the door, and I'll give you your space. But I'm not going any farther. Deal?" She was holding it in. Waiting for him to leave and fighting with everything in her to keep it all back until he did. He peeled her socks off, and tucked the blankets back over her little pink feet. Then he left the room, stepped into the hallway, closed the door, and stood for a moment, just outside it.

He heard the dam break. Heard the sobs, soft and squeaky. He didn't want to ache for this woman. But he ached all the same. And for some reason it was taking every bit of his willpower to stay out of that bedroom. There was this part of him deep down inside that was itching to go back in there, hug the woman close, and tell her he'd make everything all right for her.

"It doesn't work that way, O'Mally," he told himself.

This woman was different from the other needy women

he'd tried to rescue. She didn't want his help, didn't want him anywhere near her, and seemed determined to keep the fact that anything was at all wrong in her little world entirely to herself. She was stubbornly independent, determined to be strong, even if she wasn't.

He stiffened his spine and walked into the Newman family's kitchen. He made himself a pot of coffee. While it brewed, he slipped out to his car, and grabbed that fat envelope from underneath the seat. It had "Newman" scribbled across the front in his partner's familiar hand. Vince carried the file back inside, sat down at the kitchen table, and began reading it.

It was not a pretty story. It was long, and it was chilling.

He hadn't finished it an hour later when Holly dragged herself out of her bedroom. She looked bad. Her hair stuck up all over, and her eyes were red-rimmed. She'd changed her clothes, put on a terry robe, and he didn't know what else underneath. She was sniffling and muttering to herself as she entered the kitchen, but she stopped short when she saw him.

Blinking, she said, "What the hell are you doing here?"

"I told you I wasn't going anywhere, Red. What, you didn't believe me?" As he spoke, he shoved the papers back into the envelope. But one sheet fell free, and fluttered to the floor, faceup. It was a grainy photocopy of the missing child poster that had been plastered all over Syracuse after the abduction of little Ivy Newman—Holly's kid sister. The little girl depicted on it had been cute as hell. Chubby cheeks, and dimples. Holly stared down at it and went utterly still.

"Where did you get that?"

He picked it up, but her eyes remained riveted to the poster until he'd tucked it into the envelope, out of her sight. Then she came closer, yanked the envelope from his hand, and looked at the name scrawled across the front. Lifting her gaze to his, she looked angry and betrayed. "You had to go digging, didn't you?"

"I'm sorry, Holly. Yes. I had to."

"Why? My God, why?" She dropped the envelope onto
the table as if it were dirty. "You have no idea how difficult it's been for my mother and me to put this behind
us."

"If you think you've put it behind you, you'd better go
take a look in the mirror. This thing is eating you alive."

She turned her back to him. "It wasn't. Not until you
showed up."

He sighed and got to his feet. Walking closer to her,
he touched her shoulders. "I need your help, Holly."

She sniffed. "You're not here on vacation," she ac-
cused.

"No. I'm not. I'm here because of two kids who were
abducted not long ago. Bobby and Kara Prague."

Her body went still as a statue under his hands before
she moved away and fixed her eyes on his face. "Killed?"
Her voice had gone flat. Toneless. Lifeless.

He did not want to answer that. But she probed his eyes
with hers, and then she seemed to know. "So was my
sister," she said in that same voice. "And what about the
book? What does that have to do with any of this?"

"I found it. In the same house where I found . . . Bobby
and Kara."

"I see."

"It came from the Dilmun Library. I thought there
might be a connection. That's why I came out here."

She shook her head slowly. "There's not."

"There has to be. Look, I know you don't want to talk
about this, but honestly, can it get any worse by trying?
You're having panic attacks, flashbacks—Jesus, Red,
keeping it to yourself sure as hell hasn't been a big success so far, has it?"

She only stared at him, so he drew her to a chair, set
her down, and poured her some coffee. "Talk to me," he
said. "It can't possibly make you feel any worse."

"It won't do any good. It's a coincidence, that's all."

"What is?"

"The book. That it's the same book my sister was carrying when—"

"When what, Holly?" Reaching across the table he gripped her hands.

"You already know. You read your precious file."

He shook his head. "That file is full of dry facts. Dates and times. Cops are trained to be objective and uninvolved. I want to hear it the way you remember it."

The remaining color seemed to drain from her face.

"Come on. Come on. Tell me," he urged.

She closed her eyes. "Don't ask me to do this."

"You can help me save some little kid's life, Red. Now you know damn well you can't say no to that. So, can we skip ahead here and get on with it already?"

She opened her eyes, glared at him. "You're cruel."

"Talk to me."

She drew a deep breath, fixed her gaze on her hands where they lay flat on the table. "We were walking home from school. I decided to take the long way home. I knew better. It was my fault."

"That's bull."

She held up a hand. "If you want to hear this, don't interrupt, Vince. If I stop I may not be able to start again."

"Sorry," he said. "Go on."

She lifted her head, stared past him at some distant space, and gave him the story in short, clipped sentences with no elaboration. It was not what he wanted from her.

"There was a van. It pulled over. A man jumped out and grabbed her. She screamed. I did, too. It happened very quickly. He just threw her in, and sped away. I ran after them, screaming for help. People gathered around." She shook her head slowly. "And that was all. It was a minute—less than a minute—and it changed everything."

"Did you get a look at him?" He wanted more. He knew she had more inside her, but maybe she couldn't let it out. Maybe she couldn't even access it.

"He wore a mask."

"But you could see his eyes, couldn't you?"

"No."

"How about the van? What color was it?"

She pressed a hand to her stomach as if remembering made her queasy. "No, no more. I can't." Her breathing changed, starting to get shorter and faster. "Ivy must have been so scared. It kills me to think of how afraid she must have been, how terrified. She was so little. I hope he killed her fast. Right away. I have to hope that. I can't bear to think—"

"Okay, that's enough, Holly," he said. And he said it firmly. He understood now—why she couldn't go too deep. This was what she found when she did. "It's over now. It's not happening now. She's at peace now." Holly met his eyes, and his conscience pricked him when he saw the tortured anguish in them. "Breathe deep and slow."

She did. He took the coffee away from her and poured it down the sink. Then he rinsed the cup, refilled it with water, and set it down in front of her before taking his own seat again.

"Okay?" He watched her face.

She sipped the water and nodded. "Okay. But no more, Vince. Not about that day. I can't remember, and I don't want to go over it anymore."

He sighed in resignation. "What about the book? Did your sister have the book with her when he took her?"

Holly nodded again. "It was her favorite. We used to spend a few weeks of every summer down here, in one of Uncle Marty's cabins. He never charged us. We loved it here. Loved hanging around with our cousins, even though they were so much older."

"Cousins? I haven't met them, have I?" Vince asked.

"No. Both Kelly and Tara moved away right after Kelly dropped out of high school. Broke Aunt Jen's heart." She sighed. "I miss them. Those were some of our best times, back then, when they were home, and Ivy was still here. I don't think they minded so much having little tag-alongs in the summer. They used to put makeup on us, and fix our hair."

Vince could see her remembering now. The way her gaze turned inward, the way her eyes seemed distant. "That last summer, I got my own library card. I took the book out of the library for Ivy. *The Gingerbread Man.* It was her favorite story. She used to sing that stupid song until I wanted to pinch her lips shut." She shook her head slowly. "She loved the book so much she managed to hide it in with her things when we went home, instead of returning it to the library with the other books. She thought she could keep it."

Vince listened carefully, and he tried to find that objectivity he'd developed over the years. But it was nowhere in sight. His defenses had been torn down by the Prague kids. And now Holly Newman's pain was running rampant over his soul, even though she kept it very well hidden. Or tried to.

"I found that same book at a crime scene," he said, keeping his tone steady, as gentle as possible. "Which strongly suggests it might be the same killer. In fact, it almost has to be."

Holly gave him a puzzled frown. "I guess you didn't get all the way through those files," she said.

"No, not all the way. Not yet. Why?"

"The man who took Ivy is doing life without parole in Auburn."

Vince couldn't hide his shock. "That's impossible."

"It's a fact." She sipped more water. "It must be a sick coincidence. Some other child got a copy of the same book—"

"From the same library? No, Holly. No. The Prague kids had no connection to this town. And besides, that book was taken out in September, nineteen eighty-three, according to the date stamped on the card pocket."

She shook her head. "It's a mistake . . ."

"It's the same book. And if it's the same book, it's the same predator."

She locked her gaze with his. "No."

"It has to be. Holly, I know this isn't easy, but try to see what's staring you in the face, here. They could have the wrong man in prison for killing your sister."

"He confessed," she said.

The wheels that had been turning so rapidly in Vince's mind came to a grinding halt. "Confessed?"

She nodded, placing her hands flat on the table, getting slowly to her feet. "And then we finally managed to put some closure on things, and to try to move on with our lives. The book is a coincidence. A sick, twisted, painful irony, but a coincidence. And now that you know that, you should leave here and take all of this with you. Because I can't deal with it again. I won't."

He got up as well, went to her, gripped her shoulders. "I'm sorry. I'm sorry, I know this is hard. But, Red, look at you. You didn't deal with it the first time. And I didn't bring this anguish to you. It's been living right here, inside you, for all these years, because you won't let it out. And if you don't pretty soon, it's gonna destroy you. Trust me on this. I know."

She tipped her head up, searched his face. "How do you know?"

He closed his eyes. "I just do."

He felt her hand on his cheek, and opened his eyes again. "I see," she said. "So there's pain in your past, too." She shook her head. "I would think you, of all people, would understand my need to let this stay where it belongs, dead and buried."

He watched her, the determination in her face, the firm set of her jaw. "The only pain in my past is that I've seen too many people I cared about self-destruct because they couldn't deal. You can, I'm convinced you can. You're not weak or fragile at all, are you? You're tough, and you're smart. And stubborn and pushy and bossy. But when it comes to this—you're still playing the victim. And it's against your nature. You *can* deal with it. But you won't."

"I was over it," she insisted. "I was. I was fine until you came."

"You were ignoring it. There's a difference."

Headlights gleamed through the windows. Holly stiffened and turned away. "Don't say a word of this to my mother. Do you understand, Vince? She barely survived losing Ivy—and then Dad. She's been through enough."

He nodded, picked up the file. "If you don't want her to know anything's wrong—"

She pressed a hand to her face. "God, she can't see me like this. Tell her . . . tell her I'm feeling better and taking a shower."

With that she ran for her bedroom. Leaving Vince to tell the lie. Hell, he could see no reason to bring her mother into this. Not yet. Holly had just shot a pretty big hole in his theory. But he knew in his gut there was some connection, and he was damned well going to find out what.

The front door opened, and Doris walked in. Chief Mallory stood outside the door, hat in his hand. "Come in for coffee?" she asked.

He looked past her, nodded hello to Vince. "No. It's late, you'd better get some rest."

She leaned up to kiss the chief briefly on the mouth, then turning, finally acknowledged Vince's presence. "How is Holly doing?"

"She's feeling better. She decided to take a shower."

Doris twisted her wrist to look at her watch. "At one A.M.?"

"Go figure," Vince said. He clutched the envelope close to his chest and moved toward the door. "I should go, now that you're home. Do me a favor, Doris, and lock up from now on. Okay?"

She made a face. "I suppose it's a bit self-deluding to go through life thinking I don't have to worry about break-ins out here."

"You're right, it is," Mallory said.

Doris sighed, nodded, then paused as Vince passed. "What's that you have, Vince?"

He glanced down at the envelope. "Oh. Just some research on the case I was working before I took my vacation. I don't want to be behind when I get back on the job."

"My goodness, you certainly are conscientious."

"I try to be, ma'am. Good night." He stepped out onto the porch beside Chief Mallory, and Doris closed the door. He listened for the locks, heard them turning, and knew Mallory was listening, too.

As he started for the car, a heavy hand fell on his shoulder. "Just a minute, son."

Vince paused. Mallory took the envelope from him, turned it over, and looked at the name on the front. Vince let him. He could have stopped him easily, but he'd pretty much decided that it was time to bring the chief in on this whole thing.

"That's about what I thought. So what are you really doing out here, besides digging into someone's private hell?" Before Vince could answer, the chief said, "This have to do with those two kids who were murdered up your way?"

Startled, Vince said, "How did you know?"

"I'm the police chief of a small town, O'Mally. That doesn't necessarily mean I'm dumb as a post. That story was all over the news. I saw your picture in the paper. I knew damn well that lame stolen car tale you spun in my office was bullshit. But what's the connection with the library book?"

Vince took back his envelope, and he and Mallory walked side by side to the waiting cars. "It was found at the crime scene." He opened his car door, tossed the fat envelope onto the seat. "Have you found out who last took it out of the library?"

The chief nodded. "Holly did. Just a few weeks before her sister was taken. But you already knew that, didn't you, O'Mally?"

"I was pretty sure of it, yes," Vince admitted.

"So what's the connection? Ivy Newman's murderer is in prison—confessed to the crime. Even led the police into the woods up north to show them where he dumped the body."

Vince's head came up fast. "And did they find it?"

Chief Mallory shook his head. "No. Apparently he'd buried her somewhere in the Adirondaks. They searched several sites, but you know how it is up there. Lake after lake, and they all look pretty much the same."

Vince's jaw tightened. "There's a connection. I'll find it." He got into his Jeep.

"Vince." The chief held on to Vince's door, leaning in. "Does Holly know what you're doing?"

"She does now."

"How long has she known?"

Vince knew exactly what the man was getting at. "About an hour now. Chief, whatever is wrong with Holly was wrong with her before I started digging into this. If something has set her off, it's something besides me."

"And her mother?"

"She doesn't know anything. Holly asked me not to tell her and at the moment, I see no reason to."

"You watch your step with Holly—be careful with her," Mallory warned.

He nodded. "I intend to be." But, as he started the engine, he thought Holly Newman was one hell of a lot stronger than these people gave her credit for. The trick was in making *her* see that.

This was a puzzle. And Holly Newman was more than just one of the pieces. She was the key that would make all the others fit.

EIGHT

CHIEF Jim Mallory looked around the table at the men he'd asked to come to his home in the middle of a Saturday night. Each had a beer, but he would see to it they didn't have a second one before they left.

To his right, the town's aging doctor sipped his beer slowly from the bottle, and punctuated each sip with a fistful of chips from the bowl on the table. Ernie Graycloud was thirty pounds overweight, and wore his long, silvered hair pulled back in a ponytail, day in, day out. His face was starting to wrinkle, but it still bore the copper hue and the straight large nose that would identify him as Indian even to those who hadn't yet heard his name. He bragged that he was pureblood Cayuga, but the chief doubted anyone in this part of the state was pureblood anything at this point in history. Ernie was the finest doctor he'd ever known, though. And a good friend, besides.

So was the other man at the table, Marty Cantrell. He drank his beer in long, loving drafts that were few and far between. He looked worried, pensive.

"You didn't tell me your reasons for calling this meeting, in your phone message," Marty said to Jim.

"I didn't want to leave the details on your machine," Jim explained.

"No matter. I think I can guess. That cop, Vince O'Mally, down from Syracuse. He's poking around in things that don't concern him, isn't he?"

Jim Mallory nodded. "I'm afraid so."

"I knew there was some reason he was getting so chummy with my niece. I don't like it. I don't like it a bit."

"I don't like it any better than you do, Marty."

Ernie Graycloud was looking from one of them to the other. "I still don't understand. What is it you think he wants? Ivy's case is solved. It's closed. What can he do by digging all this up now?"

"I'll tell you what he can do," Marty said. "He can send my niece over the edge, straight into a mental ward." Marty looked the doctor dead in the eyes. "Tell me you don't think it's possible, Ernie. Say something, for crying out loud; you're her doctor."

Ernie lowered his gaze. "I don't know. I think she's stronger than we realize, but this . . . yeah. If he forces her to relive that time in her life, it could push her too far."

"So, just what is it he wants, that's worth torturing Holly that way?" Marty asked softly. "Jim? Has he confided in you, at all?"

The chief sighed heavily. "Yeah. There were a couple of kids murdered in Syracuse. It was his case. He found some things he thought linked the crime to Dilmun, and then when he found out about what happened to Holly's little sister, he thought there might be a connection."

Doc Graycloud frowned. "What could he have found to tie the Syracuse murders to Dilmun?"

"Come on, Ernie, you know I can't tell you that." The chief sipped his beer while the other two stared at him. "I will say it's pretty compelling. I don't blame him for wanting to follow up on it."

Marty set his beer bottle on the table. "I blame him. The man who killed little Ivy is in prison. That ought to be enough to convince this O'Mally he's on the wrong trail."

"That's not our concern. Our concern is Holly. This isn't going to be good for her," Doc warned.

"It's already causing problems," Marty said, leaning back in his chair. "Doris says Holly's been counting again. Having trouble sleeping. How long before the nightmares come back as well?" He shook his head slowly. "She left the bonfire early, said she wasn't feeling well."

Jim sighed again. "Yeah, and then there was the incident out at the cabin."

"What incident?" Doc asked, snapping to attention.

"She thought she saw someone moving around inside. She panicked. Vince got back and checked the place out, but there wasn't a sign anyone had been anywhere near it. The door was still locked."

"You think she imagined it?" Doc asked.

"I don't know what to think," Jim said slowly. He looked at Marty. "Doc and I have only been close with Holly and Doris for five years. Marty, you've been with them straight through the worst of it. Was there a time, even at her worst, where Holly was hallucinating?"

Marty's lips pulled tight. "She was a little girl who saw her kid sister get snatched, and then never saw her again. Yeah, she hallucinated. There were night terrors. There was survivor's guilt. There were panic attacks, and bed-wetting, and insomnia, and obsessive-compulsive disorder. There were doctors and more doctors, drugs and more drugs. Nothing helped, not for ten freaking years, until that son of a bitch confessed. That was when she finally started to put her life back together. She lost her dad soon after that, and it set her back, but she pulled out of it. I thought . . . dammit, I really thought it was finally behind her."

Ernie Graycloud nodded. "I thought so, too. She's been doing so much better since I started seeing her when she first moved out here. But Doris called me about two weeks ago. She said Holly had been talking in her sleep, saying her sister's name, stuff like that. I've been trying to talk Holly into coming in for a checkup, but you know how stubborn she can be. She says she's fine."

"She's not fine," Marty said. He took another swig of beer. "She's far from fine, and getting worse by the day."

"Wait a minute. Did you say Doris called you two weeks ago, Ernie?" Jim asked sharply.

Ernie nodded.

"Odd," Jim mused, rubbing his chin. "That's before O'Mally ever set foot in this town." He looked across the table at his friend. "What else could have triggered all this, Ernie?"

He replied with a shrug, "Anything. She could have seen a report about the missing children in Syracuse and that could have done it. Or any number of other things. I've seen people with post-traumatic stress have flashbacks triggered by nothing more than a smell that reminded them of the past event."

"So, something reminded Holly of her sister's kidnaping before this joker arrived in Dilmun?" Marty asked.

"Apparently so."

Jim shook his head slowly. "Maybe she's starting to remember something. She never was able to recall much at all, as I understand it." He looked to the doctor for confirmation.

"It's possible. Her memory about the abduction has always been spotty at best. Maybe it's starting to clear up now."

"If she was starting to remember, Doc, would that be a good thing for her?" Marty asked.

"Could be good. Could be devastating," Ernie replied. "There's just no way to know for sure, until and unless it happens."

Marty snorted. "Then, I think the best thing for all concerned would be for Vince O'Mally to get his ass back to Syracuse where he belongs, and stay the hell away from my niece, and my sister-in-law."

"I have to agree with you there," Ernie said. "You know, even though it was Holly with the symptoms, Doris went through hell, too. They've been doing well up to now. I'd hate to see anything undo all the progress they've made."

"They've really put it back together since they moved out here," Marty added. "And Jen loves having them so close. It's been good for them."

"I agree," Chief Mallory said. "Look, I'll have a talk with O'Mally. See if I can make him see reason. For what it's worth, Doris still doesn't know his real reason for being in town. I'd prefer to keep it that way."

"And what about Holly?" Ernie asked. "Does she know?"

"Yeah. Found out last night," Jim told them.

"Son of a—"

Ernie clapped Marty on the shoulder. "Don't worry. We'll help her through this."

Marty nodded, clasped his beer bottle by its neck and took another long pull. Then he wiped his mouth with the back of his hand. "Thanks for keeping us informed, Jim."

"It's the least I could do. You're her uncle, Marty. The closest thing she has to a dad. Ernie's her doctor, and I'm her employer—and in love with her mother, besides. It's up to us to protect those two, the way I see it. This meeting stays between us. Agreed?"

"Agreed," the other two said in unison.

Jim nodded. "Good. Good."

HOLLY SLEPT ONLY SPORADICALLY. EVEN though she knew Vince's theory was so much hot air, without a shred of truth to it, she couldn't stop thinking about it. What if, somehow, he was right? What if the man who'd confessed to killing Ivy had been lying?

But why? Why would anyone admit to murder if he hadn't done it? Who did something like that?

If there was even the slightest chance . . .

But, no. There was no motive. No way. Now that he knew his theory was an impossibility, Vince would pack up his envelope full of information about her and the darkest night of her soul, and go on back to the city.

She wondered why that thought brought with it a twinge of what felt like regret. Maybe, she told herself, it was simply that she sensed in him a man who didn't look at her the way everyone else in her life looked at her. He didn't see her as weak or fragile. He'd told her as much. And there was something else about him, too. Something that tugged at her. She was drawn to him in spite of herself, though it irked her to admit her mother had seen it before she had. She knew it when she woke up, rolled over in her bed, and found her face near his jacket, smelling his scent. He'd left it hanging on the bedpost. It made something tighten and yearn deep in the pit of her belly.

That part of this situation would best be set aside for now, she decided. She had more than enough to contend with.

The one thing that kept standing out was Vince's cockeyed theory that the wrong man was doing time for Ivy's murder. She couldn't just dismiss it. She had to know.

Holly sat up in bed. She had to know.

It was Sunday morning, clear and cold. No alarm clock went off on Sunday mornings. Its routine was different, though every bit as predictable. Holly and Doris slept as late as they wanted to on Sundays, then sipped coffee in the sunroom in their nightclothes, lounging lazily and catching up. After that, and only after that, they would shower and dress. At that point, the rest of Holly's routine was done with military precision. Lay out the clothes, shower, shave her legs, shampoo, always in the same order. She took more time with herself on Sundays, pampering her skin and doing her nails.

This morning she did none of those things.

Holly got out of bed, showered, and dressed immediately, even though it meant skipping several parts of the usual routine. It made her uneasy, gave her an insecure feeling, like walking on thin ice. But she had to see Vince before he left town. She had to get to the truth. Because if there was even the slightest chance that the man who'd murdered her baby sister was still free, then all the routines in the world were not going to do Holly one bit of good.

She had to know it wasn't true. That it was impossible, just as she had insisted it was.

She left her mom a hastily scrawled note on top of the coffee pot, and walked along the lakefront road to Vince's cabin. It was cool this morning. Only in the high forties, she guessed, as she hugged her jacket around her body, Vince's clasped in her arms, and gave thanks that she'd worn a woolly sweater underneath. She should have added a hat. But the sky was clear, promising a warmer day later on. A few leaves skittered over the gravel and the wind was sharp and biting. It felt good on her face. Woke her up with a smack of autumn.

The lake was dancing again with whitecaps and froth, dark water looking as secretive and sullen as Vince O'Mally's eyes. She tromped up the porch steps, and thumped the door of Vince's cabin without hesitating. If she stopped to think about this, she would change her mind and go back home.

Vince opened the door. He was wearing the same jeans he'd been wearing the night before, but with a black T-shirt and an unsnapped faded denim shirt over it. He hadn't shaved. As she looked up at him and her eyes slid over the dark stubble on his face, she got a little hitch in her breathing. He opened the screen door for her. "C'mon in."

"You don't even seem surprised to see me," she said, walking inside. She held out his jacket. He took it with a nod of thanks. The place was totally transformed from the last time she'd seen it. He had a laptop computer on the coffee table, a fax machine on the kitchen counter, what looked like a scanner on a spare kitchen chair, a portable copy machine on the floor, and stacks of papers and file folders everywhere. So many wires and cables connected the mess together it looked like a snake pit.

He closed the door behind her. "I'm glad to see you. Not surprised though. I had a feeling you had more moxy than you were letting on."

"I don't see what that has to do with my coming out here."

"It has everything to do with your coming out here. You're ready to face this thing. Up to now, it's been in charge; but you're taking over, as of today. It's a big scary step, Red, but I had a feeling you were up for it."

She turned toward the fireplace on the pretense of warming her hands. But in reality she was uncomfortable that he read her so easily and so well. "Don't be so sure I won't turn and run back home if this gets to me, Vince."

He spoke from close beside her, making her jump. "I know it's hard." He handed her a mug filled with freshly made coffee.

"Hard? You're talking about resurrecting my worst nightmares. It's more than hard." She took the mug, noticed that her hand was shaking.

"And you're up to the task."

"Maybe I am. I have a condition first."

"Name it."

"You need to give me one reason why Hubert H. Welles would have confessed to killing my sister if he didn't do it. And it needs to be a good one."

He sipped his coffee. "I finished reading the files last night, and I think I can do that."

She blinked up at him. "You can?"

"Yeah, I've been poring over that bastard's case history all night long trying to give myself that very same answer. A reasonable doubt. Anything."

"And you found one?"

"Maybe. Hubey Welles was originally arrested in connection with the abduction of a fourteen-year-old boy. When they found him, the boy's body was still in the trunk of Welles's car. They had him dead to rights. There was no doubt of a conviction, and the death penalty had just been reinstated in New York State."

"So?"

"So why is he languishing in a prison cell instead of a cemetery? A death sentence should have been a given in a case like that. So why wasn't it?"

She shrugged.

"I'll tell you what I think. I think he made a deal. He provided information on some other cases of missing children in exchange for his life."

Holly's jaw dropped when she realized where Vince was going. "Are you saying you think he made it up? Just to avoid the death penalty?"

"I'm saying his confession might have saved his life. To my way of thinking, that gives him a pretty damn good motive for lying."

"He gave them details of the crime. He led the police into the mountains to search for my sister's body." Holly's knees suddenly felt like jelly.

"Yeah. But they never found it."

Holly teetered and sank down onto the nearest chair. "Oh, my God."

"Look don't take this as gospel, not yet. It's a theory. That's all. It could be nothing. The first thing we've got to do is talk to the D. A., see what kind of deal he made with Welles, and then—"

"I have to see him."

"Who? The D.A.?"

"Welles. I have to see Welles."

"No." He said it quickly and firmly. "No. Welles is a snake. I don't want you within a hundred miles of him."

She tipped her head to one side, and searched his face. "I thought you said I was strong, deep down. That I could deal with this. This is me, dealing. I need to see him."

He hesitated, his jaw tight as he studied her. Then he shook his head, as if reaching a decision once and for all. "No. No way. We can get all the information we need

without—" He broke off there, cut off midsentence by the
bleat of his cell phone. He took the call, called the chief
by name, and spoke briefly. But before he hung up the
fax had come to life, churning out documents, and then
the cell phone rang again.

Finally, he sighed. "We're not going to be able to talk
in here."

She shook her head distractedly. "It doesn't matter.
I . . . I need to digest all of this."

"Holly . . ."

"Just . . ." She bit her lip, and as the phone began shrill-
ing again, turned, and left.

A HALF HOUR LATER, DORIS NEWMAN
called Vince, asking if he had seen her daughter.

Vince frowned at the phone. "She was here a while ago,
but she left. She didn't come home?"

"She came home—but only for a few minutes. Vince,
I— She would be furious with me for telling you this,
but I'm worried about her."

"Why?"

She didn't answer right away. He could almost see her
mulling it over. Then she continued. "She said she would
probably be gone all day. But she wouldn't say where she
was going. She took the car. She seemed agitated, Vince,
and . . . well, my gun is missing."

Vince damn near dropped the phone. "You have a gun,
Mrs. Newman?"

"It's legal. I have a license. I bought it for . . . protection."

"In a town where you don't even bother locking your
doors?"

"Oh, God, no. I bought it before we ever moved down
here. To tell you the truth, it's been packed away in my
closet for so long I'd nearly forgotten I had it. But after
Holly left, I noticed the closet door ajar, and when I

looked it was obvious someone had gone through it. The box I kept the gun in was empty."

"All right. Listen, I don't want you to worry. I'm gonna go find Holly for you," he told Doris.

"Do you have any idea where she's gone, Vince? What's going on with her?"

He did. He had a solid idea, and he hoped he was wrong. But he couldn't burden her mother with his gut feeling. "I'm not sure. I'll call you when I know, okay?"

"All right. Thank you, Vince. I . . . thanks."

"You're welcome." He hung up, pushed a hand through his hair, and took a breath. He was ninety-nine percent sure Holly Newman was on her way to see a convicted murderer, a confessed pedophile. Hubey Welles. Vince entertained the thought that someone should have blown the bastard's head off years ago, and then he shook it off and got his ass in gear. It didn't take long to gather up the papers scattered around, the faxes that had come through, his file on Holly Newman, and his laptop. He took all those things with him to his Jeep and locked up the cabin. Then he started driving, while unfolding a road map on the passenger seat and following his finger to the maximum security correctional facility at Auburn, New York.

Why the hell would she drive out there? What earthly good did she think it would do? A woman like Holly shouldn't put herself within a hundred miles of scum like Welles. Shaking his head in frustration, he got an idea, yanked out his cell phone, and dialed Jerry's cell number. He needed another favor. He just hoped he wasn't pushing too far—but he didn't think so. Jerry was his partner, and Vince would do the same for him, if their situations were reversed. Or at least he thought he would.

HOLLY'S HANDS WERE TREMBLING, HER stomach rebelling at the thought of seeing the man who

had murdered her little sister. Of looking into his eyes. It
would be horrible. A nightmare.

She drove, and she remembered. But this time she was
determined to stay in control. The memory wouldn't suck
her in like a whirlpool and drown her in emotions. She
would simply pick through the dusty recesses of her mind,
and find the facts she needed.

The van had come around the corner so slowly that
Holly hadn't even noticed it at first. Not until she caught
sight of it from the corner of her eye, creeping along the
road beside them at a snail's pace. She pinched the bridge
of her nose, and tried to remember. Details had always
eluded her. They came now, reluctantly, with great effort.
The van had been primer gray. She almost saw it, and
then the curtain of mist drew over her memory again.

All right, she had a color if nothing else. She forced
herself to remember more.

The van had stopped, and the man got out. He wore a
knit ski cap pulled over his face, with holes for the eyes.
He was tall. He was not lean. He swung his arms like
whips. One hand clutched tight around Holly's upper arm.
The other held her little sister.

Holly had looked up right into his eyes. She remembered it clearly, as if it were yesterday. She'd screamed.
He shouted at her to shut up, but for the life of her she
couldn't recall the sound of his voice. The eyes, though.
There was something about his eyes. . . .

She had twisted and fallen to the ground, forcing him
to let go. He looked at her. Just looked at her. As if to
say, fine, if that's the way you want it. Then he hurled
Ivy roughly into the van, and clambered in behind her.
He sped away. Holly ran after him, screaming her sister's
name.

"Ivy," she whispered. Tears were hot in her eyes, on
her cheeks. "Ivy . . ."

A horn blasted. Holly blinked out of the memory and
she jerked her wheel to correct the car. She'd lost control
over the memories for just a moment. The past had nearly

pulled her in again. Swallowing hard, she lifted her chin. "I'm not a little girl any more. He can't hurt me now."

But in her mind, she kept feeling his cold hands on her arm, and hearing her sister crying her name.

The howl of a siren made its way into her awareness, and she glanced up into the rearview mirror, saw the police car with its flashing lights behind her, and muttered a string of cuss words under her breath. She slowed down, moved to the side so he could go around. He didn't. He pulled off behind her. Great. A ticket would just put the topper on her day.

She stopped the car, rolled her window down, and waited. The cop took his sweet time about getting out. Didn't they always? She fished in her wallet for her license, popped open the glove compartment and rummaged inside it for the registration, then sat waiting with them in her hand.

Finally, the officer, a solid-looking man, came striding up to her car, sunglasses stereotypically mirroring her own reflection back at her as he stopped and leaned down. "Ms. Newman?"

Obviously he'd already run her plates. He knew her name. "Yes, officer?" She held up her license and registration. "I wasn't speeding. I'm sure I wasn't."

"No ma'am."

"Well, then, why did you stop me?"

He took the papers from her hand, and paused to look them over, then handed them back to her. "I'm going to have to ask you to wait here a moment."

Sighing, Holly leaned forward until her forehead touched the steering wheel. He turned to walk back to his car, and she sat up straight as an idea came to her. "Wait a minute. Don't I know you? I mean, I've probably seen you on business, being that I work at the Dilmun Police Department." She waited for his reaction. Hell, her mother was always telling her to use her connections to greater advantage. It was supposed to work. He stood there, looking at her, not responding. "You know, Dilmun?" she

went on. "That little town about twenty miles back that
way?"

"You're a police officer, ma'am?" he asked, monotone.

"No. No, I work at the department, but I'm not a cop.
I'm . . . well, I'm the chief's right hand, to be honest. Why
don't you call him and verify—?"

"That won't be necessary, ma'am. Just wait right there,
a moment, all right?"

He turned and walked the rest of the way to his patrol
car, lights still flashing. Other traffic blew by, and she sat
there, waiting for the cop to finish writing her a ticket for
whatever she'd done. Mentioning her ties to the Dilmun
police hadn't seemed to faze him in the least. Wasn't he
supposed to give her a smile, a wink, and send her on her
way?

He didn't come back, and minutes ticked by. Five, then
ten. She drummed her fingers and waited. What on earth
was taking him so long?

A red Jeep Wrangler pulled up behind the police cruiser
and came to a stop. A man got out, waved to the cop.
The cop waved back, got into his car, and then drove
away.

Blinking in disbelief, she looked again.

Vince. Vince O'Mally. *He'd* been behind this.

She opened her car door, got out and slammed it shut
again. Traffic buzzed past, sending her hair blowing in its
wake as she strode toward him. "What are you doing here,
Vince?"

"What, you thought I was going to let you go to Auburn
alone?"

"How did you know where I was going?"

He shrugged. "Did you really think I wouldn't guess?"

"And you had that cop pull me over?"

"How else was I going to catch up?"

"Will you stop answering questions with questions?"

"Will you stop giving me a hard time?"

She pursed her lips and glared at him. He met her glare
with one of his own. "Look, in the first place, Welles is

a lowlife bastard. You shouldn't be anywhere near him, much less alone."

"He'll be behind bars."

"He'll screw you up anyway. I've seen his kind do it before."

She frowned, searching his face a little more closely. Was he going all protective on her now, like everyone else in her life?

He shrugged, looking away. "In the second place, you'll never get in to see him alone. There's a process to visiting murderers in prison, you know? You just don't show up and knock."

She bit her lip in chagrin. "I guess I thought they might make an exception for the sister of one of his victims," she said softly.

He reached out, clasping her upper arms. "Listen to me. This is a bad idea. Drop this. Come back to Dilmun with me."

She looked into his eyes. A sensation washed over her, very briefly—that magnetic pull that had her body swaying closer to his. It was becoming familiar to her, this draw, this urgency to be just a little closer to him, to touch. But she caught herself in time, stopped herself, looked away. "I'm going to try to see him, with you or without you. I have to."

"You don't need to put yourself through this."

"You're the one who told me I hadn't dealt with it. That I was keeping it inside, letting it eat me alive. I'm trying to exorcize my demons, Vince. I have to do this."

The wind was blowing dust from the roadside into eddies and swirls around their legs. He held her gaze with steady eyes and she felt him looking straight to her soul. Finally, he sighed, pulled his cell phone from his pocket, punched in a number. "Chief Mallory? It's Vince O'Mally. Do me a favor and drive one of the boys out here to pick up Holly Newman's car. You'll find it on the side of route thirty-four, about twenty miles north of town. Keys are in the ashtray. And do me a favor—tell Doris that Holly's fine, and spending the day with me." He paused. "Thanks, Chief."

He tucked the phone back into his pocket when he was finished. "Now, there's the small matter of the gun."

She turned her face away from him quickly. "Gun?"

"Your mother's gun, Holly. What were you thinking? That you could smuggle it inside and blow Hubey Welles away? It might be a great way to vent your rage, Red, but he's not worth it. Trust me on this."

She still didn't look at him. "I wasn't thinking anything like that. Even I'm not naive enough to think I could get into a prison with a gun. I just wanted to have it nearby. In case of trouble from whoever broke into your place, or maybe whoever killed those kids."

"You ever shoot a gun in your life?"

Finally meeting his eyes, she shook her head.

"Do you mind if I hold on to the gun for you, then? It might be safer that way."

"Fine."

"Good. Go get it, and your purse. Drop the car keys in the ashtray. We'll take my car to Auburn."

Holly nodded slowly. Part of her wanted to tell him he was overstepping. To mind his own business and to stop butting in. But most of her was relieved. She'd been terrified of facing that monster alone. Now she wouldn't have to. Vince would be beside her. And somehow that made it better.

NINE

⊰⊱

VINCE watched her. She was nervous, fidgeting, talk-ing about anything that popped into her head. Super-ficial stuff. The weather, the scenery along the roadside. The drive took under an hour, and in that time he didn't think she'd said anything real, or showed him anything true about herself. Not once. But he saw it all the same.

She was scared. More so with every passing mile. He half expected her to change her mind. Tell him to pull over, turn the car around, take her back to Dilmun. The fact that she didn't spoke volumes. His initial guess had been right. The woman was stronger than she seemed.

He phoned ahead to make the arrangements to visit Hubey Welles. No one gave him too much trouble about it, and that didn't surprise him. No one at the prison was overly concerned with protecting the rights of a convicted child killer.

He had to leave all weapons outside, of course, and a guard checked his I.D. before they even passed through the metal detectors. Holly seemed to fade a little bit with every step through the dull, cold facility. Like a ghost losing its substance. She jumped at every electronic buzzer, every unexpected sound. But she never stopped. She kept moving forward—slowly, determinedly forward. Like Joan of Arc walking to the stake. He found himself closing his hand around hers, in spite of himself.

Finally, they were escorted into the visiting area. A long line of straight-backed chairs sat one by one, facing unbreakable windows. Every one of those chairs was empty. Small speakers were mounted on either side for talking back and forth. There was no privacy. Guards stood on either end of the room, their eyes sharp and alert.

Holly closed her hand tighter around Vince's as they stood there, waiting for Hubey Welles to appear on the other side of the glass. Her hand was cold. Her grip firm, but shaking. She was reliving her worst nightmare, he knew that.

With a buzz and the sound of locks clanging open, a sturdily built man with crew cut, gray spikes, and a boxer's face was led to the window on the other side. He looked at Holly with a sneer, then shifted his gaze to Vince, but only briefly. He focused on Holly again, ignoring Vince as if he weren't there.

"They told me I had a visitor. A cop and a lady, they said. I take it you're not the cop."

The way he licked his lips and stared at Holly just to intimidate her made Vince want to smash through the glass and grab the bastard by his throat. He thought he kept the fact concealed. When he spoke he sounded cool, he thought. Official. "I'm Detective Vince O'Mally. This is Holly Newman. She has some questions and I want you to answer them."

Welles shrugged. "I got nothing better to do." Then he sat down in the chair on his side of the glass.

Vince nodded to Holly. She just looked at him for a moment. He held her eyes, tried to send silent encouragement to her without words. They were here now. She might as well go through with this. After a brief hesitation, she sat down in the chair, clearly thrown by Welles's behavior.

"So what did you bring me, *Detective*? Mm? A little treat for good behavior?"

"Just shut up and listen to what the lady has to say," Vince snapped.

"Yeah, I'll listen. Come on in here, little girl, and I'll give you something to remember me by."

She stiffened. Vince thought she would surge to her feet and run from the room. Instead, her face hardened by degrees. She raised her chin, met his eyes. "I'm a little bit old for your tastes, Mr. Welles. By about twenty years or so."

The convict spit with laughter, his head tipping back with it. His teeth were even and white. "That's a good one," he said. "She's good, your girlfriend. She this quick in bed, Detective?"

"Shut up, Welles." It was Holly who said it, jumping in before Vince could say a word. And her voice had taken on a harshness that surprised Vince. "I'm the one you're here to talk to, so pay attention. Eight years ago you confessed to the abduction and murder of my sister. Ivy Newman."

"So what?" His gaze kept jumping from Holly to Vince and back again.

"So, I want to know if you really killed her."

Now the man seemed shaken. He tried to cover it, but Vince saw throught that. The man was nervous. "Hey, I said I did, right?"

She stared at him. "You *said* you did a lot of things."

Vince placed a hand on her shoulder, squeezed gently. She wasn't pale or fading now. Her color had risen in her cheeks. She looked as if she could kill the man on the other side of the glass without a second thought.

Vince spoke because she didn't. "I was thinking some of those confessions might have been made just to keep you off death row, Welles. I was thinking you might have confessed to anything they wanted to save yourself from lethal injection."

He shrugged. "What if I did?"

"Then we need to know. Did you kill Ivy Newman?"

The man leaned back in his seat, taking his time. "There were so many, you know. I didn't get their names."

Welles leaned forward suddenly, spearing Holly with his eyes. "They liked what I did to them, all my little ones did. They liked it. Asked for it."

She sat utterly still for a moment, then she shot to her feet and drove her fist into the window so fiercely Welles jerked backward in reaction. He fell over in his chair on the other side. Guards moved forward even as Vince grabbed Holly. "It's okay, I've got her, I've got her," he told the officers quickly. Welles got up, laughing at her. Vince turned her away, so she wouldn't see that.

She didn't fight him. Her knees gave, and she would have fallen over if he hadn't been holding her. He managed to turn her toward him, held her against his body.

"It wasn't him," she whispered. Her voice was strained and hurting. Her head was against his shoulder so when she spoke, her breath fanned his neck.

"You can't go by anything he said."

"It wasn't him, Vince. It wasn't him."

He closed his eyes for a long moment before nodding to a guard to let them out. Hubey yelled at them as they left. "Come on, now, you dragged me all the way down here. The least you can do is visit with me. Come on, honey, I promise I'll be nice."

Ignoring the shouts, Vince took Holly with him back to his car. She sat like a statue as he began to drive them home. Still, and stiff, and silent.

Finally, he said, "Holly, how can you be sure?"

She turned her head to face him. She seemed so bleak, so lost. "His eyes," she said. "I remember looking right into his eyes. Hubey Welles has brown eyes. They're small and dark. Round. When he lunged at me like that, I remembered. I looked into the eyes of the man who took my sister. Those aren't the eyes I remember. They were blue. A very pretty blue, like the earliest ice on the lake, when it's so thin the color of the water still shows through. I remember that now," she whispered.

"I believe you."

Her eyes remained on him, riveted to him. "Do you?"

"Why shouldn't I?"

She stared at him a moment longer, then sighed and leaned her head against the seat. "Because no one else will."

"Why won't they?"

She glanced sideways at him, very briefly, then shook her head. "I have a history, Vince. Come on, you read my records. You know."

"What I know is that for a kid to have gone through what you did and to still be functioning right now is pretty damned incredible."

"You call this functioning? I'm counting half the time, inside my head. The panic attacks are coming back. That one the other day at your place was just the beginning. There will be more. I can feel it. The nightmares are back. . . ."

"Yeah, but there's a difference now, Red."

She looked sceptical, but waited for him to elaborate.

"When all this stuff hit you before, you were a little girl. A helpless little girl. You're not anymore. You're a grown-up woman now."

She shook her head. "You think that's going to make a difference?"

"You're stronger than the past is, Holly. You can break its hold on you this time. But you have to turn around and face it first. You can't keep running from it."

"Don't bet the farm on that."

"You telling me you're giving up? Even now that you know your sister's killer is still out there somewhere?"

"What the hell do you want from me?"

She was no longer speaking in a normal tone. She'd raised her voice, and he knew she probably needed to. To vent and yell and get some of the turmoil that prison visit had brought to life off her chest.

"I want you to stop being a victim, Red. I want you to

stand up and fight the way I know you can. The way you did today when you insisted on looking that bastard in the eyes so you could know the truth."

"You give me one good reason why I should put myself through any more of this hell, and I'll think about it. Because I'll tell you, Vince, I can only think of one. And that would be if it could bring my little sister back to me. But it can't, can it?"

He couldn't lie to her. "No."

"Then, what is the point?"

"You want to know the point? You want the fucking point?" He pulled over to the shoulder and stopped the car. He then leaned forward, reached past her, and yanked open the glove compartment. He jerked the silver frame out of it and dropped it into her lap.

She glanced down at it. It was folded shut.

"Go on, look at it. *Look* at it, dammit."

Her hand was shaking when she reached for the frame, opened it like a book. She stared down at the angelic little faces. "Who . . . who . . . ?"

"Bobby and Kara Prague," he said.

Holly gaped at him, then back at the photo again, and then she burst into tears. Noisy, messy tears. But he didn't let up on her. "They're dead, and I'm pretty goddamn sure the guy who killed them is the same man who killed your kid sister. He's been killing little kids for eighteen years, and he's gonna keep right on killing them until somebody does something to stop him. And *that*, Red, is the point."

He had lost it with her. He hadn't meant to. She wasn't tough enough to endure his anger, and she hadn't done a damn thing to deserve it—except show signs of backing down. And why the hell did that set him off? It wasn't as if he hadn't expected it.

Or maybe it was. Maybe he'd been starting to think she wasn't one of those helpless, needy women that got him into so much trouble. Maybe he was starting to believe— or maybe to hope—she was more. That she was strong, able to fix her own life and not depend on him to do it for her. Because if she was, then what he was starting to feel toward her wasn't just a part of his recurring pattern, and to be avoided at all costs. Maybe it was something more.

She didn't talk to him for a while. She replaced the photo in the glove compartment, turned on the radio, leaned back in her seat, and stared out the window.

Finally, he said, "I'm sorry I did that. It was wrong of me."

She said nothing.

"I didn't mean to hurt you, Red."

"Don't be so vain, Vince. I just found out the man who killed my baby sister is still walking the streets. Your temper tantrum isn't even on my list of concerns." She looked at her hands, clenched tight in her lap, white and trembling. "I don't know what to tell my mother. This is going to kill her."

He felt like an assassin for having forced her to look at the photo that haunted his every thought. "Don't tell her anything, just yet. You don't have any proof."

"What do you mean?" She sent him a look out of wide, troubled eyes. "I was there. I looked into his eyes."

"I know that. But it's been years."

"It doesn't matter."

"You didn't say anything until now."

"I didn't *remember* until now. I thought you said you believed me?"

"I do. I'm just telling you what other people are liable to say."

She shook her head. "They have to reopen the case."

"They who, Holly?"

"The authorities. You, for God's sake. You keep telling me how I have to be strong enough to face this, and I have to take charge. Jesus Christ, Vince, it's not my job. There's a government, a system. They have to start looking for him again. Are you telling me my word won't be good enough to make them do that?"

"Holly . . . ," he began.

"You know he was lying. You knew it before I did. Didn't you?"

"I had a feeling, yeah." He sighed deeply, flicking on the wipers as it started to rain. "Most of these types have an m.o. and they stick to it. They prey on kids of a certain age, coloring, and gender. It didn't make a lot of sense to think Hubey Welles would have both male and female victims. When I got to checking, I found all the solid evidence they had on him was related to murdered boys. The murders he confessed to, three of them, all unsolved, were little girls. No hard evidence beyond his confession ever surfaced."

"Then you were right. He cut a deal with the D.A. He'd confess to the murders, in exchange for a life sentence rather than the death penalty."

"I have to assume he was convincing. The D.A. must have honestly believed he could have done those crimes. And God knows it would have been at least some relief to the families to be able to have closure," Vince said slowly.

"It was false closure. Now they have to admit that and reopen the cases. All three of them."

"Holly, I'm not even supposed to be working this case, if you want to know the truth. This vacation I keep saying I'm on? It wasn't by choice."

She stared hard at him, and for the life of him he couldn't believe he was telling her any of this. "Why?" she asked.

"I suppose if you asked my chief, he'd say it was due to severe stress. He thought I showed signs of losing it after I found those two kids."

Her gaze fell to the closed glove compartment. "You cared too much. Didn't you? Got too involved."

He thought for a moment. "My life is my job. You know that?"

"No, I didn't."

"It is. I've never been married. I've never wanted to do much of anything else except be a cop. Most of my pay goes into the bank, not that I give a crap how much I have. No house. I live in an apartment, a decent apartment, but nothing too nice. It wouldn't be worth it. I don't spend enough time there to make it all that important."

"You have a nice enough car," she commented.

He smiled a little. "You want to know why I bought it?"

"Yeah."

"I was on my way to a crime scene last February in my beat-up Buick, and I got stuck on an icy hill. Had to wait for a sand truck to come by before I could get up and over, and by then the case had been assigned to someone else."

"And it pissed you off so much you went out and bought a Jeep?"

"All-wheel drive," he said. "I don't get stuck anymore."

She nodded. "You sound like a good cop."

"Been at it a long time."

"Then how did you manage to get so involved in this case?"

He glanced at her, then focused on the road again, saying nothing.

"I mean, an enforced leave of absence. Digging around in it when you've been ordered not to. Carrying the kids' pictures around with you. They don't sound like the kinds of things a seasoned detective would do."

He drew a breath, sighed. "I made a mistake."

"Must have been a big one."

He nodded. "I promised Sara Prague I'd find her kids for her, and that everything would be all right."

She turned wide eyes on him. "That was a tall promise."

"It was one I never should have made. She believed me, you know. She really believed me. And I . . ."

He didn't finish, concentrating on driving instead, and on pretending his eyes weren't burning like two hot coals.

"There's a lot more to you than I thought," she said softly.

"I'm a cop. That's all, Holly. That's all I am, and all I want to be."

He shifted uncomfortably under her penetrating gaze. She was seeing a lot more than he wanted to reveal. "Does it really matter what you want to be?" She shook her head slowly. "I don't think it does, you know. I want to be a normal, well-adjusted woman. I want to be able to get through a day without turning the light switches off in the right order, or moving the pencil holder on my desk half an inch to the left." She hesitated for a moment, then went on. "Most of all, I want to be the girl who saved her little sister from an attempted kidnapping eighteen years ago. But I'm not. I'm not any of those things."

He looked at her, looked real deep into her eyes. They seemed able to see straight through him, and they touched him in places that hadn't been touched in a long time. He didn't like that a bit. And he didn't like thinking they had a lot in common, the two of them. Because he wanted to be the cop-hero who'd saved the Prague kids in the nick of time. He wanted to be the man who didn't break promises to broken mothers.

HOLLY WAS FRIGHTENED. MORE FRIGHT-ened than she had been on her way to Auburn to see Hubey Welles. More frightened than she had been in years, to be honest. She could feel the old terror creeping in like a dark shadow over her soul. And though the desire to face it, to fight it, as Vince kept insisting she must, was still strong, the fear was stronger. Her monster was still on the loose. The villain of her darkest nightmares was free. He could be anywhere. Anyone. She wasn't sure she could stand to go through her day-to-day existence knowing that. She'd only come as far as she had because she'd believed him behind bars. The case closed. Justice served. That was the foundation on which she'd rebuilt her life, her mind, her sanity. And that foundation had been ripped out from beneath her.

God, would she revert then? Would the panic attacks, and the nightmares, and the obsessive behavior slowly take over her life the way they had before?

Vince kept looking at her, searching her face with worry in his. He kept asking if she was okay. She didn't really know how to answer that.

As they rounded the corner toward Holly's house, a shadow caught Holly's attention, from the corner of her eye, and she felt an old dread in the pit of her stomach as she jerked her head toward it.

It was there, and then gone, all in the space of a heartbeat. The dark shape of the van had vanished around the bend just as she turned to look at it.

Her heartbeat slammed against her chest. "Did you see that?" she asked Vince.

He glanced at her. "See what?"

Holly closed her eyes. Hell, she'd seen the van in her dreams. Maybe it hadn't even been there. Maybe she'd just . . .

"The front door is open. Vince, the front door is open!" Holly was wrenching her passenger door open before the vehicle had even come to a complete stop. She lunged out of the car and ran toward the house, with her heart in her throat. She surged up the steps, ran through the open front door, and saw her mother, lying on the sofa, one arm dangling limply, hand dragging the floor. She took a step toward her, then stopped when her foot hit paper. She looked down.

A copy of her sister's missing-child poster lay on the floor, face up.

Holly yanked it up, bit back a scream, and lunged across the room to where her mother lay. "Mom!" She fell to her knees, skidding on the carpet, and grabbed her mother's shoulder.

Doris's eyes flew open, and she blinked at her daughter.

"What's wrong, Holly? My goodness, hon, you look like you've seen a ghost."

"You . . . you're okay." Holly sank back onto her heels, her hand still clasping her mother's shoulder. "You're okay."

"Well, of course I'm okay. Why wouldn't I be? You're the one I've been worried about."

"I . . . the door. The front door. Was open, and . . ." Holly still held the poster in one hand. She drew that hand downward slowly, slid the sheet of paper underneath her blouse, so her mother wouldn't see it.

"It was?" Doris sat up the rest of the way, frowning toward the door. "It was open?"

"Yeah, it was."

"Well, of all the . . . I'm sure it was closed when I curled up here." Then she gave her head a shake and smiled. "Hello, Vince."

"Hello, Doris. So, you don't know how the door got open?" He came up behind where Holly was crouching. She straightened, suddenly embarrassed by her instant and apparently needless panic.

"Well, no. I have no idea," her mother was saying. "I . . . oh, I'll bet I know! It was probably Bethany. I told her she could come by today to finish up the leftover cookies. She must have come while I was napping."

Holly stiffened. Again, the images played through her mind. The gray van, crawling closer. Ivy being snatched up and pulled inside. The gray van she'd thought she'd glimpsed just now, vanishing around the corner like a shark into the depths. "B-Bethany was here?"

"Look in the kitchen. She may have just come in and helped herself, you know she thinks of our house just like home."

Holly turned slowly to look into the kitchen. The lid was off the cookie jar, sitting beside it on the counter. There were some crumbs. An empty glass, with a film of milk coating the inside. She had been here. So had the van. And the front door . . .

"Bethany," she whispered.

Vince put a hand on her shoulder. "Holly, what—?"

"I'll be back in just a second." Holly went out the front door, closed it behind her, then she ran across the lawn, her heart pounding. She heard Vince calling after her, but she didn't pause. Not until she was at the Stevens's front door, pounding on it. "Bethany! Bethany, where are you?"

The door opened, and Bethany stood there, looking up at Holly with wide, frightened eyes. Her mother stood right behind her. "Holly? What's wrong?"

Holly almost wept in relief. Would have, in fact, if she hadn't felt a pair of strong hands close on her shoulders, and a deep strong voice speak from behind her. She tried to stop shaking. Instead, she dropped to her knees, and hugged Bethany as gently as she could manage under the circumstances. "Nothing's wrong," she whispered. "I just . . . I'm glad to see you, kiddo."

"You're so silly, Holly." Bethany squeezed her neck, and when she let go, Holly straightened, and hoped her terror didn't show. But Valerie Stevens was looking at her oddly.

"Mommy bought the material for my Halloween costume today, and the pattern and stuff," Bethany announced.

"Oh, that's great," Holly murmured. "I can't wait to get started."

"Me neither."

"It's . . . awfully good of you Holly," Valerie said softly. "Sewing has never been my strong suit."

"I'm glad to help. We're going to have fun doing it, aren't we Bethany?"

Bethany nodded. "I'll bring it over later and show you everything."

"Good, good, I can't wait to see it."

Vince closed his hand around one of Holly's, and spoke. "Actually the reason we came over was to ask if you had been at Holly's house today."

"Umm-hmm," Bethany said with a proud nod. "Mrs.

Newman said to help myself to the cookies, and so I did." She looked up at Holly. "She was sleepin' so I didn't wake her up. It's okay, isn't it?"

"Of course it's okay. I just wanted to make sure it was you and not some crazed cookie bandit." Holly bent, and deliberately arched one eyebrow. "Or maybe you *are* a crazed cookie bandit?" She grabbed Bethany's middle and tickled her until the child squealed. Then she let her go. "I'd better get back."

"Bye, Holly. See you later," Bethany said.

Holly turned with Vince to leave, but Valerie cleared her throat, stopping her. Val had stepped out onto the porch, and pulled the door closed behind her. "Holly, something frightened you, didn't it?"

Meeting her neighbor's eyes, Holly nodded. "I thought I saw something."

"Holly, you don't have to—"

"She's Bethany's mom, Vince." Holly faced the woman again. "The van, the one that took Ivy away. I thought I saw it, and then my door was open, and then I realized Bethany had been by, and it just all—it brought it all back. I'm sorry, Val, I didn't mean to freak out like that."

Valerie blinked a little too fast. "Oh, Holly. You sweet girl. Don't you apologize for looking out for Bethany. Not ever. I'm sorry this is still . . . so hard for you."

"If you don't mind, can we keep it between us? I don't want to worry Mom."

"Sure. Sure, hon, that's fine. You take care, okay?"

Holly nodded, and Val went back inside.

Vince drew Holly down the steps, turned her back toward her own home. They went a few steps, before the shaking that had begun deep in the core of her made its way to the surface, and her breaths came faster.

He led her around the house, toward the back yard. Out of a direct line of sight from either home. "Don't let it get you, Holly. Come on, it's all right."

"I swear I saw that van, Vince. I swear I did. Just out

of the corner of my eye, when we first pulled in. And I thought . . . I thought—"

"I know. But Bethany's safe, she's fine. Everything's fine."

She leaned back against the side of her house. Vince kept his hands on her shoulders as if to steady her, and she lifted her head. "It's not fine, Vince. *I'm* not fine. You know what's going on here as well as I do. That bastard who killed my sister isn't just free. He's here. He's right here in Dilmun."

He stared into her eyes, and she felt him searching them. What he might be looking for, she didn't know. "We have no evidence of that. None."

"Don't we?" She shook her head. "Well, it's either that, or I'm losing my mind. Imagining things. Seeing shadows that aren't there. Vans that don't exist." She pulled the sheet of paper from underneath her blouse. "This was on the living room floor, Vince."

She saw him pale when he realized what the paper was. "We could have dropped it. Remember, it was in the files the other night."

"You think we dropped it? You think something like this has been lying around my living room and I didn't see it? And Mom didn't see it?"

"It could have slipped underneath a piece of furniture. Maybe the door being open made a breeze, and it . . ." He didn't finish. He had to know how lame his words sounded.

"Either I'm completely insane," she said slowly, "or he's here. Messing with my head."

"Or it's just coincidence, combined with incredible stress . . ."

"You don't believe me."

"I don't know what to believe right now."

Holly pushed away from the house, away from his hands. "I'll tell you what I believe. I'm through letting that bastard fuck with my family, with my mind."

"Holly?"

She turned, glaring at him. Her hands curled into fists at her sides, clenching so tightly her nails dug into her palms. "I'm not going to take it anymore." She looked beyond him, toward the road, and she shouted, "Do you hear me, you son of a bitch! It's over!"

"Holly!" Vince reached out and grabbed her shoulders.

The tears exploded from her. She fell into his arms and she let them come. Vince held her hard against him, his hands in her hair, his mouth near her ear. "It's all right. It's okay," he kept saying it over and over again. But it wasn't okay. She didn't think it would ever be okay again.

TEN

〰〰〰

VINCE had seen the change. In the car, she'd been feeling panicky, frightened. In the house, when she thought another child might be at risk, her entire demeanor had changed. She found her anger.

It was good. Healthy. Oh, he didn't want her shouting challenges to a killer in the streets, but he was glad she'd found her strength. Maybe that was selfish, because it verified what he'd begun to suspect about her. He'd sensed that inner strength she hadn't tapped. Now he saw her finding it, grabbing hold.

She was something, all right. He couldn't take his eyes off her. And when she collapsed, sobbing in his arms, he found himself feeling way more than he ought to. In fact he caught her face between his palms, turned it up to his, and came within a hair's breadth of kissing her.

It was that close.

Damn.

He didn't know if she'd seen that van, or just imagined it. But he had to give her the benefit of the doubt.

Though he thought some others might not be so inclined. In fact, a short while later the chief showed up in response to Holly's call, and he looked downright skeptical. But he still promised to stay the night, just in case Holly's fears proved true.

That settled, she led Vince outside, one hand on his arm, her emotional storm long past. "Chief Mallory promised to spend the night, and to keep a close eye on Bethany next door as well," she said. "Mom will be fine."

"So, where are we going?"

"We need to talk."

He didn't realize there was more she wanted to say. "About what?"

"Look, you told me you needed me to tell you everything about that day. The things that didn't make it into the report. I'm ready to do that. I'll rip my chest open and let you wade around in my blood, if it'll help us figure out who he is so we can put him away, once and for all. But we need to be *alone*. I don't want phones and faxes interrupting every five minutes. All right?"

He nodded. "All right. I'm with you."

"No you're not. But you're all I've got right now."

He blinked, not sure what she meant. She got into the car. "Your place," she told him. And he drove.

———

"EVERYTHING HAS TO BE JUST PERFECT for the children," Reggie said as he knelt beside one of the fake tombstones on his lawn, rigging yet another special effect for the party. "I love to give them a good scare on Halloween."

"I never would have believed such a true demon lurked under your gentle exterior, Uncle Reggie." Amanda was unrolling strips of artificial turf over the various extension cords that crisscrossed the lawn. She secured them to the soil with small hooks. It wouldn't do to have anyone tripping. She didn't want to see any of the children get hurt.

"Oh, it's good for them," Reggie insisted. "What child doesn't want to be frightened on Halloween?"

"Me," she answered.

He sent her a trademark scowl and made claws of his hands. Then he knelt again. "Is this one all plugged in?"

"All set, Reg."

"Ahh, good." He tugged a remote control from his pocket and thumbed a button. The ground in front of the tombstone seemed to crumble and open, and a gnarled hand rose slowly up from the earth. In truth there was a black box there, sitting in a perfectly square hole, with a patch of turf over the top. Slices precut in the turf allowed the hand to claw its way through. "In the dark it's going to look fantastic. Sound effects for this one?"

"Another scream, perhaps?" Amanda asked. She reached to the portable CD player clipped to a belt at her waist and pressed a button. An ear-splitting shriek filled the air, coming from several speakers spaced around the lawn, all of them hidden.

"Hmm, maybe not," Reggie mused. "The little ones will probably be shrieking enough all by themselves. Especially the little girls."

"You always did like us best."

"Lucky for you, brat."

She smiled at him and hit another button. "Rattling chains?" she said, as the sound effect played. "Moaning wind?" She played that one. Then added, "Howling wolves?"

"That's it. The wolves. Children of the night!"

She rolled her eyes, smiling wider. "I swear, Uncle Reggie, I've never seen you this excited. You're like a kid at Christmas."

"I'm in my element, dear. In my element." He rubbed his hands together in mock maniacal glee and got to his feet again with effort. "Come, we still have to try out the fog machine before dark."

———

IT WAS DUSK, AND VINCE NOW KNEW
what Holly meant by "alone." They were in a rowboat,
bobbing serenely on the far side of the lake. They'd taken
turns rowing, and were near the opposite shore. They both
wore bright orange life vests. He'd objected, and she'd
insisted.

"I'm a good swimmer," had been his main attempt at
arguing.

"The water's about 45 degrees this time of year. Mark
Spitz isn't a good swimmer in that kind of cold. Besides,
it's the law. You don't want to go breaking the law, do
you?"

He'd put on the lifejacket. Was still wearing it now, as
they floated quietly in the long, narrow lake. A soft but
dense gray mist was rising from the water, even as the
sky grew darker. "I don't know how the hell we'll find
our way back," he muttered. "Did you bring a compass?"

She let him tease her, even smiled a little in response.
"Don't need one."

"You can tell by the stars where we are? What are you,
Davy Crockett?"

She shook her head. "Don't trust me, O'Mally?"

He shrugged. "This *is* the longest of the Finger Lakes,
isn't it?"

"Yep, Cayuga's the longest. Over thirty-five miles from
the southern tip to the northern."

"Mm-hmm."

"There's a light on the end of the dock that'll guide us
right back in," she told him.

"It wasn't on when we left."

"It comes on at dusk. Watch." She pointed, he presumed back toward the direction from which they'd come,
although he was already turned around and disoriented.
They watched in silence, and as the darkness grew thicker,
the light came on.

He sighed audibly. "Okay. That's better." He dipped
the oars, and rowed them farther into the depths of the
lake.

It was quiet on the water. Soothing somehow. He hadn't seen the lake this calm since he'd come out here. Every time he'd looked out over the water, it had been broken and choppy. Either spiderwebbed like cracked glass, or foaming at the mouth with whitecaps. Now it was deep and dark, a well of secrets.

"This is as good a spot as any," she said at length. He stopped rowing and the boat drifted on its own.

He pulled the oars in, leaned back in his seat. "This was a good idea. It's nice out here. You look . . . better."

"I've always loved the lake. It relaxes me." She drew a breath, sighed. "So I guess this is where I tell you about Ivy."

"When you're ready," he said. He didn't want to push her. He didn't want to do anything to cause this woman any pain.

She smiled sadly. "I'm not ready. I'll never be ready, Vince. But, the way I see it, I don't have much of a choice here."

He nodded, watching her closely. She seemed to need to prepare. First she opened the Thermos bottle he'd brought along, and poured two tin cups full of cocoa. She handed one to him, balanced hers on the rowboat's seat, while she screwed the cap back on. Then she set the jug down, picked the cup up, took a deep breath. "I was born on Christmas, you know."

"No. I didn't know that."

She sipped the cocoa, nodded. "Three years later, Ivy was born on my birthday. Mom named us for her favorite carol. 'The Holly and the Ivy.' "

"I get it. That's really cute."

She smiled just a little. "God, we used to love Christmas. It was such an event in our family." Through the darkness he could still see her eyes glow with the memories. "There would be so many presents, we wouldn't be able to get from our bedroom to the living room without unwrapping ourselves a path. Dad used to say Santa was extra good to us, because Christmas was our birthday.

Used to say we were the only kids around who got birthday presents from St. Nick."

He nodded, and he could almost picture those times in his mind. Two little girls, their eyes sparkling. The image made his chest hurt.

Then the sparkle in Holly's eyes turned to wetness, and her voice went taut. "I loved her so much."

"I know." He reached across the distance between his seat and hers, took her hand. He didn't know why he did it. He just did. And she didn't pull it away.

"Mom had told us time and time again to walk straight to school, and come straight home. I don't know why the hell I got so cocky. I loved her. I didn't know what would happen."

He nodded, but he didn't think she was seeing him now. Her gaze was distant, or maybe focused inward. It was almost completely dark now. The moon hadn't risen yet, but the stars were beginning to wink to life in the sky, one by one. They appeared and predictably, the first thing they seemed to do was check themselves out in the lake, their mirror.

"There was this boy I liked. This boy . . . I wanted to walk by his house on the way home. I don't even remember his name—Johnny . . . something—but I put him above my own baby sister."

He jerked his gaze away from the glasslike surface of the water. "No, you didn't. You had no idea you were putting her at risk. If you had, you'd have made different choices that day. You know you would."

She nodded, but her expression was vague. The nod was more an affirmation that she had heard him, not that she agreed. "I promised my mother I'd take care of her, Vince. And I didn't do it. I didn't even come close."

He knew that feeling too well to offer an objection to it. So he didn't. He just let her talk.

"This van came along. Very slowly pulled alongside us." Her breathing got a little faster. Then a little faster.

"And then he just . . . he jumped out and . . . he grabbed her, and that was—"

"No, no. Wait, slow it down for me, Holly." Vince faced her, clasped her other hand, and held both firmly enough to get her attention. "Think, very slowly. Try to see every detail you can in each moment of this thing before moving on to the next. This van came along, you said. Stop there. Don't go forward, don't think about what happened next. Just the van. Freeze-frame it in your mind, can you do that?"

"I . . . I can try."

"What did it look like? What did you see when you noticed it?"

"It was dark gray. Not like it had been painted that color. More like it hadn't been painted at all."

"Primer colored?"

She nodded. "Yes. I remember darker patches. I thought it was spotted then, but it must have been where rust had been sanded off, and something applied to it under the primer."

"That's good. That's very good. Keep going. What about the windows? Was there anything . . . ?"

She frowned. "I . . . can't be sure."

"What?"

"Well . . . they might have been kind of curved outward. Just a little."

"Like in a Volkswagon van?" he asked, all but holding his breath.

"I remember that its shape reminded me of the Mystery Machine."

Vince went blank, shaking his head, searching his mind. "I don't—"

"*Scooby Doo,*" she said. "The cartoon? That was the van they drove. All this one needed was pink paint and psychedelic flowers and it would have fit." She drew her focus back to the present, and stared at him. "My God, that's more than I've ever remembered before."

"Maybe that's because you're ready to remember it now."

Her eyes lowered. "Or maybe it's because of you."

A little alarm bell went off in his mind. He didn't want her to think that way, that he was the one to fix things for her. That he could be some kind of hero. That was the last thing he wanted. "I've got nothing to do with it, Red. This is all you. Go on now. What happened next?"

She breathed long and deeply. Her shoulders rose and fell with it. She lifted her chin. "The van stopped. A man got out. He—he—he—"

"No, no. Slow down. Freeze-frame." He held her upper arms, squeezed to remind her he was there. "Breathe slow, and just take that one image. The man got out."

She took a deep breath, then another, then nodded twice, firmly. "He was very tall. Of course, all grown-ups seemed very tall to me then. He . . . wore jeans, a blue shirt. A denim jacket. His belly hung over the top of the jeans, I remembered that much in therapy. He wore a ski mask, so all I could see of his face were his eyes. I know he was Caucasian."

"Blue eyes, you said. Anything else? Unusual shape? Any scarring? What about his lashes or brows, was there anything there?"

"Blue eyes. Icy blue." She shook her head. "Other than that, I only remember being terrified. He grabbed us both. Ivy with one hand, me with the other."

"Bare-handed or was he wearing gloves?"

She lifted her head slowly. She wasn't aware, Vince thought, of rubbing her right arm above the elbow. "Gloves," she whispered. "He hurt my arm, he held on so tight. I screamed. Ivy did, too. I twisted and he lost his grip on me. I fell on the sidewalk. He gave me this look. This *look*. And Ivy—she was screaming and reaching for me. Her eyes were so huge and so blue. And she was so afraid. He just shoved her into the van and crammed himself in after her. And then they were gone."

Tears were rolling down both her cheeks now. Her body shivering gently.

He wanted to move onto the seat beside her, pull her snugly against him. He was, in fact, actively and determinedly resisting the urge to do so.

"Are you all right?" he asked instead.

She sniffed, nodded. "Mom fell apart. Dad retreated into himself. He tried so hard to be strong for us, you know. He didn't let any of it out, not at all. I think that had a lot to do with the cancer. It was only a couple of years before the symptoms set in, and one more before the diagnosis."

"And what about you, Holly? What happened to you?"

She lifted her big eyes to his. He felt a tremor in his belly. "I never veered from my route again. Not from school to home. Not from my locker to my classroom. Not from my bed to my shower to my closet. Everything in my life suddenly had to be regimented. I developed specific patterns for everything I did, and I couldn't function if I missed a single step. The therapists called it O.C.D."

He nodded. "Obsessive Compulsive Disorder."

"Yeah. And then of course there were the night terrors. The panic attacks. The phobias. I was terrified of everything from heights to being outdoors to strangers to going to school. Mom finally had to pull me out, hire tutors."

"But you got better."

She looked at him. "I got to the point where I could function. With extreme effort. I wasn't a hell of a lot better. I was in therapy and on several medications for a long, long time."

"Until when?"

She drew a breath, sighed. "Hubey Welles confessed and went to prison. My father died the day after his sentencing. He held on all that time—by sheer will, I think. Mom put the house on the market and started looking for a place out here. Uncle Marty and Aunt Jen helped. We never would have survived that time without them. It took a while, but, once the house sold and we closed on the new one, we came out here. We hadn't been back here since before Ivy was taken. But back then, this town was our haven. It was a place where only happy memories existed for us. And I guess Mom thought, with Dad gone, and Ivy's case finally closed, we might be able to heal out here. So we came."

The night wind lifted her hair, danced with it. "And was she right?"

Holly nodded. "I started seeing Doc Graycloud. He weaned me from my meds within the first year. Put me on herbal supplements and teas, and after a while I didn't even need those. Hell, up until just a couple of weeks ago, I hadn't had a symptom. Then all of the sudden they started coming back."

"When I came to town."

"No," she said, tipping her head to one side. "No, that's not exactly true. It started before you got here. I don't know what triggered them."

"That's something to think about. Something must have triggered them, Holly. If we can pinpoint what it was, we might have a clue. Try to think back. What was the first symptom to return?"

She hesitated for a moment. "I started dreaming about Ivy."

"And when was the first dream?"

She shook her head. "I made a note of it in my journal. I can look it up when I get home tonight."

"Do that," he said. "And while you're at it, see if you can recall anything else unusual that happened within a day or two of that date. Anyone you talked to, saw, even in passing, anything that happened that wasn't a part of your normal daily routine."

"You really think that's going to help?"

"I think it's going to help."

"All right, then. But what about right now?"

He frowned, a little trill of alarm sounding. Because without realizing it his hands had moved down her arm to her hands. Her hands had turned in his, and were clasping them now, and he didn't like that. "What *about* right now?"

She lowered her eyes, then raised them again. She looked at him squarely. "You're trying very hard not to let me too close, aren't you?"

He averted his eyes. "I'm a cop, Holly. We're trained not to get too close."

"And you already got too close to this entire case, once," she added.

"I did, yeah."

She covered his hands with hers. "Do you have any idea how much I need you right now?" she whispered. "How alone I feel in this nightmare?"

He stared into her eyes. "That's what Sara Prague said. Oh, not in so many words. But it was in her eyes. That same pleading look I see in yours. You want me to promise you that I'll make this right again. Just like I promised her. But I can't get past the memory of having to face that woman—the mother—and tell her my promise was a lie. That I'd found her kids, and that they were dead."

She nodded slowly, as if she were understanding every word.

"I don't want you to promise me anything," she whispered finally. "But, could you at least . . . at least . . . ?"

"At least . . . ?"

"Hold me." The words emerged as a bare croak. A plea wrenched from the depths of her hell.

He knew damn well he was going to kiss her. Bad idea. Very Bad Idea, he told himself. Yet, he leaned forward, sliding off his seat until he knelt in the bottom of the boat, and slid his hands slowly up her arms to her shoulders. Then he tugged her down, until she knelt as well. He leaned closer, saw her tongue dart out to moisten her lips, and her eyes fall closed in expectation.

He was going to do it. In spite of everything his mind was telling him, he was going to kiss her. He *wanted* to kiss her. Possibly more than he wanted to take another breath.

A low rumble in the distance distracted him. By the time he let it interfere with his intent, his lips were already brushing hers, just barely. He felt her breath on his mouth and he tasted the merest sample of her, when the rumble became more insistent. He popped his eyes open, his hands still on her shoulders, his mouth almost touching hers. Her eyes opened, too, in response to the sound, which rumbled again, louder this time.

Sighing, she leaned into his arms as he closed them around her, held her, just as she'd asked him to. And he whispered, "Is that thunder?"

"Yeah," she murmured. "And not a moment too soon, hmm?"

"It's just as well." He stroked her hair, set her upright. "It's not a good idea, you and me, Red."

She refused to meet his eyes. "We ought to start back, before we get rained on."

He took a look around as he reached for the oars. "I, um . . . I'm probably just distracted here, but I don't see our guiding light."

Holly lifted her head, saw that he wasn't kidding, and looked around herself. Only darkness surrounded them. Darkness, and water. Clouds were rapidly obliterating the stars overhead, so that even they winked out. "The light's gone out," she said.

Then she met his eyes, held them in the darkness. "Or someone put it out."

The thunder rolled from the sky over the water. To Vince it sounded like demonic laughter.

ELEVEN

THE storm rolled closer. The wind picked up, tossing the little boat more and more ruthlessly in its grip as Vince rowed. He figured if he were heading east, or west or south, he'd be all right. They'd hit shore, if he could just keep going straight. But if he were heading north, they could row all night without reaching land.

Frankly, he didn't think the little boat would hold up that long.

The winds came harder, the waves jumping and rolling the little boat right up onto its side and back down again. They were both getting wet, and it wasn't even raining yet.

"We have to get to shore," Holly yelled. "Any shore."

"I'd do that if I knew where the hell any shore was," he shouted back.

She squinted in the distance, looking first one way and then another. "There," she yelled, pointing. "There's a light."

"Our light?"

She shook her head. "Looks like a window in someone's house. Just go that way, Vince."

He went that way, rowing for all he was worth against the waves, and the wind. But they got considerably worse, until the nose of the boat was literally bounding up and down in the water. And on one downward beat they hit something hard. One side of the boat tipped up, the other down, and the next thing he knew the little boat flipped. There was a shockingly cold impact, and then his entire world consisted of icy, cold lake water, surrounding him, filling him, pulling him down.

He'd have howled at the cold if he hadn't been underwater. As it was he swallowed a gallon of the stuff before he managed to struggle to the surface again. He blinked and swiped his eyes, looking around him in shock, for Holly. . . .

But Holly was nowhere in sight.

SHE COULDN'T BREATHE.

She was choking. Freezing. Ice entombed her and smothered her. She couldn't find air. Only ice.

A mouth sealed itself over hers, warm, wet, and life giving. Warm breath pushed into her lungs, then soughed away when the mouth rose. But it came back even before her panic set in. It came back, and it filled her, again and again, until the water rose up in her chest, and she began to choke.

Hands at her back, rolling her onto her side as she gagged and spewed water like a fountain. Hands, holding her shoulders until the spasms she thought would tear her apart finally passed. Hands, easing her down again, until her back rested against something solid. They touched her cheeks, those hands. They pushed her hair aside.

"Come on, Red, look at me. Come on."

She opened her eyes, found herself staring up at Vince O'Mally's face. His eyes were pained, worried. His hair, plastered to his head. She couldn't seem to stop shivering.

"How badly are you hurt?"

Blinking her vision clear, she looked past him, at the grim silhouettes of trees standing like demons in the darkness. Tall and hunching, watching them. Water lapped nearby, and she turned her head to the left, saw the lake, thought it was shaped wrong. And then she remembered and came upright. "The boat—"

"We must have hit a rock. Capsized. It's gone, Holly. Anywhere we go from here will have to be on foot. Are you hurt?"

She drew her gaze back to his face. "We were in the water. How did I—?"

Rolling his eyes in impatience, Vince rocked back on his heels. "If I give you the full account will you focus for me, here?" His hands drew away from her shoulders as he began ticking off items on his fingers. "We were in the rowboat. The wind and waves threw us into a rock or something, and we flipped over. We both went into the drink. You were out cold, so I had to haul your ass in. Now will you please tell me if you're hurt?"

She looked down at her body. "What happened to my life jacket?"

"For the love of—I had to take it off you, okay? I couldn't very well do CPR through a life jacket."

"Oh, my God," she whispered, her eyes welling as they locked with his. "CPR. Oh my God."

His hands clasped her shoulders again, firmly. "Holly, it wasn't necessary, but I couldn't have known that in advance. A little mouth-to-mouth and you were back. Now, come on, focus. I need to know if you're hurt."

Silently she took mental stock. "My head hurts. It hurts pretty bad. Other than that, I'm too cold to tell."

"Yeah, I know the feeling. Can you get up?"

She nodded, and he rose, taking her by her upper arms and helping her get to her feet. She tested herself, putting weight on one leg, then the other, moving her arms, flexing her fingers. She was shivering with cold, but everything else seemed to be working. Vince was eyeing her oddly, then, without warning, he pushed her hair aside, and probed a spot on her head, above her left ear. She sucked in a breath, and he muttered a curse.

"It's not bad," she said weakly.

"You haven't seen the lump. You must have hit something on the way in. Probably the same rock the boat hit."

She lifted her brows. But she wasn't thinking about the lump on her head. She was remembering what had almost happened in the boat—what had been about to happen when the wind had kicked up.

"Why are you looking at me like that?"

She shook her head, shoved the memory away, or tried to. "We'll freeze to death out here if we don't do something, Vince. We can't stay out here all night soaking wet."

Vince met her eyes, then quickly looked away. "Let's start walking. We'll find a house, a road, something sooner or later." He took her arm, started off through the woods, picking his way.

She walked beside him, but a new chill was settling over her now. "What if it was him? What if he's the one who put the light out on the shore, knowing this storm was about to kick up?"

"We can't be sure of that." He laced his fingers with hers, and stepped over stumps and brush, between limbs. "You're borrowing trouble, Red. For all we know the light blew on its own."

"That light hasn't gone out in five years, Vince."

"Then it was due."

"No. It was deliberate." She looked around. "And if the bastard saw us, he probably has a better idea where we are than we do right now."

Vince picked up the pace a little. "It doesn't matter. Even if that was true, by the time he came looking, we'd be long gone. Holed up someplace warm and dry, I hope."

She stopped walking. "Wait, there's lightning again."

She climbed up on a stump, looking out toward the water, waiting for the lightning to flash a second time. When it did, her face was more intense than any he'd ever seen as she studied the lake in that instant. Reaching for his shoulder, she got back down. She wobbled a little, and he steadied her.

She pointed. "That way's south. I'm afraid we're miles from anywhere, Vince. We came across the southern tip of the lake. To get back to town, we have to hike all the way around it." She started walking.

Vince fell into pace beside her. "There's got to be something between here and there. A house, a hunting shack, anything."

She shook her head. "The closest house is Reggie's place, and that's at least a few miles. If we make it that far, we can make it home. There's a shortcut through the woods past Reggie's place. From it we can get to Uncle Marty and Aunt Jen's, or keep going just a little farther to the cabins." Even as she finished saying it, her foot, numb with cold, hooked on a stump and she fell face first to the ground.

Vince knelt beside her, helped her sit up. "You okay?"

"Yeah, I just tripped. I'm fine." But she was shaking all over, and none too steady on her feet. She was worried about the pain in her head. She'd hit it hard in the lake, and she was still feeling dizzy and weak. It wasn't going away as she'd hoped it would.

"To hell with this," Vince muttered. Before she knew what he was thinking, he scooped her up into his arms. Then he resumed walking through the woods, carrying her now.

"Vince, that's really chivalrous and all, but come on . . . put me down."

"You're injured."

"I'm freezing. At least walking will warm me up."

"I will warm you up." He tightened his arms around her as he said it, and she felt his body heat slowly seeping through their wet clothes, into her skin where her body rested against his. She couldn't help snuggling closer. She didn't feel the least bit embarrassed about pressing as close to him as she could manage. She wrapped her arms around his neck to anchor herself as he walked. And his body grew warmer as they progressed through the trees.

"Do you really think there's a chance that light went out by accident, Vince? Or are you just trying not to frighten me?"

"Good question. I'm not real sure myself right now."

She closed her eyes, opened them again slowly. "You were . . . giving me mouth-to-mouth when I came around."

"Best part of the whole trip." He said it lightly, like a teasing joke between friends, but the words made her stomach clench into a knot.

"You saved my life, Vince."

"You saved both our lives. If you hadn't been so stubborn about the life jackets, I doubt either one of us would have made it to shore."

The wind picked up force, raking her wet clothes like a blast of ice. A shiver jostled her body, and his arms tightened around her. "Damn. If we don't get dry soon . . ."

"Let me walk for a ways," she said. "Maybe the exertion will help."

Nodding, he set her on her feet, but held her close to his side. They kept walking, and the activity should have warmed her, but it didn't. She shivered harder with every minute that ticked by, and he did, too, though his worried expression was always on her. They walked for an hour, she figured, though it seemed much longer, before he stopped and turned to face her, shaking his head as he watched her shivering violently.

"This is no good. We're barely covering any ground at all. We keep on like this we'll be frozen. And once the damn storm hits, we'll really be in trouble." He released her from his side, and shrugged out of his jacket, then his shirt. His fingers were shaking so hard he could barely maneuver the wet cloth over his hands and arms, but somehow he managed.

"What are you d-d-doing, Vince?"

"We need to dig in, Red. Just for a little while. An hour, tops. Let the wind dry our clothes at least partially. You're never going to make it back to town like this. Come on, over here." He led her deeper into the trees, until he came to a fallen trunk, surrounded by dead leaves. Then he told her to sit, and hung his shirt from a nearby limb. A moment later, he peeled off his T-shirt and did the same with it, stretching it over limbs. The stiff wind filled it like a balloon and she saw what he was going for. The wind would dry it, to some extent. Vince turned to her, held out a hand. "Strip them off and hand them over, Red. This is no time for shyness."

Nodding, too cold to refuse any suggestion that might make her warm again, she gripped her shirt with the frozen stumps that used to be fingers and peeled it off over her head. She held it out to him. The icy wind blasted her and she wrapped her arms around her upper body. "We'll f-freeze to death before they ever get dry," she stammered.

"Jeans, too. They're holding more water than anything else."

She wriggled the jeans off with difficulty—the wet denim clung to her legs. But she finally got them off, and by the time she did he'd already peeled out of his own, wrung them out, and hung them from another limb. He put hers up beside them, then came toward her in nothing but a pair of wet boxers. Kneeling beside her, he burrowed into mountain of leaves that had drifted up against the fallen tree, digging a shelter. "There," he said. "Now lie down, right there. It's dry, and there are enough leaves to cover us."

She stared at him, and she knew her eyes widened but she couldn't help it.

"It's okay," he said. "You can trust me. I'm a cop." He smiled as he said it, making the words teasing and sweet, somehow. She lay down as he told her, and he curled up beside her, turning her so her back was pressed to his chest. He pulled mounds of leaves and debris around them and over them, and then put his arms around her.

Miraculously, she began to feel warmth seeping into her, chasing away the chill. Within ten minutes she'd stopped shivering. "Where did you learn this kind of stuff?" she asked.

"I was a Boy Scout," he said. And she couldn't tell if he was kidding or not.

He wasn't trembling as much as before, either, though she had a feeling she was getting the lion's share of the body heat. His back couldn't be very well covered. She sighed in contentment and snuggled closer.

"Hey, Red?"

"Mmm?"

"Might not be a good idea to, uh . . . push back against me quite so . . . much."

She froze, and knew she'd been wriggling her backside against his groin . . . and he was responding the way most men would. She could feel him. The blood rushed to her face, but she only pulled away slightly. "Sorry."

"Me, too."

"Not your fault."

His whiskered chin moved against her bare shoulder, and she shivered anew, but not from the cold this time. "Take it as a compliment and forget about it," he suggested.

"Compliment? I'm not that innocent. You're male. You'd react that way to anyone in this . . . situation."

"No, actually, I wouldn't."

She lay there, blinking and wondering just what the hell that meant. She said, "Oh." He didn't say anything. She waited, but he didn't elaborate. Finally, she had to break the silence, because just lying there against him, in his arms, feeling his breath on the back of her neck, was too much to bear in the silence. "Do you think our clothes are dry yet?"

"It's only been twenty minutes."

"Yes, but with the way the wind's blowing . . . ?" She rolled onto her back as she said it, which made her hip

rub against his groin. When she looked up at him, he was
biting his lip.

"Will you lie still?"

She did lie still. For what must have been a half hour,
she remained perfectly still, lying there against him. He
was lying on his side, his face close enough for her to
feel his breath on her skin. She wanted to kiss him. He
must want the same thing, she reasoned. He'd been about
to kiss her in the boat, before they capsized. She lay there
thinking about it for about as long as she could stand to
before she turned her face to the side, toward his.

"Don't, Holly," he said very softly.

"Don't what?"

"I can feel what you're thinking. I told you already, it's
not a good idea."

"Why not?"

He didn't answer her, so she rolled again, onto her side,
facing him this time, and she pressed her mouth to his
mouth. His lips were stiff and unresponsive. She slid her
arms around his waist and pulled her body closer to his.
Then she nipped his bottom lip with her teeth, suckled it
just a little, and slid her tongue along the inner edge of
his lips.

He shook a little, and his arms closed around her hard
and fast. Finally he kissed her back. He kissed her like
she'd never dreamed of being kissed. He pinned her down
with his weight and drove his tongue deep into her mouth.
He wedged his knee between her legs and urged them
apart, so his hips could lower to her pelvis, and he could
press his erection hard against her. And just when she
started to feel the stirrings of panic joining the arousal in
her belly, he rolled away and sat up, his back to her. The
leaves fell away from him, and she shivered in the gust
of cold.

"Don't play with me, Red."

Breathless, she said, "What makes you think I was
playing?"

She couldn't see his face, and she thought he wanted

it that way. She couldn't read what was in his eyes, but she thought she knew. He was trying to overwhelm her. To scare her off.

"What is it you want from me, Holly? Hmm? A meaningless fuck in the woods? Cause I can give you that. Hell, I'd be more than happy to give you that." He glanced over his shoulder at her. "I'd be *goddamned* more than happy to give you that. But that's all it would be. Is that what you want from me? Is it?" His eyes were blazing.

She bit her lip. "I . . . I don't know."

"You don't know? Well if you don't know what you want, I'd suggest you not tease me again until you do. All right?"

"Tease? Tease, is that what you think—?"

"Your shirt's dry." He surged to his feet, grabbed her white button-down off the tree and, turning, held it out to her.

She rose to her feet, and his eyes devoured every inch of her. She didn't flinch or try to hide herself. She just reached out and took the shirt from him, then pulled it on. His shorts bulged. While she buttoned up, he turned away, snagged his own shirt off the tree, and put it on. Their jeans were still damp.

"I do know what I want," she said. "I want to make love to you."

He swore and tried not to look at her.

"I want to spend the night in your arms, and I want . . . to see inside you. The way you've seen inside me."

He shook his head.

"I want to know why you're so afraid of me."

He turned to face her. "You're flattering yourself, Holly." Then he pulled his damp jeans on. "Why are you so damned determined to dig into my psyche, woman? What the hell is it with you, anyway? You can't accept that I simply do not want this?"

She shrugged, pulling on her own jeans and wincing at the cold touch of the wet denim on her skin. "You're determined to dig into mine. It only seems fair. And as for what you want, well, your body is more honest about that than you are."

He stared at her for a long moment, then he shook his head, grabbed hold of her hand, and started off through the woods again.

———

HE KEPT UP A BRISK PACE AS THEY walked through the skeletal forest. Their jackets hadn't dried much at all, and they'd decided to leave them behind. Wearing them, as wet as they were, would only make them colder. Vince wasn't walking with his arm around Holly anymore. She kept a distance of at least two feet between them at all times, and he was angry at himself for his behavior. His reaction to her had taken him by surprise. He hadn't expected passion to swell up—red hot and urgent—so suddenly. And even then, he should have been able to handle it. Would have. But other feelings came with it. Protective feelings. That urge to cuddle and coddle and care for another human being. The one he'd made up his mind was bad for him.

To feel it for a woman he also wanted sexually was another shock. He'd been so disconnected from that part of himself for so long that the overwhelming heat of it left him bewildered.

Oh, sure, he had sex. When he felt the urge, he'd go out and find someone willing. But he was always completely in control. The act was always cold, calculated, thought out, and planned for. He never lost himself the way he had with Holly. And he never had sex with a woman who could need him the way she could.

Which was why it had been perfectly rational for him to think he could curl up with her in the leaves, mostly naked, and do nothing but keep her warm. And which was why he'd blown up at her when his body had almost overwhelmed his mind. He wasn't furious with her, but with himself. And if he thought to scare her off by coming

on like a caveman back there, he supposed he'd been
wrong yet again. She'd seen right through it.

Damn, where had so much longing come from?

Now she was offended. No wonder. She'd been assaulted, insulted, and rejected all in one brief interlude.
Not to mention bashed on the head, nearly drowned, and
half frozen. He was a real asshole, and he knew it.

They'd been hiking again for almost an hour, without
exchanging a word. She wouldn't even look at him. She
stomped through the decaying leaves on the ground with
her arms folded across her chest, and her shoulders
hunched.

"I'm sorry," he said. He had to force the words out.
Apologizing was not something he enjoyed doing, nor
was it something he did often. Almost never, in fact. Of
course, she had no way of knowing that.

"You're right, you are. But I suspect you're only saying
that so I won't call your department and turn your ass in
out of vengeance."

"No. I'm saying it because I acted like a jerk back
there."

She slid her eyes toward him but the minute her gaze
touched his, she jerked it back again. "Whatever."

He drew an impatient breath, blew it out again.

"I'm not a tease," she said.

"I know you're not."

"No you don't. You don't know me at all. But for the
record, I meant it when I said I wanted you. And I'm not
ashamed to admit that. And if anyone was acting like a
tease back there, you really ought to know that it was
you."

That brought him up short. He stopped walking, and
stared at her. "Me?"

She stared right back. "Yes, you. For crying out loud,
O'Mally, you strip us both down, make a bed in the
leaves, and then you hold me so close I can't breathe
without tasting you—what was I supposed to think?"

He couldn't even hold her gaze. "I was just trying to keep you warm."

"Right. And that was a nightstick prodding my backside?"

He gaped.

"I'm not a tease, O'Mally, but I am human. I'm a woman, and, for the record, I think there's something here. Something that might *be* something, you know? But you're so damned stubborn I'm not sure how we'll ever find out."

"I . . . sorry."

"I thought you wanted me, too," she said. "I mean, you gave every indication."

The words *I did*—or more accurately, *I do*—would have tumbled from his lips if he hadn't pressed them together hard. "Look, I told you, I don't do relationships, okay? I don't have that kind of staying power."

"Don't worry. I got the message."

Hell. He did not need complications like this, like her, not now. He wasn't sure if it would be better to seduce her or ignore her. Either way, things were getting muddied up and it wasn't going to do his investigation one damned bit of good.

A twig snapped off to the left, and his thoughts ground to a halt. He jerked his head around, scanning the trees in vain. He didn't have a gun, dammit. It was at the bottom of the lake somewhere.

"What the hell was that?" Holly whispered. She, too, had gone still and was searching the darkness, wide-eyed.

He examined the trees, seeing nothing. Shades of gray and brown and rust. "Deer?" he asked.

"Not unless it was wearing army boots."

He kept looking, narrowing his eyes. "I don't see anything." Then he focused on her again, saw her anger gone now, replaced by fear. Of the two he liked the anger better. He took her arm. "Let's get out of here." Then he looked up at the sky, completely obliterated now by thick clouds. The thunder was still rumbling, but it was no longer distant. It was loud, and intense. "I think the storm's held off about as long as it's going to."

"I think you're right."

They picked up the pace, and he held on to her. Kept her close to his side, tried to keep her warm. She didn't pull away, but he wasn't sure if that was because she'd forgiven him or because she needed his body heat. Every now and then he drew her to a stop, and listened for a moment. There was something—some sound—every time, but damned if he could distinguish the creak of a limb in the wind from the hurried footsteps of a squirrel. It all sounded alike to him. Rustling leaves and snapping twigs.

They walked on. They were both getting colder with every yard they trekked. If they didn't find shelter soon, he wasn't sure they'd make it.

"I felt a r-r-raindrop," Holly said unnecessarily.

He glanced down at her. Her lips were pale and she was shivering again. He didn't have a clue where the hell they were. They'd topped a small hill, and he looked around, then looked harder at what seemed to be lights coming from the top of a bigger hill just ahead. And then he realized he was seeing that crazy old actor's house, its windows alight.

"There," he said, pointing. "Come on, we'll go there."

She glanced up, following his gaze to the hulking mansion, which seemed to list slightly to one side. "Reggie's place," she said. "F-f-finally. God, I hope he d-doesn't mind. N-n-no one goes to his p-place uninvited."

"Tough."

"B-but—" She turned toward him as she spoke, and then she just flew backward. The wet ground beneath her feet crumbled, and she fell, hit the sloping hillside, and tumbled all the way to the bottom.

"Jesus! Red!" Vince ran, stumbling, after her. She lay still at the bottom, and he dropped to his knees and pulled her into his arms. "Holly? C'mon, talk to me." The rain was falling harder now. As if they needed more problems.

Lightning crashed and the wind blew even harder.

She opened her eyes slowly. They were unfocused. Her lips barely moving, her voice barely audible, she whispered, "I'm . . . ok-k-kay."

"No, you're not." Dammit, she'd hit her head again. It was bleeding. And her voice was slurred. He should have been holding on to her more tightly when they stopped at the hilltop. With a surge of guilt, he scooped her up, and carried her up the steep incline toward the isolated house of the eccentric hermit, which was farther away now than it had been before. And the storm cut loose with all its fury.

TWELVE

⎯⎯⎯⎯⎯

THE storm was brutal, and there wasn't a damn thing he could do to protect Holly from its fury. Pounding rain soaked the carpet of fallen leaves, making them slick. He carried her as fast as he could manage without falling and dumping them both. She was no longer conscious. But he was pretty sure she was alive. Bending over her as well as he could, he trudged toward the house. Yellow light spilled from its myopic windows, and the house seemed to hunch against the rain like an old man, dressed in fading goth. It tried to be imposing, like something out of one of its owner's old films, but instead it was just sad. The wind sucked up piles of leaves, then coughed them out again in great gusts. And he bowed into it and walked onward, uphill, to the pinnacle, the crown.

He'd heard sounds again and again in the dark woods, before the storm had cut loose. Footsteps, maybe. Maybe just deer and rabbits having a laugh at his expense. Who the hell knew? There could be an army trailing his ass now and he wouldn't know it.

Finally, he was at the top of the large, wet hill. Face-to-face, in fact, with the wrought-iron fence that surrounded the place. Every four feet, like clockwork, a rabid-looking iron bat perched atop a fence pole, snarling down at would-be intruders. Christ. It was supposed to be intimidating, but the effect was ruined by sections that no longer stood perfectly upright. They tilted inward here, outward there. He grabbed hold of a bar, gave it a shake, but, despite its lopsidedness, the fence was solid. Thirty yards of weed-choked lawn stood between it and the back door. He looked at the length of the damn fence he was going to have to walk to get to the front. Holly slid lower and he hiked her up, kept on walking.

Rain beaded on her face, and dripped steadily from her hair. It was pelting her cheeks, her eyes, while the wind whipped her hair, and it didn't even faze her. She didn't even flinch. Vince was cold right to his bones. His feet had morphed into frozen concrete blocks. He couldn't feel anything from them except their weight. His knuckles—those he felt. They throbbed and howled. His face burned and he thought maybe the wind had razed all the skin from his nose and cheeks and had gone to work now on the bones.

The fence turned to the right. The wind sliced him from the side now, and it had teeth. Even the leeward side of his face burned with cold. Anyone seeing him from a distance, he thought, slogging along on leaden stumps, carrying a lifeless-looking virgin toward the sagging Gothic mansion, would probably think Reginald D'Voe was filming his great comeback piece. He half expected to hear a wolf howling backup vocals to the storm.

Finally, he made it to the gate.

Closed. The fucking thing was closed, and apparently locked. Shit. Vince tipped his head back, aimed his fury beyond the gate, at the house's slab of a front door with its black iron knocker, and he let out a howl that belonged in one of Reggie D'Voe's death scenes. Swinging one of the cinderblocks he'd been using for feet, Vince kicked the gate so hard one of the gargoyle bats toppled and fell. Then he crouched, snagged the ugly little demon in one hand, and managed to hurl it at the house, all without dropping Holly. The impact made a satisfying thud, audible even in the chaos of the storm.

A minute ticked past, then another. Finally, the front door opened. Yellow light filled the crevice, and shot out in a feeble effort to penetrate the gloom. "Who's there?" Reginald D'Voe called, using his most menacing silver screen villain tone.

"I need help." Vince grunted the words. His foot was starting to register pain from the impact with the fence, and he was losing the feeling in his arms.

The man vanished inside, the door banged shut. Vince fell to his knees, partly in abject disappointment, and partly because the cinderblock effect had moved up to include his lower legs, knees, and the better part of his thighs.

But then the door opened again. That slit of yellow light, followed by a round white one. Flashlight, his mind told him. And behind it, a yellow rain slicker. And slicker and slicker, he thought, almost laughing aloud as the thing bobbed closer like some shiny, yellow, headlight-equipped ghost.

One arm went numb, started to droop, and Holly with it. Gritting his teeth he lifted her again, grunting like a goddamn caveman with the effort it took. Yellow Slicker unlatched the gate, opened it. The flashlight beam took a shot at burning out Vince's retinas. He squinted back at it and said, "The monster fucking lives." Then he was gone.

———

VOICES BLURTED WORDS IN CLIPPED fragments. As if someone were turning the radio dial back and forth, just passing the station each time.

"—but why here?"

"—sn't look to me . . . had much choice, Reg. Hell, look . . . em."

"—tective . . . up to somethi . . . he . . . suspects—"

"Quiet!"

That one came through loud and clear. It was a bark that silenced the other man midsentence. No one had turned the dial that time. Vince struggled to focus, to listen.

"He's coming around." A hand, an old hand, callused and dry, but warm, touched his face. "Detective O'Mally? Can you hear me?"

His eyes were open. Vince didn't remember opening them, but now he saw they were by the hazy blur of a human being, leaning over him. He licked his parched lips, parted them. "Yeah."

The blur smiled. A flash of white where the teeth should be. "Good. Good. I'm Ernie Graycloud. Remember? We met at the bonfire?"

He came a little clearer. Long silver and black hair, copper skin, lined with age. "You're the doctor," he muttered. "But medical or witch?"

"A little bit of both. My license to practice is from the State of New York. Most of what I know about healing, I learned from the Iroquois. You got any other smart-ass questions you want answered while I'm here?"

He swallowed hard, knowing he'd insulted the man, wondering where the hell his brain was sleeping. "Yeah. What have you done with my redhead?"

"She's over here, Detective," a female voice called.

Vince turned his head toward it, saw Amanda D'Voe in a white, floor-length satin robe, sitting beside a big white bed. In the bed, dwarfed by pillows and comforters pulled clear to her chin, Holly lay still and pale. "Is she okay?"

"Exposure, a mild concussion," Ernie Graycloud explained. "We can't tell much more until she comes around."

Vince sat up, winced, fell back down on the pillows. "She needs to be in a hospital."

"She's not in immediate danger, Detective. There's

nothing wrong with her that can't wait for this storm to pass."

"The doctor's right," Amanda said softly, in that gentle way she had. "You'd be risking her life to try to travel in this. There are trees down, power lines, too, and the phones are all out. We were lucky Ernie came by tonight, or who knows what we would have done?"

Vince frowned, processing her words, tucking them away in that mental file he kept for things that made no sense whatsoever and yet tripped his silent alarm. There was something there.

He turned back to the doctor. "Thanks. I didn't mean to insult you before. I feel like I've been on a three-day drunk." His vision cleared more and he realized he was lying on what appeared to be a chaise lounge covered in furry leopard print. Or maybe he was the one with the head injury.

"You have a bruised rib or two, by my best guess," Graycloud said, neither accepting nor rejecting Vince's pseudo-apology. "We'll need X rays to confirm that nothing's broken. Besides that and a mild case of exposure, you seem okay."

"Yes, and now that we have your diagnosis out of the way . . ." Reginald D'Voe rose to his feet as gracefully and deliberately as if someone had yelled "action!" He wore exactly what Vince would have expected him to wear. An kimono-style silk smoking jacket, red with a gold dragon pattern writhing all over it, and slippers that matched it exactly. His walking stick, gleaming hardwood under layers of shellac with a brass *something* on top, was clutched in his hand, and he leaned heavily on it, and thumped it on the floor with every other step. Vince noticed one leg stayed stiff, the foot almost dragging along the floor as he walked. Stroke, he thought. No sign of it in his face, though.

He stopped when he stood over Vince on the chaise. "What are you doing here?" D'Voe asked. One brow crooked higher than the other when he said it, and Vince couldn't help but think there should have been an orchestra somewhere playing three powerful chords to punctuate the line.

He wondered if Reginald D'Voe could be a killer. A child killer. He looked at the man's eyes. If you asked a kid what a stranger looked like, as in "don't talk to strangers," Vince figured they'd describe this guy to a T.

"Holly and I were out on the lake—"

"In this weather? Are you *mad*?"

He almost smiled. Damn, but it was such a Reginald D'Voe thing to say. "No. We were out . . ." he glanced at his watch, but the crystal was misted over and beaded with moisture. Even if it was working, which he doubted, he couldn't see its face. "I don't know. Hours before the rain started. It was clear when we left, and we had every intention of heading in before the storm hit. But the light on the dock went out, and it got foggy and dark. We tried to head to the nearest shore, but by the time we got our bearings the wind had kicked up, and the boat was being tossed around pretty badly. It smashed into some rocks or something and capsized. We made it to shore, and started walking."

"Where were you when this happened?" Doc Graycloud asked, clearly alarmed.

Vince shook his head. "We weren't sure ourselves, at first. But when the lightning flashed, Holly figured we were on the shore opposite town. I don't know what the hell it's called. Nothing but woods." He let his head rest back on the pillows just for a moment, before the cop in him made him lift it again. "What time is it?" he asked.

"A little after three A.M. It was midnight when Uncle Reg found you outside the gate," Amanda said, leaving Holly's bedside now to come across the room. "I have tea brewing downstairs. I'll bring you a cup."

Vince didn't argue. He watched her go, then he eyed the other two. "That light must have gone out around eight P.M. Where were the two of you around that time?"

They looked at each other, then at him. D'Voe put on

his most intimidating glare. "Are you asking us to provide you with an *alibi*? After we pulled you out of the storm, took you in—?"

Vince held up one hand, noticing that his fingers were throbbing as if they'd been pounded repeatedly with a hammer. "I only want to know if you saw anyone messing around out near the docks by the cabins. If you were in town, Dr. Graycloud, passing by the docks around that time, or you, Mr. D'Voe. This house has a pretty good elevation. You must have a clear view of the docks from here."

Reginald lifted one eyebrow higher than the other. Trademark. He glanced at Graycloud, then back at Vince. "I was here. So was Amanda. We spent most of the evening making preparations for the Halloween party. We were far too involved in that to notice someone on a dock on the other side of the lake. As for the doctor, he didn't arrive here until around eleven thirty, just after the storm hit."

Frowning, Vince glanced at the doctor. He nodded in full agreement. "Eleven thirty-five, or close to that, if you want to get precise. Before that I was home, watching television. I did drive past the cabins on my way here, but it was after eleven. I didn't see anyone then, for what it's worth." He glanced at Reggie, then back at Vince. "You saying you think someone put the light out on purpose?"

Vince shrugged. "Probably not."

"Then why did you ask?" Reggie asked.

"I'm a cop, Mr. D'Voe. It's in my nature to be suspicious."

D'Voe didn't look convinced.

"So, why did you decide to come over here, in the middle of the night, in a storm like this, Doc?" he asked Ernie Graycloud.

The man sent Reginald a look. One of those, *What do you want me to tell him?* looks that Vince had seen a thousand times before. The look Reg returned was another familiar one. *How the hell should I know?* Neither man answered the question.

But a soft voice from the doorway, said, "I can tell you why. He came over because of me."

Three heads turned to watch Amanda come into the room, carrying a silver tea service with cups enough for all of them, and a heaping tray of pastries beside the steaming pot. It looked way too heavy for her, but Graycloud relieved her of it in short order, and set it on a nearby stand.

"Get off your leg, Uncle Reggie. I can see it's aching," she scolded gently. Taking the older man's arm as if she were his mother, or his nurse, she urged him into the nearest chair. Then she took a blanket from the back of that chair, unfolded it, and draped it over his lap. She moved to the service, began pouring tea, and putting pastries onto tiny silver plates. "I have had a terrible fear of storms for as long as I can remember," she said. She carried a cup of tea, sweetened and creamy, and a plate of pastries to her uncle. Then she went back, and fixed a cup for Vince. "Dr. Graycloud knows I can still become quite upset. He always calls to check in on me when it storms outside." She said this with a gentle smile toward the doctor, even as she set a cup of tea and a selection of goodies on the bedside stand. Bending over Vince, her pale brown hair falling into his face, she urged him to sit up, plumped his pillows high, then leaned him back again. She put the tea and the plate in his lap, and returned to her tray. "When he called to check on me tonight, the phones were out. The storm got worse. He worries too much, so naturally he came over here to check on me."

"At which point," Reginald put in, "we convinced him to spend the night, rather than return home in such weather."

"Exactly." Amanda delivered the doctor's tea and sweets to him. He was still pacing, but she sent a meaningful glance at the chair, and he immediately took it. The two men obeyed the softspoken young woman like trained bears.

Vince was starting to see that she wasn't the meek and dependent little thing he'd at first seen. In fact, she seemed to be the caregiver in this odd little family.

Finally, she took a cup of tea for herself, crossed the room to where Holly lay in the bed, and took her seat beside it. It was, he thought, her way of ending the conversation.

Well, he wasn't finished. "Why are you so afraid of storms?" he asked her.

And it was her turn to shoot that what-do-I-say-now look at her cohorts. But it was brief, a flicker, no more. She blinked it away fast, sipped her tea, and finally met Vince's eyes. "Who knows where these things get started? I honestly don't remember."

She was good. Better than the doctor or the actor would ever be. Vince sighed, defeated. His instincts were failing him. He couldn't tell if he were in a room full of liars, or saints. There was something they weren't saying. Just what it was, he couldn't tell. Hell. He drank his damned tea.

The doctor rose. "We should let the detective get some sleep. O'Mally, you'll call me when Holly wakes? I'll be right down the hall."

Vince nodded, set his empty cup down on its saucer. "Thanks, Doc. And thank you, Mr. D'Voe, and you, Amanda, for your hospitality."

"You're welcome," Amanda replied. She was tucking the covers around Holly before leaving.

D'Voe waited for her at the door. "I wouldn't have left a stray dog out in a storm like that," he said. Then they left, the three of them. And they all knew something Vince didn't, he was convinced of that. He had no idea, though, whether their secrets had anything to do with his case.

He turned on the chaise—which had been piled high with pillows and blankets just for him—and studied

Holly. Her bed was ten feet away, and that seemed too
far. He wanted to be closer. Suppose he fell asleep, and
then she woke or had some kind of medical crisis in the
middle of the night? Suppose the killer—who may or may
not have sabotaged the dock light, indirectly causing their
accident, and may or may not have been following them
through the woods tonight—came back for another try?
His gun was gone, lost in the lake. He'd realized that
about halfway through their hike. The one he'd taken
from Holly was locked in his Jeep.

Setting his jaw, he got up. The combined pain of his
bruised ribs and throbbing feet nearly put him right back
down again, but he held on to a small hardwood table. It
didn't ease much. A little, as his body adjusted to being
upright. He hobbled across the thick carpet to Holly's bed.
Without hesitation, because he was all but dead on his
feet, he peeled her covers back. Then he stared down at
her.

She was wearing a soft, white muslin nightgown. Shit,
all she needed was a candelabra to carry around this place,
and she could be an honorary member of the D'Voe family.

He glanced down at himself, surprised to see maroon
pajamas covering his skin. They felt like silk. He lifted
his brows and said, "Hmm." Then he crawled into bed
with Holly and pulled the covers over them both.

REGINALD WAS TENSE, AND HE DOUBTED
he'd sleep a wink with that stranger under his roof. He
didn't like strangers. Didn't trust them.

He paced his bedroom, wrung his hands, and tried to
think of what he ought to be doing. Surely there was
something. Damn, things were so confusing lately. His
mind sizzled like water dripped into hot oil. So many
things dancing, jumping, and spitting all at once. Dangerous things. What the hell should he do? What?

A soft tap on his bedroom door made him start, and then Amanda stepped softly inside. "I knew I'd find you all worked up."

He tried to fool her with a false expression. One of calm, or at least something less manic. But it didn't work. It never had. Oh, his acting might have fooled millions over the decades, but it had never once fooled his darling Amanda.

She crossed the room, white gown drifting. Angelic. She took his arm, led him to the bed, and pulled the covers over him. Then her cool, soft hands drifted over his forehead, slowly, repeatedly. "We came back here to face our demons. Didn't we?"

He wanted to deny it. It might be her reason, but it had never been his. He had come back for her. For her alone. Because it was what she wanted, and because her doctors felt it was time. That it would be healthy for her.

"I'm an adult now, Uncle Reg. I'm not that frightened little girl you remember. Not anymore. No one can take me away from you now."

"I know. I know that." He did know it, on a practical, mental level. It was the rest of him that refused to believe. She was *his*, dammit. She'd been his for as long as he wanted to remember. He'd *made* her his. His little girl.

"I want you to stop worrying." Her hand moved away, and her lips replaced it on his forehead. "I love you, Uncle Reggie. I'll always love you."

That kiss, her breath warm on his skin—God, his heart twisted into a tight little knot in his chest. "You're everything to me," he whispered. "I don't want to lose you, Amanda."

"You won't. I promise, you won't."

But he would. He felt it right to his gut. If she ever remembered the things she had blocked out . . .

Amanda perched herself on the side of his bed, resumed stroking his head, and began to sing softly to him.

My redemption, he thought as she let her voice lull him, soothe his mixed-up mind. Other men washed their sins away by the blood of the lamb. Not him. His salvation was found in the touch of a child. This child. Without her, he was damned.

HOLLY HURT. SHE HURT EVERYWHERE, and she thought it must be from the running. She was running nonstop, full speed, and she was holding someone's hand as she ran, pulling them along beside her.

"Please Holly, please! I can't go on."

She turned, and saw the little girl with the hair so blonde it was nearly white, and the eyes so blue they matched the sky. Her words emerged in puffs that froze on the air and crackled and fell in glittering fragments to the ground. "It's s-so cold!"

"Ivy?"

The little girl smiled. And Holly wrapped her up tight in her arms. She wanted to say a million things, ask a thousand questions. But she could only manage to hold her baby sister close and say her name over and over again.

Then there were footsteps in the woods, and she remembered. They were running. Her happy reunion turned sad as she realized Ivy hadn't survived the attack of the monster—it hadn't happened yet. They'd gone back in time. It was happening now. Oh, things were different. The woods, instead of the street. Holly, being all grown up. But she knew—ohgodsheknew—ohgod—what was going to happen.

The footfalls crashed. The monster must have changed, too. Grown into a giant. Crush, crush, crush. He was coming closer. Holly picked up her sister and ran. That was something she hadn't been able to do before. Pick her up and run!

The monster kept coming. The woods rose up thick and impenetrable ahead, and behind the monster closed in. They were trapped!

"Over here, Red," someone called.

She looked. Vince! He stood off to the left, poking his head out of the wall of jungle, which opened around him like a curtain.

She started toward him.

The monster came closer.

She ran, but her feet were stuck. She tried to pull them free and they wouldn't move. "Vince!" She reached out a hand, and he did, too, but she couldn't make it. Then the monster was breathing hotly right down the back of her neck. She peeled Ivy off her, pushed her toward Vince. "Save her, O'Mally!"

Then the monster grabbed her from behind. She spun to face it, opened her eyes, and stared straight up at it. But it didn't have a face. No head. Just eyes. Icy blue eyes. And then she screamed.

Hands held her shoulders, hard and firm, shaking her a little. "C'mon, Red, wake up, dammit. Come on, open your eyes. Look at me."

She did.

Vince gazed down at her. His hair was all feathery and sticking up at odd angles, and he was dressed very strangely. And yet, he had her. He had hold of her, and that was really above and beyond any concerns about the odd turn her dream seemed to have taken. Her heart was pounding so hard her entire body shuddered with it. She snapped her arms around his waist and pulled him to her, hanging on for dear life.

He grunted, went stiff as his upper body slammed down on top of her chest. But then he softened. "All right, it's all right now. Easy." He slid his arms around and beneath her, rolling over, taking her with him. When he settled, he was lying on his back in the bed—*Bed? What were they doing in a bed?*—and she was curled close to him, her head on his shoulder, face near his neck. He stroked her hair, and she liked it. "It was only a dream," he murmured.

"It was Ivy," she whispered. "She was alive, and there was a monster chasing us. . . ."

"It's all right now."

"You were there. But I couldn't reach you. And then he grabbed me and—"

"Holly, it was a dream. You understand? Hmm?" He lifted her chin so he could look her in the eyes.

She blinked away tears. "It was so real."

"I know. They get that way. Is this one you've had before?"

She nodded, the motion jerky. "Yeah. I mean, not exactly. We're not usually in the woods. But the rest—the monster chasing us, me trying to save her—" She stopped there, stabbing her eyes into his. "But, he didn't get her this time. Vince, he didn't get her this time. He got me, but—but not her."

Vince curled his hand around her nape, eased her back down onto his chest. "It's survivor's guilt, Holly. I've seen it before."

"I know it's survivor's guilt. I spent years in therapy trying to deal with it. This wasn't that. This was something else."

"Yeah? What, then?"

She could hear his heart. It beat steadily against her ear. He was warm, and solid, and she relaxed against him. "It was you," she said. "It was because you were there. You saved Ivy."

He sighed softly. "It was a dream. That's all."

"I think it was more."

He tensed a little bit underneath her. "If it was more, it was the knock on the head you took earlier. Period."

She thought he wouldn't like what she was thinking. Fine. She wouldn't explore it then. Not aloud, anyway. But she knew there was something going on here. Between them. Something important.

"Vince, where are we?" She rolled over onto her back and looked around. The room was large, high ceilings with a bowl-shaped frosted glass light fixture hanging from the center. There were two tall windows, thickly draped, and it was still storming beyond them. "What is this place?"

"It's Reginald D'Voe's house," he said. "You passed out before we made it this far."

"And he took us in? I didn't think he ever let anyone past the front door unless they'd been invited."

"I think we were in such sorry shape he probably didn't feel he had a choice."

She turned toward him. "It's a big house."

He nodded.

"So whose idea was it to put us in the same bed together?"

He shifted restlessly. "Mine. But don't make anything of it, Holly. I wanted to be close, in case the maniac tried again."

"Oh. Good, I'm glad you're clear on that."

He studied her eyes for a moment, looked decidedly uncomfortable. "I'm not trying to be mean."

"So, it's effortless, then?"

He closed his eyes. "It isn't you, okay?"

"No? What is it then?"

He rolled onto his back, his head slamming down on the pillow so hard she half expected feathers to fly out the sides. "It's me. It's my past, my history. Look, I told you, I just don't do relationships, all right? And I damn well don't want some wounded dove looking at me with big green eyes that see me as some kind of hero. 'Cause I'm not. I can't save anyone for you Holly. I can't bring your sister back for you, and I can't save you from your own inner demons. I couldn't save—"

He stopped there. Broke off so suddenly it startled her, and then he was on his feet, striding across the room. She thought he was heading for the giant fake-fur-covered chaise lounge at first, but he seemed to change his mind, because he paced instead.

"The Prague kids?" she asked.

He didn't reply.

"I never asked you to save anyone for me."

"No. You dreamed it, instead."

"I dreamed you saved Ivy. I didn't dream you pulling me out of the lake, or putting your mouth on mine and breathing into my lungs. I didn't dream you carrying me through the storm, or finding me shelter. I didn't dream you coming to my bed to keep me safe." She shrugged. "So sue me if I see you as slightly heroic."

He stopped walking.

"God, you have to know I get what you're feeling, Vince. How the hell can I not get it when I couldn't save my own kid sister?"

She saw his face, in profile, saw his eyes fall closed in pain so stark she felt it to her bones.

"Listen, Red, I don't do well with women like you. I know better, but they look at me with their need in their eyes, and I end up making promises I have no chance in hell of keeping."

She frowned, tilting her head to one side.

"Sara Prague looked at me like that. Someone stole her babies, and she begged me to tell her I could fix it. And I knew better. I knew better, and yet I did it anyway. I promised her it would be okay. I would make it okay. I'd get her kids back."

"You were only trying to ease her suffering," she tried, knowing it was lame.

"And, instead, I heightened it. See, that day in my office, I think she had already begun to accept that she'd lost them. I do. But I had to give her hope, and she latched on to it like a lifeline. My God, if you could have seen that woman's face when I had to tell her . . ."

"I still don't see what this has to do with us."

He glanced at her, barely hearing her, she thought, he was so involved in his own thoughts now. "And the kids. Those kids. But I can't tell you about that. No one should know about that."

He was pacing faster now, agitated strides across the

room, then back again. He paused to look out the window once, but she thought his eyes were only seeing the nightmare he had so recently lived.

"I made another promise. To myself. I promised I'd get the son of a bitch vile enough to do—what he did. And I can't let myself get sidetracked." He looked back at her. "Not even by you, Red."

Holly couldn't stay away from him any longer. She climbed out of bed and went to him, but didn't touch him. Just stood close, looking up at him. "I want to catch him, too. So how could I sidetrack you?"

"Because you have problems, Red, and because deep down I'm fighting hard against the urge to tell you I'll make them better. To step in and try to be the hero you need me to be. I'd fail if I tried. I've been down this road often enough to know that. And what's more, I'd lose sight of the main objective."

She moved closer, took his hands. "And what else?"

He swallowed hard. She saw his Adam's apple swell with the motion, and when he turned his eyes away, she thought he would refuse to answer. But instead he said, "If I don't let you need me, I don't risk letting you down the way I did Sara Prague and her kids."

She sighed softly, nodding. "Thank you, Vince. It means a lot to me that you told me the truth, finally."

He looked at the floor, avoiding her eyes. "You needed to know. I can't play knight in shining armor to your damsel in distress, Red."

"I know." She smiled sadly. "In your own way, O'Mally, you're as screwed up as I am."

"I never said I wasn't. After what I saw in that house in Syracuse . . . I don't know if I'm ever gonna get over that."

She lifted her chin. "You may not. If you do, then maybe that's when you need to start questioning your mental state, because I don't think any caring, sane person could put something like that behind him."

He sighed, relieved maybe, that she understood.

She locked her eyes with his. "So you don't want me to need you. I can deal with that. But tell me this, Vince. Does that mean I can't want you?"

THIRTEEN

HOLLY stood close to him in the bedroom, and the storm was still raging. Outside . . . inside. Hell, he couldn't tell the difference anymore. He could smell the hint of pine and rain that still clung to her skin. And he knew better, dammit, but it didn't seem to matter. Her face tilted up toward his, and her eyes were storm-tossed lakes of phosphorous green, and he saw the need in them, despite her denial. But he also saw the desire. It blazed, green flames licking up at him, burning him. All his arguments went silent. He knew he was about to make a huge mistake, but, hell, he was only human. He was out of willpower. He curled his hands around her upper arms, pulled her against him, and he kissed her. Her mouth was cool and wet, opening willingly against his. He let go of her arms, and they twisted around his neck, pulled tighter, closer. He slid his arms around her waist, just kept on kissing her. When her tongue touched his, his body caught fire. His heart hammered and his blood boiled and his head swam with images, vivid ones, of the two of them tangled and naked. Desire, carnal and blatant, jolted through him. It was centered in his chest, that surge, but zapping outward in all directions so forcefully he was sure he must have had sparks flying from his fingertips.

He stopped. Just stopped, let go of her as if she were too hot to touch, took a backward step and felt himself shaking down deep. "Jesus."

She lowered her head, but not before he'd seen the stunned confusion in her eyes. Followed quickly by the hurt. He had not expected this. Desire was one thing. He knew he was attracted to her, he'd expected desire. He'd felt desire out there in the woods, before, but there was more now. Way more.

She shivered, rubbed her arms. She'd felt it, too.

"Holly—"

Her head snapped up, eyes alight. "Don't you dare tell me that was a mistake. Or that it can't go any further. Don't you dare, Vince."

Before he could speak, there was a perfunctory tap on the door. It opened immediately, and Graycloud stepped in without waiting for an invitation. His sharp eyes danced from Holly to Vince and back again. Vince wondered what he was seeing. The two of them standing, facing each other, looking shaken and stunned, and maybe flushed and aroused, too. Holly did, at least. He hoped he hid what he was feeling a little better than she.

"Oh, she is awake. I thought I heard her," Amanda said from behind the doctor. "Holly, you shouldn't be up on your feet. Not so soon."

"I'm fine," Holly said, but her gaze was still riveted to Vince's, and he saw the threat there. It was almost laughable that he could feel threatened by a woman her size, but he did. She meant to do him in. She wasn't going to take no for an answer, and he seriously doubted he'd be able to give it more than once or twice anyway. It was coming. It was inevitable, that's what those eyes said. Whatever it was that had just happened here, she wanted more of it.

Hell, he did, too.

"I'll be the judge of how fine you are," Graycloud said. "Into bed with you, Holly. Come on now."

She glanced at the doctor, sighed her surrender, and returned to the bed. As she got in Vince wondered what insanity had made him think even for a minute that he could curl up in a big soft bed with her—or a big pile of icy wet leaves, for that matter—and keep his hands to himself. She was too much. Screwed up enough to push all his buttons. The woman was damaged, and for good reason. He had a weakness for wounded women, and this one was wounded enough to kill him. He'd known that up front. Thought he could handle it. Then she'd gone and revealed there was more to her than the old wounds, the history, the baggage. Everything in him had resisted her far more easily before she'd decided to stand up and fight. From that moment on, he hadn't stood a chance.

Graycloud was leaning over her now, fingers on her wrist while she held a thermometer in her mouth. An old-fashioned model. No digital electronic stick for Doc Graycloud. The wind howled outside, lashing the house as if trying to break in. Vince wondered if the old actor was awake, listening to it, reliving his glory days.

A soft hand cupped his shoulder. "She's going to be just fine, you know. Holly is a very strong woman."

He glanced sideways at Amanda, saw her blue eyes on Dr. Graycloud and Holly. "I thought you two didn't know each other very well," Vince said.

"We've lived in the same small town for almost two years, Detective. We may not be intimate friends, but it would be impossible not to know a little bit about each other." She sighed, watching Dr. Graycloud remove the thermometer from Holly's mouth, and squint at its numbers. "I've always wished I were more like her. Strong, self-assured."

It occurred to him that if obsessive-compulsive, panic-attack prone Holly seemed like a pillar of stability to her, Amanda must be a virtual basket case. But that wasn't fair and he knew it. Besides, this was no time to be reminding himself of all the reasons he should avoid Holly Newman like the plague. He could do that later. This was an opportunity to gather information.

"It's a shame everyone in town doesn't agree with you," he said, dragging his gaze off Holly and fixing it on Amanda to watch her face, gauge her reactions.

She frowned at him. "What do you mean? Everyone loves Holly."

Was there a hint of resentment in her tone just then? Maybe . . . maybe just a little. "Not everyone," he said. "The person who put the light out last night so we couldn't find our way back, for example."

She looked shocked by his words. "You really think someone would do that deliberately?"

"I think there have been a few too many coincidences lately for them to be considered coincidences at all."

"Such as?"

"Someone snooping in my cabin. Someone in Holly's house while her mother was asleep."

Her eyes widened. "You think it's someone from Dilmun?"

"I've been checking around. The tourists have all gone home except for a couple of fishermen who've been coming here for twenty years. There are no strangers in town that anyone seems aware of. Other than me, that is."

"And you have no idea who it could be?"

"Nope. How about you?"

Her head came up fast, eyes snapping to his. "Goodness, no. What makes you think I'd know anything about it?"

He only shrugged. "You live here. If she has any enemies, I figured you'd know about it."

"She doesn't. Most people in this town would gladly throw themselves into the path of a speeding train for Holly Newman."

This time the emotion in the words was too obvious to ignore. "That almost sounds as if you're a little envious, Amanda."

She shook her head. "I have Reggie. He's all I need."

"Is he?" She looked at him, saying nothing. "You seem . . . lonely, to me."

Her gaze rose, even though her head stayed lowered, soft brown hair veiling her face. "Do I?" He didn't reply. She sighed. "I'm not. Not really. I don't like people. I prefer to be alone. Truly."

"Why is that, Amanda?"

She stared at him, but she didn't answer. Instead she turned toward the door. "Call me if you need anything." Then she left.

He watched her until she was out of sight, then glanced back at the bed. Holly looked away fast. Her jaw was tight, her lips pressed hard together, and her eyes angry . . . and maybe the tiniest bit jealous.

<hr />

SHE DIDN'T KNOW WHY SHE WAS LETTING herself go from disliking the man intensely to burning up for him, but she had. All in the space of a single night, though she knew damned well it had been going on far longer. From that first day, in fact.

She hadn't ever been this powerfully attracted to a man before. She didn't know if there was anything real to it or not, despite her persistent sense that there must be. She supposed it might be tied, somehow, to her psyche, and the bombs that had been going off within it for the past several days. He was connected to all of that. Maybe that was the basis for the attraction.

No. No, it was more.

It didn't matter. The cause, that is. What mattered was that, for a very long time, she'd been fairly certain she would never feel the way he made her feel. He might be her only chance at knowing that kind of passion.

But all of that was beside the point. The main point was staying alive, being safe, keeping her mother safe,

keeping all the children in the world safe from the predator who stalked them.

Vince lay on the ridiculous chaise after Dr. Graycloud
had pronounced Holly healthy and left them alone again.
He hadn't said a word since the doctor had retired, and
she hadn't either. The storm was growing more distant
with every tick of the clock, and the sky beyond the window was beginning to pale. It would be dawn soon. She
wanted to have sex with him. He knew that, she was fairly
certain she'd made it abundantly clear. She wasn't going
to beat the subject to death. Nor would she beg.

"I think we need to tell my mother what's going on,"
she said. "I think she needs to know."

He lay on his back, never turning to face her. "I think
it would upset her for no good reason."

"This person went after her, Vince. He was in the house
while she was there."

"If he'd been after her, he would've . . . she was never
a target." He altered the sentence for her benefit, she
knew. "If he was in your house, he was messing with your
head, Holly."

"Why? What purpose could that serve?"

"He's keeping you off balance. Maybe so you'll continue to question your own mind—your own memory."

"That would only make sense if there were something
more I could possibly remember. And I—I don't think
there is."

"You don't want there to be."

She swung her gaze to him sharply, met his eyes, saw
that he knew exactly what she was feeling. "You're right.
If I knew something more, something that could have
saved my sister, but blocked it—" She closed her eyes.
"This is pointless. And off the subject. We were talking
about my mother."

He nodded at her to go on.

"She has a right to know the man sitting in prison for
murdering her daughter isn't the man who did it."

Vince sighed. It was a deep, heavy sound. As if he had

more to say, and had used the sigh to keep from saying it.

"What?" she asked.

"Nothing. If you want to tell her, we'll tell her."

"Today," she said.

"Okay." He flung back the covers, got to his feet.

"What are you doing?"

"Getting up. The storm's fading fast. I have things to do."

"Or, maybe you're just in a hurry to get away from me."

He glanced across the room at her. She felt his eyes on her, sliding from her head to her toes, and warming her right through the covers. "I was planning on taking you with me."

"Oh."

"Red, you need to understand something about me."

She flung back her covers, too, got to her feet. "You don't do relationships," she said. "I got it."

He gritted his teeth. "Sex for me is a function best served by professionals. I don't like it messy. I don't like feelings and emotions involved. I like it straight up, and quick and meaningless. Like taking a shower. You jump in, you do what needs doing, and you get the hell out. Anything more is a waste of time. If it happens between us, that's the way it's going to be. Just so you know, up front."

She moved closer to him, but didn't touch him. She didn't get close enough to touch him, and when she spoke, she spoke very slowly. "I like long, slow soaks in the tub. Scented salts. Loofah sponges. Expensive shampoos and hot oil treatments. All the trimmings. You ever take baths like that?"

He had closed his eyes for some reason. "Not that I can remember, Red."

"Well, then, maybe you're due."

Ernie Graycloud offered them a ride back to Holly's house, and Vince took him up on it. They'd showered and had coffee, but passed on the full breakfast Amanda had offered. Vince stood outside the D'Voe mansion, wearing his now-dry clothes—laundered overnight by Amanda—and watching Holly as she thanked Reginald, hugged his neck gently, and moved toward the waiting car. Doc was already behind the wheel.

Vince took his cue, walked up to where Reggie and Amanda stood. He clasped Amanda's hands. "Thanks for everything," he said.

"You're more than welcome."

He reached out to shake Reggie's hand. Reginald slung an arm around Vince's shoulders instead. "I'll walk you to the car."

"No need," Vince began, but Reggie ignored that, kept on limping along beside him, while Amanda stayed where she was, standing on the front step.

"You wanted a private moment, I take it?" Vince asked.

Pausing halfway between the house and the car, Reginald removed his arm from Vince's shoulder, turned to face him. He wore the most menacing look Vince had seen him wear off screen, and the walking stick suddenly looked like a potential weapon. "I want you to stay away from Amanda. Do you understand?"

Vince blinked. "Why?"

The older man's brows lifted. "Why? Because I said so. And because I'm someone you'd be wise not to piss off, young man. I will make you very sorry if you do."

"I see."

"Good."

He wanted to argue with the man, but that was ego and pride and temper. The cop in him had it in hand. He controlled it.

Holly had her window rolled down as he turned and walked toward the car. "Good-bye Amanda," she called, waving once again.

The young woman on the front step waved back, smiling. "I'll see you both soon," she called back. "At the Halloween party. You are coming, aren't you?"

Vince couldn't help it. He should have, but he couldn't. He smiled, shot a sideways glance at Reggie, and said loudly, "We wouldn't miss it."

It was a good thing the man couldn't incinerate things with the power of his evil glare, as he had in *The Eyes of Dr. Stark*, Vince thought, or his hair would have been smoldering.

He gave a nod, and got into the car.

"I don't think Reggie likes you," Holly said.

"Really? I thought he was downright friendly."

She leaned back in the seat, sighing.

HER HOUSE SEEMED DIFFERENT SOME-how when she walked through the front door that morning. Out of order. Not . . . right. Her routines were so far out of whack she wondered if she would ever get them back again, and she consciously had to force herself not to count. No. Not to count aloud. Inside her mind, she was counting anyway. Counting the steps from the car up the sidewalk, to the front door. Counting the nine small windowpanes in the door.

She understood the psychology of it. If she stopped counting, she would have room in her mind for the other things. The fears. The memories. The guilt. The knowledge that Very Bad Things could happen to her and to those she loved, at any moment, at any time, without warning or rhyme or reason.

So, silently, she counted.

Waking up in a strange bed, having to take a ride in Dr. Graycloud's car to get back to her own kitchen for morning coffee with her mother, was not the way things were supposed to go.

Vince looked at her, watched her, all the way back to the house. He knew, she thought. He knew how she was feeling right now. He was waiting for her to fall apart, but, dammit, she wouldn't. She refused. So she counted. It was better than the alternative.

Vince opened the door and she went in, stopped walking, and glanced up at her mother. Her mother was at the kitchen table, her coffee mug in her hand. Right where she was supposed to be at this time of the morning. Thank God. Chief Mallory sat beside her. Not across from her. His being there was not part of the daily routine, but was an accepted variation on it. He was there often enough for her to adjust to him. And at least he wasn't in Holly's chair.

"Well. Good morning," her mother said. Her smile was knowing and her cheeks pink as her shining eyes shimmied back and forth between Holly and Vince.

"It's not what you think." Why those were the first words to come out of her mouth, she couldn't imagine. Not when their lives were at risk, and she was about to give her mother news that would alter hers dramatically.

Doris frowned and got to her feet. "Your head . . ." She came forward, eyeing the patch Dr. Graycloud had applied to Holly's head.

"It's fine, Mom. But . . ." She glanced at Vince for help. "We need to talk."

Chief Mallory got to his feet, but Vince held up a hand. "No, Chief, I think you need to be here for this, too. You're going to need to know about all of it, sooner or later."

Nodding, the chief sat back down.

"I don't like the way this is sounding," Doris said. "What's going on with you two?"

Sighing, Holly took her mother's hand. "Come on, Mom. Sit down. How are you feeling this morning?"

"Fine. Better than you, by the looks of you. What happened last night, Holly?"

Holly bit her lip. She walked with her mother back to the table, urged her back into her seat. Then she got two cups, poured coffee for her and Vince, and sat down in her own chair. Vince took his cup, but remained standing. Holly sent him a silent plea. She was gratified that he seemed to read it so easily.

"Last night," he said, "Holly and I took a rowboat out on the lake. The light on the dock went out after dark, and we got lost in the fog. Then the storm started kicking up, and we wound up in the water." When Doris gasped, he smiled gently at her. "It's okay. As you can see, we're both fine. We did have a heck of a time hiking back from the far side of the lake. The first place we came to was the D'Voe mansion. Reginald was good enough to let us hole up there for the night."

"We'd have called, Mom, but the phones were out."

"My God. In that storm . . . are you sure you're all right?"

"Yeah. We're fine." Holly reached across the table to squeeze her mother's hand.

Chief Mallory said, "That light is damn near indestructible. We replace it every five years or so, and it isn't due for another two yet."

Vince nodded. "So Holly tells me."

"You think it was deliberate?" the chief asked.

Vince's lips narrowed. "Possibly."

Doris sat perfectly still, just staring from face to face for a moment. "Are you saying . . . that someone tried to . . . kill you?"

"They were probably just trying to scare us, Mom," Holly said. God, she couldn't bear the fear in her mother's eyes.

But Doris was shaking her head, getting to her feet. "And last night, when you were so upset about the door being open. And the intruder at Vince's place. This is all related, isn't it?"

He nodded. "Yeah. I'm afraid it is."

"Mom, it's not going to be easy to hear any of this. I want you to sit down, and just try to listen. Hold on to me, and the chief, and let Vince explain it. Okay?"

She stared at Holly. "What are you saying? Holly, what do you mean?"

"It has to do with Ivy, Mom."

Doris's knees bent. She landed heavily in the chair. "No. No, I don't want to do this."

"I didn't, either," Holly said gently. "But we don't have a choice."

Doris looked at Holly, her eyes big and round and filling with old, old pain. She sought something in Holly's eyes. Holly held her gaze, and, finally, Doris looked away, at Vince, gave him a slight nod.

"Doris, the reason I came here had to do with the deaths of two young children in Syracuse. They were abducted and killed by a pedophile. At the scene, I found a copy of a book that came from the Dilmun Public Library."

"The Gingerbread Man," Holly said softly.

Her mother's eyes fell slowly closed. "It was Ivy's favorite."

"I checked the library's old records, for Vince," the chief told her. "It's the same copy that Holly checked out when she was seven years old."

Doris's eyes snapped open. "The same copy . . . the same copy Ivy was carrying when she was taken? But how can that be?"

Vince came closer, put a hand on Doris's shoulder. "My theory is that it's the same man, Doris."

She shook her head. "That's impossible. Holly, didn't you tell him? The man who took Ivy is in prison, Vince. He confessed and—"

"I know. Holly and I paid him a visit. We learned some . . . disturbing things."

Holly slid out of her chair now, went to kneel in front of her mother. "Mom, Hubey Welles was on a direct path to Death Row when he made that confession. In return for it, he got life in prison. There's a very good chance . . . that he lied."

Doris's face lost all color. "No. No, he knew details—"

"None that hadn't made the papers," Vince said. "He

made a deal with the D.A., Doris. It was a bad deal. But he took it. He'd have said anything to save his own life."

"Oh, my God," Doris whispered. She was shaking her head slowly, rising to her feet, and staring from one of them to the other. "No. No. This can't be true. I—"

"It's true, Mom. When I saw the man in prison—I suddenly remembered the eyes of the man who took Ivy. And they were different. Totally different. It wasn't him."

Doris looked stricken. Searching each face, almost pleading with them to tell her it wasn't true. She finally settled on Chief Mallory. "Jim?"

"I'm sorry, hon. But it all makes sense."

She stood there, fists clenched, trembling all over, eyes darting around, in search of something. Escape, maybe. Holly looked down and saw blood drip from her mother's fists. She was digging her nails into her palms. "Mom . . ." Holly reached for her mother.

Doris went limp and her eyes rolled back. The chief and Vince lunged for her at the same time. A chair went flying as the chief hit it in his rush.

It was Jim who gathered her up, held her against him. He looked stricken.

Holly found Vince's eyes, and saw the pain in them. He'd been afraid of this, it was clear. It was the last thing she had expected.

"I don't understand," she whispered. "Mom's always been the strong one."

"She had to be," Vince said. "Because you couldn't. Now you can. And she knows it. The question is, do you?"

FOURTEEN

"I don't know what I expected. Devastation, maybe. But not this."

From the uncomfortable green metal lawn chair on the patio, Holly had a clear view of her mother's bedroom door, which was closed, and locked.

"She needs time to digest it all," Vince said. "And you need to stay close to her today."

"Close to her? Close to her? Vince, she's dancing on an icy ledge, and she's going to fall, and it isn't going to matter how close I am when she does." She pressed the heel of her hand to her forehead. "You were right. God, why did I insist on telling her?"

"She had a right to know."

"I should have waited. Maybe if I'd waited until we caught the guy . . . God, what if we don't? For Mom, that would be almost like losing Ivy all over again. I don't think she could survive it."

Sighing, Vince moved to stand behind her, hands going to her shoulders, rubbing them briskly like some boxer's trainer in between rounds. "Just be there for her. It's all you can do."

Holly let her head fall forward, let her muscles warm under his touch. "Vince?"

"What?"

She swallowed, hesitated. "I think there was a part of me that wanted to tell Mom what was happening, be-cause—because—" Her throat seemed to close off.

"Because she's your mom. And that's what you do when you're in trouble. You tell your mom, and she pro-tects you from it."

"She tried. I wouldn't have survived it, Vince. She kept me together, all this time." She sniffed. "I'm not sure I can . . . get through this without her."

"What are you gonna do? Hmm? You gonna fall off that icy ledge with your mother? Leap off it, maybe? Who the hell's gonna hold on to *her* if you do?"

She shut her eyes. Vince crouched down, gripping her arms. "Ivy has been gone for almost two decades, Holly. You aren't a little girl anymore, and you aren't the deli-cate fragile thing everyone's been protecting all this time. You can do this."

She shook her head. Her eyes focused on her feet, her heart aching because she knew he was right.

"You don't have a choice, Red."

Sniffling, Holly lifted her head, nodded once. "I know that."

"Keep on knowing it." He reached up suddenly, cupped her face with his hands. "Don't quit on me. Not now."

"I won't."

He nodded, his eyes probing hers deeply, then dark-ening, and sliding lower to her lips. He licked his own, and quickly let her go, and looked at the floor.

She leaned closer and pressed her mouth against his. As kisses went, it wasn't much. Hard, cool, all too brief.

He looked at her, but he didn't scold. He sighed, in-stead, and rose to his full height. "I have some things I need to do."

"What kinds of things?"

"Come on, babe, I'm a detective. What kinds do you think?"

She sent him a scowl.

"Research. Background checks on . . . some of the players."

"Can I help?"

He shook his head. "No. You need to be here, with your mother. Besides, I need to concentrate on what I'm doing."

"You can't concentrate when I'm around?"

"No."

"Why not?"

He grimaced at her. "If you need me, use the cell phone. I'll be in and out of the cabin, but I'll have it with me, either way. Okay?"

"Okay."

He moved to the sliding doors that led to the living room, then paused. "I want you to call if you feel the slightest unease, Holly. Don't doubt your instincts at this point. Call if you need me."

"I thought you didn't want me to need you."

He closed his eyes slowly. "You know what I meant."

"Yeah. Don't worry. I'll call. Go."

So he went. She watched him move through the house, stop to speak with Chief Mallory, and then the two of them left together. Seconds after the sounds of their cars' pulling away, Holly heard another vehicle come to a stop out front. She went inside, crossed the living room and looked outside. It was one of the local officers. Bill, she thought, glimpsing his blond hair through the windows of the police cruiser. She waved. He waved back.

Holly let the curtain fall closed, and went to her mother's bedroom. Vince said to let her have some time alone. Holly wasn't so sure that was a good idea. She tried the door. It was still locked, but she'd locked herself out of her own room any number of times. The standard locks on the mass-produced door knobs were meant for privacy, not security. She went to the kitchen for a butter knife, put it into the groove in the center of the doorknob, and twisted. Then she opened the door and went inside.

Her mother was curled up on the bed, sobbing softly.

"Are you all right?"

"I'm sorry, Holly. I'm sorry," her mother said. Her voice was thick, and muffled by the pillows. "Look at me. God, I'm such a mess, and goodness knows you don't need this from me. Not now."

She rolled onto her back, and Holly almost gasped at the change in her mother's face. It was like looking back in time. The starkness in her eyes. The color of her skin, sickly pale. The tears had added their marks as well.

Holly blinked her own eyes dry, straightened her spine. "Be back in a second, Mom."

Her mother nodded, and Holly left the room, crossed the hall, and went to her own. In her bathroom, in her medicine cabinet, were several bottles of tranquilizers in various forms and doses. Some nearly empty, some all but full. She chose the Valium, a mild dose, and filled a glass with water, carrying both back to her mother's bedroom. Then she sat on the edge of the bed.

"Here. I want you take this, and no arguments."

Her mother took the pill obediently, which surprised Holly. She'd expected an argument. She slugged down half the glass of water, then handed it back to Holly, and curled up in the bed. "Remember how you and Ivy used to burrow right in between Dad and me when you couldn't sleep?" she asked.

Holly didn't want to remember. It hurt too much. She lay down, though. She wrapped her mother in her arms just the way her mom used to do for her when she was going through the worst of it. And the way she used to hold both of them, when they were afraid at night, after a scary movie or a bad dream. Ivy, with her big blue eyes and those pale lashes, and the chubby cheeks she still hadn't outgrown. Tiny little baby teeth. That was one of the images Holly carried with her. Those tiny teeth when Ivy smiled. And the dimples. And the way her eyes would scrunch when she really laughed hard. It had been a long time since she'd allowed that beautiful baby face to haunt her mind. A long time since thoughts of how Ivy's pretty, innocent face must have looked while some monster had tortured and raped and killed her. The terror.

She mustn't think of those things. She had to take care of her mother.

But somehow, she couldn't stop the memories. She heard her baby sister's screams, the last sounds she'd ever heard her make, echoing in her mind, over and over. And she couldn't erase the sound. She closed her eyes to drown it out, tried to hear anything else, think of anything else. And then she found something to focus on, and aimed her entire attention at it. The soft, steady *tick, tick, tick* of the clock beside her mother's bed. Yes. Yes, she thought silently. And inside her mind, she whispered, one, two, three, four, five, six, seven, eight . . .

⸺

VINCE LEFT. HE DIDN'T WANT TO, BUT there was work to be done, and he couldn't do it sitting around Holly's house watching her struggle with her demons.

Mostly because he didn't *want* to watch her struggle. He wanted to take her demons, slay them for her, fix everything, make it okay, make *her* okay. And he knew that if he tried he'd end up letting her down, and kicking himself for it for the rest of his life. He might be tempted to try all the same. But, damn, he didn't think she could survive another disappointment.

She had to do this on her own.

Rescue did not work with problems this big.

"You were right about the light at the dock, Vince. It looks as if it's been tampered with." Mallory sighed, waited for a reply, didn't get one. "You all right?" the chief asked.

Vince shook off his thoughts and turned to face the older man. "Just thinking."

"About Holly?"

"No," he lied. "About how quick my ass will be roasted when I call my boss today."

The chief shook his head a little. "You withheld evidence?"

"Nah. I turned over everything I had. The problem is, I was taken off this case. My leave of absence wasn't by choice."

"I see. So you kept right on working it. And now you're close to flushing out a child killer." He shook his head. "Yep, they'll hate you for that. Probably even pin a medal on you just to teach you a lesson."

"You don't know my boss."

"You weren't thinking about your boss."

He glanced sideways. "Holly has problems that I can't fix for her."

"Holly has ghosts. She's also strong, sharp, intelligent, and stubborn as they come. And if you tried fixing things for her, she'd likely club you upside the head. She's fixing things for herself. Doing just fine until all this cropped up, and she'll be doing fine again once we get past it. So what's your problem, son?"

Vince shot the man an impatient glare.

"You're afraid she's gonna fuck *you* up, is what it is. You don't want to risk it. You're scared to death of that woman."

"You don't know a thing about it, Chief."

The chief shrugged, unoffended. "Listen. Let me call your boss for you, huh?"

Vince shook his head. "It's my mess. I'll clean it up. But expect a call later on. He's gonna want to get your end of this, and more than likely there will be Feds crawling all over town by this time tomorrow. Be ready."

"Will do." He pulled into the curving drive and stopped. Vince got out of the car, held the door open and leaned down. "You're gonna keep a man on Holly's place today?"

"Only when I can't be there myself."

"Good."

"You know, you can set up in the office, if you want," the chief said before Vince could close the door. "Work from there, if you think it'll help."

"By tomorrow they'll probably have commandeered any space you have for a base of operations. No, I'll be okay right here."

"All right. Call if you need anything."

"Actually—"

"Yeah?"

Vince sighed. "Chief, how well do you know Reginald D'Voe?"

The chief's eyes clouded over. "He's got nothing to do with any of this."

"How can you be so sure?"

"You gotta trust me on this, son. Reggie has secrets, sure. But digging around in his past will only dredge up unnecessary pain for innocent folks. He's a good man."

"Okay. If you say so," Vince said, because it was clearly the only thing to say. He didn't believe it though. D'Voe had warned him off. And now the chief seemed to be doing the same. The old actor had something to hide, and Vince had a sick feeling in his belly that maybe he was starting to get an inkling of what it was.

DORIS HAD FALLEN INTO A HEAVY SLEEP within a few minutes, so Holly had slipped quietly out of the bed, run herself a long, steaming bath, and spent a good hour soaking in it. It eased her aching muscles. God, last night had beaten her up pretty good. She had bruises on her that she'd been unaware of. On her rib cage, her side, high on her thigh. Her head still ached, but it was a dull ache. Most of her distress was emotional, not physical. And the hot bath wasn't much help for that.

She lay back in the water, looked up, saw the medicine cabinet, still open wide, and the row of little brown plastic bottles on the shelf inside. They would help. She could pop a few pills and put herself on level ground again.

She'd been off her meds for a while now. A long while, and she'd been proud of it. It meant she could survive without them. But maybe she wasn't as free of them as she'd thought. After all, she'd needed to keep them nearby. Dr. Graycloud disapproved, of course, nagged her about it constantly. He'd even told her mother to keep track of the contents of the little brown bottles so he would know if she started using any of them again. But she hadn't. They were a crutch she kept around in case she needed one. She was still terrified of being without the wide array of pills.

And, now, now maybe it was a good thing they were here. Old friends. Maybe she would need them before this was all over.

There was a noise in the hall. Movement. Fear jumped in her heart, and she got up fast, water sluicing down her body. Was someone out there? How long had they been in the house? God, she'd stayed too long in the tub. Her mother was alone, across the hall. She reached blindly, found a big towel, pulled it to her and stepped onto the floor, dripping, leaving little puddles. Rivulets ran from her hair down her back as she anchored the towel around her. She ignored the trickling water and stepped slowly out of the bathroom, into her bedroom, toward the door. Someone was moving around out there in the hallway, or maybe the kitchen.

She needed a weapon. Didn't have one. She had locked the doors after Vince and the chief left. Bill was still outside, wasn't he?

Softly, she went to the bedroom door, gripped the knob, turned it slowly, pulled just a little.

In the hall, her mother strode past with a big box in her arms.

"Mom?" Holly flung the door wider, then followed her mother down the hall. "What are you doing up?"

"I couldn't sleep. But, Holly, look. Look what I found."

She emerged into the small kitchen and set the box on a chair. It was the only free spot. Holly stopped cold, and looked around her. Ivy was everywhere. Photos of her smiling, those dimples, the blue eyes. Soft hair so blonde it was nearly white. Holly's own hair had been that same pale color when she was a baby, her mother had often told her. That color didn't last. It faded, like innocence. Like Ivy. Photos were everywhere, framed, unframed, hanging, standing, propped up. And clothes. Little-girl dresses, hung from the backs of chairs. Hair ribbons dangled atop them. On the table, Ivy's favorite doll lay looking forlorn and abandoned. Its hair had been cut off, so only little nubs stuck out the holes in the top of its head. One eye was stuck open. It wore no clothes. A tea set was beside the doll. A puzzle. Some coloring books, open, with sloppily colored pages and Ivy's name scrawled in kindergarten penmanship across the tops.

She could almost hear her baby sister's laughter. She could almost see her standing there, defiantly, the baby doll in one hand, the scissors in the other, blonde locks on the floor around her chubby bare feet. She could almost hear her little voice. "Real babies don't have hair!"

"Oh, God, Mom . . ."

"I was just . . . remembering. We don't do that enough."

Holly swallowed hard. "We stopped doing that. We decided it was too painful. That's why we packed all this stuff away."

"That was before."

Holly shuddered. Jesus, she couldn't take this. Not without help. She turned back to the hallway, having made up her mind. A Valium. Maybe something stronger. Anything, just to dull reality.

"She's not at rest. She'll never be at rest until her killer pays, Holly, and if Ivy isn't at peace, we can't be either.

We can't forget her. We can't pack her things away. We can't—"

. Holly took a single step into the hallway, toward her room, her pills, her crutch, and the phone rang. It froze her in her tracks. Doris grabbed it up before it could ring again, and immediately said, "Hello? Jim, is it you? Have you caught the man yet?"

"Mom, hon, it's okay," Holly said, turning around, going back.

"Vince?" Doris said, then she shot Holly a look. "It's Vince, dear. Vince, have you caught the man yet? Have you?"

"Mom, please . . ."

Holly had her hand out. Her mother listened to whatever Vince said, then blinking back tears, handed the phone to Holly. "He hasn't arrested anyone yet. But he will. It won't be long now. Your Vince is a good man, I can see that."

She kept on walking, right past Holly, back to the table where she picked up the doll, and held it to her chest.

"Vince?"

"Jesus, Holly, what the hell is going on there?"

"Nothing. Mom's . . . I'll just give her another Valium. She'll be all right. What happened?"

"Nothing. Research. I just wanted to check on you."

"We're fine."

"You don't sound fine. Maybe you should've come with me after all."

"No." She glanced at her mother, going through yet another box of her sister's things. "She shouldn't be alone right now."

He was silent for a moment. Then, "Is Bill still outside?"

Holly glanced toward the window. "Yes. We're fine. Safe and fine. Do your job, Vince. The faster we end this, the better."

There was a pause. "Are you sure you're all right?"

"Yes."

"Okay. Okay. I'll talk to you later."

———⟐———

VINCE HUNG UP THE PHONE AND TRIED to shake the feeling that something wasn't right, but he couldn't seem to get rid of it. Holly had sounded strange. He didn't like it.

Goddamn it, what if he'd been wrong in thinking she could get through this? What if she couldn't? She'd been alone for hours with her mother, who'd sounded completely spaced out on the phone.

Hell. He had to get over there and find out for himself. Right or wrong, he had to.

Vince put in a call to Marty Cantrell, Holly's uncle. But it was his wife, Jen, who answered the phone. He'd met her, briefly, at the bonfire.

"I'm sorry, Vince. Marty's working today."

"Oh. I didn't realize he had an outside job."

"It's not much. Not even full time anymore. But when they need him, he still makes deliveries for Strofman's Bakery. They had several orders to go out today, and one of their regulars called in sick, so . . ."

"That's all right. Really. Maybe you can help."

"Well, sure, if I can. What is it? Is Holly all right?"

"Yeah, but I'm not sure about your sister. Doris isn't doing too well. I think she could use your help."

The woman listened as he told her the very essentials. A half hour later, he was pulling up to Holly's place. Jen Cantrell and Ernie Graycloud arrived immediately behind him. He thanked them for coming and went to the house. He knocked once, then walked in when there was no answer, using the key Holly had given him earlier.

"Hell," he muttered, standing there, taking in the scene. It was worse than he'd thought.

Doris sat at the small kitchen table, surrounded by toys, photos, little-girl clothes. She was smiling weakly, but there was a faraway look in her eyes. She glanced up as they entered, met his gaze. "Oh, Vince, it's you. Did you find him yet?"

Vince sighed, glanced at the Doc.

"I've got her," he said. "Go find Holly."

Vince nodded and strode through the house, into the hall, to Holly's room. She wasn't inside, but her bathroom door was open. The bedroom was dark, but the light in the bathroom was on, and it spilled out. Something quaked just a little in Vince's chest.

He moved closer, tried to make himself hurry, but found his feet unwilling to move. It was as if he was slogging through muck. Closer, he could see bottles of pills on the sides of the sink. Some standing upright, some tipped on their sides. The medicine cabinet was open.

"Jesus. Holly?"

He moved still closer, hand on the door, pushing it wider, and he glimpsed the water in the tub. It was full.

"No." He slammed the door open all the way, and lunged into the bathroom.

No one was in the tub. The water inside was clear, with a few suds floating on its surface. A damp towel was slung over the side. His entire body uncoiled, but his stomach was still clenched and churning.

He turned, glancing at the pills. The assortment would have made an addict happy.

A soft sound reached him, laughter. A child's laughter. He turned, and followed the sound out through the living room. That's when he finally saw Holly. She was outside on the back deck, beyond the glass doors. That little girl from next door was with her, and they had mounds of fabric on the table between them, along with scissors and pincushions and various other implements of stitchery.

He looked at Holly's face, her eyes. She was clear-eyed, alert. She was okay.

For just a second, he felt the power of his relief. Much greater than it should have been. He didn't want to spend time trying to probe into why that was—not now.

She looked up as if she felt his eyes on her, and met them. He saw relief there, too. Some kind of tension just vanished. She was glad to see him. More than glad. She had said she didn't need to be with him. She'd been lying.

She stood up, and he strode up to her, wrapped her in his arms, and hugged her hard. He didn't even think about it until the awkwardness set in. Then he let go, stepped back.

She shuffled her feet. "So, what are you doing here?"

"I didn't like the way you sounded on the phone," he said.

"Hi, Detective O'Mally!"

He turned and pasted an "everything's just fine" smile on his face. "Hello, there, Bethany."

She nodded. "Wait till you see what Holly and I have been doing." As she spoke, she gathered up the mounds of fabric from the table. The girl stuffed the fabric into a shopping bag, from which the very tip of a pointy black hat stuck up.

"Well, show me!" he said. "I'm dying to see it."

"No way." She picked the bag up by its twin handles. "This costume is top secret until the party at Mr. D'Voe's, tomorrow night." She tossed her blonde curls dramatically. "You'll just have to wait." Then she grinned, ran to Holly, hugged her waist. "Thank you, Holly. This is the best costume *ever*!" Then she let go. "I can't wait to show Mom." She ran off the back deck, and across the lawns toward her own house. Halfway there she shouted back. "I hope your mom feels better, Holly!"

"Me, too," Holly whispered, but not loud enough for the child to hear. She watched until the kid was inside her own place, then sighing, turned to the table, and began picking up sewing items and returning them to the basket.

"I brought your aunt and the doc," Vince said. He joined her in picking up. There were countless scraps of fabric to be tossed into a nearby wastebasket. "Thought your mom could use the help."

"I know, I saw them come in. Thanks. I don't know if it'll help but—"

"Holly, I looked for you in your room first."

"I thought I'd sit out here. I had a clear view of Mom, and I couldn't very well take Bethany in there when she came over. Not with Mom in this state." She shrugged. "It's not like I was reaching her anyway. She's withdrawn into herself."

"Yeah. Listen, I have to ask. What's up with all the pills?"

She looked up at him, frowned. "God, did I leave them out?"

"There's a goddamn pharmacy in there."

She sighed. "I haven't needed chemical help in a long time. But I keep them. I guess it's a security issue. Just knowing they're there, you know? I was looking for something for Mom. Gave her a Valium, but it didn't touch her. To be honest, I damn near took something myself." Her lips twisted.

"But you didn't."

She lifted her eyes. "No, I didn't need them." She smiled a little weakly, but, still, it was something. "I guess I learned something about myself today. I mean, it can't get much worse than this, can it?"

It could, and he was afraid it would, but he wasn't going to tell her that.

"And I didn't need them. Maybe I can throw them out at last."

"Maybe that would be a good idea."

She tilted her head. "You were worried about me, weren't you?"

He averted his eyes.

She frowned. "You walked in and saw the pills and— Vince, did you really think I'd swallowed a bunch of them, or something?"

He shrugged. "I don't know what I thought."

Moving closer, Holly grabbed his arm, studied his face. "Even at my worst, I never contemplated suicide." She paused. He knew there was more, and he just waited. She eased her grip on his arm. "That's a lie. I . . . I did think about it. But I couldn't do it. I was the only daughter my mother had left. I couldn't take that away from her."

"For the record, Red, I'm damned glad to hear it." He looked past her, back inside the house. Doc had Doris on the couch now, had his stethoscope out. "Let's go see how your mother is doing, huh?"

"I'm going to survive this."

"I know you are, Red. Most people would be in a rubber room, drooling, at this point. But you're out here in the sunshine, sewing Halloween costumes for a little girl." He ran a hand through her hair. "You're incredibly strong. And I know it. Now, can we go check on your mother?"

She nodded. "All right."

He opened the glass doors, stepped through them. Doc looked at him, and his face was stern. "What did you give her, Holly?"

She sighed, turned, walked down the hall, vanishing into her bedroom. A few moments later she came out with a pill bottle, and put it on the coffee table. "One of these," she said. "She slept for maybe an hour."

Graycloud looked at the label, then his brows raised in question, he looked at Holly again.

"No, I didn't take any. You can take it—and the rest of them—away with you. I don't need them anymore."

He smiled just a little, nodded once. "And about time. Good girl."

"What about Mom?"

Graycloud stepped away from the sofa, and Holly's aunt Jen took his place there, leaning over, holding Doris's hand, speaking softly to her. Doc huddled with Vince and Holly on the far side of the living room. "Her blood pressure is up, and her heartbeats are irregular. I don't like it. I could probably stabilize her here at home, but I think it's a bad idea. She's around all these things, and if anything more happens I'm just not sure how she might react."

Holly bit her lip. "Are you saying you want to put her in the hospital?"

"Yeah. Just for a day or two. Let me get her on some meds, get her stable, monitor her heart."

"She'll be out of harm's way, Holly," Vince said. "We can have a police guard on her door." He didn't say it aloud, but he thought it was the best answer for Holly as well. She wouldn't need to be in constant fear for her mother's safety, much less subjected to this kind of morbid behavior. "I think it's for the best, really."

"I'll go too," Jen offered. "I'll stay with her the whole time."

"Oh, Aunt Jen, that's too much to ask."

"I don't mind. Marty's away; what else do I have to do?" She smiled, patted Doris's hand. "I'll bring my knitting, some books. We'll spend some quality time. We're past due, you know."

Sighing, Holly went to her mother, looked at her, and knew she was not really there. She was lost in a sea of emotions she didn't know how to deal with. Holly knew because she'd spent a lot of time in the same place. "Mom, you're gonna go with Dr. Graycloud now, okay?"

Her mother smiled, and nodded.

"And I'm coming, too," Jen told her. "I'll be along just a few minutes behind you." She glanced over her shoulder at Holly. "I'll pick up this mess, and throw a few things in a bag for her before I go."

"Aunt Jen, I can—"

"You shouldn't even be here, Holly. This is . . ." She looked around, shook her head sadly. She was battling tears herself, Holly realized. She had loved Ivy, too. They all had. "This is too much," Jen said softly. "Go, go with Vince."

Doc was easing Doris to her feet, leading her to the door.

"Have Bill go with you, Dr. Graycloud. He can watch

Doris's room until we get him a replacement," Vince said.

"All right. I'll speak to him before we leave." The doctor led Doris to the door, opened it, and they walked together out to his car.

"Go on, Holly. Go with Vince," Jen ordered. "I've got no problem taking care of things here." Aunt Jen moved closer, ran a hand through Holly's hair. "Besides, it gives me a chance to take care of somebody. I haven't been able to do that since—well, since Kelly and Tara moved to San Francisco."

Holly hugged the woman. "Okay. Thank you, Aunt Jen."

"You're a good girl, Holly. Don't you worry about anything."

"If you need me for anything—" Holly began.

Aunt Jen held up a hand, stopping her, and dipped into her purse to pull out her cell phone. Then she frowned at it. "Oh, damn. I left it in the car overnight and the battery's down again. I am always doing that!" She sighed. "No matter, I'll plug it in and charge it up at the hospital, so I won't be out of touch at all. Okay?"

"You need a car adapter for that thing," Holly muttered. She kissed her aunt warmly. "Thank you. You don't know how much you're helping me right now, just by being here."

"That's what family's for, hon."

Vince took Holly's arm. "Lock up behind us, Mrs. Cantrell."

She nodded, tucked her cell phone into her purse, and waved them off.

FIFTEEN

HOLLY kept her spine very rigid and her chin very level on the ride back to Vince's rented cabin. She wasn't going to cry, not in front of him. She had to clench her hands into fists in her lap to keep them from trembling, and she couldn't really speak because her throat was too tight and that would give her away.

He pulled into the drive, got out, took a pile of stuff from the back seat. She opened her door the minute the Jeep stopped, and she got out, too, walked around the car, and nearly collided with him at the bottom of the steps.

"Your mother's going to be fine," he said.

"Of course she is."

"And so are you."

She forced her eyes to meet his. "I already am."

He sighed, but at least didn't argue the point. Instead, he took her arm with his free hand, led her up the steps, over the porch, then unlocked and opened the front door.

She looked around the cabin. It was no neater than it had been the last time she'd been here. Messier, maybe. Stacks of folders, with sheets of paper sticking from them. A pile of slick-surfaced faxes laid on the floor in front of the fax machine, their ends curling upward. Glitzy magazines were scattered everywhere. Movie magazines. She wondered about that.

"Weren't you concerned about another possible intruder?" she asked, looking at the mess.

"Anything vital, I took with me." As he said it he set the stuff he was carrying on the table. More file folders, and a computer disk from his shirt pocket. He walked to the fax, picked up the sheets, flipped through them. "Well, at least I don't see any notification that I've been fired. Not yet, anyway."

"I take it you finally told your chief what you were doing down here?"

"Yeah. I didn't have a choice. He notified the Feds, and passed along their orders."

"Which are?"

"That I"—he glanced at the papers in his hands, read from one of them—" 'cease and desist any and all unofficial investigation of this case until further notice.' Pretty clear and to the point."

"So what are you going to do?"

"I'm going to make some popcorn and watch old movies. Pop one into the VCR will you?" He nodded toward the floor in front of the TV set, where a stack of videos stood like a tower. Then he walked into the kitchenette and opened cupboards.

She went to the pile of movies, knelt, and perused the titles, thinking he'd lost his mind. Then she got it. "These are all Reginald D'Voe horror films."

"Well, you know, 'tis the season. I've watched all the ones in the tall pile. Take one of those others."

She opened a case, took out the cassette, and slid it into the VCR. Then she flicked on the television and watched as the opening credits of 1945's *Haunted* began to roll. "These are so old they don't even have previews on the tapes," she said.

"The newer editions do," he said. "They're re-releasing these all the time. Remastered, digitized, colorized, and

DVDs . . . These were what they had at the rental place in town, though."

"Thank God for small favors." She heard a series of beeps as he pressed buttons on the microwave, then he was standing beside her.

"They probably won't tell us much, but I'm damned if I know who else to check out. I've been running background checks on every male over thirty in this town, and so far the only person who stands out is D'Voe."

"Why? What did you find on him?" The smell of popcorn accompanied the sound of its popping.

"He was abused as a child."

"Oh, my God. I didn't know."

"I don't think many people do. I found an article about it in some fan magazine's archives on the Net. Thing was at least twenty years old. It said D'Voe ran away from his home outside London when he was twelve years old, after his father beat him bloody over a bad school report. The piece quotes D'Voe as saying that he was sure his father would have killed him, had he stayed. When he left, he said his face was purple with bruises, he had a broken arm, and a few broken ribs as well. It was the worst beating ever, though he claimed he'd had plenty."

Holly lowered her head, closed her eyes. "Poor Reggie."

Vince sighed.

Her head came up again. "What?"

He turned, walked into the kitchen, and took the popcorn out of the microwave. Opening the hot bag with two fingers, he poured it into a big bowl, brought it back with him, and sat down beside her. "I don't have to tell you that survivors of that kind of abuse often grow up to be abusers themselves."

"Not always, though. Surely not in Reggie's case."

He shrugged. "I hope not. But I've checked out practically everyone in town, and this is the first red flag to go up. If it doesn't lead us to something, I don't know where else to start digging."

Holly shook her head, but leaned back on the sofa, took a handful of popcorn, and watched the film begin to unfold. "What do you hope to find in the movies?"

"I don't know. A clue. A pattern. Maybe something similar to one of the crimes. I don't know."

"How much time do you figure we have?"

"Ah, the Feds won't get around to coming out here before nightfall."

"Well, that gives us time, then."

"Yeah."

<hr>

VINCE WATCHED HER WATCHING THE TV screen. He couldn't have told anyone much about the plots of any of the movies if he hadn't already seen most of them, but he would pick up on anything interesting. He had that extra sense on alert. That cop sense an officer developed over time. The ear that isn't listening, but hears every word when it's important. The eye that can filter all but vital images. The mind that can seem to zone out, but turns razor sharp when it needs to. He trusted his cop senses. They hadn't let him down yet.

At least, not until the Prague kids. He thought again that if he'd only found the book the first time he'd been in that house . . .

He shook the thought away, focused again on Holly. She pretended to watch the movies, and maybe she was, a little bit. But mostly she was distracted. Worried for her mother, wondering about her sister's last hours—thoughts on that subject had to be nightmarish at best. And she was scared. She would be foolish not to be.

But there was, overlying all of that, something else. A mask. She was deliberately, stubbornly trying to hide everything else behind it. And since he was the only other person in sight, he could only deduce that she was trying to hide it from him.

What he couldn't figure out was why.

As the ending credits rolled, she got to her feet, rubbed her arms as if they were chilled. "This stuff still holds up," she commented.

"They knew how to make movies back then. Now all they seem able to come up with is gore. Pour a pail of blood on a barely dressed actress and rev up a chainsaw. That's not horror."

She sent him a smile of agreement. It was an utterly false smile. "What's next?"

"I've watched all but a few of them now. There was nothing there." He nodded at the much smaller pile of tapes yet to be viewed.

"So what do you want to do?"

He didn't want to have this conversation. He wanted to take her by the shoulders and give her a shake, make her tell him what the hell was wrong with her. But he wasn't going to do that because he wasn't supposed to care that much. And he'd best remember that. "Damned if I know."

She went to the old-fashioned rotary phone on the counter, picked it up, and dialed. While she waited for an answer she put a hand over the mouthpiece. "I'm calling the hospital."

He nodded. He'd expected to hear from either Doc or Jim Mallory by now, but no calls had come in. He worried about that for a minute. Then Holly was speaking to someone, asking about her mother, nodding as if reassured. He was entirely too jumpy over things, he realized. His objectivity was shot to hell.

Then again, it had been shaky for a while. Ever since those kids . . .

"So are you really going to go to Reggie's Halloween party?"

She asked the question out of the blue, without warning. He shot her a look, almost begged off, then kicked himself. "He's my only suspect. I don't have much choice but to go—if for no other reason than to keep an eye on all the kids he'll have running around over there."

She paced away and popped the movie out, sliding another into the machine, thumbing the play button. "You know this party of his was an annual event years ago. This will be the first one since they moved back home, but before he and Amanda left town he held it every single year."

"Yeah, so you've told me."

"And so far as I know, nothing of note has happened at any of them."

"You weren't here back then, were you?"

"No. But if there had been anything dramatic, people would still be talking about it. It's a small town, Vince. Stuff like that becomes local legend in a hurry."

He sighed. "It's not like I want it to be Reggie, you know."

"I know." The film cued up, credits rolling. She walked to the sofa and sat down. "You know, you can't get into the party without a costume."

"Huh?" He glanced up at her, and his surprise probably showed.

"Reg won't allow it. Costumes are the price of admission. It's all over town."

"Can I go dressed as a cop from Syracuse?"

She smiled, and for once it was genuine. He could tell the difference without much effort. It reached her eyes when it was real. And this one did.

"Only if you wear a uniform."

"I'm a detective. This *is* my uniform." He looked her up and down. "What are you going as?"

"I have no idea."

She leaned back, grabbed popcorn, signaling an end to the conversation. The nineteen-inch screen darkened, then was filled by Reginald D'Voe's face, younger, less lined, more made up, but otherwise just the same. Brows angled to a point, eyes gleaming with evil intent. And that trademark maniacal laughter of his rolled from the speaker.

⚬⚬⚬⚬⚬

THEY WATCHED FILMS ALL AFTERNOON.
Midway through the fourth one, the only one remaining
that Vince hadn't already viewed, the phone rang. Vince
picked it up, and Jerry's voice came through. He said
three words. "They're not coming."

"What do you mean they're not . . . ?" It took Vince a
minute to process the statement. "They're not *coming*?"

Jerry's frustration was clear. "The Fed in charge of the
Prague kids' case is an asshole, Vince. Name's Selkirk—"

"Frank Selkirk?"

"You know him?"

"Yeah."

"Anyway, this Selkirk feels the book you found at the
crime scene isn't strong enough evidence to warrant pulling his team all the way down there. Says they're following up far stronger leads up here, and you're wasting your
time."

Vince cursed. "It's not the evidence. It's me he has a
problem with."

"You've had run-ins with him before, then?"

"We've butted heads. It wasn't friendly."

"Still, Vince, you think he'd rather louse up a murder
investigation than admit you might be a step or two ahead
of him on this?"

"I think he'd rather be right than wrong."

Jerry sighed. "How sure are you that you're right,
Vince?"

"I've had a break-in and an attempt on my life. How
sure would that make you?"

"Pretty damn sure. Can you tell Selkirk any of this?"

Vince swore again. "The problem is, there's not much
to tell. There was no physical sign of a break-in. No footprints or anything. But Holly says—that is, I have an eye-
witness who saw someone moving around inside the
cabin."

"Uh-huh. That's pretty flimsy evidence, pal. How about
this attempt on your life?"

"Well . . . all they really did was break a lightbulb."

"And you . . . what? Tripped in the dark and bumped your head?"

"Got lost on a thirty-five-mile-long lake, in the dark, in the fog, in a storm. We damn near drowned."

"I see," Jerry said. "We?"

"Holly and me."

"Holly again?"

"Don't even go there, Jare." Vince found Holly's eyes on him. They locked with his and held.

"I'm coming down there," Jerry announced.

"Don't bother. There's no sense in your coming down here and both of us getting written up, or worse."

"I have leave time coming. I'm taking it. E-mail me some directions, or I'll muddle through on my own. Either way, I'll see you tomorrow morning, pal."

There was a click. Jerry knew better than to give Vince time to argue. "Damn stubborn son of a—"

"Sounds like a good friend," Holly said.

Vince nodded. "The best."

"Then I'm glad he's coming. We need all the help we can get on this."

He knew that, but he was worried. He didn't want his partner getting hurt, and this thing was looking risky. At least he'd have more help protecting Holly—he needed that, because he didn't want her getting hurt, either.

She sighed, glanced at her watch, at the movie, which she'd paused for the phone call. "It's getting late. I should probably—"

"Don't say it," he said, glancing her way.

"Don't say what?"

"You're staying here. Or I can go to your place, it's up to you. But if you think you're staying alone tonight, you're dead wrong."

She held his gaze for a long stretch—he sensed she was thinking about arguing, but knowing better. Hell, she didn't want to be alone with a killer on the loose any more than he wanted her to be. And she knew that he knew it.

"My place," she said. "All my stuff's there."

Not just her stuff, but her routine. She needed it, and now wasn't the time to try to shake the habit. "Okay," he agreed. "Your place."

"You can have Mom's room. I mean, if you're sure you don't want mine." Her eyes were intense, and he got her meaning clearly.

"I'll take the couch. It's a better spot."

She cocked her head. "Better spot for what?"

"It's right between the front and back doors. I'll hear anyone who comes around."

Her face went just a hint paler. "You really think—?"

"I don't know what to think at this point. Might as well be ready for anything, though, right?"

"I . . . guess."

"Don't worry, Red. I'm good at this shit. It's what I do, remember?"

She nodded, but the fear still lingered in her eyes. He didn't like seeing it there. He preferred the flicker of heat he'd seen before, if the truth were known.

~~~

IT WASN'T THE SAME IN THE HOUSE WITH her mother away. Holly phoned the hospital again when she and Vince arrived at the house. She couldn't talk to her, though. Jim Mallory came on the line instead, saying not to worry. Her mom was sleeping soundly and he wasn't planning to leave her any time soon.

It was only slightly reassuring. She hung up the phone, and felt her shoulders slump a little as she sighed.

"Anything wrong, Holly? Your mother?"

"She's fine. Sleeping. But it ought to be me there by her bedside."

"Oh, I don't know. I kind of think she'd like the idea of Jim hanging so close by."

"I'm her daughter. It's my place."

"Maybe Jim would like it to be his place, too."

Holly tensed. "You think they're that serious?"

"You didn't see Jim's face when you and I told your mother Welles wasn't the real killer. You were totally focused on Doris. I'll tell you, Mallory looked sick with worry and fighting mad at the thought of her having to go though it all over again." Vince shook his head. "A man doesn't look like that if he doesn't care. He was all pale, kind of pinched around the eyes, and his jaw was clenched so tight I thought it would break. He cares. More than cares. You know?"

"You think he's in love with her?"

Vince nodded.

"Is it hard for you to say that, Vince? That he loves her?"

"No harder than anything else. Why?"

She shrugged. "You kind of danced around the words there."

"Did I?" He wasn't looking her in the eye now.

Sighing, Holly changed the subject. "Think we're safe here tonight?"

"I'm here. I'm armed. We're as safe as we can reasonably be."

"You're supposed to say we're perfectly safe. Tell me nothing's going to happen. What kind of hero are you, anyway?"

"No kind at all."

She rubbed her arms, glanced toward the door, the windows, beyond which she only saw black.

"Go to bed, Holly. Trust me, I'll be here and you'll be safe. I promise. Okay?"

Sending him a shaky excuse for a smile, she said, "That's better." And turning, she went to her room. She didn't stay though. She hit the closet for extra blankets, took a pillow off her own bed, and carried them into the living room for him. He'd already started a pot of coffee brewing, and was standing between the sofa and the television, thumbing the remote, flipping through channels.

She dropped the pile of soft fluff onto the sofa. "So you're planning to stay up all night?"

"At least."

"You don't have to do that, Vince."

He tossed the remote onto the coffee table and turned to face her. "No?"

She shook her head.

"So, suppose I fall asleep out here? What's to stop someone from sneaking past me?"

She swallowed the words that tried to leap out, then said them anyway. "Come to bed with me."

He felt as if she had zapped him with a stun gun. His face flushed, and a muscle twitched beside his mouth. His gaze slid lower over her face, her body. He licked his lips. "That's not gonna happen."

"You don't look like you mean that."

"Don't I?"

"No." She moved closer to him, and hesitantly, slipped her arms around his waist, pressed herself to him, and tipped her head back so she could see his eyes. "And I really hope you don't, because I need you tonight."

He parted his lips to speak. She hushed him with a forefinger.

"I know. You don't want me to need you. You can't be my hero or my savior and you can't be the love of my life. But I don't need those things tonight, Vince."

His eyes were dark as she lowered her finger from his lips. "Then what *do* you need?" he asked, and his voice was coarse.

"I need your arms tight around me," she said, and she closed her hands on his forearms, and lifted them, settling them around her waist. He tightened them there. "I need your hands touching me. I need your mouth . . ."

He didn't let her finish. He covered her mouth with his, before she could finish. One of his hands, big and callused, cupped the back of her head, holding her steady while he tasted her mouth with his tongue. His other hand curled over her buttocks, and pulled her tight to his groin.

He was hard, pressing into her, and she knew that this time, he wouldn't stop.

When his mouth slid from hers, to her jaw, to her neck, she tipped her head back. When his hand squeezed her ass, she arched into him, rubbing herself against the hard bulge behind his jeans. He swore under his breath, grabbed her shoulders, pushed her back, and held her away from him. His eyes were hungry when they probed hers. "I've told you I don't have anything to give, Red. This is here and now. That's all."

"I'm not asking for anything else." She reached for the bottom of his T-shirt, and lifted it, slid her hands over his belly and up to his chest, and dragged her nails over his nipples.

He closed his eyes, gritted his teeth. When they opened again, his eyes blazed. He grabbed her shirt with both hands, pulled it off over her head, and threw it on the floor. He didn't even pause before unhooking the bra, and throwing it to the side as well. His eyes raked her breasts. Then his hands covered them, and he squeezed. She shivered when his fingers drew together on her nipples, and she opened her mouth to gasp when he pinched them. He moved her backward until her legs hit the couch, then gave a push so she was sitting down. Peeling off his shirt, he dropped it, and knelt, and his hands went around her, palms flat to her back, arching her toward him so he could bend and suck her breasts. He sucked them hard, bit down with his teeth until sweet pain jolted through her, then licked the sting away with his tongue, and did it all over again. Each time he bit a little harder, and each time she liked it a little better.

His hands slid around to her jeans, undid them, and he jammed one hand down the front of them and inside her panties. He didn't take his time. Didn't ease her into this, just spread her folds and touched her. Rubbed her. Fingers pushed up inside her without waiting for an invitation. He lifted her a little, his fingers still in her, and held her around the waist with a free hand, and she stood there, barely balanced with her legs wide and her knees bent. "Shove the jeans off," he rasped.

She did, and he held her up until she managed to shuck free of them, panties and all, then he let her fall to the sofa again. He drew his fingers out of her and pushed her legs wider, one up on the sofa, the other stretched out to the floor, and he knelt low, and bent and pushed his face between her legs. He licked deep, and her body shivered with rapture. He lapped at her clitoris, and sucked it, and she thought her body would shake itself apart. When she started to melt into his mouth, he drew his head away, and she almost cried. But then he was on her again, his cock was pressing into her, stretching her wider, pushing inexorably deeper until she didn't think she could take any more, and then still more. She pulled her hips back. His hands closed on the cheeks of her ass, and he held her to him and pushed himself into her. Then he stayed there, waiting. He bent his head and tormented her breasts, and when his tongue and teeth did their work, she began to move. Slowly, she slid her wet body up and down the length of him. Her hands hooked under his arms, nails digging into his back, and she moved faster, harder. And then she was linking her legs around him, pulling him even deeper as her hips rocked.

She saw his face, watched the waves of pleasure wash over him as he began moving, too, thrusting in hard, fast, deeper, until he pushed her to the edge. She came, and she heard herself scream his name as she did. And then he drove into her once more, and went stiff as he held her and poured himself into her.

Slowly, her warm muscles uncoiled, then relaxed, then seemed to purr in her body. Vince lifted himself off her, kissed her mouth, and gathered her gently into his arms.

"Where are we going?" she asked as he got to his feet.

"To bed," he told her. "How do you feel?"

She opened sleepy eyes and smiled up at him. "Mmm."

He looked at her, his eyes softer than she'd ever seen

them as he lowered her onto her own bed, and reached for the covers.

She reached out and grabbed him, tugged him in with her. "Don't go. Stay here. All night, right here."

"I'll sleep if I stay in here," he said, his tone tender.

She pushed him onto his back, slid her body on top of his, and kissed his neck. "Not for a while, you won't."

HE SANK INTO A SLUMBER AS CONTENTED as that of a well-fed baby when he'd finally managed to satisfy the redhead's appetite hours later. He hadn't intended to. Hadn't expected himself to be able to sleep even if he'd wanted to, given that he'd just experienced the most incredible night of sex he'd ever had, with a woman he'd been determined not to get involved with.

He'd expected to lie awake contemplating that for a while.

But he slept. And he didn't stir until the insistent pounding on the front door woke him up. Sunlight tried to perform laser surgery on his eyes when he opened them, so he slammed them closed again. Damn.

"Someone's here," Holly muttered, lifting her head the smallest bit from his chest in order to say so.

"I hear him."

Her head came up higher, eyes just a little wider. "You think it's bad guys?"

"Bad guys don't knock."

She smiled, and dropped her head to his chest again. It was a dopey, crooked, half-asleep smile. The kind a woman who'd just had incredible sex would smile in the morning.

He managed to get up onto one elbow, and she rolled onto her back and squinted up at him. Her hair was sticking up all over, and her eyes were scrunched into tiny slits. "Good morning," she said.

"Morning, Red." Against his better judgment, he kissed her. That easy, that automatic.

When he drew back she said, "I even like your morning breath."

He rolled his eyes, wrapped himself in a blanket, then ran into the living room, picking up clothes as he went. He brought them all back into the bedroom again to put them on.

Holly was pulling on a knee-length plaid flannel night-shirt, and jamming her feet into well-worn slippers.

"It's probably Jerry," he said. "I E-mailed him before we left the cabin that we'd be here."

"Mmm-hmm," she replied.

Vince tucked his shirt in and headed back to the living room. Jerry stood on the other side of Holly's front door. He was cupping a hand beside his face, leaning forward, trying to peer through the glass between the tiny slit in the curtains. When he saw Vince, he smiled. Vince yanked the door open. "Do you have any idea what time it is?"

Jerry glanced at his watch. "Seven thirty-five. Why? You have a date?"

As he said it, an odd sound, half yawn, half something else announced Holly's emergence from the bedroom. Looking past Vince, Jerry said, "Or maybe you already had one."

"Watch it, partner."

"So, who's the girl with the feather duster on her head?" Jerry asked. But he sent Holly a warm smile as he said it. "My guess would be, oh, lemme think . . . Holly?"

"Come on, get your ass in here." Vince swung the door shut, and led Jerry toward the kitchen, which was the direction in which Holly was shuffling. "Holly Newman, Jerry, my partner."

Holly nodded to Jerry and zombie-walked the rest of the way into the kitchen. "Coffee," she moaned.

Jerry frowned at Vince. "Is she asking if we want some, or summoning it to appear?"

"A little of both, I imagine. Just tell her yes, you'll have some."

"Yes," Jerry said. "I'll have some."

Her reply was a grunt, but she grunted while running water into the carafe, so that was probably a good sign. Vince pulled out a chair at the table. Jerry sat down, setting a huge box of doughnuts in the center, opening the lid. From across the room, Holly lifted her head and turned slowly like a wolf catching a scent of blood. Her gaze fell on the doughnuts. One eyebrow rose. Vince felt something warm and liquid in his belly, and told himself it was just because he could smell that coffee brewing. A trigger response.

Right. He was usually a much better liar.

"So, is the chief ready to fire my ass yet?" Vince asked, helping himself to a doughnut.

"He was pissed at first. Then I told him what you said on the phone, about the break-in and the boating accident. I think he gets it. Oh, he's still griping, but I really think he gets it."

"It would be nice if someone did. The Feds sure as hell don't."

"They will, when we dig up something more solid, and then they'll be eating crow. Besides, the two of us are more cop than any twenty Feds."

"Three of us," Holly corrected. She sat down at the table, hitting the chair heavily, and she plunked her empty mug down in front of her. Then she turned the doughnut box toward her and began perusing its contents, taking her time. "I'm working on this case, too," she finished.

Jerry tilted his head. "So, are you Cagney or Lacy?"

She hauled a doughnut out of the box. She'd managed to locate the only one with both frosting and filling. "I haven't decided."

Jerry studied her. "Look more like one of Charlie's Angels, to me."

She lifted her eyes to meet his, and her lips curled just a little at the corners. "Thank you," she said around a mouthful of doughnut.

"It's just a guess," he said. "Hard to tell for sure at the moment, but I figure you probably clean up nice."

She shrugged.

"Nice enough to knock your socks off, partner," Vince muttered. Then he damn near kicked himself for saying what he was thinking aloud. What the hell was wrong with him?

Jerry and Holly both looked at him in surprise. Holly smiled, lowering her eyes again. Jerry lifted his brows and whistled softly, his gaze shifting from one of them to the other for long enough to make Vince uncomfortable. He sent Jerry a look, and his partner read it, nodded, moved on.

"So, what's the plan?" Jerry asked.

"For today, you mean?" Vince thought for a moment. "Today, we get ourselves some Halloween costumes."

Jerry frowned at him as if he thought his partner had lost his mind. "Halloween costumes? Why?"

"Because," Vince said. "Tonight's the big party."

Jerry frowned, looking honestly puzzled. Shrugging, he said, "Oh, well, all right then; if it's the big party." He reached for a doughnut. "That coffee done yet?"

"Almost." Vince got up, then paused when Holly picked up her cup and tapped it on the table. Fighting a smile, he reached over and took it from her, brought it with him to the pot to fill it up.

He loved her in the morning. Scratch that. He found her cute as hell in the morning. Even endearing, maybe. But that was all.

Then, as he handed her the cup, Holly's eyes met his and her face grew suddenly serious. She said, "I didn't do it in order."

He stared back at her. Jerry said, "What's that?"

"I didn't do it in order," Holly said softly. "I go the bathroom, shower, brush my teeth, get dressed, make my bed, and then come out here for coffee." She smiled up at Vince. "I didn't even notice."

It was, he realized, a major step for her. She probably hadn't started a day without thinking about her routine in years.

"That's good, Red. That's real good."

Deep down, he was worried to death. Why now? Would she try to credit his presence with her progress, and want more than he could give?

SIXTEEN

I F Reginald D'Voe's Gothic mansion had been eerie before, it had graduated to movie-quality horror. The front
lawn had been converted into a graveyard, with giant
tombstones of aging, chipped granite. They looked so real
that Vince put his hand on one as they walked past, just
to be sure. Polystyrene. The ground had vanished. It swam
beneath layers of ghostly mist, generated, no doubt, by
a professional-quality fog machine. The sour chords of a
pipe organ played backup to the heartbroken wail of a
pack of wolves. Every window of the house was occupied
by a glowing jack-o'-lantern, each one wearing a different
gruesome expression. It was damned creepy, to be frank.

Vince walked through the open iron gates, along the
path, barely able to see his feet. He wondered vaguely if
any of the props had been in place the last time he'd been
here. Then again, he hadn't exactly been in good enough
shape to notice. His ribs were still a little tender.

Holly walked beside him, Jerry bringing up the rear.
She still hadn't said much. Nothing in fact, about what
had happened between them the night before, and while

he thought that was what he wanted, it was driving him to distraction.

"You still all right with things?" he asked her softly, leaning a little closer, keeping his voice low.

She glanced up at him, eyes dark and unreadable. "I'm not all right with much of anything right now. There's a killer on the loose, my mother's in the hospital, my old methods of dealing aren't working anymore. No. I'm kind of far from all right. But I'm hanging in there."

He nodded. He thought about correcting her, telling her he meant to ask if she was still all right with what had happened between them last night, until he thought about how lame that sounded, given the dire situation they were facing. Later. There would be time later.

As costumes went, theirs were sadly lacking. Holly had thrown on a red wool cloak with a hood, and added a basket as a prop. Vince wore a cape in houndstooth checks, and the Sherlock Holmes trademark deerstalker hat his partner had found for him when they'd gone out costume shopping this morning. In a small town, on Halloween day, Vince figured they were lucky to have scored anything at all. Jerry had tried to get him to add a curving, trumpet-bowled pipe to the ensemble, but Vince had pushed his limits already. All Jerry had managed to come up with for himself were a bowler hat and a bow tie. Dr. Watson would be mortified.

As they walked, the music grew louder, and Vince swore that the bat that swooped down making him duck reflexively was real. They hit the first step. An owl hooted three times, and then the heavy hardwood door slowly groaned open. Morticia Addams stepped into the doorway, but when she smiled, he saw Amanda D'Voe underneath the raven wig and heavy makeup. "Good evening," she intoned. "Velcome." Stepping back, she swept her arm inward, black fabric trailing.

"You look great, Amanda," Holly said. But Vince noticed she was looking at him more often than Amanda. Maybe looking at him looking at Amanda, he thought.

As soon as they stepped inside, the atmosphere was different. Little goblins in every shape, size, and model were laughing and shrieking in turn. One group wore plastic ponchos over their costumes, bobbing for apples in the room's center. Another bunch gathered around a large table carving pumpkins with safety knives, under parental supervision. More were seated at a table near a Gypsy fortune teller who read their palms. The Gypsy bore a striking resemblance to the crabby town librarian, Maddie Baker.

One little witch raced up to Holly and bounded up and down with glee. "Everybody loves my costume, Holly! It's fantastic!"

"Well, stand back so I can see!" Smiling, Holly held the little girl by her shoulders, and examined her. She was dressed as the Wicked Witch of the West, complete with green face, long nose, striped socks, and singed broomstick. Her conical black hat sported a thin dusting of green glitter, and had a tiny furry spider dangling from its brim by a length of silver thread.

"You're gorgeous."

Bethany giggled. "Am not!" Then she raced off to join a group of friends. A woman cleared her throat, drawing Vince's gaze. He recognized the woman as Bethany's mother, Val Stevens, even though she wore braids and gingham. Dorothy, he presumed.

"Thank you so much for helping Bethany with the costume, Holly. I wouldn't have been able to do half the job you did."

"You did a fantastic job on the makeup, Val," Holly said. "And you look great, too!"

"Oh, this." She glanced down at herself. "Bethany insisted. If she'd had her way we'd have bought a puppy to play Toto, too." Lifting her gaze again, her expression grew more serious. "I heard your mother was taken to the hospital. How is she doing?"

Holly sighed. "She's sedated, resting."

"What happened? God, she seemed fine the last time I saw her."

Holly searched for a plausible answer. "Stress, really. An irregular heartbeat. They're doing tests."

Val sighed long and low. "I'm so sorry. She's strong, you know. I mean, to have come through what she has—she must be stronger than I can even imagine. God, to survive losing a child . . ." Her gaze strayed to where Bethany was dancing with friends to *The Monster Mash*, and Val bit her lower lip. "I think it would kill me if I lost Bethany."

"You never know what you can survive until it happens," Holly said softly.

"Oh, I know, I know. All I meant was, if your mom came through all of that, she's going to handle whatever this new problem is just fine."

Her eyes asked for more details. Holly just gave the woman's hand a squeeze and said, "Thank you for that, Val. I know you're right." Then she took Vince's hand, clutching it tightly, and led him toward the refreshment table.

He gave her hand an automatic squeeze and she sent him a grateful look.

The neon-green punch had blocks of ice the size and shape of human hands floating in it. Vince dipped her out a glass, handed it to her. Jerry helped himself. "So, is there anyone in particular we should be watching, Vince?"

Vince shrugged, looking around. "Where's Reggie?"

"Oh, he'll make his big entrance soon. He likes to wait for all the kids to arrive, give them some time to enjoy the party for a while first. Or at least that's the way Aunt Jen told me it always used to work." Holly glanced at her watch. "Any time now, if he's true to history."

Vince nodded, looking around at the costume-clad adults, trying to get a solid grip on who was who in case he needed to know later. Doc Graycloud was in character. He wore a huge coyote's head like a hood, its yellow teeth bared in a perpetual smile, black marble eyes shining, gray-brown fur hanging down and forming a cape that ended in a long, thick tail. Vince stared for a long moment, trying to decide if it was a manufactured pelt, or a real one, and then decided he didn't really want to know. Holly's uncle Marty was easy to spot. He came as a lumberjack, flannel shirt and suspenders, a rubber axe in one hand. He'd darkened his cheeks and chin to depict whiskers, and wore a knit cap on his head. Vince recognized others in the crowd as well, over the next half hour. The teenaged waitresses from the café. The kid who manned the gas pumps in town.

"Vince, Holly—how's it going?"

They both turned to see Chief Mallory standing close to them, a plastic tumbler of punch in his hand. He was eyeing Jerry curiously. "Who's this?"

"My partner, Jerry Donovan. Jerry, this is Dilmun's chief of police, Jim Mallory."

Jerry nodded hello, shook Jim's hand.

"Where's your costume, Chief?" Vince asked.

The man shrugged. "I came as a police chief." He glanced at Holly. "How you holding up, hon?"

"I'm okay, but who's with Mom?"

"Your aunt Jen is there. Bill, too. He relieved Ray of guard duty. Ray went home, got a few hours sleep, and now he's here, outside, keeping an eye out for anything suspicious. I thought it would be best we both attend this shindig, see if anything comes up. No sense taking chances in case this maniac really is in town, with all the kids here, I mean."

Holly nodded, but Vince felt the shiver that went through her.

"What happened to the Feds you were expecting?" the chief asked Vince.

"They think I'm full of hot air. I need solid evidence to get them down here."

"Hell, I hope to God we never get any."

He stopped speaking as the lights flashed on and off twice, and then remained off. Thunder rumbled like a drum roll, and a tiny explosion blasted off at the top of the old curving staircase. Smoke rolled, and when it cleared, Reginald D'Voe stood there, his Dracula costume perfectly backlit, one side of the cape drawn over the lower half of his face. He lowered it slowly as he came down the stairs. If not for his noticeable limp, it would have been perfect.

He spoke in a thick Transylvanian accent to the rapt audience. "Children of the night. Velcome to my humble abode! Now, if you have the courage to follow me, I vill lead you on a journey among the living and the dead, where surprises and perhaps a few treasures can be found!" He added his maniacal laughter, and then led them all to the front door, out it, and down the steps.

"Where's he taking them?" Vince asked, a prickle of unease dancing up the back of his neck as he stepped out into the night's chill.

"It's a parade around the yard," Amanda said, startling him by speaking from nearby. "There's junk jewelry and candy hidden in various spots, along with some theatrical scares. Watch." She pointed.

Vince watched, as did the parents who were all crowded onto and around the front steps. At every tomb-stone, some creature would spring up, or a pre-recorded growl or shriek would sound. Every kid screeched in hor-ror and delight at each and every stop along the way. The parade took them outside the house and all the way around the mock cemetery that filled the front lawn.

Vince relaxed a little as he watched. Even when they got to the farthest reaches, where it was darker and more difficult to see the children, he didn't get nervous. That wrought-iron fence surrounded the whole lawn. And the chief's cop, Ray, was out by the gate, keeping track of anyone coming or going.

A hand emerged from the earth at one tombstone. A ghostly apparition floated from another. Skeletons leaped up and danced at one more. The children squealed, but left each site with brand-new goodies for their bags.

The parade took the better part of an hour. By the time they all marched back to the house, every child had a bag full of treats, and most of the parents were wiped out, and had taken refuge in the living room, near the fireplace to await their return.

"Now what?" Vince asked as the little demons and goblins were herded back into the house.

"Now, my children," Amanda intoned, almost as if in answer to his question. "Come, come, gather near. It's time for the Count to tell you a delightfully scary Halloween ghost story. And when it's done, the party must end. And you know what happens then?"

"Trick-or-treating!" the children shouted.

Vince had to give his head a shake, and made a mental note to have his hearing checked when he got his next physical. Holly, beside him, laughed softly. "Reggie throws a hell of a party."

"Come, little ones, gather round," Reggie said in his heavily accented, scary voice. He was in an ancient rocking chair now, sitting near the fireplace in his living room.

"Man, I gotta bring my kids out here for this next year," Jerry said. "They'd love this stuff."

"You ought to be with them tonight," Vince said. "Instead of out here holding my hand."

"Kate's got it covered." Jerry looked at Vince. "She knows we're trying to make it safer for all the little demons, partner. She understands."

Vince nodded. He took a seat in the back of the room where all the other adults had been relocated. He listened only halfheartedly as the old man spun his horrific tale to the wide-eyed kids who were seated around him on the floor, staring up at him adoringly. He didn't make it too scary, Vince noted. And he watched Reggie watching the youngest kids in the group closely, making sure they didn't get too frightened.

Hard to believe he was a monster.

Chief Mallory came and stood in front of the adults in the back, motioned with his hands for them to follow him, and quietly led them all to the foyer, off the other end of the large living room.

"What's this about, Chief?" one man asked.

The chief drew a breath, glanced at Vince. Vince gave him a nod of encouragement, and he returned it. "All right, listen, I don't want to alarm anyone, here, but I have information you people have a right to know about." He paused, drew a breath. "We have reason to believe there could be a child predator in the area."

The gasp that went up, the chill that went through them all, was universal. Vince felt it move through the parents in the room.

"I don't want anyone to panic. We don't know for sure, but I figured it was better to let you know now, than to risk not telling you and having something happen to one of the kids."

"Something like what, Chief?"

He glanced at the questioner, but didn't answer. "As I said, we're probably wrong. This is a very slight possibility. But it is Halloween, and I think it will be best for all of you to be alert tonight. Don't let your kids go out trick-or-treating alone. Not even with a group of other kids. Every parent needs to be out there. Keep them close, keep a good eye on them, and get them home early."

Many voiced questions, but no one got loud, and Vince could see them gazing worriedly at their kids. He saw Holly, looking toward that glittery witch hat that poked up from the center of the group of kids and he knew she was worried, too. The chief just held up his hands until it got quiet again. "That's all I can tell you, because that's all I know. Keep a close watch, stay with 'em. That's all. Now I have to go." Turning, he headed out. Vince took Holly's arm. "Time to go."

She shook her head. "I want to see Bethany before we go," she said. Vince turned with her as the kids came in hordes from the living room, and he watched the big pointy hat with the green glitter make its way through the crowd.

Finally, the child made her way through. But the girl wearing Bethany Stevens's hat was not Bethany Stevens.

Bethany's mother stared at the child. Panic slowly made its way into her face as her gaze bounced from child to child, to every corner of the room. She knew. Vince read it in her face, and believed it. There was some kind of alarm built into mothers where their kids were concerned. He'd seen it in action. They knew things before there was a clear reason to know them. He saw that moment happen in Val Stevens's eyes.

"Oh, shit, no," he muttered.

That was just about the time Bethany's mother started screaming.

"HOLLY? HOLLY? DID THEY CATCH HIM yet?" Doris asked of the woman who sat beside her hospital bed.

Jen Cantrell leaned closer, stroking Doris's forehead, smoothing her hair. "It's all right, hon. It's okay, it's me, it's Jen. I'm right here."

Doris opened her eyes, blinking them slowly. She squinted as if it were hard to see, then tried to sit up. "Jenny?"

"Yes, sis, I'm right here."

"Poor Ivy," Doris moaned. "She's not at peace. She can't be at peace."

Jenny Cantrell closed her eyes tight at that old, familiar shaft of pain. Poor Doris. "Honey, listen to me. It's been years since we lost Ivy. And she is at peace. She's in heaven, she's fine. You know that, right? You're here, in Dilmun. Holly will be here soon to say good night."

"No. No, Jenny, you don't understand."

Jen managed to get her to lie back. She poured water from a pitcher, and held it to her sister's lips, got her to drink a little, and tried to keep her own voice soothing and level. "You're very agitated. I'll call the nurse. . . ."

"Did Holly tell you what she and Vince found out? Did she?"

"No, sweetie. But you just rest now. I'll just get the nurse and then—"

Doris's hand grabbed hers as she turned to go. "That evil man lied. He's not the killer. He's not. The man who took my Ivy is still running free." She shook her head back and forth, back and forth. "How can I live, how can I bear it?"

Jen went still. She didn't turn, didn't look, just stood there, going cold all over. "Hubey Welles confessed, Doris. Honey, don't you remember?"

"He was going to get the death penalty. By confessing to other crimes, he got life instead. That's why he said he did it."

Jen swallowed the bile that rose in her throat. "Doris, honey, how do you know all of this?"

"Vince and Holly spoke to him. They went to see him in prison. Holly remembered about the eyes being different, and Vince figured it out."

Turning slowly, Jen examined her younger sister's face, searching it for signs of dementia or delusion. Surely this couldn't be true. "Are you saying the man who killed Ivy is still running around free somewhere?"

"I'll find him. I swear, Jenny, I'll kill him myself. All this time, I thought . . . and he was—how can I bear it?"

Jen's heart seemed to turn to liquid in her chest. "Oh, Doris. Oh, sweetie, no. I'm sorry. I'm sorry." She sank onto the edge of the bed, stroking her sister's hair. It reminded her of when they were girls together. Doris would come home all upset over some trivial thing, and cry. God, she'd always been so sensitive. It was always Jen who would hold her, comfort her, just the way she was doing now.

Jen held her tight, whispering and trying to comfort while depressing the call button with a free hand. Images of her sweet, angelic niece played through her mind, and tears choked her, as her own deepest fears came back to haunt her, just as surely as her sister's had.

⸻

IT WAS AS IF THE WORLD SLOWED DOWN. Holly watched through a thick, distorted glass, heard as if listening from the farthest end of a tunnel. Panic. Mothers, gripping their children so hard their nails dug into the vinyl shoulders of their store-bought costumes. Val Stevens was running from room to room, shouting for Bethany over and over again. The chief hadn't gone six steps from the house when he heard the commotion and came tearing back. He, Jerry, and Vince spoke rapidly to one another before springing into action. The chief yanked the radio from his belt and spoke to Ray out by the gate. Jerry grabbed a phone and punched numbers. Vince started organizing men to search.

Reginald was white as a sheet, and trying to catch up with Val, to calm her. Everyone was in motion. Everyone was moving, shouting, talking, searching, doing something.

Everyone except for Holly. And one other person.

Amanda.

She sat stone still near the fireplace in the rocking chair her uncle had occupied moments before, her expression blank, eyes vacant. She looked the way Holly felt. Stunned. Shocked. Paralyzed. And for just one moment their eyes met, and Holly knew they were experiencing this in very similar ways.

"Snap out of it, Red." Vince's voice was firm, his hands tight on her forearms. "There's no time for this. Come on, focus. I need your help here. I need you pissed. Up and fighting, like you've been doing up to now. Don't quit on me."

She blinked, and made herself look at him. Her knees felt like water. She hadn't realized it before, but now she felt the shaking, the tightness in her chest as her breaths

came faster, and her heart began to batter her rib cage.
She hadn't felt the panic attack creeping up on her yet.
Vince had spotted it before she had.

"No," he commanded. "Don't you do this, Holly. Not
now. There's no time for it now." His arm clamped
around her waist like a vise, he propelled her to the punch
bowl, scooped up a half melted finger from one of the ice
hands, and laid it against the nape of her neck.

She sucked in a breath at the coldness on her skin, but
then steadied herself, let the ice do its work. It was effec-
tive. She covered his hand with her own to keep the ice
there, lifted her head and looked Vince squarely in the
eye. "Bethany?"

"Missing. We've got all the exits covered, and the chief
is leading a room-by-room search. We've got reinforce-
ments on the way."

"State police?"

He nodded, taking her back toward the fireplace, setting
her down. She looked at Amanda, knowing the woman
was still lost in fear, the way Holly had been only moments ago. Holly took her hand, squeezed it hard. "Fight
it, Amanda. If I can do it, so can you." Taking the melting
ice finger from her own neck, Holly laid it across the back
of Amanda's. The blue eyes fluttered, met hers briefly.

Vince gave a shrill whistle. Silence fell. "I want all
parents and children here by the fireplace, now."

The lights were up now, as parents and children gathered hesitantly, their eyes wide and frightened and wet
and suspicious when they fell on each other.

"We need to try to piece together what happened,"
Vince said.

"Piece together, my ass! We should be searching for
Bethany!"

"I just want to take my children home, where they're
safe!"

Vince held up his hands for silence, but, just when it
quieted down, Val Stevens's shrieking made its way from
somewhere above as she raced through the house in

search of her daughter. If Reggie had caught up to her at all, she had apparently shaken him again.

Holly gripped Vince's arm. "Go. Take care of Val, and then help with the search. I can handle this part."

"Are you sure?"

She held his gaze, clenched her jaw, nodded. "You don't want anyone to leave just yet, you need a headcount to make sure no one else is missing, you need to try to get an account from those who last saw Bethany, and you're probably going to want a list of who is here. It's not like I haven't been through the drill. I've got it. Go."

The woman screamed again, and Vince went. He paused only once on the way, to pull Doc Graycloud from the group gathered there, then the two headed up the stairs after Val Stevens.

Holly looked at the people who stood around her, drew a breath, and cleared her throat. "The state police are on their way. Rest assured they'll block off every road out of town, and begin a search immediately. I know the procedure by heart."

"How?" someone asked.

She tilted her head. "I've lived through it." She lowered her head briefly, to swallow down the lump that rose in her throat, then raised it again. "And I work for the police department. In fact, I was one of the people who helped Jim and the boys develop Dilmun's contingincy plan for missing children, and it is now in full effect. Now the thing is, we can't let anyone leave just yet. You all need to stay put until we get this organized. Anything different means we risk Bethany slipping through the cracks. You understand?"

Several heads nodded. A few people sat down, resigned, it seemed.

"Good." Holly glanced down at Amanda. She was rocking slightly back and forth in her chair. She didn't look good. If she was going to get a guest list, she'd have to get it from Reggie.

"Everyone look around you, see if you can think of

anyone who was here earlier who isn't here now. If you
do, come up to me and tell me privately. Meanwhile, just
make sure you still have sight of those you came with, sit
here, and wait. Suzy Cooper, where are you hon?" Holly
asked.

The little girl who'd been wearing Bethany's hat raised
her hand. Her face was tear-streaked and red. She clung
closer to her mother, and held Bethany's hat in one hand.

Holly moved closer, knelt down, and saw herself in the
little girl's eyes. In her face. In her horror and guilt and
fear. Gently, Holly brushed wet tendrils off the child's
cheeks. "Suzy, you didn't do anything wrong, okay? You
need to know that. No one's mad at you, and you didn't
do one thing wrong. You understand?"

Sniffling, the child nodded.

"In fact, you might be able to help us find Bethany
more than anyone else can. Do you want to try that?"

Suzy nodded again.

"You're such a good girl. And so brave. Now, can you
remember when you ended up wearing Bethany's hat?"

Suzy's lower lip trembled. "She g-gave it to me. Mine
fell off and I couldn't find it, and I started to cry, so
Bethany gave me her hat to wear."

"That's good, very good. Now do you remember where
you were when that happened?"

Again, the jerky little nod. One black curl fell, and
stuck to her cheek, glued there by tears. "We were outside. It was when Mr. D'Voe led us around the front
yard."

Amanda's head lifted slowly. "She never made it back
inside," she whispered.

Holly looked through the faces in the crowd, spotted
her uncle, sighed in relief. "Uncle Marty, I need you to
keep everyone here. Don't let anyone leave. I'll be right
back."

"You got it, hon." He came to the front of the room
and took a spot beside Amanda, patting her shoulder gently as Holly raced up the stairs. She found Vince and Dr.

Graycloud in the first bedroom at the top. Val Stevens lay in a large bed. Her eyes were closed, but moved rapidly beneath the thin lids. Her chest rose and fell in staccato breaths. An empty hypodermic needle lay on the bedside stand.

"Vince, I think Bethany was taken during the parade around the lawn. It doesn't look like she ever made it back into the house."

Lights flashed through the outer windows as the state police converged on the house. Behind Holly, Chief Mallory and Reggie entered the room.

"We've searched the entire house, including the attic and the cellars. There's no sign of her," Reggie said. His voice shook, and he looked as if he'd aged ten years in the past few moments.

"It looks as if she was snatched during the parade, outside," Vince said.

The chief swore. Reginald lifted his head. "That's impossible. I was the only adult near the children during the parade. I alone, led them around the yard . . ." He let his voice trail off then, and his eyes met Vince's.

Holly glanced from Vince to Reggie and back again, and a chill settled deeper into her bones.

SEVENTEEN

⊰⊱⊰⊱

THE state police sent teams out to search the area around the house. There were a lot of woods. *A lot* of woods. And there was the lake. Spotlights were set up, teams combed the woods, calling for Bethany. More went out on the lake in boats, shining lights on the water.

Police officers interviewed the guests, gave them clearance to leave. A pair of cops searched each vehicle before its owners were allowed to take it off the premises.

The chief had led Reggie outside. Amanda walked outside behind them like a zombie, and Vince tapped his partner, and pointed. Jerry looked, gave a nod, and went to help Amanda. Good. Less for Holly to do. She let Vince lead her to the Jeep, and rode in silence to the Dilmun Police Department.

But when she was finally left alone, on one of the small sofas in the reception area, she felt herself sliding into the distant past.

She was small, and shivering, and utterly alone, sitting on an oversized chair that all but swallowed her up, her feet dangling inches above the hard gray carpet. She didn't know if her mother was going to live through the night, because she'd never seen her mother look the way she had seen her look then. She felt sick to her stomach, and thought she might have to run for the rest room at any second. It was all her fault. It was all her fault. Her sister was gone and it was all her fault.

But they would find her soon, and everything would be okay again. They would find her by morning. Surely by morning, and it would be okay.

There was something dark and deep inside her, though, that told her that was a lie. It wouldn't be okay. It would never be okay again.

A hand closed on Holly's arm. She looked up, into Vince's face. His eyes were shadowed with concern.

"You were right about me from the start, you know," she told him.

"No, I wasn't."

She shook her head too fast, too jerky. "I need Dr. Graycloud. I need something." She glanced down at her hands, gripping the arms of the chair, white knuckled, shaking.

"What, a tranquilizer? You threw them away, Holly. You're stronger now. You don't need them." He followed her gaze to her hands, put his over them. "Look, I'll have someone get you some tea, huh? Chamomile is supposed to be calming—"

"Chamomile?" To her own ears her voice sounded brittle. But she couldn't help that. "Jesus Christ, Vince, my worst nightmare just rose up from the dead to smack me in the face. Chamomile isn't gonna cut it. I'm not sure fucking Thorazine would cut it, but I'm willing to give it a shot."

His hands closed on her arms, and he hauled her to her feet so fast her head snapped backward. His hands on her arms were hard. His face, harder. "Don't you bail on me now, goddamn it."

"Why the hell not? You knew I would. You wouldn't let yourself feel anything for me because you knew I would. Remember? You couldn't handle getting involved with a fucked-up female. A headcase like me who might need you too much. Remember, Vince? Turns out your instincts were right. You ought to be celebrating."

"I would be. If I'd listened to them." He let her go.

She sank onto the sofa, landing heavily. "What the hell is that supposed to mean?"

"You figure it out. You clear the cobwebs out of your head, stand up like you ought to, stop acting like a victim, and figure it out." He retrieved the empty cup he'd dropped on the sofa beside her, moved past her to the coffee pot and filled it. Then he turned and headed back through the reception area toward the cell in the back where he'd left the chief with Reggie D'Voe. At the doorway, though, he stopped and looked back at her. "Stop focusing on yourself Holly. Think about Val Stevens. Think about Bethany, for Christ's sake. There are other people here in far worse shape than you are right now. Take a look around."

She watched him go. Then she glanced at the waiting room around her. She had thought herself alone. She wasn't. Might as well have been, though. Amanda sat sideways in a chair in the corner, knees curled up, arms wrapped around them. Her eyes were vacant. As if she hadn't heard a damned thing.

Beyond the doorway, Vince, Jerry, and the chief were questioning Reggie. Holly leaned forward a little, and she could see them at the far end of the hall in the cell there. The cell door was open. Inside it, on a hard chair, Reggie was pale and trembling.

The sound of Ivy's screams had been echoing in Holly's ears more loudly than they ever had for over an hour. But now empathy for what Amanda and her uncle were going through crept into its place. The screams faded into the past where they belonged. Holly got to her feet, and her knees gave. She caught herself on the arm of the sofa, pushed herself up again, snapped her knees straight. With one hand, she swiped the tears from her cheeks. It stung when she wiped her eyes. She'd cried so much they were raw. "Okay," she whispered. "Okay, I have to try." Her feet wanted to scuff the floor when she walked. They felt so heavy. She forced her legs to move, to propel her forward. Into the back, into the storage closet. She took out blankets, two of them. She carried one to the cell. The door was open. She shook the folds out of the blanket, and draped it over Reggie's shoulders the way she had seen his devoted niece do so often.

He glanced up at her once. Gratitude flickered briefly from behind the mask of horror he wore. She didn't look at Vince. She didn't want to see him and be reminded how badly she had probably blown things with him by falling apart the way she had. Turning, she made her way back to the reception room. She tucked the second blanket around Amanda.

"Can I get you anything?"

Amanda kept rocking, but she did pull the blanket close around her, burrowing into it as if for protection. It occurred to Holly that she might be the one in need of some magic pills right now.

"Amanda?" Holly shook her gently.

Amanda's distracted gaze flickered, darted toward Holly. "We have to find that little girl," she said softly, urgently. "We have to. We have to."

"I know, Amanda. We will." Holly lowered her gaze. "Dr. Graycloud will be coming by soon. He took Val Stevens to the hospital. But he'll be here once he gets her settled in."

Amanda shook her head slowly. "He can't help."

"No? Then, who can? I mean, if you want to talk through it . . ."

She closed her eyes. Nodded hard. "Yes."

Holly felt stronger when she looked at the woman in the chair, how fragile and on the edge she seemed. More so than Holly had been. Maybe Vince was right. Maybe she could at least *pretend* to be the strong one here— because there was no one else to do it. And someone had to. There were only the two of them out here, and Amanda

clearly needed help. Lifting her hands, Holly gently took
the black wig off Amanda's head, removed the clips that
held her hair up, and stroked the light brown locks away
from tear-stained cheeks. She felt eyes on her, and
glanced through the doorway, down the hall. Vince's gaze
met hers, probing, searching for something she couldn't
hope to name. Then he focused on Reggie again.

<hr />

"PLEASE, I'VE TOLD YOU EVERYTHING I
can," Reginald said. It was amazing to Vince that the man
kept calm, dignified, even when he must be going crazy
inside. Guilty or not, this was traumatic. "Just tell me the
other children all got home safely. I need to know."

Sighing, the chief nodded. "The guests were questioned
one by one, their names and addresses taken down. The
cars of those few who came by car, were searched, plate
numbers noted, and then each family was given a police
escort back to their respective homes."

Reggie protested, "I can't believe the police suspect
anyone who was at my party may have been involved in
something this—this—"

"Someone at the party snatched a little girl," Vince interrupted. "There's just no way around that. It's happened.
She's gone."

Reggie closed his eyes.

"A couple of cops went out onto the lawn with flashlights," the chief said. "They walked that path you led the
kids around, during the parade."

Reggie's head came up, eyes hopeful. "And . . . ?"

"And they found Suzy Cooper's witch hat. It was near
the farthest end of the parade path from the house, where
all the parents were waiting. Bethany vanished between
that spot and the house, on the return trip, after she'd
given her own hat to Suzy."

"No. No, that's impossible. The lawn is completely
fenced in."

"Not quite, Reg." Vince sighed, glanced at the chief, and the chief nodded at him to go on. "We found a break in the fence near that farthest point. A recent one. The bars had been sawed clean through, in an area hidden by some shrubbery. Someone planned this in advance. Someone who knew the route the kids would take."

Reggie waved a dismissive hand. "The parade around my lawn has been the same ever since I started the party. It's never changed. Anyone who's ever been to one would know that."

"Think, Reg," the chief said gently. "Anyone who was at one of the parties you *used to throw* would know. But you haven't thrown one in sixteen years."

Vince met the chief's eyes. They both knew that narrowed it down. It was someone local, and someone who'd been local sixteen years ago, as well.

"Are they searching for Bethany?" Reginald asked, looking Vince squarely in the eye in a way guilty parties didn't often do.

"Teams of police officers and volunteer firemen were dispatched into the woods. Boat patrols are searching the lake. The FBI has been notified, and they'll be on the scene to take over by morning."

"God, I hope they find her."

"So do I," Vince said. He spoke quietly, glancing again toward the far end of the hall, where Holly hovered over Amanda D'Voe. Vince knew full well that Holly was teetering on the edge of what she could endure. And yet, she was hanging tough. Out in the reception area of the station, even now, she was running a wet cloth over Amanda's D'Voe's face, washing away the Halloween makeup, serving her tea, telling her not to worry. Even now, when he knew damned well she was reliving her own worst nightmares. It had been close, for a while. But she hadn't given in. She'd fought it, and she'd won. For now, at least. His admiration for her strength rose with every moment that ticked by.

Vince drew his gaze back to Reginald. The former Hollywood star, the arrogant living legend was gone. All that remained was a frightened old man who was cold, pale, trembling. "Are you sure you're telling us everything? If there's anything you're holding back, Reg, now is the time to tell us. Trust us."

"Trust you? There's nothing you can do to stop this, much less to help me. If there were, that little girl wouldn't be suffering God only knows what right now while you all wring your hands and question the innocent."

"We're doing all we can do, Reggie," Chief Mallory said.

"All you can? Well, it's not enough. Can't you see it's not enough? Look at them out there! You think it ends when you drop the case? Or when you solve it, or think you have? It doesn't, you know. Just look at that young woman in the next room. It's killing her—still. After all this time, it's still killing her. You don't know, you don't know. You think you have power, here, but you don't. He does. He has all the power."

"Who does?" Vince asked.

Reggie's shoulders slumped. "If I knew that I'd kill him myself. I swear to God I would."

Jerry came in, carrying a fax that had just come through the machine in the chief's office. Mallory scanned it, paused for a long moment before handing it to Vince.

Vince read it and, frowning, lifted his gaze. "Reggie, is it true you were an only child?"

Reginald narrowed his eyes on Vince, but said nothing. Vince continued, "According to this, there's no physical way you could have a niece."

Reggie only shrugged stiffly. " 'Uncle' is more an honorary title in this case. Amanda's parents died, and left her in my care."

"Can you prove that?"

Reg straightened his spine, glaring at them. "You can't take her from me. Not now."

"She's an adult now, Reg. No one can make her do

anything she doesn't want to," Mallory said. "But we're going to have to know where she came from. I mean, if she's not a blood relative, then her name must not have been D'Voe, unless you had it legally changed."

"Maybe we should just ask Amanda," Vince suggested softly.

Reg came out of the chair as if launched, and, in the blink of an eye, he grabbed Vince by the front of his shirt, and pressed him up against the cell wall. "Don't! You mustn't bring this up with her! You can't!"

The chief swore and gripped Reggie by the shoulders. Jerry had started forward toward them, one hand on his sidearm. Vince held up a hand to still them, but before he could say anything the old man released him suddenly and staggered backward, clutching his chest as the color drained completely from his face. He hit the floor even as Vince lunged for him.

"Jesus! Call an ambulance—and get hold of Graycloud!" Vince shouted.

"He's already here. Just pulled up out front," Jerry said.

"Uncle Reggie?" Amanda came running, and in a moment she was on the floor beside the old man, bent over him, crying her heart out.

Holly tugged her gently away when Dr. Graycloud burst through the doors. She turned into Holly's arms, sobbing. "He's all I have," she moaned. "Oh, God, please don't let him die."

<hr />

BETHANY HUDDLED IN THE DARKNESS, hugging her arms as she shook. At first she'd thought it was just a game. Just a part of Mr. D'Voe's Halloween party tricks. The large arms had snapped around her from out of the darkness, and pulled her through the fence and into the woods. She screamed. But then, everyone was shrieking with every ghost or ghoul that popped up on the parade around the lawn. Who would notice one more scream? Something smelly and damp was pressed to her face. It burned. She thought there had been some kind of hole in the ground but then everything went dark. She knew it was the smelly stuff on the cloth at her face that made her go to sleep.

Until now. She woke up in darkness so complete she couldn't see a thing. She could feel only the wall at her back and the floor beneath her. Metallic, and cold. When she moved, something jangled and tugged tight. She reached down and felt cold metal clasped tight around her ankle, and a heavy chain attached. She closed her hands around that chain, yanked on it with all her might, but it didn't give. It was attached to something. If there had ever been a hole in the ground, she wasn't in it now. This area felt large. As big as a room, but not a room, somehow.

Oh, gosh. She didn't know where she was, or who had brought her here. But she knew this was bad. This was very bad. She was in serious trouble. Hot tears ran down Bethany's face. She pounded on the wall, shouted for her mother, but she had a feeling no one could hear her. Her voice bounced off the walls of the big dark room. No one answered. Nothing moved.

She sank to the floor, sobbing softly. She thought about how she had missed trick-or-treating this year. She thought about how worried her mom must be. And Daddy was out of town. Mommy would probably call him, though. He would rush home, and then he would come and find her.

She hoped he would hurry.

❧

It WASN'T A LARGE HOSPITAL. IT WAS THE size of a small Holiday Inn, only four floors, and a total of three treatment rooms in the E.R. They wheeled Reginald D'Voe through the hall, a comet's tail of onlookers trailing right behind. The gurney slid through the doors of a treatment room. Doc Graycloud passed through, as well. Then one nurse, who appeared to have drawn crowd-control duty, stepped into the doorway, effectively cutting off the comet's tail. She moved forward into the sea of bodies, closed the door firmly behind her, and crossed her arms over her chest. She was dark skinned, with a cap of gleaming curls that should have softened her harsh expression, but didn't. "Does this *look* like a circus to you?" she asked them.

Vince was the first one to pull out a badge. "I'm a police officer, and that man needs to be under guard."

She tipped her head to one side, looked at him as if he were drooling when he talked. "*That man* is having a heart attack. I assure you, he's not going anywhere."

Beyond her, through the glass in the closed door, Vince saw others: white coats, latex gloves, working over Reggie. He felt responsible and weighed like lead on his shoulders. "Is this the only way in or out?"

"Umm-hmm," she said.

"Can I post someone outside the door?"

She puckered, but finally nodded. "One man. And he'd best stand to the side if he doesn't want to get knocked flat on his fanny." Her frown grew as an orderly pushing a cart had to fight his way through all of them to get into the treatment room. "The rest of you, get your badges and your backsides to the waiting room. *Now.*" The nurse pointed. It was ten feet away, around a corner to the right, and it was small. Close enough, though. Vince nodded, and, turning, did his best to herd everyone back there. The chief, his officers, the handful of state cops who'd heard the call and come on their heels, Jerry, Holly, and Amanda . . .

Wait a minute, he'd lost Holly and Amanda.

"Vince?"

He turned at the sound of her voice, and saw Holly holding Amanda's shoulders. The blonde was bent double, trying to catch the breaths that rushed in and out of her lungs at breakneck speed. That same nurse reached the two at the same moment Vince did. She moved fast, locating a wheelchair, then easing Amanda down into it. She had her seated and breathing into a paper bag within seconds.

Holly said, "The man we just brought in is her uncle."

The nurse nodded, addressing Amanda, not Holly. "Well, no wonder you're upset, all this fuss." She gripped the wheelchair from behind, pushing it down the hall, leaning close to speak. "Let's just get you out of all this chaos for starters." She wheeled Amanda into a small room, out of the way.

Vince slid an arm around Holly's waist as they followed. He glanced down at her. "You all right?"

Her eyes were steady and clear when they met his. She nodded once. He wasn't sure he believed her. But she *looked* all right.

"What's your name, child?" the nurse asked.

Amanda didn't answer. "Amanda D'Voe," Holly answered for her, while Amanda continued inflating the paper bag over and over again.

"I'm Sally," the nurse said. "Now you rest assured, your uncle is in very good hands. And he didn't look all that bad to me when they brought him in. Hell, I've seen 'em come in way worse off than him, and walk out again in a few days."

Amanda's breathing slowed still more. She lifted her head, moved the bag away from her face. "Really?"

"Yes. Really."

"You . . . you think he's going to be all right?"

"I'll bring you out a report just as soon as we know anything, okay?"

Amanda nodded. Sally glanced up at Vince. "You keep all those cops off her case, you hear me? And you," she said, looking at Holly. "You stay with her. You two ought to be all right in here for a while. Anyone gives you any crap, you tell 'em to take it up with Sally. All right?"

Amanda nodded. Vince thanked the woman for her help and glanced at the room. It was a break room for the staff, from the looks of it. There were a sofa, a couple of chairs, a large cafeteria-type table with benches attached, a coffee pot, fridge, and some vending machines.

As Nurse Sally left, Vince glanced through the open door, down the hall to the waiting room, caught the chief's eye. Assured Mallory knew where to find him should he need to, Vince closed the door. Then he went to Amanda, knelt in front of the chair. "Are you better now?"

She met his eyes. "I will be, when they tell me Uncle Reggie is going to be all right." She licked her lips. "What happened, Detective?"

He shook his head. He couldn't bring himself to tell Amanda that her beloved uncle was looking more and more like a suspect in a string of brutal child murders. He didn't find it all that believable himself. How the hell could he suggest it to her? "I think it was my fault. I asked him about you, your past I mean, before you came to live with him, and he became extremely agitated."

Amanda lowered her head. "He's very protective of me. And he was already upset over . . ." She closed her eyes. "Poor little Bethany."

"Yes, I know." Vince got to his feet, took a seat on the edge of the bench nearest her. He thought before he spoke. He was half afraid to talk to her at all and risk bringing on another episode. But, hell, it was his job. "Maybe you can help me, Amanda. Answer the questions that your uncle didn't."

Slowly, she looked at him. "I can't."

"Why not?"

"Vince, don't," Holly urged. "Please, she's been through enough. And how relevant can something like that be, anyway?"

Vince met Holly's eyes. "I'm afraid it might be very relevant." Then, turning to Amanda, he tried to speak as gently as he could. "Now isn't the best time, Amanda, I realize that. But sooner or later, you're going to have to tell someone about your past."

She only shook her head from side to side. "It's impossible."

Vince's brows pulled tight, and he started to ask why, but a tap on the door interrupted, and he got to his feet again. When he opened the door, Chief Mallory was standing on the other side, and he jerked his head toward the waiting room. Vince looked that way, saw the new arrivals. Dark suits, stiff jaws, shined shoes. Feds. He glanced back at Holly. "You two stay here, okay? I'll be back."

Holly nodded, and he took just a second to notice how together she seemed. A far cry from the mess she'd been a few hours ago. He held her eyes for a moment. "You're doing great, you know."

"That's what you think," she told him with a ghost of a smile.

He left her there, headed back out to the waiting area.

A tall, dour-faced man with steel gray hair and eyes to match watched him all the way in. "Well, Detective Vince O'Mally," he said. "Been a long time."

"Not long enough, Selkirk. How are you?"

"I'm considering whether to let you keep you badge or have you brought up on charges of impending a federal investigation, to be blunt." He walked back out through the entrance doors. They opened automatically with a whoosh of Halloween night air so cold it was like the breath of the Reaper.

Vince followed. He could see his breath in the tall goosenecked streetlights that lined the parking lot. Beyond their reach, the night was a black abyss. Sighing, he turned toward the special agent. "So . . . ?"

"So what?"

"So if you think you have the grounds and the balls to go after my badge, be my guest."

Selkirk jammed his hands into his pockets. Hunched a little against the cold. "If you think I don't, keep on pushing, Detective."

"Right. So you wanna tell me what your problem is,

Selkirk? That I stepped on a few toes and bent a few regs, or that I got to the bottom of this case before you did?"

"I don't give a rat's ass who solves this case, so long as it gets solved."

"No?" Vince blew a sigh. "Then why are you breathing fire at me, Selkirk? I followed a hunch and came down here on my own time. The hunch panned out and we're closer than ever to catching this asshole. End of story."

"Not quite the end. You forgot the part where another kid gets snatched *before* we catch this asshole."

Vince stiffened because the guy hit him in his raw spot. "Are you implying that's my fault? The perp lives here, for crying out loud."

"If he does, he's never hunted in his hometown before, O'Mally. He was pressured into it—your presence pushed him too far."

"And you're what, reading his mind now? You ever think maybe it was something else that pushed him? Like us finding the Prague kids' bodies before he dumped them—when we've never recovered the bodies of this guy's victims before? Maybe that was what threw him. You ever think of that, Selkirk?"

Selkirk hesitated, rather than shooting right back. Vince frowned, looked at him, wondering why.

"Actually, we have," he said at length.

That bought Vince up short. "Have what?"

"Found the bodies before. Two in Pennsylvania, one in Jersey, another in Massachusetts."

Vince backed off a step. Lowered his head. His righteous indignation drained slowly. "All identified?"

"Yeah."

"And how do you know they were all his?"

"All female blue-eyed blondes, small for their age, five to seven years old. All the bodies were moved after death. All sexually assaulted. Same M.O. He keeps them for anywhere from a few days to a couple of weeks, before he kills them. Keeps the bodies around awhile before he hides them. Almost like he's daring us to find them. The sick son of a bitch."

Vince watched Selkirk's shuttered face as he spoke. "There's more."

"Look, this is a federal case now. I've said all I can say." Selkirk paced away from Vince a few steps, stared out over the parking lot. "What's the story on D'Voe?"

"I don't think he's our guy."

"Why not?"

Vince shrugged. "Give me the common denominator on the victims, and I'll give you what I know about D'Voe."

For a long moment Selkirk stood there with his back to Vince. Then, slowly, he turned. "I want this guy, O'Mally. Not for the collar. For the kids."

"Sure you do."

"Hey, I've seen some of them. Same as you. I've been working this case for three years. You think it's pushed you to the edge? What the hell do you think it's done to me?"

Vince held the man's eyes steadily. In them he saw his own frustration and rage, mirrored right back at him. He saw the same hell he'd fallen into when he'd walked into that room to find Kara and Bobby Prague.

He sighed. "You're right. We want the same thing here."

Selkirk nodded. "He marks them," he told Vince. His voice had gone softer, lower. As if he were speaking of something that shouldn't be said aloud. "Every one of them had a brand burned into their backs. Right between the shoulder blades. Four-leaf clover. Probably made by a heated piece of jewelry. Ring or a pendant, that sort of thing."

"Jesus Christ." He wanted to ask if the kids were branded before or after death. But he didn't really want to know. He didn't know if he could stand knowing.

Turning now, Selkirk reached into his pocket for a cigarette, lit it. "Your turn."

"You already know most of it. I dug around in D'Voe's past as deeply as I could. He comes from an abusive family himself," Vince told him.

Selkirk lifted his brows. "That's something we didn't know."

"His father beat the hell out of him back in England," Vince said. "Reggie ran away young, came to the States, grew up to be a famous horror star."

"Any of his films involve torturing kids?"

Vince shook his head. "No. Believe me, I checked. As far as anyone around here can tell, the guy loves kids. He used to throw this big Halloween party for them every year. Moved away for a while, came back the year before last, and this year, he reinstated the tradition. Candy, prizes, special effects."

"And one kid doesn't get to go home."

Vince looked up fast. "This is the first time anything bad has happened to a kid in connection with D'Voe or the party."

"Except maybe for his niece. The niece who's not a niece. You saw the fax?"

"I saw it."

"So what have you got on Amanda D'Voe?"

"Reggie says he was more an honorary uncle. Got real upset when we asked him to prove it."

"So Chief Mallory told me. Have you asked her?"

Vince nodded. "She said she couldn't talk about it." When Selkirk frowned at him, Vince went on. "She's fragile. Was in the middle of an anxiety attack at the time. Maybe it's just a painful memory."

"Or maybe she was his first victim."

Vince narrowed his eyes. "What, and he decided to keep her?"

"It's more common than you would believe. They don't start out killing, you know. They molest. They rape. They even fall in love with their victims, at least it's love in their sick, twisted minds. It's the closest thing to it for them. He may very well have decided to keep her. Raise her. Especially if she was his first. God knows there are enough missing kids on the books who've never been found."

Vince blinked, frowned hard.

"What?"

"Nothing." He gave his head a shake. "Nothing, never mind." He focused on the crisis at hand again. "Listen, don't you think she would know? I mean, if she were kidnaped, assaulted, abused that way, do you really think she would have grown up utterly devoted to the guy?"

Selkirk heaved a sigh. "It's possible. It happens. Been documented." He took a long drag on his cigarette, then tossed it to the ground, crushed it with his toe as he blew the smoke out into the night. "One way to find out."

"How's that?"

"Check her for the mark. That four-leaf-clover brand. It's probably something he's been doing for a while. Maybe even from the very first time. If she has it, he's our man. We oughtta get a blood sample, too, find out once and for all if she's related to D'Voe."

"He already admitted she wasn't," Vince said. "Why would he do that if she were a blood relative?"

"You never know. Maybe he started out snatching kids related to him. Most of these guys warm up molesting their own before they start in with the kids of strangers, you know."

Vince lowered his head, wondering how the hell he was going to explain any of this to Amanda without sending her into hysterics. But there was no getting around it. It had to be done.

EIGHTEEN

"THEY'RE going to be a while," Holly said, about the fourth time Amanda peeked out the door down the hall toward where they'd taken her uncle. "Sitting in here isn't doing you any good."

"I can't leave."

Holly took her hand. "We won't go far. My mother's upstairs. I'd like to check in on her."

"Your mother?" Amanda met her eyes. She was still pale, still shaky, but she had control now.

"Yeah. She . . . this has brought back some memories. Bad ones." Holly looked away. "I'm sure you've heard the story. Dr. Graycloud . . . thought Mom needed to rest."

Blinking slowly, Amanda seemed to forget her panic for a moment. "I've only heard rumors. You . . . had a sister."

Holly nodded, felt her eyes heating, welling up. "Yeah. She was taken—just like Bethany."

"And you never got her back?"

Holly gave a quick, sharp shake of her head. "It was a long, long time ago."

"I'm sorry, Holly." Amanda touched her arm.

"It won't be the same for Bethany. We'll find her."

"We will," Amanda agreed with a nod. Holly started for the door, opened it, and Amanda hesitated. "What if Reggie needs me?"

"We can leave a note for that nurse. We won't be gone long. I just . . . I don't really want to go by myself."

Eyes lowering, Amanda rubbed her arms. "I know what you mean. All right. If we leave a note."

Holly nodded, then rummaged in the room, finding a paper and pen, scribbling a note. She left it on the table, face up. "There. Okay?"

She took Amanda's hand, opened the door, and they stepped into the hall. To the right, they could see through the window of the treatment room, where doctors and nurses still surrounded Reggie. To the left and across the hall was the waiting room, but Holly didn't see Vince there. To the immediate left, there were elevators. That was where she turned, only to be stopped by Nurse Sally, carrying a little tray by its center handle. Test tubes filled small square sections. "Can I bother you two for just a minute?"

Amanda's eyes widened. "Is it Uncle Reggie? Is he—?"

"No, no. It's related, though. There's a slim chance— but a possibility—that he may need a transfusion before this is over. We're short on blood so Dr. Graycloud asked me to get some samples typed and cross-matched, just to see if we have a donor on hand should we need one."

"Oh." Amanda sighed, nodded. "I'm afraid I won't be much use," she said. "We're not really blood relatives."

Holly glanced at her. "You're not? I didn't realize."

"Oh, that doesn't matter," the nurse said. "Anyone might be a match, related or not. We can do it right in here. Come on." She walked back into the break room, and set Amanda in a chair. Amanda rolled up her sleeve, and Sally tied a large rubber band around her bicep. She flicked her finger against the crook of Amanda's elbow. "Ah, that's a nice one. You ready, hon?"

Amanda nodded, and Sally stuck a needle into her arm.

As the crimson liquid rushed into the glass tube, she untied the rubber band. When the tube was full, she drew the needle out, holding a gauze pad to the puncture wound, and adding a bandage. "There. All done. Told you it would only take a minute." Smiling she labeled the tube and dropped it into the tray, then turned as if to go.

"Well, wait a minute," Holly said. "What about me?"

Sally turned, looking puzzled.

"You said the donor doesn't need to be a blood relative. So, why don't you take a sample from me, as well? I'd be glad to give blood if Reggie needs it."

Amanda sent Holly a grateful look. The nurse blinked, but finally shrugged and came forward, repeated the entire procedure on Holly. As the blood surged into the tube, Holly asked, "How much longer, do you think, before we'll know something about Reggie's condition?"

"It's liable to be a while, hon." Sally must have heard Amanda's sigh as she withdrew her needled and applied a bandage to Holly. She looked up, met Amanda's eyes. "Let me just tell you this much, child. It's looking good in the E.R. Now they won't call him stable yet, but I'd say it's close to that."

Amanda's relief was palpable. Holly felt it, along with a sizable measure of her own. "My mother is on the third floor," Holly said. "We're going up to look in on her. Please make sure to come for us the second there's any news."

"I promise," the nurse said. "The second there's any news."

When Sally left them, they headed to the elevators. No one else was aboard. They rode two floors up, and the doors opened again.

It was quieter there. A hushed hallway, lights all dimmed. Just a few nurses padding softly up and down the halls with their rubber-soled shoes and white pant-suits. Holly wondered if they wore white because it made them look like angels. So much more soothing to a frightened patient than looking up into the face of a woman dressed in scarlet or purple, she imagined.

"That's my mom's room." She pointed down the hall to the door marked 317. "She's probably sleeping at this hour. But . . . Well, we can just peek in at her."

Amanda nodded, and the two walked softly to the door. Heads close, they looked through the mesh-lined glass. Holly expected to see her mother lying still on the pillow, looking peaceful as she slept.

It wasn't what she saw. There was a woman curled in the fetal position in the bed. It was not her mother. Her mother was sitting up in the bed, cradling the other woman, stroking her hair as if she were holding a small frightened child.

Doris looked up and saw Holly in the window. She crooked a finger at her to come in, but added a warning to be quiet by putting that same finger to her lips.

Nodding, Holly pushed the door open, stepped inside, tugging Amanda along beside her. Holly moved close to the bed, leaned down, and kissed her mother's cheek. Then she touched it. "You've been crying," she said in a whisper.

Doris's cheeks were tear-stained, eyes red. "Not as much as she has," she said, nodding at the woman who slept in her arms. "God, it's as if she's me, eighteen years ago. I remember this. I remember everything she's feeling. It's like I've gone back in time as an onlooker, as if I'm seeing my own history replay."

Holly looked down. Amanda did, too. Amanda said, "It's Bethany's mother."

"Yes. They gave her something, but she just kept crying. I could hear her in the room next door." She shook her head slowly, stroking, stroking. "They couldn't help her. I'm the only one who can help her. Because I know. Because she's me."

The woman was definitely out cold now. She hadn't even stirred. "Mom, you shouldn't be putting yourself through this." Holly leaned forward, reaching for the call button.

Her mother's hand closed over hers. "No, Holly. She's staying right here. She needs me. And I need her."

Holly frowned, not liking this.

"She's right," Amanda said. "I feel more in control when I'm helping someone else. I was losing ground fast until Uncle Reggie . . . and you know it's the same for you, Holly. You were falling apart until you noticed that I was in worse shape that you were."

"That's it exactly," Doris said, smiling gently up at Amanda. "Helping Val through this night is my way of helping myself through it, as well." Then she frowned, searching Holly's face. "Is there any sign . . . ?"

"No. Not yet."

Doris's gaze shifted to Amanda. "Your uncle must be beside himself."

Amanda lowered her head. "He had a heart attack while the police were questioning him about what happened. He's down in the E.R. right now."

Doris's brows rose, her lips parted on a soft "Oh," and she opened her arms. Amanda leaned over the bed, accepted the hug, returned it. Doris said, "I know it doesn't seem like it now, child, but you're going to be all right. You will."

"Sometimes I have trouble believing that," Amanda whispered.

Holly looked on, until a tapping sound on the door behind her made her turn.

Vince peered in through the glass. His face was expressionless. Holly opened the door. "What is it?" Beside him a grim-faced man in a dark suit and tan coat stood like a soldier awaiting orders.

"We need to see Amanda for a sec," Vince said softly. "Can you have her come out?"

"Is it Reggie?"

Vince shook his head immediately. "No, we haven't heard a thing about Reg yet. It's something else."

Holly frowned at him, but he just sent her an appeal with his eyes. *Please.* "Okay. Wait here." She ducked back inside. "Amanda, we have to go. No word on Reggie yet, but we're being summoned anyway."

Amanda straightened away from the bed, and Holly hurried forward, hugged her mother. "Are you all right, Mom?"

"Yes. Yes, I am. I'm sorry I fell apart the way I did, honey. I didn't mean to do that to you. How about you, how are you doing through all of this?"

"Better than I expected I'd be by now. I'm surprising myself."

"Not me," Doris said. "Be strong, honey. I need you."

"I know. Don't worry." She glanced at the bed, the other woman in it. "Try to get some rest tonight."

"I will."

Holly backed out of the room, blew her mother a kiss, and let the door fall closed as she turned to face the two men. Amanda was already standing beside her, facing them expectantly. "So, what's this about?"

"Is there a place where we can have some privacy?" the stranger asked.

"I'm sorry," Holly said, and if her tone had an edge to it, it was because she disliked the man, instantly and instinctively. Something about his brisk tone, his cold eyes, made her bristle. "Do I know you?"

"This is Special Agent Frank Selkirk with the FBI, Holly," Vince said quickly. To Selkirk, he said, "Holly Newman, and Amanda D'Voe."

He acknowledged the women with the barest nod. "Privacy?"

Holly glanced at the empty room beside her mother's. "In here," she said, leading the way, opening the door. "It was Val Stevens's room, but she's in with my mother and I don't think she'll be back anytime soon." She held the door wide while Vince led Amanda in, and Selkirk followed. Stepping in herself, Holly let it close again. "Okay, so what's the big secret?"

"Miss D'Voe," Selkirk began, ignoring Holly completely. "Do you have an unusual scar in the middle of your back?"

Amanda blinked. She swung her gaze to Holly, then to Vince.

"Right about . . ."—Selkirk poked her between the shoulder blades with a long finger—"there?"

"How could you know . . . what is this about?"

"I'm going to have to ask you to show me that scar, ma'am."

"Show you . . . *No*. This is inappropriate. Don't you need a warrant or something to—?"

"Amanda, it's all right. I . . ." Vince seemed to struggle for words. "It's relevant to the case, believe me. I wouldn't ask you to do this if it wasn't."

Amanda blinked, her face softening. Holly tugged her arm, pulling Amanda back a step, then moved forward, putting herself between her and Selkirk. She thrust her chin at Vince. "*How* is it relevant?"

"Holly, I can't—"

"How is it relevant, Vince?"

"It's all right," Amanda said softly. "If it could help find Bethany, I don't mind all that much." Turning her back to them all, she pulled her sweater upward, baring first her slender waist, then the long curve of her spine. Arms crossed over her head, she lifted it higher. The sweater rose past the strap of the white bra across her back. Higher, just above the strap, in the center of Amanda's back was a scar. The scar was old, faded, but there. Holly squinted, leaning closer.

"It looks like a shamrock."

"Four-leaf clover," Selkirk murmured. "I'll be damned."

Amanda lowered the shirt, turning slowly. "I've had it for as long as I can remember. What does it mean? What does it have to do with what's happened to Bethany?"

Her blue eyes were wide, and she was showing signs of panic again. Holly grabbed Vince's arm. "Dammit, don't put her through this shit. Tell us what's going on."

Vince sighed. "Maybe nothing—"

" 'Maybe nothing' my ass," Selkirk said. "Every one of this child killer's victims—the ones we've found at least—had that same mark on her back, Miss D'Voe. Which tells me you were one of this man's victims, too. Maybe his first one. Maybe before he'd started killing them after he'd finished—"

"Shut the fuck up, Selkirk," Vince snapped. He turned, reached for Amanda.

She was backing away, shaking her head from side to side. "But—but I would remember. I would know . . ."

"It's all right. We can't be sure what this means," Vince was saying, but there was no recalling Selkirk's words.

"Of course you are!" Amanda shouted. She spun, right into Holly's arms, and clung there, shaking. "It means I could save Bethany . . . if I could only remember. Dammit, Holly, why can't I remember?"

Holly held her, stroked her soft brown hair down her back, and sent a fierce scowl at Vince.

"You don't remember?" Vince asked urgently. "Amanda, are you saying you don't remember anything about your life before you went to live with Reggie?"

She shook her head against Holly's shoulder. "Nothing," she said. "Except pain."

"I'm getting an arrest warrant," Selkirk said, turning for the door. "If that old bastard survives, he's going down."

Amanda broke free of Holly, and stared after him. "Are you talking about Reggie? You think Reggie did this? My God, you *do*! Reggie would never—you can't believe . . . No. No, no, *no*—" She dragged in a ragged breath, followed by another, clutched her chest, bent at the waist.

Holly held her firmly and ordered, "Go out to the nurse's desk and have them get the doctor back up here. Now." Amanda was starting to hyperventilate again. Holly soothed her as best she could, while Vince gripped

Selkirk's upper arm and propelled him bodily out of the room.

The minute the door closed on them, Amanda stopped panting. She straightened her back and met Holly's eyes; hers were clear. It was so sudden a change that Holly blinked and shook herself. "Amanda? I don't understand, what—?"

"It wasn't Reggie." She said it calmly, her voice deeper than Holly had ever heard it, soft and quiet, but perfectly firm.

"I believe you."

"I have to remember. I have to. It's the only way."

"What *do* you remember? Maybe if we start with that. . . ."

Amanda glanced toward the door as footsteps approached. "Not now," she said quickly. "Just . . . tell me you'll help me. You will, won't you?"

"Amanda, whoever put that mark on you murdered my baby sister. I'll do whatever you want."

Amanda nodded. The door burst open, and she bent over again, sank onto the edge of the bed, resumed gasping for breath.

Dr. Graycloud crowded into the room, flanked by Vince and Selkirk. He took hold of Amanda's shoulders, and eased her down onto the pillows. He held a paper bag to her mouth.

Amanda looked past him, her eyes on Holly's, then rolling toward the men. Holly gave a nearly imperceptible nod, and turned to Vince. "You two get out of here, will you? You've upset her enough."

Vince met her eyes. He looked puzzled and a little hurt before he controlled his expression. "I'm sorry. I didn't mean—"

"You're doing your job," Holly said, and her tone was gentler with him. "But I know what she's going through. You know I do. Don't second-guess me on this. She needs some space. Please, can you take your FBI friend out of here? Just for a little while?"

Vince nodded, holding her eyes with his. He saw something. She knew he did, it showed in that slight narrowing of his eyes and the way they dug and probed. He curled his hand around the nape of her neck, leaned in close. "Are you okay?" He asked it quietly, for her ears alone.

She nodded firmly.

"You sure?" He looked as if he doubted it.

"I promise. I'm okay."

Vince moved closer, kissed her on the mouth, lingering there. "We need to talk."

"Later, Vince."

Finally, he let her go. Then he turned. "Come on, Selkirk, we're outta here."

"I need to question her," the agent protested.

"She just told you, she doesn't remember anything. It'll do you no good, and maybe do her some harm if you push her too hard right now."

"I'm going to sedate her anyway," Dr. Graycloud told them. "You can ask your questions in the morning." He straightened away from Amanda, who was breathing slowly now into the bag, and he turned to Selkirk. "I'm in charge here. This girl's been through enough tonight. Come back in the morning. That's final."

Scowling fiercely and looking mean, Selkirk warned, "I can get the authority to question her now. If you force me to, I will."

"Go get it then. By the time you come back she'll be out for the night. I promise you, you will not be questioning this girl before morning."

Sighing, the agent glared at the doctor, then finally turned and stomped out of the room. Some of the tension left with him.

"You should know that Reggie is past the crisis, Amanda," Dr. Graycloud said. His voice was gentle now. "He's stable. He'll be here for several days, but he's stable."

She started to sit up, but he put his hands on her shoulders. "You can't see him before morning. He'll be unconscious until then. But he's going to be all right, child. I promise you that." He took the crushed paper bag from her hand, set it aside as he went on, giving her more gentle, encouraging news about her uncle's condition.

Holly didn't catch all of it, because Vince was tugging her into the hall. He glanced around, she guessed for Selkirk, but he was gone. Then Vince stared hard at her, started to say something, stopped again, and finally just pulled her close, and held her against him. Her head on his chest, Holly hesitantly lifted her arms, settled them around his waist.

"You're so tense you feel like you might snap in two." He ran a palm across the small of her back. His touch was warm. Firm. "How are you holding up—and tell me the truth this time, Holly, I mean it."

"Fine."

Frowning, he stepped back slightly, looking down at her. "That's not an answer."

She closed her eyes. "What do you want me to say? I can lie to you and tell you that I'm rock solid here, but what would that accomplish? I can tell you the truth and watch that look come into your eyes again. But I don't want to see it, Vince. Not now."

"What look?"

"The one that tells me you can't wait to get the hell away from me."

"You've got it all wrong, Red."

"Do I? Fine. I'll tell you how I'm holding up, and then we'll see. I'm sick inside. I'm wide awake and tense as hell, and I know, every part of me knows, that if I go to sleep tonight—or maybe any night, ever again—the nightmares will come. If I lower my guard for as much as a second, even enough to take a deep breath, my heart's gonna start pounding like a racehorse in the homestretch, and I won't be able to breathe. My darkness is squatting like a demon, right around the next corner, lurking in every shadow, just waiting for me to slip. And when I do it's gonna grab me, Vince, and I don't know if I can fight

my way free the next time it does. I really don't." She
paused, looking back toward the hospital room she'd just
left, and the one beside it, taking a breath. "The only thing
keeping me from curling into the fetal position, in a corner
somewhere, is knowing that Amanda needs me, and my
mother needs me, and Bethany needs me. And all of the
sudden I get it. I totally get why you don't want that
burden of being needed put on you. I get it, Vince, because I'm scared to death I'm going to let them down.
The way I let my sister down."

He didn't say anything for a long time. Didn't touch
her. Just stood there, looking at her until she forced herself
to lift her head and look back. She expected to see pity
in his eyes. The kind of pity you feel when you pass a
homeless person talking to herself on the streets in a big
city. But she didn't see anything like that.

"I got news for you, Holly Newman. I need you, too."

She sucked in a breath, wondering what the hell that
was supposed to mean.

"You are one of the strongest people I've ever met. And
you *can* fight your demons. And you *will* win."

"That's bullshit and you know it."

A muted, cotton muffled voice came over the P.A. system. "Detective O'Mally to the E.R. Detective O'Mally
to the E.R."

He lifted a hand, stroked her hair. "You're doing great.
Stay here, keep Amanda company, see to your mother.
Hang tough just a little longer. I have a feeling things are
gonna be all right this time, Red. I really do."

She shook her head. "I'm gonna lose it and you're
gonna walk away. Bethany's either going to be scarred
for the rest of her life, or die in the next day or so. I don't
see anything all right about any of this."

Doc Graycloud came out of the room, cleared his
throat. "Detective, I need a word with you."

"Walk with me down to the E.R. then," Vince told him.
He kept his eyes riveted on Holly. "I'll be back up later

on. As soon as I can. Wait for me. We really do need to talk."

She nodded, but turned away. She didn't watch him go. She felt his eyes on her though, as he left with Doc. She felt them on her until she heard the elevator doors slide closed, and the soft ping of its bell.

Holly went back into the room, and saw Amanda on her feet, putting on her coat.

"What are you doing?"

"We have to get out of here," Amanda said. "I'll never remember anything here, and they aren't going to leave me alone. Dr. Graycloud will order meds. The nurses will be in with them soon. Will you help me, Holly? Will you help me go to where I can remember?"

Holding the other woman's gaze, Holly nodded. "You're damn right I will."

NINETEEN

"DID you get a blood sample from Amanda?" Vince asked, as he and Dr. Graycloud rode the elevator down two levels.

"Yes, though I can't imagine why you need it. Reggie has already admitted to you that she's not a blood relative."

"Yeah, well that begs the question of just who the hell she *is,* then, doesn't it?"

The doctor grunted as the doors opened, and they headed down the hall toward the E.R. Halfway there, Chief Mallory met them, Selkirk on his heels. "They're ready to move Reggie to a regular room. I think you should be there when they go in to question him, but Selkirk and his cohorts disagree."

"It's our case now," Selkirk said. "O'Mally has no jurisdiction."

"Well I do." The aging doctor straightened to his full height and looked Selkirk right in the eye. "And I don't want you or your men anywhere near him until I give the okay. Good God, if I won't allow you to question Amanda when she's on the verge of emotional collapse, what makes you think I'd let you grill a man who's just suffered a coronary?"

"We need to question him as soon as possible," the agent said, his tone dismissive. "There's a little girl's life at stake, Doctor. I suggest you keep that in mind."

"I'm keeping it firmly in mind, Agent Selkirk. What you need to keep in mind is that if you push Mr. D'Voe into another heart attack, you'll never get the chance to question him at all. And any information he might have that could help save that little girl will be gone with him."

That brought Selkirk to attention, and the doctor rose a notch in Vince's eyes. He was holding his own and then some with the imposing federal agents, and looked as proud and powerful as a tribal chieftain. Then he delivered the clincher. "The man won't be conscious for several hours anyway. You couldn't question him if you wanted to until then."

"Fine. We'll wait," Selkirk said grudgingly. "But we'll post a guard at his door. One of ours," he added with a meaningful look at Vince, and then the chief.

Jim Mallory nodded. "Fine by me. I'm shorthanded as it is."

Several attendants rolled the gurney out of the treatment room, and the men stopped speaking to watch. Reggie's skin was nearly indistinguishable from the sheets around him. He was chalk white, except for the blue veins showing through his thin eyelids, and ghostly gray of his lips.

"So you wanted to talk to me?" Vince reminded the doctor as he watched the man's friend being wheeled away.

Graycloud looked up at him as if he'd forgotten, then gave a nod. "Yes. My office will do." He led Vince back up the hall, past the elevator doors that closed on three nurses, two federal agents, and Reggie on his rolling bed. Around a corner, the doctor opened a door, flipped on a light switch, and then stood aside for Vince to enter before closing it. Moving behind a large desk, he sank into his

chair, as if he were exhausted, and Vince sank into one
in front of the desk just like it.

"Been a hell of a night, huh?"

Dr. Graycloud nodded wearily. "*Hell* of a night. You
get nights like this around here every now and then."

"Around Dilmun, you mean?" Vince asked.

"Nah. Around an emergency room. Oh, nothing this
dark. Farming accidents, hunting accidents, drunk drivers,
that sort of thing. But death is a tough combatant, no
matter the form he takes or the victims he comes for.
Fighting him off is exhausting." He gestured at the room
around him. "That's why I keep a little haven for myself
in here."

Vince looked around. It was a cozy space. Coffee pot,
hot cocoa in a cannister beside a tiny microwave. A cup
tree held mugs with nature scenes painted on them. Deer,
birds, mountains. The chairs were overstuffed and cozy,
and there was a cot around a corner in a spot that might
once have been a closet.

"I think it's time I told you what I know about Amanda
and Reggie. I think maybe Reg would want me to, at this
point. I don't like that Selkirk character, and I think the
chief already knows, or at least, suspects."

Vince sat forward in his seat.

"I don't believe Reggie's guilty of anything at all, you
know. Most certainly not of harming children."

Vince nodded slowly. "I don't think he is either, Doc,
but I gotta tell you, it's gonna be tough to find someone
who looks more guilty than he does right now."

"Unless we find the real culprit, you mean."

Vince sighed, not answering that one.

The doctor leaned forward in his chair, taking keys
from a pocket and unlocking a file drawer in his desk. He
pulled it open, took out a folder, and closed the drawer
again. Then he tossed the file down on the desk.

Vince saw the name "Amanda" across the top, and
frowned. "That's an odd way to mark her file. No last
name?"

Doc shrugged. "I didn't see any need. I knew who I meant. The fact is, we didn't know her last name. We didn't even know her *first* name when Amanda came to us."

Vince took the file, flipped through it. "Maybe you'd better start at the beginning, Doc."

Graycloud nodded, leaning back again, getting comfortable. "It was late fall, 1983. The exact date is in the folder there. It was in November, as I recall. Close to Thanksgiving. I remember it was storming. Made that thunderstorm we had the other night look like child's play. Blew up a real banger that night. No snow just then, but it moved in by week's end, as I recall. But this, this was a thunderstorm, and it was blowing full throttle when I got a phone call from Reggie. Said to come to his house right away. Said not to say a word to anyone about where I was going."

Vince was fully alert now. Weariness no longer held a candle to anticipation. "So, you went."

"Of course I went. When I got there, I found Reggie pacing. And there sitting by the fire, was this little girl. Skinny as a rail, pale, soaked to the bone." He hesitated for a moment. "She was bruised, and there were these . . ." He lifted a hand, ran his thumb around his wrist. "These red rings around her little wrists. Like she'd been bound, but not with rope. Cuffs of some kind, was my best guess. Metal. She wouldn't let Reggie near her. Wouldn't let either one of us near her for a time. And her eyes, they were just . . ." Sighing, he shook his head slowly. "I don't know. Hollow. Empty. I don't know how to describe it. She looked . . . bleak."

Vince was on the edge of his chair. "What did you do?"

"We got her some food, warm milk to drink. Reg had already given her blankets to wrap up in. She reacted well to the food. Like she hadn't eaten in days. And I think that was when she started to trust us just a little. We finally got her calm enough to sleep, and I managed to examine her. Once she was out, I'll tell you, she was out."

"And what did you find?"

Doc looked away. "She'd been raped. More than once. There was internal damage. I doubt she'll ever be able to have children of her own. She was malnourished and suffering from exposure and post-traumatic stress. Nothing life threatening. She'd been drugged. Sedated. I wanted to call in authorities. And that's when Reggie started lying."

"What do you mean?"

"When I first arrived, he'd told me this little thing had just shown up at his front gate, in the middle of the night, right in the full brunt of that storm, not wearing a stitch of clothes. That he just got up and looked out the window and saw her out by the gate. But the minute I wanted to report this to the police and Social Services, his story changed. He said he knew who she was. He said she was the child of a relative of his, and he made up the name. Amanda, he called her. Hell, I knew he was lying. And he knew I knew it."

"Why? Why would he lie, Doc?"

The doctor looked Vince squarely in the eye. "Reggie ran away from his father six times, Vince. The first time he was only seven years old. Every time he was found by police or social workers, no matter how many burns or broken bones or bruises they found on that kid's little body, the authorities sent him right back. And every time they sent him back, he got beaten ten times worse than he had before he'd run. Every time, he would wait until he was healed up, strong, and then he'd try again. Five times they sent him back for more. The sixth time, he made his escape." Doc shook his head. "Why do you think he lied?"

"He was afraid she would be sent back to whomever hurt her."

Doc nodded. "She wouldn't talk much that first night. Barely at all. Wouldn't tell us her name, her age, anything. But the one thing she did say was all it took to convince Reg to do whatever it took to keep her with him."

"And what was that?"

"When we asked her who hurt her this way, she replied, 'Daddy.' "

Vince closed his eyes, got to his feet, and leaned over to flip open the file folder. Inside were photos of a little girl who looked haunted, skinny, ill. He fought against waves of nausea as he studied the snapshots.

"I went along with the lie," Doc went on. "I knew what he was doing, but I pretended not to. It was the best thing for the child. I believed that at the time, and I still do. Look, flip the pages. There's a photo taken six months later."

Vince did, and found the snapshot of a beautiful light-haired girl, smiling, with dimples, having what looked like a birthday party. Her eyes were still shadowed by the past, but she looked about a thousand percent better than in the first photos.

"Reg had no idea when her birthday was, of course. He just picked a date. Just like he picked a name. And even after Amanda's body healed, she couldn't remember what happened before Reggie found her. Except that her daddy had hurt her. The idea of going back sent her into hysterics."

Vince nodded, closed the file. "When you examined her that first night, did she have a mark on her back?"

Doc looked up fast. "Yes. A burn, seared into her flesh, right between the shoulder blades. Four-leaf clover. There's a photo of it in the file."

Vince bent his head, thinking that if this version of the story was true, they needed to know who Amanda's abusive father had been. Because he might very well be the killer they sought. If it was true. "Thank you, Doc. Thanks a lot."

"Amanda still doesn't remember what came before, Vince. Hell, it's probably better that way."

Vince picked up the file, tucked it under his arm. "Maybe you're right." But deep down he knew these revelations didn't prove a thing. Not really. Doc hadn't seen the child arrive. Vince knew the way a good prosecutor's mind would work. Doc's testimony only went so far. For all he knew, Reg could have had the girl captive for weeks, and only called the doctor in when she seemed too ill to survive without help. Perhaps Reggie was a sick child molester who had decided to keep the girl and raise her as his own. How could anyone know for sure, if Amanda herself couldn't even remember?

HOLLY AND AMANDA RAN FROM THE hospital's side entrance, through gathering rain and utter slick, shiny darkness, to Amanda's car. "You drive," Amanda said. "I'm still too shaky."

Holly nodded, taking the keys and getting into the driver's side. Amanda slid in the passenger side and brushed the droplets from her hair, as Holly started the engine and turned on the wipers and the heat.

"Where do you want to go?"

"Back home. To Reggie's house."

Holly wiped a hole in the fogged-up windshield and pulled out of the parking lot. "You realize that's the first place they'll look, don't you, Amanda?"

"It's all right. We won't be there long." She glanced at Holly. "I mean, I won't. You can do whatever you want. I don't want to pull you any further into my nightmare. You helped me get back here, that's all I can ask you to do."

Holly reached across the seat, closed her hand around Amanda's. "It's everyone's nightmare now. And I want to—I need to help you through to the end of this thing, Amanda. But, I'm not sure I understand. . . ."

"I need to remember," Amanda said. "It's time for me to remember."

"The time before you came to live with Reggie."

Amanda nodded.

"How much do you remember, Amanda? You never

got the chance to tell me back at the hospital."

Amanda closed her eyes. "I remember pain."

"And nothing else?"

"No, there's more. Fear. Darkness, and rain, and thunder, and cold. Those are the things I remember, the only things I remember when I try to think of the time before Reggie. The things I was feeling. Mostly the cold and the fear. I was so cold I couldn't feel my bare feet anymore. And the thunder kept getting louder."

Holly waited for her to continue, but she didn't. "You were outside, in your bare feet, in the middle of a thunderstorm?"

Amanda nodded. "At night. I don't think I knew where I was."

"So, you were not in a town you knew, or at least not a neighborhood you knew," Holly suggested. Then she bit her lip. "Then again, to a small child, any neighborhood would probably seem foreign in the dark, in the rain."

"Yes." Amanda's brows knitted in concentration. "I saw light, and I went toward it, but then I couldn't go anymore, and I just sank to the ground. I remember looking up and into the kindest eyes I thought I had ever seen. I was . . . yes, I was curled up on the wet ground, outside the front gate of Reggie's place. He picked me up, and he carried me inside, and he wrapped me in warm blankets."

"And then what happened?"

"It gets clearer after that. The next thing I remember is Dr. Graycloud and Reggie, feeding me warm, sweetened milk and telling me that I was safe. That no one would hurt me anymore. That I could trust them. They were warmth and light. And after a while, they made the pain go away."

"They fed you, gave you a warm bed, promised you they'd keep you safe."

"Yes," Amanda said. "Yes, and I needed to believe that so badly that I did. I remember in the morning, Reggie told me whatever happened before didn't matter. That I should try to forget about it, because it couldn't hurt me ever again. That it was gone, as if it had never been. That I was starting all over again." She looked at Holly squarely. "And I think I took those words to heart, I really do. Because I forgot everything. My name. My history. Whatever horrible things had been done to me . . ."

"Have you tried therapy?"

Amanda sighed. "Therapy, hypnosis, drugs. Uncle Reg got me the best doctors money could buy. Most of them agreed that if I couldn't remember my past, it would be a bad idea to try to force it." She sent Holly a worried look. "They said the human mind knows what it can and cannot withstand. That if I'd blocked something out that completely, maybe there was a reason."

"Maybe you couldn't handle remembering."

Amanda swallowed hard. "Maybe. But that's no longer relevant."

"Of course it's relevant!"

"No, it's not. If I don't remember now, that little girl could end up dead. And I'll be responsible for it. No. No, I have to remember. And I can only think of one way. I have to go back. I have to go right back there, to the gate where Reggie found me that night."

Holly frowned at her, shifting her gaze rapidly from Amanda's determined face to the road and back again. "And do what? Try to backtrack?"

Amanda nodded. "If I can retrace my steps, make it as much like it was before as I possibly can, then maybe . . ." Sighing, she lowered her head. "It's a long shot, I know, but I just can't see any other way."

When thunder rumbled softly in the distance, Holly said, "Sounds like the weather's going to cooperate."

Amanda looked up, eyes probing the black depths of the sky. "Yeah." And she shivered. "God, I hate thunderstorms."

"DR. GRAYCLOUD?"

The doctor held up a hand toward the nurse, and kept on with his conversation with Vince and the federal agent guarding Reggie's hospital room door. "I don't want to catch anyone trying to get into this room again, do you understand me, young man?"

"With all due respect, doctor, Special Agent Selkirk is my superior."

"But he has no right to put my patient's life at risk," Graycloud insisted.

Vince cut in. "Listen, kid, if the suspect dies because you didn't do your job, it'll be your ass, not Selkirk's. You got that?" His own methods were a bit more direct, but he didn't have time to dick around with the rookie. He and the doctor had come along the hall to see Selkirk with his hand on the hospital room door, about to go inside, and the guard looking the other way. "If you're too scared of Selkirk to stand up to him, then just call one of us next time he tries to get into the room."

"I'm not scared of Agent Selkirk, Detective."

"Shoot, you wouldn't know it to look at you." Vince shook his head. "Can you do the job, kid, or should we ask for someone else?"

"I can do it just fine, sir."

"Good."

"Doctor, please," the nurse said again.

"Just a moment, will you? Listen, son, if we hadn't come by just as Agent Selkirk was heading in there, I can't even predict what would have happened. Now, I know what you're thinking—so he dies, no great loss. But keep in mind that we have no solid evidence of that man's guilt. But we have very good reason to believe he might be the only hope we have of finding little Bethany Stevens alive. So you think about that, all right? You're not protecting a suspected child killer. You're protecting the life of a little girl."

"Yes, sir," the agent said, and he looked, for once, as if he meant it.

Sighing, Graycloud nodded, turned away. "Now, what is it nurse?"

She walked beside the doctor and Vince through the hallway, flipping open a folder as she did. "They messed up the blood samples you requested," she said. "Must have been a glitch in the hospital lab; either way, we're gonna have to do them over again."

"Why's that?" Frowning hard, Doc pulled a pair of bifocals from a pocket and slipped them on, then took the chart from her, scowling at the pages inside.

"Miss D'Voe's friend insisted on being tested as well. And as you can see, the results between her workup and Miss D'Voe's are, well they're . . ."

"They're damn near identical." He lifted his gaze to Vince's.

Vince swallowed hard and felt the blood drain from his face.

"Exactly," the nurse went on. "I had the lab double-check. They swear the results are right, but it's obvious they must have mislabeled the samples, or tested the same one twice. For two adults to test this way they would practically have to be—"

"Siblings," Doc said.

Vince shut his eyes tight. "My God."

"Thank you for the information nurse. I'll, uh, I'll take it from here," Graycloud muttered, and the nurse left them with an odd look.

"We can't breathe a word of this," Vince said. "Not to anyone, not until we're absolutely sure. I don't think Doris could take the shock, much less the heartbreak if it turns out we're wrong. And as for Holly . . ." He shook his head slowly. "I don't know how she'll take this, but I do know we have to be sure. I don't want to hurt those

two—those three—any more than they've already been
hurt by all of this."

"I'll have further tests run," Doc said. "We'll need fresh
samples from the two women. We'll get this confirmed
and—" He was turning as he spoke, walking quickly, but
he stopped all at once, braced a hand on the wall to keep
him upright. His head dropped forward.

Vince quickly gripped his arm. "Whoa, hold on."

The doctor hung there a moment, closed his eyes. "My
God, O'Mally, what if I took part in keeping a secret that
should never have been kept? What if I'm partly to blame
for what that family went through?" He opened his eyes,
and they were wet. "I thought I was saving her. Not hiding
her from a loving family! I swear I did."

The man looked stricken. And Vince felt sorry for him.
He could imagine making the same choices, if he'd believed what they had that night. "Look, you did what you
thought you had to do. And who the hell knows, maybe
you did save her. You said yourself, she told you and
Reggie her daddy had been the one who hurt her."

Lifting his brows and his head at once, Doc paled.
"You think Holly's father—then, what about her? What
about Holly?"

"I don't know," Vince admitted. But it galled him to
think she may have been a victim of the same thing.

"No. No, Vince, it wasn't him," Dr. Graycloud said. "I
knew the man. And, besides, if it were him, that would
mean he was the one who took Bethany. And those children in Syracuse, he would have done that as well. But
he couldn't have. He's dead. He's been dead for seven
years."

"Let's not get carried away. Maybe this really was just
a mistake in the hospital lab."

Doc nodded. "We'd better get those samples from
Holly and Amanda."

Vince headed for the elevator, and thought about Holly.
About Amanda. He kept putting their faces side by side
in his mind, and seeing similarities. Or was that wishful

thinking? Why hadn't he noticed before if there were a resemblance?

⬥⬥⬥

DORIS NEWMAN STOPPED WALKING when she heard the two men arguing outside Mr. D'Voe's room. She'd been on her way to look in on him, since she couldn't sleep anyway. He seemed like such a kind man, and she honestly hoped he was going to be all right.

But the words of the two men brought her up short.

"Look, I'm sorry I got you into trouble," one man was saying. "I shouldn't have done that. I just don't want to wait until morning to question this guy."

"I know," the younger man said. He was the one who seemed to be guarding the door. "The idea of protecting a child killer makes me sick. But are you sure he's the one?"

"As sure as I need to be. He took that kid last night. Near as we can figure he's been killing little girls for eighteen years. Maybe longer. There's a guy in prison right now for one of those deaths."

The guard sighed deeply. "Still, we'd better stick with procedure."

"We will kid. I'll question him in the morning, with the doctor standing there protecting him. The piece of shit."

Doris's eyes were frozen wide open, and her heart was skipping beats and swelling. Reginald D'Voe? A killer? Was it possible? Was *he* the man who had murdered her precious little girl? She felt herself sinking to her knees, one hand pressed to the wall, the other to her heart.

"Ma'am? Are you all right, ma'am?" someone asked.

She ignored her. Ignored the hands pulling her to her feet, the chair she was eased into. Someone looked at her wristband, and said, "Mrs. Newman? Doris, can you hear me? Honey, what are you doing down here? You belong up on the third floor."

She blinked, lifted her head, and tried to see through swimming eyes. But she couldn't. "I was just going to look in on Mr. D'Voe," she said. "He's a neighbor of mine."

A neighbor. A neighbor, who had stolen her baby. Who'd killed her, and nearly driven Holly insane with grief and guilt. Him. He'd done it. But why? She'd never even met D'Voe until she and Holly had moved here. She'd known of him, even driven the girls past his house a few times when they visited every summer. But D'Voe had always summered elsewhere. The Keys, she'd once heard someone say. He'd never even been in town when she and the girls had been here. Why had he targeted her Ivy? Why?

They pushed her chair into an elevator. She was shaking. Too much, it was too much to feel all at once.

The doors opened, and the nurse pushed her back toward her room, as one of the nurses at the desk came forward to take over. "What happened? Doris? I thought you were doing better?" the nurse said. "I'll take it from here," she told the other nurse. Then she leaned over Doris again. "God, hon, you're white as a sheet."

She shook her head. "Just tired. I . . . need to rest."

"Well, we'll see to that. I've put Mrs. Stevens back in her own room for now. She'll be out till morning. Do you need anything to help you sleep?"

What she needed, she thought, was a gun. Or a knife. Or a vat of deadly poison. Reginald D'Voe had taken her baby, and God only knew what he'd done to her before he'd finally killed her. He'd put Holly through hell, and he'd caused the cancer that had killed her husband. She had no doubt about that. Never had. The man had all but destroyed her family. He couldn't get away with that. He couldn't.

He wouldn't.

As the nurse pushed her toward her room past the nurses desk, she saw a large pair of shiny silver sheers on a tray. She bumped the tray with her foot, knocking some of the lighter items to the floor. When the nurse bent to pick them up, Doris grabbed the sheers and hid them in the folds of her hospital gown.

TWENTY

⊰⊱

"YOU did it!" the woman shrieked from the middle of the trashed kitchen. Every drawer was opened, every cupboard. Papers, photos, old notebooks were strewn over the table and counters. She'd been searching for something. Evidence of his guilt, he supposed. "You did, didn't you? *Didn't you?*"

"I don't know what you're talking about, honey. Why don't you calm down and stop looking at me like that?"

His wife was wild-eyed. Her eyes were red and bulging and her hair a mess, as if she'd been repeatedly running tear-dampened hands through it. He'd never meant for her to find out. But he supposed, deep down, he'd always known she would. How could she not?

The truck was in the back driveway, behind the house, its precious cargo bound and gagged and drugged and frightened. God, he loved it when they were frightened. It made it so much better. He'd only come home for a bite to eat, a change of clothes. Hadn't intended to stay long. Hadn't expected her to be home. God knew how little time he could take with his girls these days. It was getting shorter and shorter every time.

"Our own daughters," his wife sobbed. "You did it to our own daughters."

"Don't be ridiculous." He reached out for her, but she backed away fast. Past the little round table, one hand dragging over it, knocking papers and old news clippings to the floor.

"Our own daughters," she said again, shaking her head while new tears welled and rolled. "They tried to tell me what you were doing to them. And I didn't believe them. I chose you over our own daughters. That's why they ran away. That's why they left us. Because I wouldn't believe them."

He tried to look stricken as he moved closer to her. One step, then another on the little square tiles. She was still backing up, but his steps covered more ground. "How can you even think something like that?" he asked softly.

"And then, when little Ivy was taken—it hit me then, that maybe it was you. Maybe the girls had been telling the truth and I'd been blind—but then that other man confessed. I was so relieved. God, I was so relieved to know it wasn't you!"

"He confessed because he was guilty," he said reasonably. "That proves it wasn't me. It was never me."

She didn't just shake her head this time, she flung it from side to side so fiercely he thought she would wrench her neck. Not that it mattered. Not now. "No! No, he didn't confess because he was guilty. Doris told me he only confessed to cop a plea. He didn't kill Ivy. Someone else did. *You did!* And I could have saved her. I could have saved Ivy if only I hadn't wanted so badly to believe you!"

"Oh, honey, come on. You're upset. This whole incident with little Bethany has you thinking crazy." He was close now. He reached out and caught her upper arm.

She slapped him. Her hand whipped his face so hard he rocked backward, releasing her arm in the process. "Where is that little girl? What have you done to her? Tell me!"

He didn't speak this time. Just stared at her and felt his cheek heating, reddening. She had never hit him. In all their years of marriage, she had never once hit him.

Her voice came broken now, softer, her body shaking. "How could you do it? How could you kill a child? How?"

He sighed deeply. Damn, he hadn't wanted it to come to this. He knew he shouldn't have made a move on the Stevens girl so soon. Not until he'd gotten that nosy cop the hell out of town, at least. But he'd planned this for so long. He'd never taken a child from Dilmun before—but this one was special. He'd been watching her for two years. Soon she would have been too old.

He'd been planning for Bethany for months. Then things started going wrong. They'd seen his old van, the one no one knew he kept. So he had to use his work truck. They found his hideaway in the city. The place where he liked to use them and keep them. It was there he'd kept Ivy. But he'd kept her too long. She'd been an important lesson in his education. You couldn't keep them too long.

Then that cop had shown up in town—and now this. His wife knew. She knew.

She looked at his eyes as he started toward her again, and she backed up still more. Through the arching doorway into the dining room. He paused in the kitchen, near the counter. She was halfway across the dining room now—she couldn't see. Reaching out with one hand, he drew the meat cleaver from its rack, brought it behind his back so smoothly she never noticed.

"How could you? How could you murder a child?" she kept asking.

"Hell, honey, it isn't like I wanted to. It's just—well, if you give them what they want—oh, yeah, they want it. They all want it. I never touched a girl that didn't—but once you give it to them, they talk. Our girls, for example. Ungrateful little . . ."

She brought her hand to her lips, eyes going even wider. "Oh, my God . . ."

"So you go younger, and you take 'em someplace where you can keep 'em quiet, use 'em till they're all used up. Shoot, I was still trying to decide how to finish it all when the first one got away." Sighing, he shook his head slowly. "See, it's their fault. You *have to* kill 'em, or they run away. You can only keep 'em for a short while at the most. And then you have to kill 'em. It's the only way."

"No," she whispered. "No, no, no." She closed her eyes, backing into the hallway now, and turning, stumbling into the bedroom, slamming the door.

"Yes," he told her, raising his voice enough so she could still hear, through the closed door. "I've been doing this awhile. You can trust me on it, there's no other way." He stepped into the hallway, too. She'd thrown the locks. He slammed his hip against the door, and it popped open easily enough. She whirled to face him, cowering. "Tell you what, though, honey. They die happy. Those little girls die just squirming with pleasure. I make sure of that."

She made a face and gripped her stomach as if she were ill. "Where is she?" she asked. "Where is Bethany Stevens?"

He licked his lips. "You don't think I'm gonna share, now, do you?"

"God, you're insane!" She tried to duck past him, toward the door, but he punched her in the belly. Gave her such a blow that she doubled over, stumbled away from him. She fell to her knees, hunched, gagging. He walked up behind her. Lifted the cleaver. "I'll tell you the real trick to the whole process," he said, keeping his tone conversational. "Keep the bodies around until all the commotion dies down. Then you bury 'em far from where you use them. And never, *ever* leave any witnesses. That's really the main thing."

⟷

THE RAIN WAS FALLING HARDER THAN BE-
fore. Amanda opened the gates in front of Reginald
D'Voe's place, still wearing its Halloween decor, only
now there was crime scene tape added to the mix. Holly
drove the car through. Then Amanda took her inside,
where they gathered up what they needed. Raincoats.
Flashlights. Amanda ran from room to room, gathering
the items, bringing them to Holly. They were ready now.
It was to be on foot from there on. It was understood.
Holly didn't need to ask why. It made perfect sense to
her, though she supposed it wouldn't have to most normal
people.

Holly was worried about Amanda. She didn't look
steady on her feet physically, much less emotionally
steady. They walked back outside in the pouring rain,
down the path to the open gate, and stepped through it.
Amanda closed the gate, then they just stood there, with
the rain pounding down on their yellow hoods, on their
backs and shoulders. Facing the mansion, Amanda stood
staring for a long moment. And then she nodded, and
turned to the left, and said, "I came from this way."

"Then we go this way," Holly told her. She stayed close
to Amanda as the two of them walked back along the
road. The gravel was wet, shiny in the beams of their
flashlights. Trees lined both sides. They walked for twenty
yards, and then Amanda stopped, lifting her head so the
rain peppered her face, looking left, then right. "Here,"
she said. "Here is where I found the road again. Before
that, I'd wandered through"—lifting her head, she looked
at the trees off the right—"woods."

"You came through the woods? Here, are you sure?"

She nodded, and plunged into the wetness of the trees
with barely any hesitation. "Yes. Yes, this way. Look, the
trail is still here."

Holly shone her light ahead, saw the one area through
the woods that was clear of brush and trees. Even the
weeds on the three-foot-wide strip were trimmed low.
There was a yellow pole with black stripes sticking up

out of the ground. "It's where the natural gas line runs through, underground," Holly said. "They keep the brush trimmed off it, so they can get to it to dig it up for maintenance. Local kids use it as a shortcut to town. I use it myself."

"It seemed like a trail to me." Amanda hurried onto the path and began walking at a brisk pace along the cleared section. Holly tried to keep up. She was freezing. Her hands were cold and wet, and she dearly wished she had grabbed a pair of gloves. She thought belatedly that they should have called Vince from the house, told him what they were doing. But Amanda didn't trust Vince right now. And Holly couldn't really say she blamed her after he'd convinced her to reveal her scar to the federal agent, knowing it would implicate Reggie.

"This trail cuts through the woods, right along the south edge of the lake, and comes out at the edge of town, near the cabins," she explained to Amanda. "Does any of that sound familiar to you?"

Amanda shook her head. "No, not town. There were no cabins." Her steps were slowing, until finally she stopped, and stood still, head tipped back to the rain, eyes closed. "There were more woods. Woods with no path. I came . . . I came . . ." She tugged off her hood, and let the rain pour onto her head until it darkened her hair. She turned in a slow circle. "I came from the woods. I came through the woods a little ways before I found the path. And when I found it I thought it was put there to help me. Like when Snow White ran through the woods to escape the wicked queen. I thought the animals—" She stopped there, turning to face Holly, her eyes wide. "I remember that! There was a deer—a deer—standing right on the path, that's how I found it. I went toward the deer. It ran off, but not until I had found the path."

Holly moved closer, gently touching Amanda's arm. "That's good. It's good, Amanda, it's coming back to you now." She studied Amanda's wet face, reached out to tug her hood back up. Then she fastened the snap at her neck to keep it there. "Are you okay?"

Amanda nodded, spinning away, jogging a few more yards along the path. Then she stopped again, looking around. "This way." She pointed.

"Are you sure, Amanda? I mean, town is only another hundred yards or so that way. The cabins are less. The only thing up this way is . . . Amanda? Wait up."

Amanda was already hiking off the trail, angling away from it.

And then lights shone through the trees, and she went faster. Holly tried to stop her, but she couldn't catch her as Amanda moved faster and faster. Then the trees ended at the edge of a nicely manicured lawn. And Amanda stopped, and stared at the red house with the white shutters.

"Here," she said. "I came from here." Her eyes closed tight, Amanda pressed a hand to her head as if in great pain.

"But, Amanda, that doesn't make any sense. This is my uncle Marty's house."

THE NURSES ON DORIS NEWMAN'S FLOOR hadn't seen Holly or Amanda. They were not in Doris's room. Mrs. Stevens was sleeping, though restlessly, thanks to the sedatives she'd been given. Reggie's guard said he'd had no visitors, and the doctor had searched the entire hospital.

Vince, Jerry, Agent Selkirk, and Chief Mallory stood in the parking lot outside the hospital, in the rain, and Mallory said, "It's not here. Amanda D'Voe's car was parked out here earlier, right there." He pointed to an empty space. "She pulled in right behind me."

"Still think she's an innocent in all of this, O'Mally?" Selkirk crossed his arms over his chest. "Panic attacks my ass. The bitch needs to be interrogated, and when we find her, you can bet I'll be the one doing it."

"She's a victim, Frank," Vince snapped. He swiped a hand across his face to wipe away the rain that was running from his hair.

"She *was* a victim. Now she's an accessory. And if the Newman woman is helping her evade questioning, then so is she."

"That's bull and you know it," Chief Mallory protested. "Amanda wasn't in custody."

"She was told not to leave the hospital without clearance," Selkirk said.

The chief shot Vince a pleading look. Vince read it clearly. He didn't want this asshole to be the one to find Amanda D'Voe. Vince didn't want him to be the one to find Holly. But he was worried about more than that. Holly had a look about her the last time they'd spoken. It was one he had seen before, one that said she was keeping something from him.

"Look at the sign," Vince said, pointing. " 'Emergency Parking Only.' They probably moved the car, and then found a place to get some sleep." He caught the chief's eye.

Mallory was blank for a second, then he lifted his brows and jumped in. "That's right. I think one of the hospital staff was saying the vehicles were going to have to be moved." He glanced out over the lot. "Vince, Jerry, you two check the front lot out, row by row, if necessary. Agent Selkirk and I will cover the lot in the back." He looked at Selkirk. "It's right around the corner. Come on." Then he just started walking, leaving no time for arguments.

Selkirk followed Mallory as Vince led Jerry out into the parking lot, toward his own car. And as soon as the chief and Selkirk were out of sight, he yanked his keys out of his pocket, slapped Jerry on the back, and said, "Let's hit it."

They were in the Jeep, pulling out of the parking lot seconds later.

"So, where do we begin?"

"I don't know," Vince said. "Holly's house. Amanda's house. Whatever the hell they're up to, I imagine it started with a stop at home. Seems like they'd want an umbrella if nothing else."

"I suppose that makes as much sense as anything." Jerry shook his head. "Why do you think they took off?"

"I don't know."

"Do you think they could have reached the same conclusion we did, back there?"

Vince's fingers tightened on the steering wheel. "I hope so."

"Really?" Jerry looked at Vince in surprise. "I thought you wanted them kept in the dark until we knew for sure."

"I do. But the only other reason I can think of for them to take off like this is that maybe Amanda started to remember something."

Jerry blinked, then his eyes widened. "About the killer? Holy shit. You think they've gone after him?"

"God, I hope not," Vince said grimly. He remembered all too well what it had done to him to walk into that room in the rundown house and find the bodies of Kara and Bobby Prague. Holly couldn't survive something like that. Amanda probably couldn't either. "I hope not."

───✦───

"THIS IS YOUR UNCLE'S HOUSE?" AMANDA asked, searching Holly's face.

Holly nodded. "I don't understand this. Are you sure, Amanda?"

Amanda looked at the house, at the lighted windows, the shutters. "I remember standing right here, looking at that house, and knowing I had to get away. Away from that house. *He* was in there." She covered her face with her hands, and Holly wrapped her arms around Amanda protectively, instinctively holding her hard and close.

"It's all right. Nothing can hurt you now."

Amanda looked up, tears mixing with the rain on her face. "We aren't frightened little girls anymore."

"No." Holly's head was still spinning. Uncle Marty. It made no sense. But there was no time to work it all out, not now. "But Bethany is. And she needs us. I can go in alone, if you want."

"No. No, I'll go with you."

Nodding, Holly hooked her arm through Amanda's, and they walked across the lawn, toward the back door. Holly reached up to ring the bell, but Amanda caught her hand. "Just . . . try the door."

Holly glanced sideways, saw the closed garage door, and beyond its windows, the glint of metal. "Looks like Aunt Jen is home. Her car's in the garage." She couldn't see if Uncle Marty's bread truck was back from its most recent run. It would be around the far side where the driveway looped around the house. "It's going to be all right, Amanda." She gripped the knob, and turned it slowly.

It wasn't locked.

There was nothing strange about that. It was a small town. Folks rarely locked their doors when they were away, much less when they were at home. She pushed the door open and stepped inside.

The lights were on, and the living room was a mess. Cabinets and drawers, the closet, everything open and things strewn everywhere. The cushions on the sofa were askew, as if someone had pulled them off and then tossed them carelessly back down again. "My God," she whispered. "Someone must have broken in. Aunt Jen?" she called.

A door slammed. The side door.

Holly jumped out of her skin, and Amanda gripped her arm. "Come on."

Slowly, they moved forward, into the dining room. The kitchen and its side door were off to the right, but Holly could see nothing that way except more chaos. Certainly no one was out there. The screen door was banging in the wind, though. That must have been the slam she had heard.

To the left was a short hallway, leading to the bedroom. She turned in that direction, with Amanda clinging to her arm, and went to the master bedroom door. "Aunt Jen?"

No sound came in reply.

She pushed the door open. The light in there was off, so she reached around to snap it on.

In the middle of the floor, Aunt Jen was curled into a tight ball, in a pool of crimson. It looked as if a pile of raw meat had been dumped on her back, but only at first glance. A large meat cleaver was implanted in the back of her head.

Amanda made a choking sound, and twisted away, stumbling back down the hall.

Holly, shaking all over, didn't. She moved forward. "Aunt Jen? Oh, God, Aunt Jen?"

Her feet stopping at the outermost edge of the blood pool, she reached down to grip her aunt's warm wrist. She had to. The edge of Aunt Jen's sleeve was soaked in crimson. It touched Holly's fingers as she searched for a pulse, but she found none.

Vaguely she heard a motor start. She dropped her aunt's wrist and left the bedroom. Amanda was standing in the dining room, staring out a window, and looking close to the edge of endurance. Eyes wide, pupils dilated, not even blinking. Holly went to her. "Are you all right?"

"I was never in this house, but I saw him come in here. That's why I had to run away from it. That's why I saw it from outside. I was never in the house. I was in the truck."

Holly looked, just in time to see the taillights of the familiar bakery truck drive away. It was her uncle's truck. He'd driven it for years. The familiarity of it now seemed ominous rather than comforting.

"I was in the truck!" Amanda shouted. "Holly, he's getting away!"

"I know, I know. But we'll never catch him on foot." Holly ran to the phone in the kitchen, yanked it up. Silence greeted her. She looked at the line, saw it cut cleanly in two. "Damn!" Then her gaze hit the keyrack hanging beside the phone. Aunt Jen's car keys, or God she hoped they were. She snatched them. "Come on, Amanda! We'll take my aunt's car. We have to stop him."

Amanda nodded, running into the kitchen. They ran through the door at the far end that led to the attached garage, and Holly hit the button to raise the overhead door as she passed.

She got behind the wheel. Amanda grabbed something off the workbench in the garage as she passed, before diving into the passenger side, while Holly frantically jammed keys into the switch until one fit. She twisted it. The car started. "Thank God." As she shoved it into gear and pulled out into the pouring rain, she glanced sideways at Amanda.

In her lap were a hammer and a tire iron.

HOLLY'S HOUSE HAD BEEN EMPTY, AND Vince saw no signs that anyone had been near it. But at Reginald D'Voe's, it was a different story. The gate was unlocked, closed, but unlocked. Amanda's car was in the driveway. No one in it, though. And the house was pitch dark.

He went to the door, rang the bell, pounded on the wood. "Amanda! Holly, open up, it's Vince!"

No answer. He tried only once more before drawing his gun, breaking the glass, and reaching through it to unlock the door.

"Jesus, Vince, you don't have a warrant," Jerry said.

He said nothing, just ducked inside, Jerry right on his heels. He paused there, flipping on the lights, and looking around. Wet footprints still dampened the floor in the foyer. "They've been here. But why the hell would they leave on foot?" He crept through the darkened mausoleum, calling, but there was no reply.

———※———

HOLLY STEERED THE CAR IN THE DIRECtion Uncle Marty's bakery truck had gone.

"What if we've lost him?" Amanda asked, knuckles flexing and releasing on the tire iron, eyes wide and fixed straight ahead.

"We won't. There are no turns off this road for miles, and the truck can only go so fast." She hit a pothole as if to emphasize her point.

"Where does it go?" Amanda asked.

"It hugs the lake, most of the way around it. Passes through some towns farther north, but it's damn barren up to that point." She glanced sideways at Amanda. She was rocking now, slowly, steadily back and forth in her seat. "Amanda?"

Amanda gave her head a shake, pressed the heels of her hands to her temples. "It's coming back. It's all coming back, and I don't want it. Dammit, I don't want it."

"I'm sorry, Amanda." Holly reached out to stroke the girl's hair, but Amanda pulled away from her touch.

"There was a room. In a house. He kept me there. Oh, God, for so long, I don't know. It seemed forever. Chains. My wrists." She rubbed at the phantom marks that must have once been on her wrists. "Water, once in awhile. Hardly any food. And I was alone a lot of the time. All alone, in the dark. No lights. It was so cold there at night. But it was worse when he was there. It was so much worse."

"Amanda . . ."

"He . . . *hurt me.*"

Those three words, spoken so softly, carried more pain in them than Holly had ever heard before.

"If I could make the memories stop, I would."

Amanda turned toward Holly. "You can't."

"I know."

Thunder cracked like a rifle shot and Amanda cringed, closed her eyes. "It was just like this. There was a storm, and I was so afraid in the dark, with the thunder and lightning crashing, that I pulled, and I pulled. And my wrist slipped right through the metal bands." She looked down at her own hands in wonder.

"You'd probably lost enough weight that it made the difference," Holly said.

Amanda nodded. "I heard him coming. So I ran. I found my way out of the house. I was so weak. And so cold. And then I saw a truck. It was parked down the street. I just wanted to get in out of the rain, and I thought it was safe. Something about the truck . . . told me it would be safe. I couldn't reach the doors in the front, but the back wasn't shut tight. And I could smell the bread. It smelled so good. I crawled inside. I ate and ate. And then I wrapped up in a piece of canvas or something I found back there, and I went to sleep." She looked at Holly again, eyes wide. "I didn't know it was *his* truck. When I woke up it was moving. And when it stopped again, I peered out through the crack where the back door was still open just a little. And I saw your aunt's house. And I saw *him* going into it."

"You recognized him?" Holly asked.

"Not his face. I'd never seen his face. He always wore a mask when he was with me."

Holly's memory flashed back to the man in the mask, tearing her sister from her life. And suddenly those ice blue eyes were familiar. They were her own uncle's eyes.

"But I knew it was him," Amanda went on. "His walk. His shape. His way. I just knew. And it was still storming. But I realized I still wasn't safe—the truck I thought would be my escape was his truck. It was his truck, and I had to get away. So, as soon as he went inside the house,

I climbed out, and I ran away from the truck, away from the house."

"Into the woods," Holly said softly. "And you wound up at Reggie's."

Nodding, Amanda sniffed and swiped at her tears. "Reggie never hurt me."

"I never thought he did."

Amanda nodded, lifting her head. Then she froze. "Look. Taillights."

Holly looked ahead and saw them. She quickly turned off the car's headlights so Marty wouldn't see them coming. "Uncle Marty and Aunt Jen have two daughters," she told Amanda. "Kelly and Tara. Five and seven years older than me. When I was a little girl I thought they were the wisest, the coolest girls in the world." She sighed, shaking her head. "When Kelly turned eighteen she dropped out of high school, took Tara, and ran away. They turned up months later, living on the west coast, making their own way. I never knew why." She bit her lip at the inevitable conclusion.

"They must have been his first victims."

Holly nodded. "And my sister was his next."

"Oh, God. Holly, I'm so sorry." Amanda's hand, cool and soft, smoothed back a lock of Holly's hair, and stroked a path down her cheek. "I'm so sorry. I shouldn't have told you all I did. It was cruel."

Holly looked at her, her own eyes welling with tears. "At least you got away. I'm so glad of that."

Amanda nodded hard. "And Bethany will, too. We'll see to it."

Suddenly a soft tone beeped.

"What was that?" Amanda looked around, her eyes wide. Holly checked the lights on the dashboard.

"None of the warning lights are on. Oil, gas—"

It beeped again.

"It's in here." Amanda popped open the glove compartment. Then she released a loud breath. "Oh, God, it's a phone!" She yanked it out, looking at its face. "It's the low battery signal."

"Pray there's enough for one call," Holly said.

Amanda looked at her. "Who should we call. Nine-one-one? Chief Mallory? The hospital?"

Holly met her eyes. There was only one person she wanted to call right now. "Vince," she said. "We have to call Vince."

Amanda's lids lowered quickly.

"I know you don't trust him, Amanda, but I do. And you trust me, don't you?"

Lifting her gaze again, Amanda hesitated, then finally, she nodded. "What's the number?"

Holly rattled it off and Amanda punched the buttons, then handed her the phone. She heard Vince's cell phone ring once. Then again.

"He'd better answer fast," Amanda said. "The bakery truck is stopping."

Holly hit the brakes, pulling off to the side of the road as much as she could, as the truck did the same a short distance ahead. She drove into the darkest, most shadowy section of the roadside she could see. Then she cut the engine, staring dead ahead.

"Answer, Vince. Dammit, pick up your phone!"

TWENTY-ONE

※

VINCE'S cell phone bleated as he was wandering around a make-believe Halloween graveyard in the pouring rain in the dead of night. Which explained why he jumped out of his skin, fumbled for the phone, and then dropped it.

It had rung three more times by the time he fished it out of the mud, wiped it on his coat, and punched the right button.

"Hello?" he said, when he brought it to his ear.

"Vince! We need help."

"Holly, where the hell are you? What's going on?"

A static buzz hit his ear. Then, "It was Uncle Marty. Aunt—*zzz*—house—*zzz*—dead."

"What? Holly I can barely hear you. Are you all right?"

"Lake Road," she said, between further buzzing. "—ing north."

"Holly—"

"Hurry!"

And that was it. The connection was dead.

"Jesus Christ," Jerry said. "Look at this."

Vince turned, and looked beyond the broken section of

fence, just inside the woods. Jerry was there, holding up what seemed to be a rectangle of the ground, like a door. "It's some kind of old root cellar. The top was completely covered in soil and leaves." Jerry flipped the door all the way over and left it open.

Gabbing Jerry's arm, Vince started back to the car. "Ten to one that's how he got the kid," Vince said. "He slipped away from the party, came out here, and waited. Grabbed her when she passed closely enough. Drugged her, hid her there in that freaking tomb, and rejoined the party. It would have only taken a few minutes. Then he came back for her later, after the party was over, and the searchers had moved farther out into the woods."

"And when he did, he left the top, slightly askew. Otherwise I'd have never seen it. But how do you know he was at the party?"

Vince looked at the phone. "I'm pretty sure Holly just told me it was her uncle Marty."

"The guy you rented the cabin from?" Jerry asked, hurrying to keep up with Vince.

"The same." He was thumbing the buttons of the cell phone even as he opened the car door and got behind the wheel. "Mallory? It's Vince. Holly's in trouble. It was a bad connection, but I got 'Lake Road' and 'North.' How do I get there fastest from the D'Voe place?"

The chief gave directions as Vince drove, back wheels slipping sideways in the mud.

"Meet me out there," Vince said. "Bring everyone you can muster. Feds included. And some ambulances. God only knows what we'll find when we catch up to them."

He hung up and looked at Jerry as he negotiated the rain-wet, unpaved road, and turned onto the one called Lake Road. No one would ever know it. It didn't bear a sign. "Mallory says this road runs for seventy miles, around the lake. God only knows how far ahead of us they are."

"Just don't kill us before we get there," Jerry suggested.

———

HOLLY WAS STILL SPEAKING INTO THE
cell phone when she realized that Vince was no longer
replying. Twisting the phone in her hand, she scowled at
the panel that had gone dark. "Damn, damn, damn." She
punched buttons to no avail. The thing lit up only once,
just long enough to flicker "no power" on its face before
it died again. Holly flung it into the back seat.

A hand clutched her arm. "Look."

She glanced at Amanda, then toward where Amanda
was staring. The taillights on the bakery truck went out,
leaving the deserted road almost pitch dark. Then the
truck's door opened, and an interior light spilled out just
enough to illuminate Uncle Marty as he got out. He
hopped from the step, down to the road, then slammed
the truck's door closed. Pausing a moment, he looked up
and down the wood-lined road, then he came walking
straight toward Holly and Amanda.

"Oh, God, he sees us!" Amanda said. She reached for
the door handle.

"No." Grabbing Amanda's hand, Holly dug the nails of
her free hand into the car's upholstery. "I don't think so.
We're in the shadow of the pines. Just wait."

They sat there, frozen, and Holly swore she could hear
both their heartbeats pounding in her ears. He kept coming, kept coming, all the way to the back end of the truck.
And then he turned away from them to open the truck's
rear door. It slid upward when he yanked on it.

"He's going after Bethany," Amanda whispered. "She's
in the back of the truck—just like I was. Only when I
was in there, he didn't know it."

"He probably still doesn't know what ever happened to
you," Holly said softly.

"We can't let him hurt that little girl."

"I know."

Marty grabbed a handhold, stepped up onto the back

of the truck, and was swallowed up by the darker shadows within. Holly grabbed her door handle.

Amanda touched her shoulder. "Wait." Then she pulled the keys from the switch.

Holly sighed with relief that she hadn't opened the door and caused the car's "door ajar" tone to sound in the silence of this deserted place. "Good thinking, Amanda." As an afterthought she reached above their heads, moved the switch on the overhead light to off, so it wouldn't come on when she opened the door and give them away.

"That, too." Amanda clasped Holly's hand once. Then she pushed something into it. The hammer she'd taken from the garage. The implication made Holly's stomach lurch. But she closed her hand around the thing anyway. "Ready?" Amanda asked.

"No, but I don't see that it matters. Let's go."

Holly opened her door, and Amanda opened hers. They stepped out of the car, and pushed the doors closed again so gently they didn't catch, or make a sound.

It wasn't raining as hard. The trees that lined the road on both sides grew so thick and lush that they formed a canopy overhead. Driving this stretch was like driving through a tunnel. Earlier in the fall, it was a stunning ride, with the colors bright and fiery. Now, the canopy was intact only where the evergreens grew. In between, the hard maples, the white-skinned birches, and the gangly poplars were bare. Skeleton hands joined above the road as if shaking to seal some macabre bargain. It was in such a spot Marty had stopped his truck, so a meager amount of light touched it. It wasn't much, but it allowed them to see shape and shadow.

Holly's feet made soft squishing sounds in the mud of the road. She clutched the hammer tighter, tried to walk more softly. The car was behind them now. They were maybe two hundred feet from the back of the truck when they heard the soft crying. The plaintive voice. They were too far away to make out the words, but the child was obviously begging. Pleading.

Holly went stiff, and some kind of heat rose up from somewhere deep inside her. It suffused her chest, then crept up her neck into her face. Her scalp prickled with it, as if it were trying to burst through. She didn't feel the cold kiss of the wet night wind anymore. Her shivering stopped. Her hand closed more tightly around the hammer.

Then Uncle Marty appeared in the open back door of the truck, with the child tossed carelessly over his shoulder. Bethany hung oddly, and in a moment Holly realized her arms and legs must be bound. Marty leaped down, turned to the left, and stalked off into the woods.

"She was still wearing clothes," Amanda whispered, moving closer to Holly as the two of them hurried to the spot where he'd vanished amid the trees.

"The Halloween costume I made for her," Holly murmured.

"Maybe he hasn't . . ." Amanda didn't finish the sentence. Her eyes said enough, and Holly read them clearly and hoped to God she was right.

They got to the truck, crept to the edge of the woods. Holly could hear the crashing sounds of Uncle Marty stomping through the brush. "He's making so much noise he won't hear us coming. God, where is he taking her?"

"Is Vince coming?" Amanda asked.

"I don't know. The phone died. I don't know how much of the message he got." She jumped the small ditch on the roadside, and reached back to help Amanda across.

"We'd better make sure he can find us if he does come." Amanda reached behind her head, and yanked the snaps that attached the yellow hood to her raincoat. They were noisy as they popped apart, but Holly didn't think Marty could hear. Then Amanda hung the hood from a branch, gave a nod. "At least he'll know which way we went."

"Come on." Holly led the way, and they moved quickly, despite the utter darkness, slick ground, and thick underbrush. Certainly more quickly than a man as physically unfit as Uncle Marty, carrying a child, could go. Every few steps, they would stop and listen to the cracking and snapping of brush to be sure they were moving in the right direction.

It was a long walk.

Finally, they stopped to listen, and didn't hear any more brush cracking. Instead they heard soft crying, only a few yards ahead.

It was killing Holly to take her time now, to move as quietly as possible through the woods. Killing her, because she kept flashing on images of what that bastard was doing to Bethany now that he'd stopped walking. It was two minutes before they reached them. Maybe less. It felt like hours. Every time the little girl's cries got louder, every time her tone changed, Holly was sure he was hurting her.

Finally, the woods ended, and they stepped into a clearing. In the center, in utter darkness, she could make out the silhouettes. Uncle Marty was hunched over the little girl. Bethany lay on her back on the ground, sobbing softly and saying, "I want my mommy. Don't hurt me. My daddy will come, he'll come, you'll see."

Marty was bending over her, reaching down, touching her. "From now on, I'm your daddy. Understand? Say it. Call me daddy. Do it!"

Holly didn't need to see more. "Get your filthy hands off her, you slimy bastard!" She ran at him as she shouted, lifting the hammer as she did.

He spun before she got to him, swinging a beefy arm at her. Her hammer connected with his shoulder instead of his head. Then he punched her in the chest so hard her hand lost its grip on the hammer as she buckled and dropped to the wet, cold ground. He looked down at her, hulking over her. "Damn you, Holly, you never could mind your own business, could you?"

Holly scrambled on her hands and knees until she was beside Bethany.

"Holly?" the soft voice squeaked.

"It's me, honey. It's all right, it's going to be all right now." The child pressed herself close to Holly, sobbing and shaking uncontrollably. She was blindfolded, her hands still bound, but there was no time to untie her now.

Uncle Marty bent down, picked up the hammer, and leaned over them. "Well, no matter. I can plant you in my little garden, too, I suppose." He lifted the hammer, and Holly folded herself over Bethany to protect her from the coming blow.

The sound of the impact was dull, and it cracked. But Holly never felt it land. Stunned, she looked up. Amanda stood there, the tire iron in her hands. Marty cowered on the ground at her feet.

"You will never hurt another little girl the way you hurt me," she said, her voice deep, haunting. Not high-pitched or hysterical, but level and icy cold.

"No. No!" Marty wailed.

Amanda lifted the tire iron, and brought it down again. And a third time. The impact sounded wet.

Holly struggled to her feet, gripped Amanda's hands as she lifted the tire iron overhead yet again, stopping her. She stared down at Uncle Marty. He lay still on the ground, and his head was no longer shaped like a head.

"He's dead, Amanda. He's gone; it's all right now."

"He's dead?"

"Yes. Put it down."

Shaking, Amanda lowered her arms. But she didn't drop the weapon.

"Holly? Holly, where are you?" On the cold, wet ground three feet from Marty, Bethany was sitting up, unable to see them, her hands still bound behind her back.

"Right here, honey. It's all right now."

As she made her way to the child, hugging Amanda to her side, Holly heard more crashing brush, saw two lights bobbing closer through the forest. Vince's voice shouted her name. Holly released Amanda, who only stared blankly at Vince and Jerry as they burst into the clearing.

She heard sirens as she bent to untie Bethany's hands. The others couldn't be far behind.

Vince flicked his light around the clearing until it landed on Holly, and then he came running. He wrapped her in his arms, and Bethany with her. "I've never been so scared in my entire life, Red. Jesus, I'm glad you're all right."

"Vince?" That was Jerry's voice now. Holly looked his way, still locked in Vince's arms, and she saw where his attention and his light were focused.

Amanda stood over what was left of Marty. His head didn't look as if it had ever been human. There was blood and other stuff splattered on the front of Amanda's yellow raincoat, and she still clutched the tire iron.

More feet came crashing through the brush.

"Vince?" Holly whispered. "Will they arrest her? She couldn't bear—"

"It's all right, it's all right." He released Holly, took his gun from his holster, tossed it to the ground. Going to Amanda, he gently took the tire iron from her hands. "You listening Jare?"

"I'm listening."

"I pulled my weapon. Marty knocked it out of my hands and came after me with—" He glanced at Holly. "Did he have any other weapon on him?"

"A hammer," she said. "He took it from me."

He studied Holly's face for a second as she knelt there with the child, gently removing her blindfold, and keeping her head from turning toward the ugly scene.

Vince continued. "Marty attacked me with the hammer, and I clubbed him with the tire iron."

"He got up and came at you and you had to club him a couple more times, by the look of it, partner."

"Two decorated officers, two eyewitnesses." Vince tossed the tire iron down. "And my prints on the weapon."

"Open and shut," Jerry said. "I saw the whole thing."

"Why didn't you draw your own gun and fire?"

"Kid was too close." Jerry replied.

People swarmed into the clearing. Holly met Vince's eyes. "Thank you," she whispered.

"Get Bethany out of here," Vince said. "I'll be right behind you."

Holly nodded, gathered Bethany up into her arms, keeping her head tucked close to her until she got into the woods, so the little girl wouldn't see what was left of her attacker.

The child was cold to the touch, utterly traumatized as she searched Holly's face and then burst into tears. Holly just held her tight, and closed her eyes. Police officers crowded around her, but she wouldn't let Bethany go. She waited for Vince to come with Amanda, just inside the woods beyond the clearing. Bethany buried her face in the crook of Holly's neck, as Holly turned to look back.

Cops swarmed past her into the clearing. There were uniforms everywhere, and men in suits and raincoats as well. They all had flashlights, and there was a crisscrossing of beams over the clearing that looked like a checkerboard.

The rain had stopped. And almost as if it were preordained, the clouds chose that moment to drift apart, allowing the bright light of the waxing moon to spill down onto the clearing. Holly wasn't sure what she was seeing when her gaze was first drawn to the moonlight-washed ground. It was Jerry who said, "Sweet merciful Christ, do you see what I'm seeing?"

Vince frowned, and looked. He had Amanda anchored to his side. She wasn't looking at anything at all, just staring blankly into space. The clearing was not a natural one. There were mounds in the ground. Neat rows of them. Perfectly spaced, each roughly the same size and shape. And one hole, freshly dug—shallow, and open, and waiting. Bethany tried to lift her head, but Holly held her hand to the back of it. "No, no, baby. You stay still. I'm taking you back to your mom now, okay? You're gonna be just fine." Holly's eyes welled with hot tears as she glanced one last time at the open grave that had been meant for the little girl in her arms. Vaguely, she wondered which of those graves held Ivy's body. Her throat closed off at the thought. "You're gonna be just fine, honey. You're just fine." She spun away and carried the child rapidly through the woods, away from the nightmare.

***

VINCE CAUGHT UP TO HOLLY BEFORE SHE got back to the road, extricated the little girl from her arms. "Let me, hon. It's all right, Bethany," he said. "I've got you. You're safe now."

She hugged his neck, and Holly linked her arms through one of his. "What about Amanda?"

"Jerry and the chief are bringing her out. She seems to want to move slowly. No one wants to push her right now."

He carried the child out of the woods, onto the muddy excuse for a road, and into the flood of flashing lights. Holly kept her body pressed to his side. She had to be close, had to be touching him. Two ambulances were waiting on the narrow dirt road.

"I'm scared," Bethany whimpered. "I'm so scared."

"You don't have to be afraid anymore," Holly told her, her voice gentle, soothing. "It's over now, this nightmare is all over. You're safe now, I promise."

"You came for me," Bethany went on. "I'm so glad you really came for me, Holly."

An attendant came running from the back of an ambulance with a blanket, as the three of them stepped into the flood of light. He wrapped it around Bethany as she shivered.

"This man is going to take you to your mom, okay?" Vince said to the child.

Bethany looked afraid, wide eyes shooting to Holly's then to Vince's, as if asking them to come with her. But then Vince saw yet another vehicle pull in—Ernie Graycloud's car. The doors opened. The doctor got out of one side and a man he'd never seen before helped a woman get out of the other. He recognized the woman, guessed the man to be her husband.

"Looks like your mom decided to come to you instead, Bethany," Vince told the child. He nodded toward the woman, and Bethany looked.

"Mommy! Daddy!" She twisted out of Vince's arms and ran, letting the blanket fall away behind her. Val Stevens was running, too, arms open, and then she was on her knees, heedless of the mud, hugging her little girl, sobbing, speaking too quickly to be understood. Her husband came, too, wrapping his arms around them both, drawing his wife gently to her feet.

Graycloud met Vince's eyes, gave him a nod. Vince put an arm around Holly's shoulders, grateful to have one arm free to hug her with, as they met the old man halfway.

"Get them straight back to the hospital," Vince said. "This is no place for that kid. We'll be along."

"Holly?" the doctor asked, a brow crooked.

"I'm okay. Amanda, too. Physically, at least."

"She's going to be fine," Vince assured the doctor. "They both are."

Graycloud nodded, turning toward the reunited family, urging them back toward his car. But Val Stevens stopped with her daughter wrapped tight around her, and then she turned back toward Holly with her tears still flowing full force. "I can't find the words . . . there aren't any words, Holly."

Holly shook her head. "Don't. Please. Just . . . just go. Take her out of here." Holly averted her eyes, lowered her head.

The woman turned and carried her daughter into the doctor's waiting car.

"You're not okay at all, are you?" Vince asked her as the car backed up, turned around and moved away.

"No. I'm not."

"Tell me," he urged. He lifted her chin, tried to search

her eyes, but the flashing lights made them impossible to read. "Tell me what you're feeling."

She seemed to search his face. "Why?"

"Because I care, Red. More than I wanted to, more than thought I could. I want to make it good for you again."

Her tears welled, making her eyes shimmer beneath them. "I wish you could."

"Tell me what you're feeling," he urged.

She pressed her lips tightly together, as if willing the words to remain inside. But then they spilled out all the same. "Why couldn't I save my own sister, Vince? Why couldn't I be the hero, the protector, until now? Why did it have to take me so long?" She paused, sucked in a gulp of air, and everything in him was screaming at him to tell her what he suspected about Amanda D'Voe, but he couldn't just yet, not until he was certain.

"Did you see all those mounds out there? My God, why did so many kids have to die, Vince? Why did my sister have to die? Why?"

"Not because of you," he said. "Not because of you, Holly. You understand me?"

"She's out there. She's out there in one of those muddy graves. Ivy." She fell against him, and he held her tight, stroked her back, her hair. But, hell, he couldn't say much to ease the gut wrenching feelings inside her, because he felt them, too. All those graves in the woods.

"Over here, Vince," Jerry called. He was just helping the chief get Amanda over the ditch onto the road. Her yellow raincoat was splattered with gray and red.

Holly lifted her head, turned to look as they stepped onto the muddy road. "Take that thing off her," she said, straightening her spine, unconsciously squaring her shoulders. She was now drawing on that core of steel she didn't know she had. But Vince knew. She took her own raincoat off as they moved toward the others. Jerry tossed the soiled one aside, Holly draped hers over Amanda's shoulders.

"I found the hood," Vince said, pulling the yellow piece

from his pocket. "That was smart thinking, leaving it there so I'd know which way to go."

They stood there, on the muddy road, beside the bakery truck, Holly touching Amanda's face. "It was Amanda's idea," she said softly. "Wasn't it, Amanda?"

Amanda didn't answer. She'd retreated somewhere deep inside. Vince kept looking from one of them to the other, seeing things he hadn't seen before. Similarities in their cheekbones, in their noses, and the shape of their eyes.

"Come on, Amanda. Come on. Look at me," Holly urged. "You're going to be all right. It's over. It's finally over."

Amanda obeyed, meeting Holly's eyes, nodding but only briefly. Her head came up farther, and her eyes locked on to the bakery truck, and she just stood there, staring.

Agent Selkirk came out of the woods. He started toward the women, and Jerry held up a hand. "Don't even suggest questioning them about Marty's death. Not yet."

"He's right," the chief said. "We can get 'em in out of the cold, get them warm and dry, and take their statements there."

Selkirk started to speak, but Holly spoke first. "You're not going to charge anyone with any crimes here, Agent Selkirk." Her gaze shot to Vince's, fiercely protective. "I'll say I did it. You try to prosecute Vince for Marty's death, and I'll take the blame myself, do you understand?"

Vince's stomach knotted up. "Holly—"

Selkirk said, "We'll take your statements inside where it's warm and dry. But I honestly don't know what you're talking about, Ms. Newman. It's clear from what I've seen that the man was killed in self-defense." He met Vince's eyes. "And that's exactly what will be going into my report."

"There'll be an autopsy," Vince said softly.

"It'll be handled."

The man meant it. Vince had told his version of things

out there, briefly, and he'd known full well Selkirk saw
right through it. The truth had been all over the front of
Amanda D'Voe's raincoat. But the Fed wasn't going to
push that. Maybe he was a decent human being after all.

Vince thrust out a hand, and shook Frank Selkirk's.
"Thanks."

Selkirk nodded and turned to go to a car, where he
pulled out a microphone and spoke into a radio.

"Run, run, run, fast as you can," Amanda half whispered, her voice a low monotone, and utterly chilling. Her
eyes were still glued to the bakery truck.

Holly went stiff, and turned slowly. "Amanda?"

"Can't catch me, I'm the Gingerbread Man."

Holly followed Amanda's gaze to the side of Marty's
truck. There a brown gingerbread man with pink icing
smiled back at her in the flashing lights.

"It was always my favorite story," Amanda said softly.
She frowned, and tilted her head. "I lost my book you
know. But then I saw the picture on the side of the truck.
That's why I went to it when I got away. That's why I
got inside. 'Run, run, run, fast as you can.' I thought I
could run, that he'd never catch me if I could run with
the gingerbread man."

Holly was staring at the woman. Her lips were parted,
and her eyes riveted. She reached out a hand, then drew
it back without touching. Almost as if she were afraid.

"Amanda?" Holly whispered. "Amanda this is very important."

Amanda's eyes flickered, and she looked at Holly.

"Where did you get the book? The one you lost?"

Amanda frowned hard. "I . . . my sister got it for me.
From the library." She shook her head. "I promised I'd
take care of it, and then I lost it. God, Holly's going to
be so mad when I . . ." she let her voice trail off, and fixed
her gaze on Holly.

"Ivy?" Holly lifted a hand. "Is it . . . are you . . . ?"
Holly turned her stunned eyes to Vince.

He spoke softly, slowly, choosing his words with care.

"At the hospital, they said your blood and hers were too close a match not to be siblings. Doc thought it might be a mistake. We wanted to run another test to be sure before we said anything, but . . ."

Amanda's face twisted, lips pulled tight. "I . . . remember . . . oh, God, I remember. Mom and Dad and . . . and . . . Holly?"

"Ivy?"

"Holly!" She launched herself at her sister, and the two clung, held, fell to their knees still locked together sobbing, holding tight and sobbing softly.

Vince looked on, and tried to wipe the dampness from his cheeks without drawing undue attention.

TWENTY-TWO

※

DORIS Newman didn't know where everyone had gone. Dr. Graycloud had come and taken Mrs. Stevens off someplace. All the police who had been milling around earlier had gone, and the guard was no longer at Reginald D'Voe's door.

It was early in the morning, not even daylight yet. The hospital was eerily quiet.

She slipped out of her room without drawing any notice, took the elevator down, and held tightly to the large pair of scissors she had taken earlier.

Reggie D'Voe had been the man who had taken her little girl so long ago. And the system had let him get away with it all this time. She wasn't going to leave justice to the system any longer.

She crept up to his room, opened the door, and slipped silently inside.

Then she saw that girl, Amanda, sitting beside Reggie's bed, holding his hand, and her face was wet with tears.

Reggie lifted his head off the pillows. His eyes were tear-stained as well. "Mrs. Newman . . . Doris," he said. And his lips were compressed tightly as if in pain. His eyes welled with fresh tears. "I won't even ask if you can forgive me for the wrong I have done you and your family. There is no way I can ever make it up to you."

"Then you admit it?" she asked, rage welling inside.

He blinked, frowned, glanced at Amanda. Amanda said, "She doesn't know, Reg. Holly and Vince went to find her, but she must have already left her room. She still doesn't know what really happened to Ivy."

Reginald gasped and turned even paler. "Oh. Oh, God, you poor woman."

"It's okay. It's okay, Mrs. Newman," Amanda said, rising slowly to her feet. "I know what you must be thinking right now. But we know the truth, finally. Holly knows. So does Vince. Reggie didn't do any of this."

Doris narrowed her eyes on the girl. "How do you know?"

Amanda looked at her in an odd way. Her blue eyes seemed to move constantly over Doris's face, as if trying to memorize every line. "Because Ivy escaped from her abductor. He didn't kill her. He never killed her. She got away."

Doris's knees weakened. The scissors fell from her hands to the floor, and she lifted a hand to her trembling lips. "Are you telling me . . . my baby . . . is still alive?"

Amanda nodded. A tear ran slowly down her cheek. "She got away," the girl went on. "And wound up wandering, lost and alone in a storm."

"And that's where I found her," Reginald D'Voe said softly.

Doris frowned, her gaze shifting from him to his niece and back again. "You—*you* found her?"

"She was delirious," Amanda said. "She told Reggie that her father was the one who hurt her. Her abductor was a sick man, who used to make her call him 'Daddy.' She was confused, and she'd been drugged a lot of the time. So her mind was muddled. She didn't remember who she really was."

"She couldn't even remember her real name," Reginald

went on. "I thought I was protecting her from an abusive parent, like the one who tortured me as a boy. I claimed her as my own niece, and I raised her. I swear to God, Mrs. Newman, I didn't know she was your daughter. I didn't know."

"You saved me, Reggie," the girl said. "You saved me, and you cherished me, and you helped me to heal."

Doris blinked, her eyes sliding to the young woman, who was moving slowly closer to her. She looked at the blue, blue eyes. The soft, light-brown hair that had once been white-blonde. The shape of her nose and chin. And she saw . . . what she was almost afraid to believe she was seeing. "Ivy?"

The girl nodded. "Mommy." She moved into Doris's arms, and hugged her as Doris closed her eyes and started weeping, holding her daughter as if she'd never let go, ever again.

VINCE AND HOLLY OPENED THE DOOR TO Reg's room, saw what was going on inside, and withdrew quietly. "Let's give them some time," Holly whispered. "They've lost so much time. They need it. God, I just want to sit down. I'm so tired."

Vince held Holly to his side, led her to the nearest place he could think of where they could find quiet, which turned out to be Dr. Graycloud's office. He knew the man wouldn't mind. He set her down in a comfortable chair, knelt in front of her, and peeled off her shoes.

"How many bodies?" she asked. She was drained, emotionally, physically, mentally.

"I don't know."

"Come on Vince, someone's counted the mounds by now. You've been on your phone ten times since we got back here. And it'll be in the papers by tomorrow anyway. How many?"

He sighed, not wanting to tell her. He had hoped for a

lighter moment, but maybe it was impossible, given the circumstances. "Fifteen is the best guess so far. Seventeen when you add in the two most recent victims in Syracuse. He'd have probably buried them here as well, but I found them before he moved them. Selkirk said there were four others whose bodies were found before Marty had buried them."

"That's twenty-one." She closed her eyes. "Twenty-one innocent little girls."

"Twenty girls. One was a boy. Bobby Prague." Vince shook his head. "He must have got in the way, seen too much, something. Marty never took boys."

Holly winced. "And how many more victims did dear Uncle Marty leave scarred and damaged, who lived to tell the tale?"

"No one's even begun to count yet." Vince tugged a blanket off a gurney in the hall, just outside the door, then came back in and draped it over her. "But, he did have a prior conviction."

She sat up in the chair. "He *what*?"

"Before he married your aunt, he served two years for molesting three seven-year-old girls."

She narrowed her eyes. "Two years? And that's it? They just let him go after that?"

"Yep. Even though they knew full well he'd do it again."

She swallowed hard. "That's not right. Why didn't you know about it? You must have checked for convicted sex offenders in the area."

"He lived in a different state, used a different name. Local authorities are supposed to be notified when a convicted sex offender moves into their area, but it doesn't always happen. Marty fell through the cracks. A lot of them fall through the cracks." He shook his head. "What's even harder to take is that your cousins, when they were contacted by California State Police to be notified about all of this, said their father had molested them. They told their mother, and she refused to believe them."

"That's why they left home," Holly said softly. "I kind of pieced that together on my own over the past several hours."

"They found the gray van he used for the abductions, you know. He kept it in an old barn, outside town," Vince said. "This could have been prevented. All those kids could still be alive, if he had been taken out of society permanently the first time he was convicted. Or if his wife had believed her children and filed charges against him."

"What about Bethany?" Holly asked.

Vince shook his head. "Doc says she wasn't raped. You and your sister got to her in time."

"My sister." She sighed, settling back in the chair. "My sister. God, I like saying those words, hearing them. I just want to hold her for days on end, you know?"

"Your mother is probably feeling the same way about now."

"I remember now when all my symptoms started coming back. It was right after that day when Mom was late for lunch, and I had coffee with Amanda—with Ivy—in the cafe. Almost as if something in me knew . . . I just wish the families of all those other children could have had the ending we did."

"So do I." He thought of Kara and Bobby Prague, the lifeless eyes of their mother, and his regret was bitter, despite that justice had finally been served.

"We should put a marker on that site," Holly said. "Something to honor those children. Something to remind us what can happen."

"I think it's a good idea." Vince got to his feet. By now he knew his way around Doc's office pretty well. He took cups from the rack, hot cocoa from the canister beside the coffeemaker. Added water, and put the mugs into the little microwave.

"So, it's over," she said. "You solved the case. You found the owner of that mysterious missing library book."

"Hell, you haven't seen the fine yet. You're gonna need

to mortgage the house." As an effort to lighten the mood, he figured it was lame at best.

She smiled a little though. Softly, halfheartedly. The timer bell pinged, and he took the cocoa out, gave her cup a good stir, and put it into her hands. She sipped, and seemed to absorb the heat.

"You did this, you know," Holly said softly. "If you hadn't followed your instincts and that one silly book, and come out here and dug into my personal hell, I might never have known the truth. Marty might have gone on hurting kids for years to come, and I might never have found my sister again. You did this."

He shook his head. "You're the one who found Marty, rescued Bethany. I was just doing my job."

She narrowed her lips. "No, you weren't. You disobeyed orders to come out here. I know you said you didn't want to be anyone's hero, Vince, but there are a lot of people in this town who think you are just that. And even though you didn't want to be, you're a hero to me, too."

He couldn't look at her when she said that. He didn't doubt that he wanted the job of being Holly Newman's personal hero. Hell, in retrospect, it had never been that he didn't *want* the job. It had been fear that he'd fail at it, and let her down.

"I've learned something about you in the time I've spent down here, Red," he told her.

"Really? What?"

"That you don't need a hero. You do just fine playing that role for yourself."

She let her lips curl up at the corners. "You know something? You're right, I do."

He smiled, glad she had reclaimed her power.

"So I suppose you'll be going back to Syracuse now. Back to the illustrious S.P.D."

He looked at her. "They'll probably give me a promotion."

"You deserve a medal."

"Hey, you get the medal for this one, not me. You and your sister. Hell of a team."

She shook her head. "Don't try to draft us, Detective. We're gonna stick around here, where life is usually slow and easy, and everyone knows everyone else. Nothing bad ever happens in Dilmun, you know."

"So I've heard." He nodded. "I was thinking along the same lines myself, as a matter of fact."

Holly lifted her head, frowned at him over the coffee mug.

He pulled a chair up to face hers, and sat down in it. "I misjudged this town and the people in it from the start, Holly. It's tight, and close, and caring. I like that." He drew Holly's bare feet up off the floor along with the tail end of the blanket, which he tucked snugly around them. Then he set her feet in his lap and rubbed them warm again. "Most of all, though, I misjudged myself."

She tipped her head sideways. "About what, Vince?"

"Oh, you're gonna laugh at this one. I thought, I honestly thought, I could keep from falling in love with you."

She went very still, not quite meeting his eyes. "And you, um, you were wrong about that?"

"Wronger than I've ever been about anything."

He took her cup from her hands, set it aside on the doctor's desk. "So, what do you say, Red?" His stomach clenched tight. Leaning forward in his chair, he took both of her hands, held them in his own. "Jim Mallory says he could use another officer."

"You're saying—you want to stay?"

"I want to stay. I like it here. And I want to be where you are, where your family is."

Her eyes teared up again as she held his gaze. If she didn't say she loved him back pretty soon he was going to break something. But, damn, she looked so vulnerable right now. Her lips were trembling. Maybe it was too soon. . . .

"Promise not to hurt me, Vince," she whispered. "And I'll promise not to hurt you. Not ever."

He closed his eyes, realizing she was still scared of the same old thing. Of losing the one you loved. That fear would probably never go away. He pulled her close and kissed her tenderly. He took his time about it, made it long, and slow, and gentle. It was a kiss of promise, and one of healing, he thought. For both of them.

When he lifted his head, he looked into her eyes, not blinking. "I won't hurt you, Red," he promised. "I swear to God, I will never, ever hurt you."

A sigh escaped her, along with a lot of tension, he thought. "I love you, Vince," she whispered against his lips as he tasted her tears on them. "I love you so much."

"I'm damn glad to hear that."